Praise for
the
Summer
Guests

"Fast-paced and fluid . . . heartache as well as joy make this a most enjoyable read."

—*New York Journal of Books*

"Authentic, generous, and heartfelt!"

—Mary Kay Andrews, *New York Times* bestselling author

"Following the dramatic arc of the hurricane's progress, from buildup to landfall to dispersal, *The Summer Guests* escalates to a satisfying resolution. Loyal readers will recognize Monroe's signature love of animals, while fans of Elin Hilderbrand and Wendy Wax will enjoy the picturesque setting and heartwarmingly intertwined character arcs."

—*Booklist*

"Mary Alice Monroe writes gorgeously, with authority and tenderness, about the natural world and its power to inspire, transport, and to heal."

—Susan Wiggs, #1 *New York Times* bestselling author

"*The Summer Guests* is the story of mothers and daughters, a love story or two, and [about] the mystical connection that happens between a rider and a horse."

—*Belle*

Praise for
Beach House Reunion

"This atmospheric novel depicts a lush sanctuary that draws in the needy and provides heartwarming inspiration."

—*Library Journal*, starred review

"A beautiful novel and a fantastic read that is perfect for the start of summer."

—*RT Book Reviews*

"Fans of Elin Hilderbrand and Mary Kay Andrews will adore this tender and openhearted novel of familial expectations, new boundaries, and the power of forgiveness."

—*Booklist*

"Monroe's trademark mix of environmental awareness, coastal nostalgia, and gentle wish fulfillment should be catnip for the hordes of recreational readers who've made her a *New York Times* bestseller."

—*Wilmington Star-News*

Also by Mary Alice Monroe

BEACH HOUSE SERIES

The Beach House

Beach House Memories

Swimming Lessons

Beach House for Rent

Beach House Reunion

LOWCOUNTRY SUMMER SERIES

The Summer Girls

The Summer Wind

The Summer's End

A Lowcountry Wedding

A Lowcountry Christmas

The Butterfly's Daughter

Last Light over Carolina

Time Is a River

Mary Alice Monroe

the Summer Guests

POCKET BOOKS

New York   London   Toronto   Sydney   New Delhi

Pocket Books
An Imprint of Simon & Schuster, Inc.
1230 Avenue of the Americas
New York, NY 10020

This Pocket Books paperback edition May 2021

POCKET and colophon are registered trademarks of Simon & Schuster, Inc.

For information about special discounts for bulk purchases, please contact Simon & Schuster Special Sales at 1-866-506-1949 or business@simonandschuster.com.

The Simon & Schuster Speakers Bureau can bring authors to your live event. For more information or to book an event, contact the Simon & Schuster Speakers Bureau at 1-866-248-3049 or visit our website at www.simonspeakers.com.

Interior design by Davina Mock-Maniscalco

Manufactured in the United States of America

10 9 8 7 6 5 4 3 2 1

ISBN 978-1-9821-7151-3
ISBN 978-1-5011-9364-4 (ebook)

This book is dedicated to Cynthia Boyle

My dear muse

FOREWORD

Fourteen years ago our pony-loving family relocated to Wellington, Florida, to begin a new chapter in our lives. The northeast winters were too long, dark, and cold and we were unable to find a balance between the growing demands of equestrian sport and family life. Little did we know that within two years we would be owning and operating the largest and longest-running equestrian competition in the world.

The venture was a combined effort of friends and other equestrian enthusiasts, and after several expansions within the industry in Wellington, we found ourselves drawn to Tryon, North Carolina.

We had spent time in this area, also referred to as the Foothills, with our dear friends and partners Roger and Jennifer Smith. The Smiths had settled in the area several years earlier and had participated in foxhunting as well as show jumping. This part of the Carolinas had suffered greatly during the most recent recession, and we believed our equestrian lifestyle industry model would translate well for many reasons into Tryon's footprint, with the added benefit of infusing economic stimulus into the community.

One of the greatest benefits of being involved in the equestrian community is that I meet fascinating people from all over the world and various walks of life. One of those individuals is Mary Alice Monroe.

Three years ago Mary Alice and I attended a charity luncheon at our Tryon facility for a horse rescue organization. Mutual friends had introduced Mary Alice to the equestrian world, and of course she agreed to contribute to the event's fund-raising efforts. We became fast friends and spent a memorable evening together in 2018 when she evacuated from the coast and was staying at my neighbor's farm.

Mary Alice was among a wildly eclectic group of "evacuees" from South Carolina and Florida being housed at our friend Cindy's farm. This particular evening will forever be referred to as "Women, Daughters, Babies, Dogs, Wine, Cheese, and Makeup," not to mention the birth of *The Summer Guests*.

Any of Mary Alice's readers knows that each of her stories presents itself as a beautiful and intricately wrapped gift. The reader constantly struggles with wanting to quickly tear off the wrapping and rapidly delve into the book versus carefully appreciating and removing each thoughtfully crafted component that makes up the whole.

The Summer Guests parallels Mary Alice's journey from the South Carolina coast to the beautiful foothills of North Carolina surrounded by the Blue Ridge Mountains. Dolphins and turtles are replaced with horses and dogs. But true to form, Mary Alice brings her characters with her, thereby also introducing her prior readers to the equestrian world.

The horse community in the United States in particular has the reputation of only being accessible to the wealthy. Although competitive horse sport is by no means inexpensive, the opportunities for exposure and interaction with horses are vast and the ensuing benefits are immeasurable.

The overriding mission of our equestrian partnerships in Wellington, Tryon, and Colorado is to afford everyone across all demographics the opportunity to experience a connection to the horse, whether it be a free ride on a carousel, interacting with our miniature rescue horses, taking a lesson on the riding simulator, or an actual trail ride. The love and appreciation of these incredible animals is nonexclusive.

My life has become far more enriched from having horses in it. I have been able to share experiences with my children that have transcended the mother-child relationship. I have witnessed the miraculous therapeutic benefits of the horse not only for the physically and mentally impaired but also for those suffering from post-traumatic stress disorder. In addition, through my affiliation with Brooke USA as a board member, I have been able to contribute in a real way to helping relieve the suffering of working equines and their families in the most impoverished parts of the world.

Mary Alice builds these connections between humans and horses into the story line of *The Summer Guests*. Interwoven are other familiar themes in her books: mother-daughter connections and conflicts, the beauty of multigeneration families, and, of course, dogs.

Horse people love their horses, but with every horse comes at least one dog. In addition to supporting "their own" philanthropically, equestrians are wonderfully charitable with both their time and money when it comes to dog rescues. Our family has adopted three rescues just this year.

The Summer Guests weaves these wonderful creatures brilliantly into the story as indispensable companions to their owners as well as hilarious characters.

Natural disaster brings people together. The urgency of evacuation makes you focus on those possessions that you believe are most important to you. This is the powerful theme of *The Summer Guests*. People's lives are in immediate upheaval, and they become dependent on the generosity of friends and strangers to house them. Oftentimes there is no clear end to the stay nor a guarantee of return home. Strangers become friends, friendships are tested, and lessons are learned.

Enjoy the story.

Katherine Kaneb Bellissimo
Founding Partner and CMO
Tryon Equestrian Properties
The Winter Equestrian Festival
The Adequan Global Dressage Festival
International Polo Club
Tryon International Equestrian Center
Colorado Horse Park
The Rolex Central Park Horse Show
Publisher, *The Chronicle of the Horse Untacked*

CHARACTERS
IN THE NOVEL

Grace Phillips, 55, co-owner of Freehold Farm in North Carolina. Married to Charles. Mother of Moira.

Charles Phillips, 65, co-owner of Freehold Farm in North Carolina. Married to Grace. Father of Moira.

Moira Phillips Stevens, 30, daughter of Grace and Charles. Married to Thom Stevens. Lives in Kiawah, South Carolina.

Gerta Klug, 55, friend of Grace Phillips. Owns a Trakehner horse-breeding farm in Wellington, Florida.

Elise Klug, 29, daughter of Gerta. Grand Prix dressage rider. Lives with her mother in Wellington, Florida.

Hannah McLain, 52, friend of Grace Phillips. In a relationship with Javier Angel de la Cruz. Former model, owns a makeup company, Nature's Beauty. Lives in Palm Beach, Florida.

Javier Angel de la Cruz, 45, Olympic medalist, international event jumper from Venezuela. In a relationship with Hannah McLain. Lives in Palm Beach, Florida.

Karl Reiter, 34, trainer of dressage, employed by Gerta Klug. Lives in Palm Beach, Florida.

GLOSSARY OF TERMS

Dressage: A sport involving the execution of precise movements by a trained horse in response to barely perceptible signals from its rider. The word *dressage* means "training" in French. Particularly important are the animal's pace and bearing in performing walks, trots, canters, and more specialized maneuvers.

Show Jumping: Also known as "stadium jumping," "open jumping," or simply "jumping." A sport in which horses with riders jump a series of fences as quickly and skillfully as possible. It is nationally and internationally one of the most popular and perhaps most recognizable equestrian events. At its highest competitive level, Jumping is recognized as one of the three Olympic equestrian disciplines alongside both Dressage and Eventing.

Grand Prix: Grand Prix Level is the highest level of dressage and Show Jumping. This level is governed by the International Federation for Equestrian Sports (FEI) rules and tests the horse and rider to the highest standards.

Para-Equestrian: Para-equestrian is an equestrian sport governed by the International Federation for Equestrian Sports (FEI), and includes two competitive events: para-equestrian dressage and para-equestrian driving.

PROLOGUE

The storm originated as a tropical wave off the coast of Africa, but during the next forty-eight hours, it grew highly organized. As it veered west, it met with favorable, warm surface-water temperatures and low wind shear. It rapidly intensified, developing a distinct eye feature. When the sustained winds reached seventy-five miles per hour, the storm was given a name: Hurricane Noelle.

The hurricane wobbled, shifting directions and sending the experts racing back to their computers to create updated tracking cones. This, in turn, sent another group of residents into panic mode. Everyone living in the Caribbean and along the southeastern coast of the United States was stocking up on supplies and preparing for evacuation.

The only thing the experts agreed upon was that Hurricane Noelle was fast becoming an extremely powerful, Cape Verde–type hurricane, typical in August and September and potentially deadly. As the storm plowed west across the Atlantic and intensified, it was becoming possibly the most catastrophic hurricane to reach land in more than a decade.

PART ONE

———

EVACUATION

ONE

August 15, 2018, 7:15 a.m.
Isle of Palms, South Carolina
*Tropical Storm Noelle intensifies into a hurricane
in the Atlantic Ocean*

Cara Rutledge rubbed her arms and looked out over the Atlantic Ocean. The mercurial sea rolled in and out in its metronome fashion, reflecting the blue-gray color of the sky. The beach was nearly empty, the vast expanse of sand scarred only by her footprints. All seemed calm. Even the golden panicles of the sea oats hung still in the pensive air. Yet she sensed a heightened tension coiling under the calm façade of the water, like some great beast rippling, lying in wait to pounce.

Cara shivered, though it wasn't cold. She was a tall, slender woman accustomed to daily walks along the beach with her daughter, Hope. She'd spent her childhood on this beach, and had returned as an adult to make the quaint beach house, Primrose Cottage, her home. From May until October she was on the Island

Turtle Team, like her mother before her. After a lifetime living beside the ocean, she felt attuned to the moods of her old friend. And today, something felt *off*.

The sun was shining, but thin streaks of clouds stretched from the sea toward land, eerie fingers reaching out from the incoming storm.

Cara inhaled the salty air and placed her hand against her chest. There was an unusual heaviness in the air. A moistness that tasted of rain. She was no stranger to summer storms, or the havoc they could wreak. She also knew that she was unusually skittish when it came to storms. Cara had lived through too many hurricanes not to be on guard. And yet, she didn't want to panic. There was a wave out in the Atlantic the meteorologists were keeping an eye on, but it was August, the height of the hurricane season. There were a lot of storms that lost steam or changed direction long before they neared landfall.

She was leaving the island this afternoon to visit the mountains of North Carolina with David Wyatt and his family. It would be a welcome change of pace with the lush green foliage, cooler air, and hiking. She might even get some horseback riding in. She exhaled slowly. Yes, she thought with relief. She was working herself up over nothing. Whatever storm was coming would likely blow in and out by the time she returned. And, she thought with a hint of a smile on her face, she was bringing along with her the one thing she treasured most in the world—her daughter, Hope.

Cara turned her back on the ocean and, swinging her arms, began her trek across the beach toward home.

TWO

August 20, 6:30 a.m.
Palm Beach, Florida
*72 hours till Hurricane Noelle's expected landfall
in southeastern Florida*

Hannah McLain brushed away a shank of blond hair to hold the phone to her ear. The male voice at the other end of the line rattled off instructions in staccato.

"Do not forget the medals," Angel told her in his heavily accented English. "Most important is Olympic medals. *Sí?* You won't forget."

"Yes, okay. Got them," Hannah said as she pulled the gold and silver medals from their perch over the fireplace mantel. She tossed them into the leather duffel bag with the other awards he'd won in his fabled equestrian career.

The living room, usually bathed in southern light, today was shadowy. Outside the plate glass windows of her condo overlooking the Atlantic Ocean, an armada of silvery clouds streaked across the sky. Her television was tuned to the weather station, as it had been for the past twenty-four hours. A hurricane had developed in the Atlantic, and as of last night its path was predicted to hit southeastern Florida. Suddenly all the inhabitants of the eastern coast had shifted into emergency mode—especially those inhabitants with prize horses. The owners wouldn't take the chance of leaving their horses to fend for themselves and were scrambling to leave the area early, a minimum of seventy-two hours before the arrival of the storm. Every owner's nightmare was to get stuck in traffic with a trailer full of horses and a hurricane approaching.

Windows were boarded; store shelves had been stripped of essentials like milk, bottled water, and batteries; and plans were being made should the governor call for a mandatory evacuation. The arrival of the hurricane was no longer a question: now it was a matter of *when* and *how big*.

Angel was at the stable in Wellington loading up his horse. His decision to leave had come quickly, which was typical of him. He could be impulsive, but once a decision was made, he followed through with remarkable efficiency. And Javier Angel de la Cruz had very good instincts. On the phone, Angel continued listing all the things he wanted Hannah to pack up for him.

"Javi," she said with a hint of impatience. Javier Angel de la Cruz was known as Angel by his adoring fans in the equestrian world, which made her private nickname for her lover more . . . intimate. "Stop! I can't bring all this, and I really have to go."

"It's okay. I know. But—"

"¡No más!" she exclaimed, raking her hand through her long hair. Already a huge pile of riding gear, trophies, and files was on the bed. "We can only take those few things we truly treasure. Everything else must be left behind. There's no room in my car."

There was a long pause. "I understand. Yes." She could hear him suck in his breath. "You decide. I must deal with Butterhead." He paused. "Except for medals. Bring those."

"Of course."

"You coming now?"

"Once I load up all your crap . . ."

He chuckled. "Oh yes, *sí*, my Olympic medals *son* crap."

She laughed softly, conceding the point. "I'll be there soon. Please say you'll be ready to go when I get there. I don't want to get caught in too much traffic."

"Yes. Much to do, but yes. Come now. Oh, and Hannah . . ."

She liked the way he said her name. The *H* was silent, so it sounded more like "Ana." "Be nice to Max, okay? Very nice. You know he is scared of thunder. The storms, they make him crazy."

Hannah's smile fell as her gaze slid across the room to the giant black schnauzer lying on the tile, watching her. That dog was always staring. It was creepy. Max was Angel's beloved dog, and for the past ten years—throughout all his tabloid-fodder relationships—that dog had been his one constant companion. Even though she and Angel had been together for nearly six months, she still had the niggling feeling that she was in second place behind the dog in Angel's heart.

"I will. But, Javi, be ready, okay? Don't make me—and Max—wait."

"Okay. And Hannah?" Pause. "Pick the right stuff, okay?"

She hung up the phone, stunned by the responsibility entailed in that last request. He trusted her to choose for him what he valued. An impossible task.

Her gaze swept across the gleaming, modern, all-white condo.

Two large paintings of blue ocean waves dominated the walls. A bronze statue of a horse and a few coffee-table books sat on the glass coffee table. Hannah didn't like clutter and kept her apartment spare. The large white phalaenopsis orchid and the lemons that filled the crystal bowl were all faux. No bugs, no mess. She spied black hairs on the white sofa again and with a huff of frustration brushed them off, muttering, "Bad dog."

She finished and straightened to look around the room. What did *she* value? she wondered. There wasn't much here she'd miss, she realized with sudden clarity. It wasn't a grand apartment; it had only two bedrooms, but the building was desirable in Palm Beach. Though small, it had been enough space for her after her divorce. She'd taken precious little from the divorce, signing away a fortune in the prenuptial agreement. She'd left Randall's spacious mansion after seven years of marriage and moved into this small condo wanting—needing—an uncluttered lifestyle and the soul-saving vista of blue water more than square footage.

Her divorce had been a life-changing decision. She'd given up her modeling career to marry Randall, though in truth after age forty the calls were winding down. She'd always been street-smart and had planned for the inevitable. So during her long career, Hannah had studied makeup artistry. She had a talent for it, understood the science of the compounds that went into making beauty products. She'd worked with some of the biggest talents in the fashion world, both in front of the camera and making up other models to practice. She'd been consumed by the dream of developing her own line of natural beauty products. With her divorce settlement finally out of the way, Hannah had committed herself financially and emotionally to her vision, carefully curating a selection

THE SUMMER GUESTS   11

of essential makeup. And she being an animal lover, they were all cruelty-free.

She'd launched her line, Nature's Beauty, and was generating interest when she'd met Angel de la Cruz during a photo shoot for the cover of the *Chronicle of the Horse* magazine. An amateur competitive rider herself, she was the perfect choice to model with de la Cruz in the multipage shoot that would have her posing on and around horses. She'd heard of Javier Angel de la Cruz before the shoot—who in the horse world had not? His reputation as a medaled rider was well established. As was his reputation with the ladies. The equestrian world could be very closed and chatty.

It always struck her as ridiculous that the sport was stereotyped as a feminine one in the United States and that male riders were commonly regarded as "girly men." Equestrian sports required extreme amounts of toughness and control to manage 1,500 pounds of spirited muscle. That was certainly masculine. In fact, in her experience, male riders were the best lovers.

So she'd been a bit nervous to meet Angel, expected him to be haughty, entitled. But he was anything but. Angel was charming, agreeable, willing to please. She, like everyone else on the set, was enamored with him. Then, during the shoot, their gazes had locked, and in those dreamy hazel eyes her life had spun on its axis.

Angel was like no one she'd ever met. What attracted her most was his charisma. When Angel was in the room, he was a magnet. Quick-witted and bold, he was both creator and destroyer, heroic and villainous, foolish and wise. So very wise, in fact, that fools often misunderstood his jests, much to the amusement of those who did. Their love life had burned hot. Not long after they met,

Angel had moved in with her. She was quickly consumed by his world of competitive show jumping, and in the early days of their relationship, she planned her life around his hectic schedule.

But lately, her gaze had shifted back to her own dreams. In the past few months there had been renewed interest in her product line from serious investors.

Hannah glanced at the enormous mass of belongings on her bed. There was no way she would be able to load all that into her small Audi. She'd have to decide what to take and what to leave behind to fate. She glanced at her watch, and with a renewed burst of adrenaline grabbed the leather duffel bag filled with Angel's medals. These were a must-go, she knew. The rest she would leave behind. Her own roll-on luggage was packed with just enough to last the few days of evacuation. Her closets were bursting with beautiful clothes, but as a model she'd always worn couture. They were, she knew, replaceable.

Her gaze fell on a cosmetic travel case. In it were the makeup samples for Nature's Beauty. Years of study and development were all held in that one box. A small smile of pride slipped across her face. This was the one thing that mattered to her.

Grabbing the case handle, she made her way to the front door. She cast a final glance out the wide expanse of glass windows. Outside, the ocean roiled, a tempest of burgeoning power. What chance would those windows have against such fury? she wondered. Hannah shrugged and whistled sharply.

"Come on, Max. We're out of here." The dog looked back at her blankly. "And thanks for nothing. You've been absolutely no help at all."

She tugged at the leash and could've sworn the dog smiled.

. . .

August 20, 7:00 a.m.
Kiawah, South Carolina

Moira Stevens's house was a five-minute walk from the beach. Facing a lagoon, the soft-gray cedar-shake house looked like it belonged in New England more than it did beside the pale-colored lowcountry architecture. It seemed displaced . . . rather like Moira herself.

She'd lived in the coastal town of Kiawah since her marriage four years earlier. Kiawah was rich with long stretches of beach, lush maritime forests, and a wealth of wildlife. The community she lived in had a well-run stable. Moira, no longer a competitive rider, could ride purely for pleasure.

The windows and doors of her house, like so many others, were boarded up in readiness for Hurricane Noelle. From a distance, the homes resembled massive monoliths, cold and deserted. Her gardeners had moved all the planters and outdoor furniture inside, lest they become missiles in the high winds. All was in readiness for the storm. Walking through the house now, it was eerie how utterly silent it was, bathed in silvery light. Gigi's nails clicking on the polished floors seemed to echo in the boarded-up house. The crisp white and pale-blue beach décor couldn't disguise the shadowed, closed-in feeling. Without the usual sunshine or the sound of sea breezes filtering in through the windows, the house felt like a tomb.

She remembered reading the description of the house the first time she stumbled upon it in a real estate ad, when she and Thom were looking to purchase: "Its generously sized living spaces and four bedrooms will accommodate intimate family gatherings and large parties with equal ease. And the kitchen is a chef's dream!" A young bride at the time, she'd imagined filling the rooms with children, and grandparents visiting often.

The children didn't come, however, and her parents rarely came to Kiawah. Instead, whenever Thom was out of town on business travel, Moira returned to Freehold Farm, her parents' sprawling horse farm in North Carolina, instead of staying by herself in the big, empty house.

It was a sad state of affairs to admit that she visited often.

Moira was headed there now. Her packed suitcases were waiting by the door. She just had to get a few personal items and she'd head out, like thousands of others, to the interstate on a northbound evacuation.

She glanced at her wristwatch, a Longines her parents had given her on her graduation from Auburn University in equine science. The day was slipping away. She wanted to be on the road. All that was left was to gather her jewelry and she'd be off.

She'd evacuated Kiawah for hurricanes two of the four years that she'd lived here. Each time she felt like a horse bolting, her flight instinct in high gear. After every storm, there were those who swore they'd never evacuate again. Moira always heeded the experts' advice. One of these years, that monster hurricane would hit full-on, and she didn't want to be stuck on a barrier island when it did. Not to mention that every year more and more people moved south, which meant that every year more and more people crowded the highways during an evacuation. Leaving promptly was key.

Her cell phone rang as she crossed the living room. Moira picked up her pace to run to the master bedroom and grab it from her purse. The name GRACE PHILLIPS popped up on the screen.

"Hi, Mama," Moira said breathlessly when the phone was at her ear.

"Have you left yet?"

Moira held back her smile. This was typical of her mother: abrupt and to-the-point. Grace was always multitasking and didn't have time for idle chitchat. Long and meaningful conversations, yes. When the time was right, Grace would sit in a comfortable chair, coffee or wine served, and give you the full impact of her undistracted, razor-sharp attention. But when she was on a roll, her decisions came quickly, and she didn't suffer fools.

"I'm about out the door."

"Why haven't you left?" The shock with a hint of scold registered with Moira. "The traffic is already building, and the governor is a breath away from declaring a mandatory evacuation for the barrier islands. You'll be trapped on the interstate."

As usual, her mother had all the up-to-date information. Moira could envision the large computer screen on her desk and the television on the wall of her home office, blaring the news.

"I'll be trapped anyway. Take a chill pill. I'm just grabbing a few last things. What's going on up there?" she asked, referring to Freehold Farm.

"Chaos," Grace said. "Panic is setting in. Everyone I ever knew or met is calling to ask if I have a place for them and their horse. There just isn't anything available. The hurricane wobbled again, and it looks like Wellington is going to be hit hard. Everyone is scrambling."

"Who's coming to the farm?" Moira asked while throwing things into a bag.

"The Klugs, of course. Gerta had her ducks in a row the moment the first wave was spotted off Sierra Leone. Gerta knows she always has a place with me if she needs it."

Moira knew Mrs. Klug and her daughter, Elise, very well. Gerta and Grace had trained together as young women in Germany, and their friendship had endured after each woman married. Grace had given up competitive riding after she'd married. Gerta, too, had stopped competing after her terrible fall and focused instead on her husband's breeding program. Trakehners from the Klug stable in Bavaria were highly sought after, and many had reached international competition. Grace and Gerta had maintained their friendship, despite the long distance. The Phillips family often traveled to the Klug estate, and when the girls were older, Moira had gone to Germany to study under a noted German dressage trainer with Elise. Like their mothers, the girls had become friends, bonding over their shared love of horses and competing.

Yet unlike their mothers, Moira and Elise had let go of that bond. After Gerta had divorced her husband more than a decade earlier, she and Elise had left Germany and moved to Wellington, Florida, where Gerta established her own equestrian facility. One would have thought that the move would have brought the two young women closer together. But Moira, like her mother, had given up competitive riding after her marriage to Thom, while Elise had continued competing hard in dressage.

"It'll be nice to see Elise again," Moira said. "It's been ages. I hear she's covering the circuit."

"That's an understatement," Grace replied. "Gerta told me she's getting ready for the Devon show in September, then after a break she has a big push during the Wellington winter season at the Adequan Global Dressage Festival."

"That's impressive."

"She hopes that Robert Dover will encourage her to join the team going to compete in Europe during the spring and summer."

Moira paused, stunned. "She's going for the Olympic team."

"You got it."

Moira took a moment to digest that. To make the Olympic team would place Elise at the pinnacle of riders. She remembered how she and Elise had talked wistfully about someday riding in the Olympics. How they'd cheer each other on. As happy as she was for Elise, she couldn't help but also feel a twinge of jealousy.

Elise had done it. She'd made her dream come true. While Moira . . . *What?* she asked herself impatiently. *What do I want?*

Grace spoke again. "Moira? You there?"

"Uh, yes, sorry. The connection went weak. Is anyone else coming?" she asked, changing the subject.

"Hannah," Grace replied. "And," she added with import, "she's bringing her current beau. You'll never guess who."

Moira rolled her eyes. It was anyone's guess as to who her current attachment might be. Be they wealthy, famous, or poor as church mice, Hannah went through men at such a pace that Moira's father had nicknamed her the Man-Eater.

"I'm in a hurry, remember? Who is he?" Moira asked as she made her way across the dark wood floor of her master bedroom to a lowcountry beach landscape painting. She pulled on a corner of the ornate frame and it opened on a hinge to reveal a wall safe. Moira rested the phone in the crook of her neck as she punched in the combination.

"Angel de la Cruz."

Moira's fingers stilled as her attention sharpened. Javier Angel de la Cruz was a famous, even notorious, show jumper, winner of two team gold medals and a silver individual medal on the Venezuelan team.

Thom often said that his wife "didn't like sports." But this wasn't true. Unlike Thom, she had no interest in football, baseball, hockey, or basketball. But Moira was a devoted fan of equestrian sports: show jumping, hunting, and dressage. Though she no longer rode competitively, she avidly kept up with the sport and the who's-who. And in the equestrian world, Angel de la Cruz was a rock star.

"You're kidding. Are you serious?"

"I am," Grace replied, and Moira could almost see her smiling.

"If anyone could bag Angel, it's Hannah. But isn't she a little old for him?"

"Not really," her mother replied, seemingly affronted. "She's just a tad younger than me." Grace was in excellent shape and took pride that at fifty-five, she looked years younger.

"Yeah . . . and Angel's what? Forty?"

"Forty-five, but who's counting? They're both ageless."

Moira wisely let that drop. "Are you putting them in the lake house?"

"They'll be comfortable there, and besides, Gerta is accustomed to the cottage."

"I have to admit I'm stunned. And kind of fan-girling at the moment. Is he bringing his horse?" Moira paused to scan her brain for the mare's name. "Rogue's Fancy?"

"Right. But he calls her Butterhead. And yes, she's coming."

"And Hannah's horse?"

"She is currently without a horse. She leases one. She says she doesn't have the time. She's working on her makeup business. But that's another story."

"So. A full house."

"That's not the half of it. Hold on a minute."

Moira waited for what she knew was another phone call coming in. Her mother had two cell phones, often going back and forth between the two.

"Here we go!" Grace exclaimed, coming back on the line. Her voice was clipped. "The governor of Florida just declared a mandatory evacuation for the southeastern coast."

Moira sucked in her breath.

"The update shows Hurricane Noelle gaining strength and heading straight for Miami."

Moira felt the old flutter of panic wash over her. "If Florida called it, then South Carolina won't be far behind."

"Wait, there's the phone again."

While she waited for her mother, Moira swung open the safe's metal door. Reaching into the back, she pulled out a leather case and carried it to the dresser, laying it beside the silver-framed wedding photo of her and Thom. She looked radiant in that photo, with her dark hair pulled back and an intricately embroidered lace veil flowing from the crown of her head. Beside her, Thom was smiling his winner's smile, the one she'd seen whenever he closed a big deal for the international pipe and valve company where he worked. She shoved the photo aside to make room for the case. Opening it, she began sifting through its contents.

What should I bring with me? she wondered. *What pieces couldn't I live without?*

Moira pulled out an opera-length necklace of large pearls with a ruby and diamond clasp. It was the one she'd worn in the wedding photograph and, like the veil, it had been handed down to her from her grandmother. She put that into the small silk travel bag. She riffled through the rest of the case's contents: a yellowed bracelet of ancient seed pearls given to her at her birth, a few family rings, and the emerald ring she'd purchased for herself in a pique when Thom had been gone on a business trip for the third wedding anniversary in a row. Most of her other pieces of jewelry were not of any great financial or emotional value. She paused, her left hand resting on the leather chest, when Grace returned to the line.

"It's really heating up now. Everyone is running for the hills. We've got to do something to help those poor people."

"Can I do anything to help?"

"Yes. Get your precious ass up here."

Moira ignored that. "What was that last phone call?"

"That was Danny and Ron's dog rescue. They're expecting a new load of rescue dogs after this storm. They're bringing the dogs rescued in Florida to their facility in South Carolina. But first, they have to empty the facility there. Time is of the essence. Do you know anyone who lives near Camden who can bring the dogs to Freehold Farm?"

"*To Freehold Farm?*" Her mother could dive into a rescue mission headfirst. "Mother," she said, trying to interject calm. "How many dogs are we talking about?"

"Not too many. Maybe eight. Tops."

"*Eight?* Where are you going to put them?"

"I've thought it all through," Grace said in a dismissive tone. "Don't worry about it. I'll make the garage a temporary kennel. It opens right up to the fenced-in yard. Randy is here now, clearing everything out of the garage. It's all under control."

Moira was silent. Leave it to her mother to prepare an animal shelter in her yard at a moment's notice.

"I hear that long pause of disapproval. I couldn't say no. They're desperate."

This too was typical of her mother. She always leaped to lend a helping hand. If there was a fund-raiser needed for a charity she believed in, she was there to run it. If a friend needed support, she was the first to offer it. And Moira was her mother's daughter.

"I'll get the dogs."

"Absolutely not. You need to get on the road and come straight here."

"It's almost on my way. It'll be a minor detour. I have one of your small horse trailers here. Don't you remember? I borrowed it when I brought down that load of furniture."

"I can get someone—"

Moira interrupted. "Mama, I *want* to do it, so let's not waste time arguing about it. Text me the address and tell Ron to alert the shelter to be ready for me in about"—she quickly calculated the time—"three hours."

After a pause, Grace said in a softer tone, "I'm proud of you."

"Thank you." It had been a while since she'd heard that. "I'll call you from the road."

Moira hung up and walked directly into her spacious closet. There, she stripped off her J.McLaughlin pants and top, then slipped into a pair of jeans and a chambray shirt. Paddock boots, leather gloves . . . She was ready to pick up a truckload of dogs. Her own tricolor Cavalier King Charles spaniel sat patiently by the door, following Moira's every movement. *Dear little dog,* Moira thought. Gigi had spent many a lonely night with Moira while Thom was away on business. He traveled so often to faraway places in Europe, Russia, and Asia. Trips that took weeks at a time. Moira used to wonder how anyone could call a pet their baby. She better understood that emotion now.

"Come on, baby, let's go do some good."

Gigi leaped to her feet, her liquid brown eyes on Moira's face, tail wagging.

Moira went to the dresser to grab the small jewelry bag filled with her treasures and tossed it into her purse. As she took hold of the leather case, her hand brushed against the framed photograph, knocking it to the hardwood floor. The sound of the shattering glass ricocheted in the shuttered room.

Moira gasped and stared at the image of her and Thom's smiling faces behind the broken glass. It seemed like an omen. She felt as though the walls of the house were closing in on her and she couldn't breathe. She tugged her diamond engagement ring from her finger with a determination edged with desperation. The wedding band resisted. The ring of gold hurt her tender skin as she wrestled it away. But off it came, and in a swift move, she opened the jewelry case, tossed the rings inside, and snapped the lid shut. Sniffing, she walked across the room to return the case to the wall safe, closed the door, and moved the painting back. It closed with a satisfying click.

Without a backward glance, Moira led Gigi from the house.

. . .

Hannah heaved a sigh as she pulled into the palatial Medici, one of the jewels of the fabled equestrian community of Wellington. Angel kept his prize horse, Rogue's Fancy, stalled there at the invitation of the owners—a mutually beneficial arrangement that allowed the owners to boast of having the great Javier Angel de la Cruz there, while Angel was able to house his horse at a top-tier stable at no cost to him.

They were drawn to Wellington because it had fast become a premier equestrian destination. The Village of Wellington— something of a misnomer, given its current population of more than sixty thousand—owed its name to Charles Oliver Wellington, a Massachusetts businessman who purchased some 18,000 acres of swampland due west of Palm Beach in the 1950s.

In the late 1970s, the International Polo Club Palm Beach was created and that was when the growth really began to happen. By 2006 the Palm Beach International Equestrian Center was respected as an international center for equestrian sports and hosted world events. It was also where the wealthy and famous horse lovers went during the winter.

Medici was a stunning facility with Mediterranean-style features. The barn was vastly expansive, and no expense had been spared in the creation of an Olympic-quality facility. Hannah rounded the fountain in the circular driveway and parked her sports car in the welcome shade of a large oak tree. She got out and opened up the back of her Cosmos blue Audi Sportback for Max, and was almost knocked over by the excited dog in the process. She cursed as he took off toward the stables, his leash dragging behind him.

Hannah put her hands on the small of her back and stretched. That dog would find his master without any problem. She reached into the car to gather her purse, then at a leisurely pace made her way toward the stables. She knew this area well. Hannah had lived down the road in Palm Beach for nearly twenty years. This was her turf. She had business contacts in the fashion world in Miami and contacts within the social elite in Palm Beach. She'd been smitten with horses since she was ten years old, like so many other girls, and had taken riding lessons and later worked in stables as a groom. She'd left the sport when she left for New York City.

She'd only begun to ride seriously again after she married Randall and retired from her modeling career at forty. Accidents were too common in the horse world, and a broken leg or injured back was out of the question as long as she depended on making her own living. Nor could she dedicate the time that the sport required. Once those issues no longer weighed on her, Hannah regularly took the short drive from Palm Beach to where she boarded her horse in Wellington. With her long legs and trim, well-honed body, Hannah had a natural ability. She made fast progress, reaching low junior amateur jumper status. After a lifetime of taking orders from parents, agents, and photographers, Hannah felt exhilarated when leaning far forward over the neck of her horse and becoming one with the animal as they soared over the jumps as equals. Horses gave her the connection in life she hadn't felt with people.

The more her life circled around horses, the more she enjoyed the rollicking camaraderie of horse people. Marriage to an older man was confining. Hannah fit in with the crowd of young people who worked hard—and partied harder. She was honest enough with herself to admit that this lifestyle was the major element that had torn her marriage apart. Since the divorce, she'd sold her horse and concentrated on her business career. She still rode, but strictly for pleasure. Her connection to the equestrian world today was largely through Angel.

Hannah heard the barking before she entered the courtyard. There she saw three horse trailers with their doors open, ready to board. A tall, slim groom at the opposite fence held his horse tightly on the lead as it pranced uneasily in front of a barking Max. The groom shot her a nasty look as she ran up to grab his leash, effusive with apologies. She was glad she couldn't understand his heavily accented English or the undoubtedly scathing remarks as she walked away with Max, who tugged the entire way toward the barn. She wanted to strangle him as he pranced jauntily at her side, pleased with himself. She jerked the leash back at the entrance to the enormous barn.

It was quiet, despite the action in the courtyard. Only two horses remained in the twelve roomy stalls; the other stalls appeared recently cleared out. Despite the high ceilings and numerous electric lights, the overcast skies infused a gloomy grayness into the interior. Peering around the shadowy stalls, she spied movement, recognizing Angel standing in one of them with his horse, Butterhead. Angel wasn't a tall man, so she saw only the top of his dark head over the open stall door. He stood in front of the palomino mare, his forehead pressed against Butterhead's in silent communication.

Hannah stepped back, halfway hidden by the arch of the door.

She remained quiet, thinking as she watched how Angel had taught her to trust her instincts when she was near a horse.

"Just because she puts her nose near you doesn't mean she wants you to touch it," he'd told her the first time he introduced her to Butterhead. Hannah had reached out to pet Butterhead's muzzle and the horse had swung her head away. Hannah had felt rebuffed, but Angel made her understand the horse's thinking. "She comes to you because she's curious. Maybe wants to be nice. But when you reach up, you stop her. Horses don't like that. Do you want me to reach out and touch your nose, eh?" he'd asked, playfully tapping her nose with his fingers. "It's annoying, no? You think, *Go away! You bother me! Show some respect, man!* What you do is stand quiet and let the horse come to you."

Hannah had stood quietly, and sure enough, Butterhead had drawn near again. She felt the horse's breath on her hair, her cheek, warm and welcoming. She remained still and felt the horse's whiskers, her energy. When Butterhead nudged her gently, Hannah smiled and leaned against her, feeling a profound connection.

Since then Hannah never marched up to a horse and patted its nose. She always waited for the horse to invite her into its space, to show affection on its own terms. Watching Angel standing with Butterhead, she recognized the profound devotion that was being shared between them. He loved that horse, and she trusted and loved him right back. They demonstrated that bond daily in their exercises, in the recognition of subtle body movements, and in a mutual respect.

It was Max who broke the moment with a husky bark. Angel turned around, and broke into a wide grin upon seeing them. He stepped out of the stall with arms spread wide from his slim body, dressed in riding breeches and a black shirt.

"You're here!"

Angel was always expansive, full of heart. Max tore away from Hannah's grasp and lunged into Angel's arms. Angel bent down to rub the big dog's head.

"Good boy. I love you."

Hannah waited her turn.

"You okay?" he asked her, lifting his face from the dog.

She refrained from teasing him about greeting his dog first. "I'm good," she replied, walking into his embrace. At five foot nine to Angel's five foot six, Hannah might have felt awkward about the height difference—but Angel's commanding hold always made her feel safe and protected. They kissed briefly, but he gave her an additional squeeze of reassurance.

Drawing back, she asked, "Why isn't Butterhead in the trailer? That hurricane is on our tail."

"Is all good," he said placatingly. "We have plenty of time to get on the road. But for all this craziness, I tell you, Hannah, it is good fortune that this hurricane is coming."

Hannah looked at him like he was nuts. "What?"

"Yes! You have us staying with your good friend Grace Phillips. This is good." He kissed her. "I hear something important today. How good do you know the husband of Grace, Mr. Charles Phillips?"

Hannah was curious where this was going. "I've known him for years, in a casual way. Grace is a good friend and he's the husband. You know how that works."

"Did you know he is looking to buy a dressage horse?"

"That can't be right. Charles is a jumper."

"No!" Angel put his finger in the air as one making a point.

"Charles *was* a jumper. No more. Now he is doing dressage. And . . . he is looking for a good dressage horse."

Hannah lifted one shoulder in slight irritation. "Dressage, jumping, what does it matter? The skies are about to open up. Can we talk horses later?"

"It is important now because . . ." Angel paused, then said in a rush, "Because I have decided I am going to sell him Butterhead."

Hannah gaped at Angel in disbelief. She wasn't sure she'd understood his accented English correctly. "Sell Butterhead?"

"*Sí.* Yes."

"B-but . . ." she stammered. "You love Butterhead."

"Yes, I do. Of course."

"I don't understand. How could you sell her?"

"Hannah, you know why. I can't ride her for Grand Prix. Butterhead can't jump the one-point-five meters anymore. She makes too many mistakes. She wants to and it makes her feel bad. In her heart, you know? Butterhead, she has great heart."

"Then retire her."

He shook his head. "She is still too young. And she can still jump lower levels. But you know how it is," he said with exasperation. "I *need* another horse. A great horse. And Mr. Charles, he is looking for a great horse. He is lucky to have such a horse as her. But"—he lifted his hand to stop the argument at Hannah's lips—"it is also good for Butterhead. She will have good life at his farm. Not so hard."

"But . . ." Hannah put her palm on her forehead. "I'm sorry, but I'm trying to make sense of this. And it's hard when we've got a hurricane riding our asses."

"Don't get mad," Angel said, bringing his hands to her shoulders and staring into her eyes. "I need a horse for the Olympics. I need to train now. There is no time to wait. No time for mistakes, eh? I know what I have to do."

"But, Javi, Butterhead is a jumper. Not a dressage horse."

Angel released his hold and waved his hand dismissively. "But of course, Butterhead is trained in dressage. It is discipline, no? She will be good enough for a novice like Charles."

He turned to look at Butterhead, and in that fleeting glance Hannah saw pain flicker across his expression, even longing, that contradicted his enthusiasm.

"She still is a magnificent horse. The best."

"Don't do it," Hannah told him. "You'll regret it."

A groom, short and athletic, came to Angel's side. "Excuse me, Mr. Angel, sir. We're ready to load up Rogue's Fancy. What do you want us to pack?"

Angel's tanned, chiseled face shifted to reflect his hard-won decision. "Pack everything. She won't be coming back."

He turned and began walking out of the barn. Max lunged after him, his leash trailing on the ground. Hannah took a final look at the beautiful golden mare. The horse's dark eyes were fixed on the departing figure of Angel, full of longing and devotion. And sadness.

"I know how you feel," she said to the horse, then hurried to catch up.

In the circular drive, Angel opened the back door of the car and whistled for Max, then walked over to open the passenger-side door for Hannah. This done, he quickly skirted around the front and hopped into the driver's seat. Before Hannah could get in, however, Max bolted into the front passenger seat and sat staring straight ahead.

"Oh, no, you don't," Hannah said to Max. "Get out. Go on, get out, you rangy mutt."

"It's okay if he rides there, no?"

"Dogs in the back. Family rule."

"Come on, hop in back."

"Who in this scenario is a dog? And you'd better think carefully about your answer."

"Hannah," he said pleadingly, "let's just go. It'll take too much time to make him move."

Hannah looked up at the sky. An army of clouds was moving in, dark and menacing. The wind gusted, sending dust into the air, stinging her skin and making her squint. Finally, eager to be off, she slammed the front passenger door shut and climbed into the narrow backseat of the sport sedan. Her long legs folded tightly, putting her knees practically under her chin. In front, Angel moved the driver's seat forward, adjusted the mirrors, opened a bottle of water, and took a long drink. Then he slipped on his sunglasses and looked into the rearview mirror at Hannah, a boyish smile on his face.

"We are on a road trip, right? You buckled? Okay. This is good. I love you!" Angel stepped on the gas and the car lurched forward. "Hannah!" he called over his shoulder as they exited the Medici. "You have directions, no?"

August 20, 7:50 a.m.
Wellington, Florida

The early morning sky was a melancholy steel gray. Elise Klug's gloved hands clenched and unclenched at her sides as she approached the barn. She was dressed in a button-down shirt, jeans, and paddock boots, and her blond hair was bound in a long braid that fell down her back.

She could hear the low chatter of the grooms and the occasional, higher-pitched whinny of a horse as she approached. It was a large, airy facility with high ceilings and glass cupolas and open-style stalls that allowed the horses to see and interact with each other. Her mother, Gerta, had spared no expense in the building of it, and light usually filled every corner of the space. Today, however, the light was as gray as the sky outside.

The air inside the barn was heavy with the sweet smell of leather, feed, and pine shavings, the stalls full of horses. The stalls had already been mucked out. The feed buckets were clean; the water buckets brimming full and fresh. Elise greeted the two additional grooms that her mother had hired to help board the seven Klug horses onto trailers for evacuation. It was a dangerous business to load and unload horses, and the Klug horses represented an investment of multiple millions of dollars. This morning they were restless, aware that something was different today. They hung their heads out of their palatial abodes.

Pausing to pet a few of the horses' noses or give them a reassuring whisper, Elise headed toward her horse: Whirlwind, a nine-year-old Trakehner stallion. Whirlwind was in a special stall, separate from the mares, at the far end of the stable. He watched her approach, head erect and ears pricked forward. At nearly seventeen hands in height, with a velvety coat as black as night, he was a formidable horse. And he had always been that way.

Her mother had first heard about him—a young horse with exceptional potential—in the World Breeding Championships for Young Horses. Without a word to Elise, she had made the trip to

Europe to see him for herself and had returned soon after with the proud, spirited animal. His German name was Wirbelwind. The deal had been whispered about; word eventually reached Elise that Gerta had preempted the auction with a record purchase price of 1.2 million euros for a two-year-old horse. She'd presented the horse to Elise as a birthday gift at a grand affair, more to promote her stables than to celebrate her daughter. Elise had never been consulted, nor asked what type of horse she'd prefer. What was understood between mother and daughter, beneath the fanfare of the magnificent acquisition, was that the gift meant that Gerta had great hopes for her daughter. The bar had been set high. Whirlwind had a reputation for being spirited and difficult to handle, but Gerta knew that this horse could carry her daughter to Olympic gold.

Elise tried to love Whirlwind, she truly did. He was gorgeous and willing. She, like her mother, could sense his strength and potential. But he was aloof. She had worked daily with Whirlwind for seven years, yet she'd still never felt a bond with him. That connection between a horse and rider was not merely desired, it was necessary for success in competition. It indicated a true partnership, a willingness to work together to lead them both to victory.

But Elise had always felt hesitant around Whirlwind, and he likely sensed it. Maybe, she thought, their inability to work together was on both of them. Was she holding back from Whirlwind as well?

She felt his eyes on her as she approached, tension already rippling in his body. Two horses were being led out of stalls by the grooms. The clatter of their hooves echoed in the barn. As Elise glanced at Whirlwind, their gazes locked. His eyes flashed and his head pulled up as he snorted, then pawed the ground. There was a change of routine this morning, and Whirlwind was sensitive to change.

"Hey, there," she crooned softly. "It's all right. I'm going to take care of you." When she reached out her hand toward his muzzle, he jerked his head back, refusing to let her touch him.

Elise felt her stomach drop. Whirlwind had a lot of anxiety around trailers. He'd had a trailer accident and, though it had been years ago, he'd never forgotten it. His resistance was already beginning, and she knew it could spiral as soon as he saw the trailer.

Elise let herself into his stall, padded to protect him from his kicking. She was careful to keep her movements easy and her voice low. Whirlwind shifted back when she reached up to put the shipping halter on him, but she was firm, securing the halter and lead rope in one easy motion. She then covered his legs with special wraps for protection during transport. Taking a deep breath, she led him out of his stall, through the barn, and into the yard. Once in the open air she paused, catching her breath as she assessed the situation. Every step would have to be calculated to get Whirlwind into the trailer without causing damage to him . . . or to her. She measured the distance to the trailer in her mind and considered the best approach.

"Uh, Miss Elise," a groom called out.

She turned toward the voice, seeing a lanky, ruddy-faced man with hair the color of a raven's wing walking toward her, one hand raised to flag her attention. She didn't know him—she only saw him around the barn every once in a while—but she was vaguely annoyed at the interruption nevertheless.

"Yes, what is it?"

"Mr. Karl, see . . . he told me that no one was supposed to go near that horse 'cepting him."

A flare of anger surged up in Elise's chest. Karl Reiter was

Whirlwind's trainer, a brilliant dressage rider in his own right. Like the horse he trained, Karl was young and had great potential. He had joined the Klug stable in hopes of one day being allowed to ride one of the excellent horses in competition. He wasn't so much handsome as he was striking, with his tall, lean, athletic body and fine Germanic features. He had the self-confidence, courage, and patience required in a good trainer, and Elise couldn't help but admit that she admired him. But his confidence often bordered on an arrogance that irritated her, as did the obvious bond he shared with Whirlwind. In Elise's opinion, Karl had too strong a sense of ownership over *her* horse. He was, after all, an employee—not Whirlwind's owner.

"Did he?" Elise asked the groom slowly with narrowed eyes. "Well, you can tell *Mr. Karl* that Whirlwind is *my* horse, and I'll thank him not to interfere."

"Yes'm." The groom was clearly eager not to get between his boss and this young woman. He turned and trotted away behind the barn.

Elise was aware of the dangers involved in attempting to load Whirlwind onto the trailer herself, but she'd done it countless times with other horses in her ten years on the circuit. Traveling with horses was part of the equestrian world, where a rider competed in one event after another, sometimes in foreign countries. Yes, Whirlwind was a challenge. But Elise was determined to prove that she could handle it. She could hear in her mind her mother's words that very morning: *If you can't handle that animal, I'll find a rider who can.*

"Come on, big boy," Elise said in a calming voice. "There's nothing to be afraid of. We're just going for a ride."

She took her first steps toward the top-of-the-line trailer. Like a stretch limo, it was capable of carrying multiple passengers and was set up with box stalls, fans, and even videos for the horses. "Such a fancy trailer. Only the best for you," she crooned, hoping her voice would soothe him.

But Whirlwind was having none of it. Having caught sight of the trailer, he laid his ears back, and she could feel him bow up for a fight. The closer they drew to the trailer, the more she could see his muscles tighten. Suddenly he stopped short and yanked his head back. The power of his move almost lifted Elise's petite frame from the ground, but she held tight to the lead rope.

"Whirlwind, no!" she cried out. "Come on, it's okay . . ." Once she got him under control again, she tried to reach up to pat his neck, but he haughtily pulled back his head and looked at her with disdain. Clearly he had no intention of letting her touch him or of getting close to the trailer. He backed away farther, snorting, jerking the lead, refusing her. She could hear her mother's voice in her head yelling, *Get him under control!*

"Come on!" Elise tugged on the lead to make him move forward. This time when he raised his head, his nostrils flared and his eyes rolled back. She could see the whites. She froze: the horse was in full panic.

Whirlwind reared up on his hind legs, whinnying loudly. Elise held tight to the lead, pulling back with the weight of her body. It was a contest of wills between a 115-pound body and a 1,700-pound one. Elise was going to lose. For the first time, she was afraid.

Suddenly she felt a strong arm grab the lead and jerk it out of her grip, the owner's other hand pushing her farther away. She stumbled back a few steps and looked up to see Karl standing in front of the panicked horse, his legs wide and his right hand up. Rather than pull back on the lead, he allowed slack, wiggling the rope back and forth gently.

"Whoa," he called out calmly. "Whoa, *Schätzchen.*"

Elise felt shamed by the sheen of tears in her eyes as Karl brought Whirlwind down from his panic, guiding him to walk backward. Karl was confident. Patient. All the things she wasn't. She saw not one glimmer of fear in Karl's blue eyes as he stared up at the great horse. Only a calm concern that radiated to Whirlwind.

Watching, Elise felt her self-esteem wither, and her heart was filled with self-recrimination. She knew better than to tighten the lead on a panicking horse, but she'd panicked too, escalating Whirlwind's fear. The air was thick with humidity from the oncoming storm and the kicked-up dust stuck to her skin. She could taste its bitterness in her mouth.

When Whirlwind quieted, Karl petted his neck, then made soothing remarks as he began walking the horse in wide circles as though he had all the time in the world. Whirlwind snorted, his hooves kicking up the dust in his spirited prance. The other grooms kept their distance, waiting to load their charges until after Whirlwind was settled. Whirlwind was like the oncoming hurricane, moving in an unpredictable, dangerous path. After several more rounds the stallion had calmed down completely. Only then did Karl turn his attention to Elise. Under his shock of blond hair, his eyes sparked with fury.

"I told you I would load him," Karl said in his slight German accent.

She lifted her chin in defiance. "He's *my* horse."

"Well, you almost killed *your* horse. And yourself along with him!"

The tension in his rising voice was spooking the horse. Karl shook his head and muttered under his breath, *"Scheisse."* When he spoke again, his voice was low but it vibrated with emotion. Spearing her with his gaze, he said, "You know he's afraid of the trailer. What were you thinking? You can't just expect him to walk straight in. You have to guide him to it. Very slowly. Give him the chance to see that it's not some dark, terrible cave but a place he can tolerate. Help him past his fear. Walk him past the trailer, over and over, each time closer and closer."

"I know that, but we don't have all day," she exclaimed. "We're evacuating now. My mother wants to leave."

Karl's face set. "It's going to take as long as it's going to take."

Elise didn't have time to reply. Nor did she have to. A pale-yellow, vintage Mercedes drew close and slowed to a stop near them, crunching gravel. The driver's-side window slid down, and Elise could see her mother's face in the shadows.

By classic standards, Gerta was a striking woman. Her patrician features were elegant and fine, like the horses she bred. Her skin was unblemished and so pale that her blue eyes appeared as chips of ice. Her blond hair was perpetually smoothed back into a chignon, as slick and polished as wood. No hair would deign to slip out of its tight hold. But her perfection was broken by the downward curve of her nose, like the curved beak of a hawk. It was the Voelker nose, her father's nose, one she was proud to have inherited. She knew the power the strong profile lent when she lifted her nose in disdain.

Elise knew immediately that she had seen the entire humiliating scene.

"Get in the car," she ordered Elise in her clipped, German-accented voice.

Elise tightened her lips and, ducking her head, walked around the car to slide into the backseat. The door shut with a muffled sound.

In the front, she saw Gerta's gaze flicker to Karl. Her lips pursed in annoyance. "You," she ordered the trainer, speaking in German. "Get that beast into the trailer. I'll meet you at Freehold Farm. Understood?"

Karl nodded and drawled in English, "Yes, ma'am."

Gerta stared at the young man as the dark window slid back up. She slowly pulled away from the barn; on hitting the road, gravel spun as the engine purred and the great Mercedes sped off toward the north.

August 20, 4:00 p.m.
Tryon, North Carolina

Cara sat in a rocker on the expansive deck of David Wyatt's mountain home. A soft, sweet-smelling breeze caressed her cheek and ruffled Hope's soft hair, the child a comforting weight in her lap. The massive log house stood in the middle of a clearing of soft green grass, a breathtaking view of the Blue Ridge Mountain range just in the distance. The mountains lived up to their name as a deep, purpling dusk settled over the valley, their looming shadows cast in blue light.

The vista was so different from the ocean view Cara usually enjoyed from her deck on Isle of Palms in South Carolina. They both had their own unique charm, though, she decided, on the island the air tasted of salt. Here, the heady scent of freshly mowed grass filled every corner of the house, and tonight there was an added note of rain in the air, sweet and moist. She leaned her head back against the chair, sighing in pleasure.

She pushed on her foot, bringing the rocker into a lazy swing. The trip had been a wonderful time of reconnection. She and David had been dating for only a year, yet they were so compatible, so easy together that she felt she'd always known him. Cara was also very fond of David's daughter, Heather, her husband, Bo, and their son, Rory. She'd known Heather before she got acquainted with David, and the woman was both friend and daughter to her. Little Rory was nearly the same age as Cara's two-year-old daughter, Hope. They played so well together. It was a joy to hear their laughter over the silliest games. This time away in the mountains had been filled with conversation, good meals, great wine, and laughter. The only shadow on the vacation was the worry of a storm building in the Caribbean.

She heard the house door open behind her, followed by a heavy footfall. A moment later she felt a firm yet gentle hand on her shoulder. Cara looked away from the mesmerizing view to smile at David.

His face was tanned from a summer spent sailing off Dewees Island, his home in South Carolina. There was a new tension in his face, however, a worry flashing in his eyes that had her sitting straighter in her chair.

"Cara," David said, and took the chair beside her. "There's something I want to talk to you about." His voice sounded strangely calm, which usually meant that what he had to say was serious.

"All right," she said, trying to sound casual. "What's up?"

"I just heard the latest weather report."

Cara swallowed the lump in her throat. They'd been monitoring the weather ever since they'd heard a storm was heading toward the southeastern coast. If she'd been in her home on Isle of Palms, a vulnerable barrier island, she would have been glued to the weather reports. Islanders didn't take hurricanes lightly. The TV would be blaring 24/7 once a hurricane formed somewhere in the Atlantic. They were like sprinters at the starting line, poised to spring into action.

In the mountains, however, one felt detached from coastal storms. They seemed so far away. When she lived in Chicago, Cara had been only vaguely aware of the hurricane reports. But since she'd returned to the coast of South Carolina sixteen years earlier and a hurricane had hit during that first summer home, she'd learned to pay attention. Here she'd once again grown complacent. Now David's comment slammed the reality into the forefront of her mind. Her heart started beating rapidly.

"What's happening?"

"It's the hurricane. It's getting tightly organized."

Though he kept his voice calm, Cara involuntarily wrapped her arms tighter around Hope.

David, always perceptive of her emotions, added in an encouraging tone, "It's still far out there, of course. It's hitting Puerto Rico now. It could lose strength when it goes over the island."

She heard the door open again and, looking over her shoulder, saw Heather and Bo step out to join them on the porch. Their tense faces were grim.

"You heard?" Heather asked Cara, jiggling Rory in her arms.

Cara nodded. "Just. God, I hate hurricane season. Have they pinpointed where it's headed?"

Bo leaned against the railing, tucking his fingertips into his jeans. "I just checked Weather Underground. The cone has it heading straight up the southeastern coast." He paused. "Charleston's on its path."

"Damn," Cara said on an exhale. She had endured too many Category One storms on the island, as high a category as anyone with any survival instinct would endure. Now, at the first alert, she leaped up and began making preparations and laying in supplies. Even high on a mountaintop, her fight-or-flight instinct was kicking in. She wasn't on the island and didn't need to flee. Yet with so much at stake on the island, she knew she couldn't stay put. Cara would put up the good fight.

She stood up abruptly from the rocker, cradling Hope. "I've got to get back."

"Back?" Heather asked, eyebrows raised. "Why would you go back to the island? You're safe here in the mountains."

"The beach house," Cara said, her tone implying that was the only reason she needed. "I have to board up the windows. It's completely open."

"It's just a house," Heather said, trying both to assuage her fears and encourage her to stay. "Your safety is more important. And Hope's."

"It's not just a house to me," Cara said, panic bubbling under her cool surface. "I love that house. It's very important to me. You know that."

Chastened, Heather didn't reply, but kissed Rory's head.

Resolve stirred in Cara's veins. "I'd better start packing."

"You stay here," David said, standing up. "I'll go down to Isle of Palms and close it up."

"I'll help you," Bo offered.

"Bo?" Heather's voice was high with worry.

Rory lifted his head, alarmed by the tone of his mother's voice.

Bo slipped an arm around her and winked at his son. "Don't you worry. It won't take long. We'll be back before the hurricane hits."

Cara looked at Heather's uneasy expression. She was four months pregnant with their second child, and emotions were running high.

"You stay with Heather," Cara told Bo. "I know where everything is and it'll go quicker. Plus, it's my house. I won't feel easy if I don't see it secured myself." She looked at David. "I should've boarded it up before we left for the mountains, like you did."

"Don't be hard on yourself," David said kindly. "You were only going away for a week, and I was staying for a month. You couldn't have planned this. I'll go down with you," he said in a decisive tone. "Bo, you stay here with Heather. She needs you up here in her condition."

Heather nodded, relief shining in her eyes. "I'll take care of Hope," she volunteered. "She knows us, and she and Rory are best pals."

"Mama? I wanna go with you," Hope said, her lower lip trembling.

"Mama will be back real fast, you'll see," she told her daughter with an attempt at a reassuring smile. Then, resting her hand on Hope's soft curls, she looked at Heather. "Thank you. That would be amazing. Of course, I couldn't take her." She turned to David, rocking Hope on her hip. "How long do you think it'll take?"

"Not long. It's a small house."

"With a lot of windows."

"Right," he said with chagrin. He crossed his arms across his denim shirt as he considered. "A day down. A day to board. A day back. Three days. That should do it."

Cara turned to Bo. "When is it due to hit?"

Bo shrugged. "Hard to tell. It's too far out for them to be sure, but probably not for at least five days, maybe six. Less, if it picks up speed."

Cara nodded with sober acceptance. "Okay. That gives us time."

David came to wrap his long arms around her. She felt their strength and leaned into them. He rested his chin atop her head, then spoke in a low voice.

"Don't worry. We'll leave first thing in the morning."

Cara shifted her gaze to the south. Her view was shrouded by thick foliage, but in her mind's eye she envisioned her beloved 1930s cottage perched on a dune surrounded by primrose and sea oats. Small and vulnerable, it faced the ocean she both loved and feared. Her mother had always said a wise woman never turned her back on the ocean.

Cara felt the breeze again on her cheek. This time, however, the wind felt menacing.

PART TWO

ARRIVAL

THREE

August 20, 6:00 p.m.
Tryon, North Carolina
*Mandatory evacuations called
for southeastern coast of Florida*

Hannah glanced in the rearview mirror. Angel was snoring softly, curled in the cramped backseat of the car. She chuckled to herself. He could fall asleep at the drop of a hat anytime and anywhere. Unlike herself, who struggled to fall asleep anywhere but in her own bed, and even then she usually awoke in the early hours of the morning—the witching hour—her mind spinning with thoughts, recriminations, and dire warnings. Angel slept like a baby, then awakened refreshed and eager to start the day. In so many ways, he was like a child.

She turned her head toward the passenger seat and her smile fell. Max had curled into the front seat as he also slept. His enormous, hairy body kept sliding, annoyingly, over the gearshift. She shoved his butt out of the way as she turned off the interstate.

Hannah had taken the last leg of the arduous drive. They'd been smart to get out of town early. The traffic on I-95 North was heavy and steady, but it moved. At long last they bade farewell to the hardscape highway and, after a few turns, entered a world of lush green. The winding road was bordered by thick forests and steep hillsides that pushed upward into the sky. As the road moved farther into the countryside, the landscape grew more rolling, with well-managed acres dotted with trees and bordered by long stretches of white rail fencing. Here and there, in clusters, horses grazed. Hannah turned off the air-conditioning and rolled down the windows. The stale air was swept away by the fresh breeze smelling of new-mown grass that blew into the car. She breathed in great, soothing gulps, then laughed when she saw Max rise up, stick his head out of the front window, and do the same.

The North Carolina mountains were a world away from the merciless sun, heat, and scrubby landscape of Florida in August. Palm trees had given way to oaks and elms, birch and beech, sandy soil to red clay. She'd forgotten what crisp mountain air smelled like.

Hannah had lived in Florida for so long she thought of it as home. But in truth, she'd been born in Virginia, in a tiny town with a population of fewer than 1,500 humans, big horse farms, and a premier equestrian facility. Neither of her parents had known much about horses. Hannah, however, was one of those star-eyed girls who fell head over heels in love with the horses that surrounded her.

She wouldn't say her childhood had been hard. It was simply that, unlike her horse-set friends, nothing was handed to her. She didn't come from a wealthy family like the other girls. They lived on horse farms with big houses and elaborate barns, one more impressive than the last. Each girl had her own horse, private riding lessons, and prized trainers. And clothes . . . It was a different world from the one Hannah inhabited. The girls had thought she was "poor."

She and her mother lived in a small rental house on the outskirts of the privileged town. Her father had died not long after Hannah was born. Her mother singlehandedly supported them. Delia had found a job as a waitress in a local restaurant. With her strong work ethic and diligence, she worked her way from waitress to manager. Delia was a proud woman who had refused public assistance or charity. She lived within her means and paid her bills. Pride didn't pay for extras, however.

So, like her mother, Hannah went to work. At age twelve she started in the local stables as a groom, rising at dawn each morning to muck out stalls, and feed and brush someone else's horses in exchange for lessons with top trainers. As she got older, she was given more responsibilities and was asked to exercise the horses. Her hope was that an owner would one day choose her to ride one of his great horses in competition. She went to the public school and knew these private-school girls only from the horse world. She most likely would've been ignored except for her exceptional beauty.

At seventeen, Hannah was spotted in Middleburg at a horse event by a scout for the Wilhelmina modeling agency. One look at the coltish, leggy blonde who moved with the grace and light feet of a dressage horse, and he signed her for his agency. Hannah looked at the shiny city and alluring offerings and left for New York City with surprising ease. She was a young, beautiful girl, suddenly the envy of her friends. Her career took off from the gate and she never looked back.

Not until twenty years later when she married business tycoon

Randall. He was a good man, twenty years her senior. After a life-time of being a single career woman, for her Randall had been the right man at the right time. Hannah had turned forty, her career was waning, and in truth, she'd been bored with modeling for some time. Suddenly she found herself free from the burdens of a career and earning a living. For the first time in her life she had the time and the money to return seriously to the equestrian world—and this time she could buy her own horse. Looking back, her marriage had been a good chapter in her life. And though her marriage had ended, her love of horses raged on.

Horses. She smiled. They enhanced her life. Hannah felt the breeze ruffle her hair as she looked out at the fields dotted with horses. She loved the noble beasts. Yet, she knew, they did not ful-fill it. She glanced in the rearview mirror. Angel slept on his back, an arm thrown over his eyes, dark stubble on his chin, his legs bent in the cramped space. He looked sexy even while asleep. A soft snore sounded from his slightly open, full lips. Hannah sighed. She did not know if Angel fulfilled her either.

The paved country road changed suddenly and without warn-ing to dirt and gravel. Hannah slowed and focused on the road as her GPS announced that her destination was approaching. She squinted in the dimmed light of the thick canopy of trees and slowed further. Max sat up again, alert, sensing that the car was coming to a stop.

The entrance to Freehold was simply marked: a stone and wood gate and a plain black mailbox. Hannah thought she could have found the place without GPS. Grace always did things with a quiet elegance.

She smoothed her hair and added a bit of lip gloss. Grace Phillips had a condo in Palm Beach and took four weeks every year to bask in the sun and catch up on her reading while Charles pursued jumping at the equestrian center. "Pure indulgence," Grace called it, but everyone who knew her knew that it was an important time for her to recharge her batteries. Hannah had met her at one of the many equestrian season parties in Wellington. Grace had taken an immediate interest in Hannah's makeup company. Grace had been, in fact, one of her first financial backers. But their primary connection had been friendship. Grace had a daring streak in her that matched Hannah's own. They both loved a good glass of wine and a spontaneous laugh. Hannah felt a sudden excitement to see her friend.

"Javi!" Hannah called out. She reached back to jostle his arm. "Javi, wake up. We're here."

August 20, 6:00 p.m.
Freehold Farm, Tryon, North Carolina

Grace Phillips was a maestro leading a symphony. On the dining room table were four clear glass vases of various shapes and sizes filled with flowers she had arranged, one for each of the two guest cottages, one for Moira's bedroom, and one for her dining table. She'd overseen the thorough cleaning of all the houses, fresh linens on the beds, pantries stocked, and both red and white bottles of wine on the counters along with baskets of fruit. Out in the barn, additional feed, hay, and supplies were being unloaded.

She stood in front of her substantial Viking stove, a large Le

Creuset pot simmering. She glanced at the kitchen wall clock. Six o'clock already! She felt a flutter of anticipation. Her guests should begin arriving anytime. She'd seen reports on television of how traffic on the interstate was a parking lot, with many drivers taking alternate routes. It was impossible to plan with any surety when they'd all arrive. She kept checking her phones, but no one had texted. It was frustrating for Grace, who liked her dinners to flow seamlessly.

She had decided on a meal that could be served impromptu. It was her favorite recipe, a no-fail concoction that she'd finessed over the years. She picked up a wooden spoon and gave the beef bourguignon a good stirring, releasing the scents of browned filet of beef, chunks of garlic, and seasonings.

It was a large kitchen, filled with sunshine gleaming off all the latest appliances and long lengths of marble counters. Grace loved to cook and spent a lot of time in her kitchen. Still, she was a multitasker and liked to know what was going on in her house and the world, so she'd designed a large open wall over her stove through which she could oversee the family room and the large television. Charles called it her "command module." Today the television was tuned to the weather station. Outside the windows the sun shone in a cerulean sky. But on the TV the perpetual drone of the voices of meteorologists reporting on the storm created an undercurrent of tension.

The house had the elegant aura and comfort of an old home, with its tapestries, velvets, and oriental rugs—and all the advantages of newer construction: central heating, efficient plumbing, a bathroom for each bedroom, and the expansive, modern kitchen Grace called the heart of the home.

The rear of the kitchen had large, paned windows overlooking the garden, lush with mature boxwoods, hydrangeas, and perennials. It was a small, neat park bordered by a fence that kept her small terrier in and the deer out. Beyond the iron fence was a thick forest, the branches of the trees screening the small lake on the other side from view. The recent addition was a kidney-shaped swimming pool. Grace had had it built for Charles after his terrible accident two years earlier. The rest of the farm's seventy-five acres was fenced rolling pastures.

Grace gave the stew another stir, then reached for the bottle of burgundy and poured the entire contents into the stew.

"I hope you saved a glass for me," Charles said, entering the room.

Grace looked up and smiled, even as her sharp eyes swept over the sheen of sweat on his face and his slight limp.

Charles approached, one of his thick, graying brows rising over his pale-blue eyes. He picked up the empty wine bottle from the counter. "That was a damn good bottle of wine for stew."

Grace offered her cheek for a kiss. He smelled of leathery sweat and horse feed, a scent she'd fallen in love with when she met him at a hunt a little more than thirty years earlier. Charles came from an equestrian family. Though they both enjoyed riding and Grace was an avid hunter, Charles was the true equestrian. He had neared the exalted Grand Prix level of show jumping before the terrible fall that had broken not only his bones but his spirit.

He didn't have to tell her that he'd worked himself to a lather in the barn getting all in readiness for the arrival of the famous visiting horses. Although Charles no longer rode, his devotion to horses had not dimmed. He worked in the barn as hard as his stable hand,

Jose, taking care of the animals he loved. He was a natural horseman and treated each horse with both affection and respect. His willingness to give his time and effort without any expectation of reward or praise in a field that was fiercely competitive was the quality that she loved most about him. She found him noble and worthy of her devotion.

"Julia Child said one should only cook with wine that one would drink." Grace grabbed a wooden spoon, then ladled a steaming spoonful of the simmering beef bourguignon. After blowing on it, she raised it to her lips, then rolled her eyes. "Oh, yes. This *is* good." She offered him a taste. Charles stepped forward and helped himself. His eyes met hers.

"Score one for Julia Child."

"Right? Some warm baguettes, a crispy salad, my summer fruit trifle, and we have dinner." She shrugged. "Whenever they get here." She put the lid on the heavy orange Le Creuset pot. It clattered as she called out, "Lois?"

A heavyset middle-aged woman with prematurely graying hair pulled back into a ponytail popped her head around the corner. "Yes, Mrs. Phillips?"

"Are you finished with the silver?"

"Just. I'm putting it all back in the silver box."

"No, leave it out. I'll set the table." She glanced again at the clock and began untying her apron. "We have to get a move on," she said with the edge in her voice that prompted her help and horses alike. "Could you deliver these flowers right away?"

Lois stepped into the room.

Without waiting for a response, Grace continued, "The two large bouquets with the freesia go to the guest cottages. The freesia smells so wonderful and will freshen the stale air. The pink roses to Moira's room. She's always loved them, you know. Ever since she was a little girl. And the hydrangea arrangement stays in the dining room. Got it?"

"Yes, ma'am. I'm on my way." Lois had worked for Grace Phillips for ten years and knew her employer to be both demanding and generous.

"Thank you. I want the flowers in the houses before they arrive," Grace added.

Lois disappeared behind the door. Grace put her hands on her hips, surveying the kitchen, mentally checking off her to-do list.

Charles watched her, crossing his arms and leaning against the kitchen counter. "You're in your element, aren't you?"

He had the patrician features befitting his historic family, a once-firm jawline slightly sagging with age, an aquiline nose, and full lips. What kept his expression from being haughty was his soulful blue eyes. She smiled into them, acknowledging his tone that implied he knew her as well as, or better than, she knew herself.

"Whatever do you mean?" she asked blithely.

"All these guests arriving, organizing your troops with the strategy of a general . . ."

"I'm a woman. I excel at multitasking," she replied smugly, then laughed. "But this *is* a challenge. So much to do and so many uncertainties. Everyone's on edge with this storm. And I confess, I'm a little nervous about Angel de la Cruz coming."

"Why?"

She looked at him askance. "Because he is Angel de la Cruz. I've heard he can be very temperamental. You never know what he's going to say or do."

Charles gave a *who cares?* shrug. "I heard he's a womanizer."

Grace smirked and reached for a measuring cup half-filled with wine. "I hadn't heard that." She sipped. "Interesting."

"Don't get your hopes up. I won't let him get within ten feet of you."

Grace laughed, and came to wrap her arms around Charles. They were the same height and she almost always wore flats, so his body fit perfectly against hers, strong and firm from a lifetime of riding. At sixty-five, Charles had the body of a man twenty years his junior. He kissed her possessively.

"I love it when you're jealous," she quipped.

"Who said I'm jealous? I just want a taste of your wine."

Grace chuckled as she slid away and returned with another bottle of the burgundy. She handed it to him to open. Though she smiled, his comment pricked her heart. Ever since the horrific jumping accident two years earlier, Charles had been more aloof when it came to showing affection. At the beginning she'd assumed it was due to the severity of his injuries. The poor man had endured surgery, immobility, a wheelchair, and a year of therapy. Hardly conducive to romance. She never doubted he still loved her. Truth be told, Grace hoped he would never ride again. She discouraged it. God knew she'd sleep better. Yet his inability to get back on a horse had created a chasm in his soul, as though a large part of himself was missing.

Suddenly their terrier, Bunny, began barking. Grace hurried to the window to peer out at the driveway. Coming up the gravel drive was a blue Audi. And hanging out the front passenger window was the black head of a massive dog.

"They're here!" she called to Charles.

• • •

As Hannah pulled the dusty Audi to a stop in front of the stately stone house, the front door flew open and Grace emerged, preceded by a bolt of brown fur that took off down the stairs, barking uproariously. Grace was a striking woman with the tall, lean, girlish body of a rider. She was dressed as usual in a crisp white shirt, tight jeans with a belt sporting a large Hermès buckle, and the ever-present pearls. Her memorable hair, a mane of dark curls, was drawn back from her face and piled on her head, held precariously with a clasp. Grace took long strides toward her, smiling broadly, arms held out in welcome.

Hannah felt shabby by comparison after her long drive. She strained to tug her stiff, long legs wrapped in tight jeans out from the cramped car. Her blood was still racing with the miles, making her a bit light-headed as she rose. She knew she smelled stale, but she raced into Grace's arms, holding her in a tight embrace of reconnection.

"Welcome!" Grace whispered in her ear, then, smiling, pulled back to look at her closely.

Hannah beamed, doing the same. Grace's face was deeply tanned after a summer in the sun, revealing new lines at the eyes. But she looked healthy and well.

"It's so good to see you again," said Hannah.

"Welcome!" echoed Charles as he stepped forward to kiss her cheek.

"Charles! How long has it been?"

"Two years, but who's counting?"

When he leaned in, Hannah smelled faint aftershave, very subtle and pleasant, that hinted at a fresh shower after a day with the horses. Tanned and smiling, Charles was one of those men who never aged. He too wore jeans and a crisp, pale-blue button-down shirt the same color as his eyes. He'd been a distinguished gentleman when she'd met him years ago, and he still was. Though he was usually reserved, he always gave her the feeling that he liked her. Which was deeply appreciated, for Grace was her friend and she rarely spent any real time with Charles when the couple visited Palm Beach.

"Why did you stop coming to Florida with Grace? Are we too boring for you?" Hannah teased, then froze as a flicker of pain crossed his face.

"No, no. . . . I've been staying close to home. You know . . . since the accident . . ."

"Oh." Hannah blanched. "Of course. I'm sorry, I didn't mean—"

Charles smiled benignly. "Of course not."

Hannah rolled her eyes. "You know me. I always have a quip. I don't know when to keep my mouth shut sometimes." She laughed. "I'm hopeless. What can I say? Seriously, though, Angel's tour schedule is insane. It feels like we're always on the road. Like a Barnum and Bailey circus. And I'm one of the clowns."

Grace linked arms. "You're here now."

Grace's eyes slid from her face to the car, where Angel was emerging from the backseat. Max was already running down the gravel drive to the grass, where he promptly lifted his leg against a tree. Angel put his hands on his back and stretched, then dropped his arms and strode toward his hosts. He ran his hands through his longish dark hair, nonchalant about being disheveled. His wrinkled black shirt was hanging out from his black jeans and he had a day's shadow on his chin, yet he still managed to look sexy. Angel strode toward them with confidence and refinement, his arm out and a genuine grin on his face.

"You must be Grace Phillips!" Angel exclaimed as he took her hand. He put his other hand over hers. "Hannah told me about you. But not how beautiful you are." She demurred as he looked around the property appraisingly. "Your home is beautiful too. It is, how do you say it, quaint?"

Grace's smile slipped.

"I don't think you mean *quaint*," Hannah quickly interjected. *Quaint* implied small, like a cottage, and this house was anything but a cottage. "Maybe *impressive* is the word you're looking for?" She gave him a stern look.

Angel shook his head. "No, that's not it."

Hannah groaned inwardly. Angel wasn't even aware he was being insulting. "His English," she said to Grace by way of explanation.

"I'm impressed he speaks two languages."

"Three, actually. Spanish, English, and German. And Portuguese. So I guess that's four."

"Well, then—" The sound of furious yapping some distance away drew Grace's attention. "Bunny! Come!" she called after her dog.

The little terrier, which Hannah now knew was called Bunny, ignored its mistress and continued barking at the massive schnauzer.

"You train Bunny yourself?" Hannah teased.

"Hopeless," said Grace. "Too bad we love him so much."

Suddenly Angel's eyes lit up and he exclaimed, "Charming! This is the word I am trying to find. Your house, it is very charming."

This was met with relieved laughter. Behind him, however, she heard a disgruntled snort from Charles. She couldn't tell if Angel heard, but he moved to Charles, his hand out and his smile engaging.

"And you are Mr. Charles, no? I'm so glad to meet you," he said, pumping Charles's hand. "It is an honor. Truly. I met you at a competition when I was just starting out. You were very good." He corrected himself. "*Are* very good. . . ."

Charles raised his brows, seeming flattered by the recognition. "You remember me? That was years ago. It was a good competition," he said. Rubbing his chin, he added, "You won that one, if I recall. You were just a boy. What? Seventeen?"

Angel's smile broadened. "Fifteen."

Charles smirked. "Ouch, that stings."

Hannah added, "Angel was also the youngest rider to win the World Cup. Were you even eighteen?"

"Just eighteen," he conceded as a matter of fact, his smile not the least conceited. "That was in Sweden. A good year for me. But the best years were on Butterhead. She was my partner."

Hannah could see that Angel was about to launch into Butterhead's achievements. Trying to ward him off, she went to link arms with Angel and said, "Don't be modest. You've had many good years."

He shrugged. "Not so many recently."

"Well, you know what they say," Charles blustered, well-meaning. "Sometimes you win and sometimes you lose, but the game goes on."

"Oh, yes! I am going on," Angel said, and his eyes flashed. "I do not quit."

"He didn't mean you should quit, Javi," said Hannah, startled by the degree of Angel's emotion.

"No, not at all," said Charles placatingly.

"Good. Because I never quit. *Nunca!*"

After an awkward pause, Grace said smoothly, "Why don't we go inside? I'm sure you're parched after that long, god-awful trip. How about a glass of ice water?" She paused. "Perhaps with something a little stronger added."

Hannah tossed her a grateful glance and nudged Angel toward the front door.

Angel stopped and turned toward the two dogs far out in the grass. They were getting along better now, sniffing and making each other's acquaintance. He whistled sharply. Immediately the giant schnauzer came running, followed closely by the Norfolk terrier. Angel reached out to vigorously pat Max when he arrived at his side.

Grace let out a short, surprised laugh. "Well. That's certainly a big dog."

Angel heard the tone and looked her way. "Is it okay to have a dog? We had to bring him. But I will go if it is not okay. No problem."

Hannah paled. In all the rush of evacuation, shuttering the condo, and moving Butterhead, she'd utterly forgotten to ask Grace if it was all right for her to bring a dog. Especially one as large as Max. It was an unforgivable faux pas.

Grace's gaze swept the black dog appraisingly. "He *is* house-broken?"

"Of course," Angel replied. "In fact, he is an old dog. Eleven. Very old and very quiet. He doesn't do much but sleep."

Grace was not one to be led down the garden path. Hannah

recognized the tolerant smile that slid across her face and released a sigh.

"I suppose it's all right. As long as he doesn't tear my house up." Grace looked at Max again and shook her head. "Are you sure you don't want to put him in the barn with the other horses?"

FOUR

August 20, 7:00 p.m.
Freehold Farm, North Carolina
*Hurricane surge and storm warnings issued
for Florida and the Keys*

The mood was relaxed once the gin did its work. Charles enjoyed playing the role of host, seeing to his guests' comfort. He'd made the gin and tonics stiff, with thick chunks of sliced lime, pleased with the grateful response. At first the hurricane dominated the conversation. They'd turned on the Weather Channel to watch the updates in a nervous silence.

The commentators were discussing the increasing frequency and intensity of hurricanes. Though they came every year and mainly threatened the southern coast, what everyone had to remember was that the hurricanes then moved north. Sometimes the storms pushed out to sea. Some went farther up the coast toward Maine. When the hurricanes moved inland, they brought horrific flooding and damage. With extreme weather escalating, the one-hundred-year storms were happening with shocking regularity.

Charles glanced at the group clustered around the television. They stood in a semicircle in tense silence, arms crossed, hands clutching their drinks. Living in the mountains, he often watched hurricane notices with vague interest. But in recent years the devastation of monster hurricanes had demanded attention. His friends in Panama City, Florida, wept for a city that would never be the same.

Now this Hurricane Noelle was on a march for the United States coastline. It had skirted the tip of Puerto Rico and was hitting the Bahamas hard. A bone-numbing fear seeped through them as it advanced, slow and unpredictable. The news reported on people still boarding up their houses in Florida. Still deciding whether to evacuate.

Charles shook his head. "They're like a herd of horses. The decision whether to fight or flee is racing in their minds."

Hannah moved to slip her arms around Angel's waist.

Angel groaned, muttering in Spanish, as he pointed at the television. The first photographs of the devastation of the Caribbean islands were being shown. Trees were misshapen stubs, houses leveled, cars and boats tossed into the streets like toys.

"It is terrible," he said with feeling. "The people, they have nothing. Nowhere to go."

Charles felt the couple's fear radiate as they stared, mesmerized by the screen. "It hit as a Cat Four. That makes it one of the strongest Atlantic hurricanes in recorded history, if not the strongest. And it's still going to pass through warm water before it hits us. They say the ocean's like a bathtub. That'll feed it."

Hannah lifted her head from Angel's shoulder. "No one ever anticipates this kind of catastrophe," she said soberly. "I remember when Hurricane Andrew hit." Hannah released her hold on Angel and took a long sip from her drink. "That was, what? More than twenty years ago."

"Nineteen ninety-two," Grace chimed in.

Hannah blew a strand of hair from her face. "Wow. That long ago. I remember it was just about this time of year. I was visiting friends in Miami. I didn't live in Florida full-time yet." She shook her head. "No one took the warnings seriously. We were so unprepared. Naïve. I mean, not just me. Everyone! It was my first hurricane, and I was up for it. I didn't go fleeing back north. Heck no, I wanted to experience it. Imagine that. Not only didn't I evacuate—I was excited. For a Category Five storm. My friends had a hurricane party!" She snorted at their foolishness.

Charles shook his head, finding that mentality hard to believe today. Yet he clearly remembered the country's shock and disbelief at the repercussions of that giant storm.

"Well, let me tell you, the party ended pretty quickly. We were scared straight," Hannah continued. "The hurricane intensified so fast. We ended up huddled in the living room, plunged into darkness while objects hit the roof and windows. It was terrifying. The only sounds were of ferocious wind, rain, and the shriek of all those car alarms that were set off. And our crying and praying . . . Some of us hid in the closet. People were grabbing mattresses and hunkering down under them. It's a miracle the roof didn't blow off. I'm telling you, I'm never living through one of those things again." She turned to Grace. Her face was raw with emotion just remembering. "Thank you for letting us come here."

Grace reached out to place her hand on her shoulder. "Of course. You always have a place to run." She let her hand drop. "I didn't know you were in Florida for Hurricane Andrew. That storm was some kind of biblical milestone. Not only Florida. The whole eastern coast changed the way they prepared for hurricanes. Building codes have changed. Today, people know to get prepared for storms."

"People get out," Hannah added.

"We learn from every storm," said Charles. "But not fast enough. Think of Hurricane Katrina. Another Cat Five, but far more people died. More than fifteen hundred. And that was in 2005!"

"I'll never forget the images of people standing on their roofs, waiting to be rescued."

"I was in Europe," Angel said. "And it was big news there too."

"Most people think only the coast gets hit by hurricanes," Grace said. "Let me tell you about the shocking damage hurricanes can do inland. Flash flooding, dangerous mudslides, countless fallen trees and power outages. You're out of the brunt of the storm," she said to Hannah and Angel, "but we'll feel it if it comes our way."

There was a stunned silence. Behind them, the meteorologists were droning on about what to pack for evacuation.

"Let's turn this off for a while," Charles suggested, and was met with a chorus of agreement.

He refreshed their drinks, and the group strolled to the cluster of sofas and chairs. Charles cleaned up the bar before joining them. He sank onto the sofa beside Grace, leaning back against the smooth brown suede and sliding his arm around his wife's shoulders. Bunny jumped into his lap, curled, and settled. Across the room, the giant schnauzer lay at Angel's feet.

Angel began an animated story about some horse at the Pan American Games. Charles was grateful for his effort at cheer and watched the Venezuelan gesticulate with his arms as he spoke. The man was as entertaining as a court jester, he thought, slightly annoyed at Angel's skill at storytelling. Though he wasn't a large man—neither, for that matter, was Charles—Angel had a presence that dominated the room. You couldn't take your attention from him.

He glanced at his wife, then Hannah. Certainly the women could not. They were utterly enamored of his dark good looks and sharp wit. Charles's brows rose when Grace burst out with a hearty laugh. Across the room beside Angel, Hannah did the same, leaning into Angel, resting her head on his shoulder. Charles glanced at his wife. Her cheeks were flushed, her eyes were alive with mirth, and her long, curly hair was slipping out of its clasp, allowing tendrils to slide down her graceful neck. He couldn't help but smile himself as he looked down into his drink. It had been a long time since she'd laughed like that.

His thoughts were interrupted by the ringing of a cell phone. Angel pulled his phone from his shirt pocket and brought it to his ear. The room quieted as he spoke in rapid Spanish. When he lowered the phone, he looked up at Grace, his expression boyish with anticipation.

"They are here! Butterhead has arrived!"

As one, they all set down their glasses and rose from the deep, cushiony sofas.

"Hop in my car," Charles said as they exited the house. He indicated his white BMW SUV.

"No way—I can't bear to get back in a car," Hannah said in a groan. "I'll walk."

"Yes. We can walk," Angel agreed, and, grabbing hold of Hannah's hand, strode forward in a strong gait.

Charles and Grace shared a commiserating glance. Charles offered his arm.

"Shall we?"

Grace and Charles arrived at the barn just as a sleek white horse trailer was pulling up the drive. The tires scrunched as it came around the curve. The early evening sun cast golden light and a merciful, cooling breeze gently shook the leaves of the massive trees surrounding the barn. Angel was calling out directions to the driver, waving his arms as he guided the van to park parallel to the barn, narrowly missing a pickup truck. With a shift of gears, the engine halted and went silent.

Grace crossed her arms and stood beside Hannah on the slope of the hill, well out of the way of the commotion. Enclosed in a metal box, naturally the horses were skittish, eager to escape. When they felt the pressure from a butt-bar or strap lessen behind them, they knew that they would be asked to unload—a nerve-racking, tricky maneuver, since horses are blind to objects directly behind them. Some would comply. Others, however, could panic and bolt.

Angel knew his horse and allowed Butterhead the time she needed to settle before disembarking. The groom opened the front door while he did the windows, allowing fresh, moist air to flow through. Angel approached, his attention riveted on his horse, speaking gently to her in a stream of encouragements as he came up behind to unbolt the rear strap. He immediately moved to her head.

Patting and giving verbal cues in Spanish, he gently, slowly guided her backward, giving her time to feel her way with her hooves in a halting gait blindly down the ramp. It was a move of mutual trust.

Grace craned her neck to catch sight of the well-known horse as she emerged from the trailer. Butterhead was a beautiful palomino mare, with a thick golden mane and strong, fit muscles. Grace admired the mare's calm behavior as she backed out of the trailer. Clearly this horse was a pro. She glanced at Charles. He stood with his arms crossed, chin down, watching keenly as the horse reached the tar and gravel surface, shook her head, and got her bearings. Angel began walking her in circles around the open barnyard.

"The stall's this way," Charles called out, extending his hand. He guided them toward the barn entrance, Angel leading the horse behind him.

Hannah sighed and smiled into Grace's face. "All's right with the world," she exclaimed with relief. "He's got his baby back."

Grace chuckled as they descended the hill and followed the procession to the barn. Each time she entered it, she felt a flush of pride. Built in the New England Craftsman style, it had a stone foundation, wood paneling, and vaulted ceilings to provide air circulation. She'd embellished the barn with hunter-green metal grilles topped by freshly shined brass finials, and on each of the two gambrel roofs was a weathervane with a fox. Under her feet the hall and stalls were padded with cushy rubber herringbone pavers. She and Charles treasured their horses and provided the best living conditions they could afford.

The air was thick with humidity that clung to the skin, but inside the barn the large and low-speed overhead fans moved air comfortably throughout the space. Charles ushered Butterhead into the first stall, closest to the entrance. Angel slipped the halter off, then gave her ears an affectionate scratch, tracing a finger over the narrow white marking down her nose. His affection for the horse was obvious.

The three other horses in the barn, hearing the commotion, stuck their heads far out of their stalls to check out the newcomer.

"Curious, are you?" Grace asked as she walked to the stall across from Butterhead's. Inside stood her Percheron/Thoroughbred, Andy. His ancestry was part draft horse, so he was a massive animal. His coat felt like velvet against her palms as she stroked his neck.

"He's got his eye on the pretty lady," teased Hannah, also reaching out to pat Andy's neck.

"Too bad, too sad," Grace said. "He's a gelding."

Grace moved on to greet the two other horses waiting for attention down the avenue of stalls. "This old boy was Moira's ride in competition," she said, standing before Quicksand, a gray Irish Sport Horse. "And you remember Superman, Charles's horse?"

"Yes, he brought him to Florida." Hannah paused. "Isn't that the horse that caused the accident?"

Superman, a Dutch Warmblood, moved to the gate and stuck his head out. Grace reached up to stroke his neck. "No, that horse passed."

"Does Charles have any, you know . . ." Hannah hesitated. "Bad feelings?"

"No, not at all. He took care of him until the day he died. They both were great jumpers in their time. Comrades." She deftly sidestepped the issue. "All these horses," she said, letting her gaze sweep across the stalls. "They gave us their all. Now, they'll enjoy their final years in the pasture. They've earned it."

Hannah turned her head to glance at Butterhead. "It breaks my heart to hear of a horse being discarded when it's no longer needed." She nudged Grace. "You can bet that's not going to happen to me."

"Don't get me started," said Grace with a short laugh. "Seriously, though, Charles and I work with a team that rescues horses from kill lots. Some truly great horses are just tossed aside when they're used up. It's heartless. Owning an animal is a lifelong commitment. When their work is done, they've earned their rest. And our care." She paused, then added with a chuckle, "Though we sometimes call this part of the barn the old folks' home." She gave Superman a final pat, then turned to walk back toward the stall where Angel and Charles had settled Butterhead.

The mare had fresh water and hay and Angel was brushing her shining coat. Charles opened the stall window that offered the horse a view overlooking the green, rolling hills in the distance. Fresh air circulated with the sounds of chewing as Butterhead bent to her hay.

"She's one beautiful horse," Charles said, crossing his arms and watching the mare.

Angel didn't reply as he tended to his horse.

Grace moved closer. "Where did you get the name Butterhead?"

Hannah burst out with a short laugh. "You tell them," she said to Angel.

Angel looked up from his task, his dark eyes sparkling with mirth. "It's, how do you say it, a nickname. My name for her, you know?" Angel looked at his horse affectionately. "She has great bloodlines. Her lines are perfect. Her movement is fabulous." He shrugged. "But she has pig eyes. And her nose . . . Roman," he said, and ran his palm gently down her slightly convex nose. "She is perfect." He shrugged lightly and cut Grace a telling look. "But for her head."

"But her head," Grace repeated, a smile twitching at her lips. "Got it. But I have to ask, what are pig eyes?"

"Oh, you know," Charles prodded. "Eyes that are too small for the head."

"And . . ." Angel faced Charles and made a show of narrowing his eyes.

"Squint?" asked Charles.

"*Sí*, that's it. They squint."

"No, they don't," Hannah exclaimed, walking up to pat Butterhead's head. "Don't you listen to them."

"Who cares about her eyes?" asked Charles. "She's a great athlete."

"Yes!" Angel exclaimed, latching on to that comment. "Exactly. For dressage, maybe looks are important." He lifted his shoulders as if to say, *who cares about that?* "But for jumping. We care how high the horse can jump. How fast. And how great a heart. A champion needs that most of all."

"I agree." Charles reached out to stroke the mare's neck, the hair smooth and glossy over her taut muscles. "You are fortunate to have such a fine horse."

"Yes," Angel said, running the brush down Butterhead's coat. "But my heart is broken. Butterhead is no longer able to do Grand Prix. She can still jump lower jumps," he hurried to add. "That is good enough for most riders, eh?" He looked over his shoulder to Charles for agreement.

Charles nodded. Grand Prix heights were for a select few.

Angel began brushing again, using long strokes. "But I need a

Grand Prix horse. Of course, eh? For the Olympics. I must begin training soon. I must find a home for my Butterhead."

Charles visibly straightened at the remark. "You're letting Butterhead go?" he asked, his voice tinged with disbelief.

Angel paused again to look at Charles. He shrugged sadly. "I don't know." Angel looked down at the brush in his hands, then moved to the horse's other side. "I only want what is best for her."

Grace could see Charles's blue eyes gleam. Oh, he wanted that horse. Every muscle in his body was twitching. Grace felt her own body shaking, but with fear. She didn't want to see Charles on any horse again, to see him take the risk of another fall. And a famed jumper like Butterhead? Grace could feel her blood pressure rising.

"Charles," she said, stepping closer to him. She wanted to break the spell that Angel was casting. "Remember? D or D." She said this last part in a foreboding tone.

"What's D or D?" asked Hannah. "Drunk and disorderly?"

Charles cast Grace a half-smile of acknowledgment, then moved closer to pat Butterhead's neck, letting Grace answer the question.

Alarmed by his budding attachment to the horse, she spoke loudly so he—and Angel—could hear inside the stall.

"A couple years ago," she answered Hannah, "after that horrible accident that left him in a wheelchair, I was a wreck. I told Charles I'd had enough. I mean, he's probably broken nearly every bone in his body. I was done," she said without malice. Enough time had gone by that she could talk about the accident without despair or tears. "I can't stand by and watch him in pain any longer. If he went back to jumping, I just knew he'd end up dead or paralyzed. So I told him he had a choice. The two Ds." She lifted two fingers. "Divorce or dressage." She smiled smugly. "He chose dressage." Grace lowered her hand to point teasingly at Charles. "Don't get tempted. No more jumping."

Charles smiled back amiably.

Angel stroked Butterhead's flank slowly as the comment sank in. In the resulting silence, he stepped out of the stall and closed the gate. He looked at Charles, then let his gaze slide to Grace and smiled benignly.

The sound of an engine roaring up the drive forestalled further conversation. As a group they walked out of the barn in time to see a gleaming silver and black luxury trailer cruise up the sloping ridge.

Charles put his hands on his hips and whistled softly. "That thing has to be at least fifty feet long."

"It's a frigging luxury liner. I'll bet it has a sleeping compartment," added Hannah.

Grace watched as the trailer slowed, then came to a stop, its mighty engine purring in idle. This top-of-the-line trailer that she knew cost as much as a house covered the outer edge of the courtyard.

"This must be Whirlwind," Angel said, his voice low with awe.

FIVE

August 20, 7:30 p.m.
Freehold Farm, North Carolina
*Noelle intensifies to a major
Category Five hurricane*

Gerta Klug lowered her window as the Mercedes rolled past the entrance gate of Freehold Farm. She slowed to a stop, lowered her glasses, and peered out at the rolling hills. Her experienced eyes noted the new-mown grass filling the air with its sweet green scent, the trimmed boxwoods at the gate, and the riot of summer flowers in front of the imposing barn. They'd arrived. At long last they were off the dry, traffic-clogged highway and here at this green oasis in North Carolina.

She felt dusty and displaced, like a refugee in search of a place to sleep. Her leg was aching something fierce from too many hours in the car. What she needed was a cool drink, a hot meal. To feel safe. Gerta repressed a shiver as she glanced again at the sky. Here the clouds were not dark and threatening, though hints of the advancing storm were apparent in the long, slender gray clouds stretching northward. Yet she felt a stirring of hope in the ripening colors of sunset that tinged the clouds in ochre and gold.

Taking a steadying breath, Gerta drove slowly along the winding driveway, allowing her gaze to roam the extensive property. River rock was neatly collected alongside the road, forming a culvert that channeled the spring water trickling down the road to the pond. The large trees were thinned and trimmed, the rolling hills neatly manicured, and in the distant meadow she spotted a herd of six deer, heads up, ears pricked and alert. Gerta owned several large properties and knew that only a large labor force and an attention to detail could provide such an idyllic setting. A small smile of approval eased across her face. Anything less wouldn't be Grace.

Gerta Werner Klug and Grace Scott Phillips had been friends since they'd met at a private boarding school in Switzerland. By the age of thirteen, both girls had won medals in jumping. Each girl had selected the school for its excellence in equestrian sports. Though their backgrounds were different, they shared a love for horses and a competitive spirit.

Gerta had been born into an equestrian family in Stuttgart, Germany, where her father was an executive at the Daimler Corporation. She couldn't remember a time she didn't ride horses. She'd learned to ride when she'd learned to walk. Riding was in her blood. She'd started in dressage, the sport her parents pursued. Dressage had strong and historic ties in Europe and was considered fundamental to most equestrian sports. But Gerta loved jumping. She loved the adrenaline rush, the feeling of oneness with the horse as they flew over the jumps. And she was good.

Grace came from a United States military family. For most of her early years her family had moved from state to state as her father advanced in rank. When her father made colonel, they'd moved to Virginia while her father worked at the Pentagon. Grace was in horse heaven in Virginia, a bastion of hunters and jumpers. During these formative years, she focused on her riding lessons and had done fairly well in local shows. When she was thirteen, her father was promoted to general and sent to Germany. Grace was offered the opportunity to attend the ultra-elite boarding school in Switzerland. She was over-the-moon excited to be taught by some of the world's greatest equestrian trainers.

But their friendship didn't get off to an easy start. Grace's German was stumbling at best, so she tended to hang around with the English-speaking girls. Gerta, who was fluent in three languages, had taken an instant dislike to the leggy American girl with dark hair that flowed from her head like a wild horse's mane. Gerta's own blond hair was neatly tied back. Many of the girls, especially those from Europe, brought their own horses to school. Those who didn't—including Grace—rode one of the thirty-some horses in the stable. On the first day of riding class, Grace was given a spirited horse, one that required an experienced rider. Gerta and three other girls who knew the horse's reputation clustered together expectantly, watching Grace mount. Gerta was ashamed to admit they all hoped she'd land on her pretty ass.

Grace settled in the seat readily and held the reins loosely. The horse, an Irish Thoroughbred, was skittish, but Grace brought him under control with seeming ease. She started smoothly, but on the first jump her horse refused and dumped Grace ungracefully on the ground. As the trainer ran to assist, some of the girls snickered. Not Gerta. She watched the pretty brunette to see what she'd do. Having grown up in an equestrian family, she knew that how one handled a fall spoke of character.

Grace slowly rose, calling out assurances to all that she was fine. She brushed herself off, then walked back to the horse, trying to disguise her limp. Rather than scold or, worse, walk away and not get back on, Grace stroked the horse warmly and apologized to the animal for her mixed signals. She smoothed back her mane of hair, readjusted her helmet, then mounted again. Her eyes focused and her jaw set, Grace guided the horse to successfully make the jump, and together they finished the round beautifully.

Gerta respected her calm confidence, and even more the connection Grace had made with the horse. When Grace dismounted, Gerta walked up to her and, in slightly accented English, introduced herself. From that day on, they were inseparable. If someone saw Grace, they saw Gerta nearby, and vice versa. They trained together and competed against each other in school and at events. For four years they compared grades, medals, points at competitions. Nonetheless, they were also each other's top cheerleaders.

They went on to different colleges, but continued to visit each other during the summer. More often, Grace traveled to the Werner estate in Stuttgart to study with German trainers. Gerta also came to the United States as a working student to experience American show jumping competitions.

After college, Grace chose to stop competing. Gerta had never understood her friend's decision and had argued against it. But as with most things, once Grace had made up her mind she didn't go back. Gerta persevered with competitive jumping, reaching the ultimate Grand Prix level. It was common knowledge she had her eye on the Olympics.

Still, their friendship endured. They were in each other's bridal parties and subsequently were delighted that they each had a daughter. Their friendship had weathered four decades of life's vicissitudes, but like the horsewomen they were, they crossed each hurdle—the great distance, sparse communication, and the occasional argument. Now in their fifties and successful, they appreciated each other all the more in light of experience.

Gerta may not have won her Olympic medal, but she did succeed in creating one of the most respected and sought after breeding programs for Grand Prix horses in the United States. Grace's success was her family, first and foremost. She was a major force in horse rescue and the hunting community. Grace believed staunchly in the idea of giving back. Gerta thought that in the end, both of their lives were busy and fulfilled, and in this, Gerta knew they were indeed fortunate women.

Still, with her wealth and position, Gerta didn't have many friends and her relationship with her daughter was strained. Grace was one of the precious few women she could trust. One who knew the secrets of her heart. One who always had her back. And there was comfort in knowing the feeling was mutual.

Gerta's mind was filled with these thoughts as she drove into Freehold Farm and wound up the gentle curve that led to the barn. She saw that the enormous trailer was already here. She glided the Mercedes past its long length to park in front of it, then turned off the engine and sighed, letting her hands rest on the wheel. She glanced in the rearview mirror and frowned with disapproval. Elise lay sprawled on the backseat, her long, unbrushed blond hair looped into an erupting bun on top of her head, earbuds in her ears. She was pale and appeared bored to tears.

"We're here," announced Gerta.

Her redundant statement went ignored. Gerta sighed and pressed the button to raise the window. It had been a punishing seven-hundred-mile drive from Florida to North Carolina. Elise had barely spoken a word to her, and when she did, she'd found a way to make each statement negative or some sort of rebuke. Gerta was too tired to argue with her recalcitrant daughter and too eager to see her old friend.

She pushed open the car door and felt the evening air, moist yet sweet. She set one brown leather shoe on the pavement and, with effort, slowly pulled herself up from the car. Her prosthesis chafed, and she grimaced. There'd be hell to pay tonight when she removed the leg. But she'd deal with it later, she resolved. She hated weak people and would die if someone considered her as such. Gerta smoothed the tan pants over her false leg and straightened, gathering her balance and composure.

"Gerta!" Grace called.

Gerta felt a spark light up in her chest and a smile burst onto her face. Lifting her chin, she scanned the area. Across the courtyard Grace shot an arm into the air and waved it in an arc over her head. Her dark hair, still thick and curly, was barely restrained, and Grace's wide smile lit up her face as she began walking toward Gerta.

Gerta moved forward; then almost on cue, both women lost all sense of decorum and broke into a trot straight into each other's arms. Gerta felt her friend's strong arms tighten around her shoulders as they rocked from side to side, caught the scent of her perfume, closed her eyes and felt the years peel back. They were teenagers again, squeezing tight at seeing each other again, hopping up and down in excitement.

"I've missed you," Gerta whispered into her ear.

"Me too." Grace pulled back, eyes blinking away tears. She looked off, gesturing toward the trailer. "You certainly arrive with panache!"

Grace often deflected the rush of emotions with humor, which spared them both. Gerta gave a slight, dismissive wave of her hand and stepped back.

"Oh, *ja*, that . . ." She laughed, her German accent flaring a bit in her otherwise impeccable English. "It's just a trailer. *Mein Gott*," she added with a hint of distress. "I had to evacuate twelve horses in a rush. I can't tell you what a scramble it was. I bought this one, but rented a fleet of trailers, not to mention hired additional grooms. Evacuation is a trauma. All hands on deck. And then all that driving." She sighed dramatically. "I'm exhausted."

Grace offered a reassuring smile. "We have the cottage all set up for you and a hot meal waiting." She looked up. "Where's Elise?"

"In the car." Gerta made a face. "We're hardly speaking. It's been hell on wheels, I can tell you. She is always mad at me. At the world. Sulking. I'm at my wits' end."

Grace's eyes reflected concern. "And Whirlwind is here?"

"Of course. I'm boarding the other horses at the equestrian center. But Whirlwind—he must come with us. Thank you for letting us board him here."

"You know all you need ever do is ask."

Gerta met her gaze and felt as she always did the strength of the bond between them. "I know."

There was an explosion of noise inside the trailer, followed by a loud, low-pitched whinny echoing with frustration. A kind of *how dare you make me wait in here?*

"That horse . . ." Gerta shook her head with impatience. "He'll either be the making of us, or the end of us."

Grace smirked. "Well, I'm voting for the former."

At the horse's demanding neigh, the narrow metal door of the trailer's front living quarters opened. A lean young man with bluntly cut blond hair and dressed in jeans and a blue WEG T-shirt, stepped out.

Karl Reiter, Whirlwind's trainer, squinted in the sunlight and then, spotting Gerta, raised a hand in silent greeting. She tightened her lips as she nodded in acknowledgment. Karl was a well-respected trainer, though still young. Like the horse he trained, he had great promise. She'd brought Karl from Germany soon after she'd acquired Whirlwind, at the recommendation of the breeder. He'd been Whirlwind's trainer in Germany, and the horse had bonded with the young man. Over the years Gerta had further trained Karl, and he was fast becoming a dressage master in his own right.

But Whirlwind was for Elise. She would be the one to ride him to the Olympics. Gerta was aware of the struggle between Elise and Karl over who truly managed the spirited horse. Gerta wanted Elise to handle him—but conceded that, up till now, only Karl could. She watched as Karl descended the trailer steps and walked in his rolling gait toward the rear of the trailer, putting on gloves en route. As he passed the Mercedes, its rear door opened, blocking his path. It nearly hit Karl, and it was too close not to be deliberate.

Elise emerged from the car in form-fitting black yoga pants and a cut-off T-shirt that bared a slim midriff. She had the body of a ballerina, small and lithe, but slammed the door like a truck driver. She turned on her heel to glare at the young man.

"You are *not* unloading Whirlwind," Elise shouted. Her fists were balled at her thighs. "*I* am."

"No, I am. It is your mother's wish."

"It is not my mother's horse! It is my horse. I'm sick and tired of you refusing to get that."

"Stop acting like a spoiled child and let me do my job."

Their voices rang out, and everyone stood openmouthed, watching the spectacle.

Gerta strode toward them muttering, "Such children!" She was fed up with Elise's theatrics. She reared on her daughter, eyes blazing. Unlike theirs, her voice came out in a low hiss, which had a greater effect.

"How many times do I have to put my foot down about this?"

Elise glared back at her but remained silent.

"Stop embarrassing me in front of my friends. And *you* . . ." She faced Karl, her nose lifted. "Do your job and unload that horse." Gerta turned and walked away.

Karl's face went cold as he turned his back to Elise, pounded twice on the large trailer in a signal to the driver, then marched at an angry pace to the side opening. The vehicle's engine quieted, and a dark-haired young man climbed out of the cab and trotted over to help Karl begin unbolting the ramp.

Elise remained by the trailer, but Gerta returned to stand beside Grace. The two women shared a commiserating glance, mother to mother. Then Grace focused on the action at the trailer.

"Mrs. Klug?"

Irritated at the interruption, Gerta turned to cast a quick glance at the lean, compactly built man with longish dark hair and piercing, hazel eyes. She recognized the famed equestrian, but her face gave no indication. As far as she was concerned, riders were no more important than the grooms. They had their job to do and she expected them to do it well. Or they'd be fired.

She looked brusquely at him, then turned away.

"We met before," he continued with an almost eager cheerfulness. "I am Javier Angel de la Cruz." He smiled, as though waiting for her reaction.

Without turning her head, she said, "Yes. I remember."

Angel blinked. "It is good to see you again. And your daughter. Elise?"

"Yes, that's right." She turned to face him, suspicious. "You've met?"

Angel's eyes registered her coolness, yet he pushed on. "Not formally. But I've watched her compete. She is doing very well this year. You must be proud."

Gerta didn't reply. The noise at the trailer drew her attention, and she turned to see the two men pull out the ramp. It landed with a great clatter. Then Karl climbed up the ramp and began opening the side swing door as another high-pitched whinny sounded from within. Anxiety spiked within her; Gerta wasn't aware that she was clenching her hands at her thighs. Her gaze searched out Elise and found her hovering nearby, one arm crossed, her other hand at her mouth as she chewed her nails.

Karl slid open the metal door, and immediately the head of a black stallion, ears forward in an alert posture, appeared. His eyes were bright, and he shook his head imperiously and snorted in the fresh air.

Charles had stepped closer. "That is Whirlwind?"

"Yes," Gerta said, not shifting her gaze from the horse.

He whistled softly. "Magnificent animal!"

She turned to Grace. "I am always nervous when Whirlwind loads and unloads a trailer. A few years ago he had a bad scare in transport that resulted in an injury. He's never forgotten it. He can be a terror backing out. Which is why I purchased this side loader. He can walk out headfirst." She sighed with worry. "I can't let him get hurt. Or, of course, hurt the groom," she said, but with less heart. "This is why I will not allow Elise to load or unload him. She is furious with me about that." Then added, "But then, she is always so."

Whirlwind appeared anxious to disembark, lifting his head and sniffing, eyes wild. Karl stood stoically at the top of the ramp with the lead in his hand. At the base of the steep ramp the driver was waiting to assist. Still Karl didn't move. He waited for Whirlwind to collect himself.

Charles put his palm to his chin as he watched the young trainer's technique, impressed with the young man's calm and efficiency with the great horse. He knew these show ponies, especially the young ones, could be unpredictable. All the obvious precautions had been taken. The trailer would, he knew, be padded to prevent injuries. Whirlwind's legs were also wrapped in padding, as was the halter.

At last the young man began moving the horse down the ramp. Charles had seen photographs of the stallion but was unprepared for the impact of him. Whirlwind was a powerhouse, strong-muscled and confident. His coat could only be called gleaming. But there was something more. Charles had seen a lot of good horses in his time, some of the best. Whirlwind high-stepped and shook his head, as regal as any king. This horse had star power—and he knew it.

Despite Karl's control, midway down the ramp Bunny, Charles's Norwich terrier, came running down the path, barking, and spooked Whirlwind. The horse balked, backed up, and refused to move forward. Karl held firm to the line, but Whirlwind was high-stepping and, on the narrow ramp, dropped his hoof on Karl's foot. Karl blanched and scrunched his eyes shut in obvious pain.

"Mein Gott," Gerta said under her breath.

To his credit, Karl ignored his injury and instead focused on the horse. It was a tense few moments as he limped with the skittish horse to the ground. Elise drew near, and this time Karl obliged and handed her the lead. Anyone could see her satisfaction in her body language as she began walking Whirlwind around the open area. Karl limped to the side of the barn and leaned against it, shooing away the other groom, muttering, "I'm fine. See to the horse."

Grace clapped her hands and called cheerily to the dog. Bunny came promptly in a jaunty trot. Charles could see that Grace was not pleased. She slipped her Hermès belt under the dog's collar and began walking him back up the road to the kennel with an angry stride.

Meanwhile, Elise swiftly moved in to guide Whirlwind with an impressive assurance in wide circles around the area, allowing him to stretch his legs and get his bearings. Everyone watched, mesmerized by the sight of the beautiful stallion in the last of the day's light. His raven coat seemed to glisten against the golden sky. Even in the barn curiosity reigned. The horses stuck their heads out the stall windows, ears pricked forward, checking out the new arrival. They whinnied calls.

When Elise led Whirlwind close to the barn windows, he pranced by the other geldings with a stallion's arrogance. As he neared Butterhead, however, Whirlwind abruptly stopped and jerked his head up. He stretched his nose closer to the mare, his wide nostrils flaring. In response, Butterhead lowered her head and nickered, her tail swishing behind her.

Charles let his fingers cover his grin at the amorous display. *Well, well, well,* he thought. He glanced covertly at Gerta. She stood still, her face unchanged, but her eyes blazed at the display. Then he shifted his gaze to Angel. As expected, he was fixed on the exchange as intently as a hound on the scent.

Gerta rounded on Angel. "Your mare is in heat?" she demanded, her tone accusatory.

"I did not know it until this moment. Hormones, anxiety . . ." He shrugged, taking the situation lightly. He seemed amused by the stallion's reaction.

Gerta was furious. "You let your mare in heat near my stallion?" She didn't give Angel a chance to respond. She turned her back on him and walked toward Elise. "Such incompetence," she said, loud enough for Angel to hear.

Angel appeared stricken. Charles patted him on the back. "No worries. We can't control nature." He indicated the sky. "In any shape or form. We've already decided to put Whirlwind in the small barn across from the main one. His stall is prepared. It's never a good idea to put a stallion in with the others."

He turned to watch as Karl limped with barely concealed pain as he returned to the stallion. He too had witnessed the exchange between Whirlwind and Butterhead and obviously wanted to move the stallion to a different area. Elise relinquished the lead without an argument. Karl wiggled the lead, prompting the horse to walk forward. Whirlwind jerked his head back and shook his mane, but it was more a show. He followed Karl, but as they walked off, Butter-head kept a keen eye on Whirlwind across the square.

A sudden gust of wind swirled and stirred the dust, causing it to spiral high in the air as around them leaves were torn from branches and sent scattering across the grass. The horses retreated into their stalls while the humans raised hands over their eyes, blinking hard.

Looking skyward, Charles saw the low-lying clouds moving in from the southeast across a crimson sky. That stallion wasn't the only thing getting stirred up, he thought. The wind was a reminder of why they were all congregating here. That storm was coming. The horses were settled. Now it was time to take care of the people.

"Let's all go inside for a drink and some dinner," he called to the group. Then, taking Gerta's elbow, he led his guests back up the winding road to the house.

SIX

August 20, 9:15 p.m.
Freehold Farm, North Carolina
Hurricane Noelle pummels Caribbean islands

The delicious scents of garlic and simmering beef bourguignon welcomed the guests into the house. Grace closed the door on the deepening hush of twilight. Inside, candles flickered on the long, damask-draped table like early stars.

An hour later, Grace leaned back in her chair, wineglass in her hand, and gazed around her table. Through the comfortable haze of wine and good food, the white flowers seemed to shimmer in the candlelight. Yet though her guests were sated, they were anything but relaxed. The conversation had been awkward and stilted throughout dinner. When she'd agreed to let them come, she'd had concerns whether her friends, who for the most part didn't know one another, would get along.

Charles sat opposite her at the head of the table. He and Angel at his left were engaged in earnest discussion. Well, mostly Charles was listening and Angel was talking in his exuberant, hands-in-the-air style.

At her left, Karl was leaning toward Elise. They talked heatedly, heads bent. They could be an advertisement for a picture-perfect German couple, she thought, with their blond hair and blue eyes. And they had so much in common: their culture, language, love of horses—one in particular. But all they did was continually, annoyingly snipe at each other.

Hannah sat between Angel and Gerta, circling her wineglass with her finger. She seemed to be listening to Angel's conversation, but not participating. Grace watched and wondered what Hannah's position was on the sale of Butterhead. She hadn't had a chance to talk to her friend yet.

She shifted her gaze to the friend sitting at her right. Gerta too sat with one elbow on the table and her long, slender fingers folded near her chin. She looked out under lids at half-mast with an air of elegant ennui. It was a disappointment to Grace that her two friends didn't get along. Hannah and Gerta were polite when they were together and she didn't sense animosity between them. Rather, they didn't have much to say to each other. Looking at Gerta's plate, Grace saw that she'd not touched her dinner.

Grace leaned closer. "Are you all right?"

Gerta turned her head and a faint smile crossed her face. "It's my leg. The drive was, perhaps, too long. I'm afraid I'll have to pay the piper."

Grace could see the pain reflected in her expression and felt awash in embarrassment. She should've known Gerta would be tired. She was failing as a hostess . . . a friend. But in truth, she often forgot that Gerta had lost her leg. She puffed out a plume of air. Well, of course she didn't forget, not really. But Gerta camouflaged her injury so well, like a wounded wild bird that would spend its last breath trying to look healthy. Gerta was a determined, dynamic woman, one who wielded strong opinions. A woman of influence. And she always wore pants to cover her prosthesis. Seeing Gerta, one never thought of her as handicapped. Grace smiled ruefully. And, of course, wasn't that the point? Gerta would never let others know that after twenty-five years using a prosthesis, she still suffered.

Grace folded her napkin and placed it on the table, ready to rise and bring the dinner to a close. "It's time for you to go to bed."

Gerta placed her hand on Grace's, stilling her. "One moment. I want to hear how this ends." She nodded discreetly toward Charles and Angel. "I think your husband is being sold a horse."

Grace grimaced and darted her gaze back to Charles. Of course Gerta would not be sitting idly by. She was hawking the conversation, feigning disinterest. Hannah too, Grace noted, was leaning toward the two men. Grace was mildly irked at herself for being so oblivious. Like the other two women, she leaned forward in her seat to hear better. Grace groaned inwardly. Sure enough, they were talking about Butterhead.

"The sad truth, my friend," Charles said in a gentle voice, "is that my jumping days are over. Once upon a time, I'd have jumped at the chance for a horse like Butterhead. Pun intended." He shrugged slightly. "But I'm not looking for a jumper."

"Butterhead is a superstar jumper, this is true," Angel conceded. "But she is older and doesn't want"—he made a sigh of concession—"or *can't* take the high jumps any longer. She knows this and it hurts her." He fisted his chest. "She's proud, eh? But

Butterhead also knows dressage. The fundamentals of any riding discipline come from dressage, no?" He spread out his hands. "Butterhead will be able to transition into dressage so smoothly you would think it had been her first profession."

"Oh, please . . ." Gerta's voice rose over the table. Everyone swung their heads around to look at her. "You make it sound so simple."

Angel cocked his head, surprised that she had joined their conversation. Then he smiled. "Because it is simple."

Gerta lowered her hand to rest on the table. Her multi-carat diamond caught the light. "You *simply* will not have the necessary support in the saddle unless the rider is able to sit properly balanced."

Angel scoffed, "There are different saddles, of course."

"Saddles are the least of it. Switching disciplines is much more than a change in tack. It requires a change in a rider's seat and aids. Switching can leave even the most experienced rider feeling as if he is learning to ride all over again."

Angel leaned back in his chair and slid an arm along the back in an insolently relaxed manner. "But any beginner"—he nodded toward Charles—"must learn all this on any horse he rides, correct?" He paused and moved again to place his elbows on the table and clasped his hands. "And Butterhead is not just any horse." His eyes gleamed. "She is one of those rare, superb athletes that has had great training. She will take care of the rider. And a rider can expect that *this* horse will maintain the highest standards." He flattened his palms on the table and leaned forward, chin high as though to prove his point.

Hannah put her hand lightly on Angel's arm, indicating he should stop.

Karl spoke up. "I think you are both missing the most important point." Heads turned toward him. "It is not merely a matter of technique. While I acknowledge that there is a connection between rider and horse in any discipline, dressage pushes that relationship to its greatest heights. The riding pair is a *team*. In body and mind."

"And you think that is not true of a jumper and rider?" Angel said, sitting straighter, as if affronted.

Karl shook his head. "No, not to the same extent."

Angel made a sound of exasperation. "This spoken by a trainer of dressage."

Karl pushed on. "Try to think of it as if they were dancers. And they all learned the basics of ballet. What are they called . . . ?"

"The barre exercises," said Grace.

"Yes. This is fundamental." Karl spread out his palms. "Dressage is the dance in the horse world. It's a ballet where the rider and horse are harmonious." He moved his hands. "It's one fluid motion. They are one mind. The first time you get a moment like that is an exhilarating, almost spiritual experience. You remember it for the rest of your life."

A hush settled over the table. Grace saw that Charles was mesmerized by the possibilities. It had been a long time since he had felt a connection like that to a horse. The possibility of feeling it again was like a lifeline thrown to a drowning man. In contrast, Elise's brows furrowed as she slumped back in her chair.

"That said . . ." Gerta paused. She had picked up a knife and was gently tracing a line in the linen. Grace studied her friend's face. She looked like a feline ready to pounce. Grace waited pensively. She knew Gerta hated to lose an argument. Gerta let the knife rest on the table and raised her head to fix her hawkish gaze on Angel.

"Your horse . . ." she said as though she'd forgotten its name. "Butterhead."

Angel stiffened as though slapped. Gerta Klug was an expert and raised some of the world's finest horses. Her opinion mattered.

"She could, I suppose, be retrained in dressage. But I do not believe she is the right horse for a beginner in the sport." She turned her attention to Charles. "My friend, though you are an experienced jumper, you are not experienced in dressage. You need a horse that can help *you* make the transition. You don't need a horse that you have to help make that transition as well. That is a recipe for failure."

Angel's face colored. He opened his mouth to speak, but Grace beat him to it.

"I think," Grace said, setting both hands on the table and cutting off the discussion, "we can continue this conversation tomorrow. My friends, it's late, and you haven't yet settled into your houses. Before we adjourn, there are a few things we must discuss. First, as always, the horses. We have only one groom, Jose. There are too many horses for him to tend alone. I realize you will all take care of your own horses' needs in the morning and evening. But we'll need to take turns going down for the late-night barn checks. Especially with Karl injured. We can draw straws, or . . ." She smiled and let her palms flip up.

"I'll take tonight," Charles volunteered. "You're all exhausted."

"I'll go tomorrow night," Angel volunteered.

"I'll take the following night," said Gerta, raising a hand and wiggling her fingers.

In short order, the nights were assigned. Grace sensed a universal urge to retreat as people dabbed their mouths with napkins and set them on the table.

"There's coffee in your houses. I'll have breakfast here every morning by seven, should you choose to join us. Dinner we can take in our strides. I love to cook. We can go out too. There are some lovely restaurants nearby. Now, leave everything and go," she told them, her fingers wiggling as though chasing them all away. "I have your keys."

The group began to rise, exchanging comments of farewell. They were gathering at the door when a new sound rose up over the rest. It was the high-pitched grind of a truck coming up the driveway. Grace felt her heart quicken. She swung open the door and stepped out on the stoop. Coming around the curve she saw the front grille of her daughter's mud-splattered Range Rover, a horse trailer behind it.

"Moira's arrived!"

"Mama!"

Moira waved, then stepped down from the cab of her big black Range Rover, feeling the blood circulate through her legs. Ever since she could remember, just seeing her mother's face meant being home. She was beyond exhausted, but a sudden burst of adrenaline spurred her to run into Grace's arms.

"You're here!" Grace exclaimed by her ear as she squeezed Moira in a rocking motion. "I was beginning to worry."

"Oh, Mama, it's good to be here."

"Thank you," Grace said. "You did heroic work to go to Camden and fetch the dogs." She pulled back to look at Moira's face. Moira saw fatigue etched in her mother's tanned skin, but her eyes were bright with excitement. "Which reminds me. Ron called and told me to tell you again how grateful they are. They're in Palm Beach now, hunkering down for the storm. He said the entire state is in mayhem, fleeing the storm or madly boarding up houses. I feel for them."

"I feel for the whole coast. My own house included."

Moira felt the gentle squeeze of reassurance on her arm. Oddly, she wasn't afraid for her house. At this moment, now that she was back at Freehold Farm, she didn't care if the whole house just blew away. There wasn't time to think about that, however. There was work to be done. Moira inhaled the scent of her mother's perfume and treasured the feeling of her arms around her for one second longer, then slowly released her.

A high-pitched yapping sounded from the car. Moira turned to see Gigi standing on the seat, her rear wiggling as she tried to determine if she could make the jump to the ground.

"Gigi, wait," Moira ordered as she hurried to the car.

At seeing Moira, Gigi of course did not wait. In her excitement she leaped from the car and began dancing around the clustered cars, running to the guests and leaping on legs.

"Mama, can you put Gigi inside the house? She's in heat, and the last thing I need is for a bunch of randy dogs to start howling."

"In heat? Good God," Grace exclaimed as she hurried after the dog dancing around her friends. Angel scooped her up in his arms and, a smitten female, Gigi began eagerly licking his face. Laughing, he handed Gigi to Grace, who took her inside.

That done, Moira looked at the trailer and sighed with resignation at the havoc she was about to unleash. "I'd better get all these dogs out, watered, and fed, pronto."

Her father stepped up, beaming at her. "Daddy," she whispered on a sigh as she gave him an equally long, heartfelt hug, feeling as she always did on returning home how strong their bond remained. As Moira pulled from her father's embrace, she looked over his shoulder to see other guests emerging from the house in that hesitant gait of uncertainty.

She immediately recognized Gerta. Though small boned like Elise, with her height and carriage, she tended to stand out in a crowd. Behind her she spotted Hannah, also tall with her long blond hair pulled back in a ponytail—always beautiful and chic, even in jeans, always with her makeup perfect. Then her breath hitched when she caught sight of Angel de la Cruz. It was startling to see him here, in the flesh. He looked just as he did in his pictures, only perhaps even more handsome, all scruffy and . . . real.

But her smile widened at seeing her old friend Elise. It had been years. She seemed smaller and thinner, if possible. She looked like a Pre-Raphaelite with her strong cheekbones and her piercing blue eyes, and her blond hair flowing in ripples nearly to her waist. Elise hung back, but her eyes were gleaming with expectation.

Moira politely made her way through the group, kissing Gerta's cheek, then Hannah's. She put out her hand to Angel, but he moved to kiss both her cheeks in the European style. She caught the faint scent of cologne and his body that was very masculine. Then, at last, Elise. She felt awkward hugging her friend. The gesture seemed to emphasize the estranged years.

"You look great," Moira told her. "I like your hair down."

Elise's hand shot to her hair. "I look horrible. I just spent the day in a car." She rolled her eyes. "With my mother."

Moira laughed. "Hey, try driving with eight dogs!"

Elise barked out a short laugh. "Wait. What?"

"There are eight rescue dogs in that horse trailer," Moira explained, pointing. "Rescues from Danny and Ron." She saw Elise's eyes spark at the names. When they were young, the girls had volunteered together at the pair's dog shelter in Florida. Gerta had told them in her inimitable way that if they brought a dog home with them, *they'd* be sent to the doghouse.

Moira continued, "They're gearing up for the storm. These dogs needed to be moved so more rescue dogs could be brought in. They're expecting a lot of lost dogs from the hurricane. People leave them. Or they can't take them. I don't know."

"I can't imagine leaving a pet behind."

"Anyway, they put out the call for transport, and I volunteered. Speaking of which, the dogs need to get out. Like, *now*. Help me, okay?"

"Yeah, of course." Elise hurried to accompany Moira to the rear of the trailer.

"Mom?" Moira called out. "Want to open the garage door?"

Moira unlocked the latch of the trailer and, with a heave, slid open the door. There was an immediate cacophony of high-pitched yelps and low, gruff barks of anxious dogs.

Elise waved her hand before her face. "Whew. Man, smells like it was a long trip."

"It was." Moira sighed, chagrined by the foul smell. "I walked them at each rest stop. That's what added so much time to the trip." She made a face. "They're nervous."

"No good deed goes unpunished," Elise quipped as she stepped into the trailer. "Let's get them out of there."

Each of the dogs had arrived with paperwork that was attached to its crate, including its name, breed, health records, and whatever was known about the dog's disposition. There were crates of all sizes—several large ones, a medium, and several small ones. In each, bright eyes stared out, fearful, curious, begging to be released.

To their credit, all the guests hurried to the trailer to help. Everyone except Gerta. She promptly went to Grace and made her apologies, and then came to Elise.

"Darling, I'm sorry. I must go."

"Well, I can't leave Moira when she needs help."

"No, of course not."

"I can drive Elise to the cottage or she can stay here," Moira assured her before Gerta could say anything more. Gerta thanked her and took her leave.

Moira and Elise began the process of picking up one crate after another and passing it to waiting arms. A couple of the crates were so large that it took two people to carry them.

"Carry the crates to the fenced yard and let them run!" Grace called out, immediately taking charge. She trotted to open the iron gate into the large yard and swung it wide for Hannah and Angel to stagger through with the first one. Once inside, they opened the large crate, and a coonhound mix lumbered out.

"That's a good-looking dog," Angel said, watching the coonhound take long, graceful leaps.

"You like any dog as long as it's big," Hannah said, bending to close the crate's latch. "Where is Max, anyway?"

Angel pointed. Hannah turned to see a long line of paned windows from the family room; standing there, noses pressed to the glass and barking, were Max, Bunny, and Gigi.

Some dogs calmly strolled out of their crates and stretched, then lumbered to the grass; others, a bit disoriented, spun around, then stood stiff-legged and barked at no one in particular. There were eight dogs in total, different sizes, shapes, and fur. Finally the last one was released to the yard, and the helpers began to disperse. Hannah and Angel called out their good-byes. Then Charles said that he and Karl were going to the barn to check on the horses. Karl had been given the loft above the stable to stay in.

Moira felt fatigue descend as she turned to watch the dogs running in the yard. She thought how much they needed and deserved this time. From the moment she'd taken charge of their welfare, she'd felt an onerous sense of responsibility.

Elise came to her side. "Once we settle the dogs down, you'll have to tell me how you got roped into this."

"It's a long story," Moira replied, swiping a lock of hair from her brow, "and a good one. But I'll need a glass of wine to tell it." She went to the now empty horse trailer. Tufts of fur lay in the corners and the scent of urine was pervasive. She sighed heavily. "But I've got eight dog crates that need cleaning."

"I'll help."

Moira looked at her askance. "Are you up to helping to carry the crates over to the hose there? If you do that much, I'll wash them."

"I'll help wash too," said Elise.

"You sure? It's a dirty job."

"Hey, you forget I've done it before."

"Thanks," said Moira.

"I'll help too," said Grace. "I've mucked out my share of stalls. A little poop doesn't scare me. But first, come check out the new kennel." She ushered them toward the garage that stood open.

Moira stepped into a three-car garage that had been transformed. Her mama had done it up proper. It had been scrubbed clean and still smelled a bit of Pine-Sol. Metal shelves lined one wall; each shelf held neatly stacked plastic bins filled with supplies. A tall pile of new dog mats for the crates rested on a nearby table. In the opposite corner was a food prep area complete with a long table, a small fridge, and sealed plastic bins filled with dog kibble and canned food. Nearby a thick rubber pad lay on the floor beside a laundry basket filled with assorted dog toys.

"It's dog heaven," Moira said with a laugh. She wouldn't have expected anything less from her mother. "You've created a dog rescue shelter."

"Not just me. Randy was here, and Darryl. They worked for hours to clean it and move in all the supplies." She pointed to the long back wall. "The dog crates will go along that wall, so if you ever want to open the door, they can look out." Grace put her hands on her hips and took a final survey. "Like it?"

"What's not to like? It's perfect. Take lots of pictures for Danny and Ron so they won't be worried."

"With that storm coming, I doubt they'll have time to worry."

Moira thought of the oncoming hurricane and all those heroes like Danny and Ron, and the firemen and police and city workers who would hunker down, and the residents who had decided, foolishly, to stay and ignore the evacuation orders. They all had to face the oncoming monster.

"God bless them all."

SEVEN

August 20, 10:45 p.m.
Lake Lure, North Carolina
*Hurricane Noelle makes landfall on Cuba
with sustained winds of 160 mph*

The beam from the Audi's headlights tilted and dipped as they wound along the road to the Phillipses' lake house. Angel drove too fast on the country roads for Hannah's comfort, but she was too weary to voice a complaint and, like him, was eager to put her head on the pillow and close her eyes.

"You laid it on pretty thick about Butterhead tonight," she told him.

"What? I did not. I didn't once mention selling her. Not once."

"You didn't have to. Please, Javi. You heard Grace. She doesn't want Charles to get a jumper. She's my friend." Her voice held a note of warning as well as a plea.

"Mr. Charles is a big boy. He can make up his own mind, eh?

But I will not press. I will present the facts. That is all. Okay?" He swiftly turned his head to gauge her reaction.

Hannah gritted her teeth and didn't reply. Angel didn't know how *not* to lay it on thick. She tightened her arms around herself in a huff and swung her head to look out the window. They made the turn into the residential community that bordered the lake.

Angel slowed to a crawl on the serpentine road that wound around nooks and crannies of the lake that was visible only as a shimmering blackness in the distance. Cars sat in the driveways, lights burned in the eclectic houses that rimmed the lake, and the occasional dog erupted in barking as they drove past. Angel inched along while Hannah peered out the window seeking the correct address on a mailbox.

"I hope we didn't pass it," she said worriedly.

Angel swore something in Spanish.

"If we did, we'll just circle back." She hoped he wouldn't lose his good humor, which she counted on at tense times. At the sound of his master's voice, Max rose up on the backseat and stuck his enormous head through the opening between the seats. Hannah could feel his hot breath on her neck.

"Sit down, Max," she ordered. And was ignored. "Oh, there it is!" she exclaimed with relief, spotting the correct number on a black mailbox by the road.

Angel turned into a long, narrow driveway that dipped steeply toward the lake. She could make out a two-story house in the shadows, but the porch lights were shining in welcome. Beyond, tiny lights from distant houses shimmered around the dark expanse of water.

"It's bigger than I expected," Angel said, pulling up the parking brake.

"And thoughtful of Grace to leave the porch lights on." They provided a welcoming glow in the darkness.

Angel pushed open the car door, and immediately Max bounded into the darkness, madly sniffing the ground. They dragged their suitcases to the front porch and were relieved when the key easily clicked. Stepping inside, they found themselves in a gracious home with overstuffed furniture, a stone fireplace, black-and-red-checked curtains, and country décor. Hannah was immediately cheered to find the place immaculately clean, with fresh flowers on the dining table and bottles of wine, coffee, and sundries at the ready.

"Isn't this charming?" she said, feeling that sense of joy and relief one does when arriving at an unfamiliar guest house or hotel room and finding it delightful. Upstairs there were three bedrooms, and without a word they both carried their suitcases to the large master bedroom with windows overlooking the lake.

"I'll take the first shower," Hannah volunteered, her travel bag in her hand. She couldn't play the polite game of you-go-first. She was too damn tired and stinky.

The bathroom was small but tidy and had all the necessities. Hannah closed her eyes and stood under the stream of hot water, sighing heavily, feeling the miles wash away. It seemed forever ago that they'd packed up and evacuated Florida. All the panic, the decisions, the heartbreak. The raw fear. Here in the mountains, she felt safe.

She washed her hair, taking her time to scrub the tension from her scalp. Then she buffed her body with thirsty towels and slipped into a silk and lace nightgown. She felt bonelessly tired now. She didn't do a beauty routine. She barely brushed her teeth, ran a comb through her long hair, and dabbed moisturizing lotion on her skin. Then she stepped out of the steamy bathroom into the bedroom.

The spacious room had a cushy navy sofa piped in white before the windows. The white curtains at the windows were matched by a plump white comforter on the bed piled with an overabundance of pillows. On the bedside table Angel's phone was already plugged in and recharging, and his boots were set neatly by the door.

Angel was standing in his stocking feet, shirttails out, before the television, holding two wineglasses amply filled with what she hoped was a robust red. On the screen a trio of weathermen looking professional in pressed shirts stood in front of a map of the southeastern United States. They all spoke in the same urgent tone as they pointed to several dark blue lines running from a circular hurricane in the Atlantic and skimming the eastern coast of Florida. Like the dogs in Pavlov's famed experiment, she and Angel responded by drawing closer to the television, their attention riveted.

"Your turn," Hannah said.

Angel moved toward her and handed her one of the wineglasses. She took it gratefully and sipped, eyes glued to the screen.

"What's the update?"

Angel frowned. "They are calling it extremely dangerous," he said in a taut voice. "It looks like Miami's going to get hit. It could be ground zero."

It was an odd phenomenon. While listening to the reports, you were always grateful and relieved when your town was not the bull's-eye. But that relief you felt for your own safety made you feel guilty and worry for the neighbors in the bull's-eye. "But they always say Miami's going to get hit. . . ."

"Yeah, sure. Because it's right there at the tip of the state like a chin sticking out. But look," Angel said, pointing. "Some of the models are veering more north now."

Hannah felt a surge of worry for her condo. "I know that'll be bad for me, but think of the worry for Gerta. At least it's a relief most of the horses got out."

"A lot, but there are still many there. We'll just have to wait and see, no?"

"I hate this waiting. Waiting for a hurricane is like waiting for a turtle."

Angel lowered the volume on the television and tossed the remote on the nearby chair. "Speaking of Gerta, what's with her?" he asked, gaining heat. "What a bitch. Who does she think she is, eh? Talking about my horse like that."

"She's Gerta Klug," Hannah deadpanned. "And she was getting under your skin. I know her. She likes to play with people. Like a cat with a mouse."

Angel bowed up. "A mouse? That's what she thinks I am? A *ratón*?"

"*Ay! Un ratoncito,*" she teased.

He shot her an angry look and paced across the room, muttering furiously in Spanish. He stopped short in the middle of the room and spun to face Hannah, indignant. "And what was that about with her leaving early tonight, eh?" he demanded, his arms lifted in emphasis. "We were all tired, but we all came out to help with the dogs. Aiee, so many dogs. . . . But she cuts out? Everyone else, you know, they helped. Even Karl. He is hurt! He can barely walk. What was her excuse?" He snorted. "Is she too good to work with the peasants?"

Hannah heard the annoyance in his voice and wondered if he

was angrier at Gerta for not helping out with the dogs or for blocking his sale of Butterhead.

"No," she said in a calm voice, trying to defuse his frustration. "That's not it. Grace told me her leg was hurting her. She barely made it through dinner."

Angel looked perplexed. "Her leg?"

"Her prosthesis," Hannah explained. When Angel stumbled on the translation, she added, "Her false leg."

Angel's eyes widened with surprise. "Her what?"

"Oh, come on, Javi. You know Gerta lost her leg."

He shook his head. "No! I never knew."

That surprised her. The equestrian world was like a small village in terms of gossip. And Gerta Klug was a major figure. "I thought it was common knowledge."

Angel merely shrugged. She had to remember that he was Venezuelan and he had only been staying in Wellington for a short while. While the Klug horse breeding program was known and respected throughout the world, the gossip about Gerta might not have reached him.

"What happened to her?" he asked.

It was a long story. Hannah walked to the queen-size bed and plopped onto the fluffy white down coverlet. The soft cushiness was inviting and, careful not to spill her wine, she propped up a few pillows and leaned back against them, stretching out her long legs. She sighed and took a second to enjoy the high-quality cotton against her skin. Dear Grace. Small pleasures like these meant the world when one was exhausted. She looked over at Angel. He looked pale and drawn, his clothes wrinkled from the exceedingly long day. She patted the mattress. Moving soundlessly in his stocking feet, he came to perch on the bed beside her. Promptly, Max rose with a groan like an old man and padded across the red oriental rug to the bedside, then collapsed on the floor with a thump beside Angel's feet. He settled his big head with a grunt that implied he was put out at having to move.

Angel swirled his wine, his eyes bright with curiosity. "So?"

Hannah stifled a yawn as she tried to dredge up all the details in her mind. "It all happened a long time ago," she said on a sigh. It struck her suddenly how much older she was than Angel. He was in his midforties, but he seemed forever young. Though Hannah had aged well, with a little help from plastic surgery and cosmetology, she was fifty-two years old. Gerta and Grace were fifty-five. They knew a history in the horse world that preceded him.

"It was when she was in her late twenties, I think. Or maybe early thirties." She paused, but her foggy brain couldn't remember exactly. She knew Angel got impatient when a story stalled, so she plowed on. "Anyway, Gerta was a top rider in her day. She won many international show jumping competitions. A rising star. She rode one horse in particular . . ." Once again her tired brain failed her. She took a sip and waved her hand. "Ugh, I can't remember the name. But he was one of those once-in-a-lifetime horses. They were always in the top three at jumping events."

"This I knew. He was a famous horse. His name, I think, was Razzmajazz."

"That's right," she said, the name clicking in her brain. She saw the big bay in her mind's eye. "A beautiful horse. They were a winning combination." She paused and lifted her glass. "Is there more wine?"

Angel rose and walked to the table for the bottle. Max lifted his head, watching. When Angel returned to the bed, Max settled his head back on his paws with a satisfied grunt.

"Thanks, *mi amor*," Hannah said as Angel refilled her glass. She took a small sip. Angel filled his glass, put the bottle on the bedside table beside the brass lamp, and settled once again on the bed.

"I think it was during the Olympic trials," she continued. "She was taking a final jump. It was a good run. Maybe flawless. Razzmajazz made the jump. Everyone cheered. But on landing . . . he just collapsed. They said he suffered an aneurysm. A heart attack," she clarified. "Unfortunately, when he hit the ground, he rolled over onto Gerta. Her leg was pinned. Crushed, really." She shook her head sadly.

He frowned. "That's terrible!" Angel said, seeming truly shocked. "That was *her*? I remember now that this horse died during a jump. But I didn't put it together with Gerta."

"It was so sad. Heartbreaking. They had to put the horse down on the spot, of course. And Gerta—she lost her leg. Her career was over."

She watched him digest this. After a moment, he shook his head. "No. Her career was not over. She went on to create a world-class breeding program. I would be honored to ride a horse from the Klug stable. And all this time I didn't know she lost her leg. What a remarkable woman."

"She's tough, that's for sure."

"Yeah. I thought she walked stiffly because she carried a crop in her boot," Angel said with a laugh.

Hannah laughed lightly at the joke she'd heard before. Her boot wasn't the only place she'd heard people say Gerta's crop was stuck. Gerta was the boss. Respected. But because she was a woman, the men bristled under her authority where they'd expect it from a man. The stables were still a man's world. She'd heard the slurs slapped on Gerta by the guys: Brunhilda, Der Führer, the Dragon Lady, the Sloane Ranger, Darth Vader, which Hannah thought especially cruel considering the lost leg. Angel had never stooped to that level, but still, like her, he'd laughed at the quips. She was glad he now knew the full story.

He appeared lost in thought, staring into his drink. Hannah nudged him. "So, you've changed your opinion of Gerta Klug? She's not the slacker you thought she was."

Angel offered a crooked smile that soon slipped as he slowly shook his head. "No, she's not." He paused. "Quite the contrary. I admire her."

The Cottage, Freehold Farm

The teakettle whistled shrilly. Gerta hurried to the stove, grabbing a towel en route. She winced as she walked, each step in her prosthesis causing her pain. Not just her leg—tonight every muscle of her body ached after the long car journey. But her amputated leg pulsed an angry pain, scolding her for overdoing.

"Damn knob," she muttered. That was what she called her stump. She thought of it in the third person, an appendage she had to deal with on a daily basis but one that was not really part of herself, like her arm or foot.

She gratefully removed her stale clothes and slipped into her long, white cotton Calida nightgown. Then she went into the bathroom to prepare for her shower. Once she removed her prosthesis, all had to be in the ready. Gerta noticed that Grace had put a shower bench in place, bless her heart. Without it, showering was a clumsy affair of crawling and hoisting her body on wobbly arms.

Gerta always stayed at Grace's cottage when she traveled to Tryon for horse shows. The lake house might be bigger, but the cottage was one floor that Gerta could readily navigate. And at this point in her life, comfort mattered so much more than luxury. The other reason, of course, was that the cottage was closer to her dear friend. She could zip over to the big house for breakfast, a sauna, or a glass of wine.

Before removing her leg, Gerta made herself a bracing cup of tea. Then after her shower, she could, at long last, sleep. That's all she wanted from the world tonight. As she poured the water, she wondered when Elise would return. Moira had promised to give her a ride.

Elise . . . Gerta huffed out a short laugh. Elise was more trouble than help these days. Nothing Gerta did made her intractable daughter happy. Quite the opposite. Everything she said was met with skepticism, doubt, or even anger. It was a classic mother-daughter stalemate. And it was exhausting. She'd have to talk to Grace about it. Idly, she wondered if Grace had the same problem with Moira. She doubted it. Moira was married now. From all she'd read, didn't that change the nature of the mother-daughter relationship?

Gerta wrestled with those thoughts as she carried the scalding tea to her bedroom and set it on the bedside stand to cool. It was a comfortable room with a king-size bed, two big lamps for light, and an upholstered chair—and, of course, the hunting décor that adorned the rest of the cottage.

Grace loved to hunt. She found the sport of men and women in black and red coats riding behind baying hounds on the scent through crisp woodland exhilarating. Despite the dress and decorum, however, neither the hunters nor their dogs actually chased a fox anymore. Instead, the dogs followed a scented path. In Europe, foxhunting was banned in many countries—in fact, though most people didn't realize it, Hitler had been a pioneer of hunting bans. Gerta often wondered how the Führer could consider killing foxes unsporting but not have an issue with killing fellow human Jews.

Grace's passion for hunting was the theme of the cottage, done in a scheme of hunter green and white with splashes of red. Prints of horsemen jumping over fences on the hunt beside hounds decorated pillows, plates on the wall, and curtains. There was a fox door knocker, fox brass lamps, and a few fox figurines. When she'd first stayed at the cottage, Gerta had begged Grace to remove the stuffed fox from the living room.

Gerta found that in the equestrian world, people who hunted tended to be mad for their sport in a different way than those who pursued dressage or jumping. They took the sport home with them, relished the folklore, and were chummy with friends in the club. By contrast, the jumping world could be catty, as could the world of dressage. Competition brought out the best and the worst in people.

She was content, even happy, that Grace had found her niche in hunting. When they were young they'd both aspired to event jumping. Grace was good. Very. But she didn't have the drive needed to excel in competition. She was too good at other things that mattered to her. By the time they were in college, she wanted to date and enjoy being a young, beautiful woman. She continued to jump, but only in local shows. She loved sponsoring events rather than jumping in them. When she met Charles at twenty-five, that was it. In her indomitable style, Grace had made him her top priority. Her life. After they married, she had put her energy and determination into his equestrian career. A few years later, her focus included Moira.

Gerta gathered her bag of supplies for her leg, then settled on the bed. She took a deep breath before beginning. It was a process she knew well. She'd gone through several models of prosthetic legs in the twenty-five years she'd worn them. The first one hadn't been far from the wooden leg of Captain Ahab. It was like walking on a stilt. Science had come a long way since then. Now she wore a top-of-the-line leg with a microprocessor knee that had a computer and hydraulics on board, not to mention a foot that allowed her to walk with a natural gait over uneven terrain and to take stairs step over step. That had been life-changing.

Still, care of the prosthesis and the knob involved a process that required due diligence. Her German mentality and eye to perfection had kept her relatively infection-free all these years, knock on wood. She playfully knocked on the leg, though it was a far cry from wood.

She pulled back her long nightgown to reveal the black, high-tech carbon-fiber socket that enveloped the stump of her leg. She pushed the white button on its side. A soft hiss sounded as the vacuum suction was released. After that, the leg was easy to remove. She slipped it off and set it aside. Next she peeled off the liner. This cushioning material fit over her limb for comfort and to prevent chapping and blisters. Rolling it off felt a bit like removing an old-fashioned stocking—if the stocking had been made of silicone instead of silk. Guys jokingly called it the leg condom.

Gerta released a soft moan at being free. The flesh of her stump hung loose and was ribbed with scars. Each year she lost a little more of it. Tonight the skin appeared chafed and bruised. She delicately let her fingertips graze the tender skin, and winced. But she was lucky. Despite the overuse, she didn't see any blisters. Those were the enemies. They'd keep her from using her leg until they healed. She reached for the cream in her bag, then began to massage in the anti-chafing cream, her fingernails blood red against her pale skin. Another moan escaped her lips.

The cream felt restorative but the wretched knob continued to throb. She pulled out a bottle of Vicodin and tapped two pills into her palm. She reached for the tea, cooler now, and downed the pills with a hearty swallow. Gerta closed her eyes and felt the pills slide down. Then she put away the bag and lay back on the pillows, letting the fatigue and pills do their work.

Her thoughts drifted back to Grace and their time together as young women. Grace had had the luxury of choosing to give up competitive jumping. Gerta had had that option wrenched from her unwilling hands. She no longer felt cheated or angry at God for that tragic accident—not anymore. The years had a way of rounding off the pointed edges of anger. Still, she sometimes wondered how far she might have gone if fate had allowed her to continue. She liked to think she'd have made it to the Olympics. She felt sure she would have. That had been her most cherished dream. A hard one to let go.

She'd never been as motherly as Grace. It was not in her nature. Even as girls, Grace had taken care of her friends, watched out for them, always seeming to know what Gerta needed and when, while Gerta was laser-focused on whatever competition she was preparing for. It had never occurred to her to think about what others might need—at least not during events. Gerta could be very generous with her friends. Giving to them gave her great pleasure in return. She found that being able to be generous was one of the great perks of having money to spend on causes and people she cared about. But for Grace, the giving came naturally and was a constant in her life.

That quality was probably one of the main reasons she was such a good wife and mother. Charles adored her. Gerta huffed out a short laugh. She couldn't imagine her ex-husband, Paul, agreeing to the D or D demand. Or any demand, for that matter. After nearly twenty years of marriage, Paul had been furious at the division of property. He'd always resented her meteoric rise and felt she deserved little or nothing for not giving him a son. Gerta's lip curled as she brought the teacup to her mouth. The misogynist . . .

Without a husband, a home, or a leg, Gerta had left Germany and fled to southeastern Florida, where friends of hers were developing a new horse community. She'd needed to get in on the ground floor of something important that she could become passionate about. And she had Elise. Together, she'd dreamed of creating in the United States a breeding stable that rivaled her ex-husband's in Europe. In less than fifteen years, Gerta felt she'd largely succeeded in her business goal. But her dream of creating the Klug dynasty with Elise was so far failing miserably.

Gerta yawned, feeing the pain lessen and the sleepiness take hold. She couldn't think of Elise tonight. She was too tired. Too defenseless. As the Vicodin took effect, she felt her self-control slide and she began to slip into the vortex of uncertainty. Old fears and doubts stirred in her brain to infest her heart. She curled up on her side, one knee bent closer to her chest, and drew up the blanket to tuck under her neck. Where was Elise? she worried. How were her other horses? The people who worked for her in Florida? Her home? What devastation would this hurricane bring? What would she return to in Florida?

During the day Gerta put on a strong front. Gerta Klug was always in control. *Large and in charge*, Elise would say, not in a kind way. But at night, in the dark, she was just a woman. Alone. Vulnerable.

And, yes, afraid.

Freehold Farm, North Carolina

Grace sat against the plush pillows in the king-size mahogany four-poster bed, spreading cream on her hands and watching her husband pace about the room getting ready for bed. In his sixties, Charles was still as slender and fit as a younger man. His core strength from a lifetime riding horses kept his abdomen firm. He turned his back to her as he stepped into his pajama bottoms. A ferocious scar ran down his back. Another one cut into his left shoulder. She never saw them without a shiver of fear and a surge of gratitude that he'd survived so many falls and surgeries.

Injuries were expected, even common, in the equestrian world. It was an unspoken code of honor among them: you fall, you get back on the horse. Broken bones were commonplace. There were serious spinal breaks that meant weeks, even months, of healing. And still the rider got back on the horse.

But there was, for a few, the fall that changed one's life. Some gave up riding from fear of the next fall that could cripple. There were those both lucky and determined enough, like Charles, that they could endure the near-fatal fall, struggle, and against all odds and the doctors' predictions, succeed in walking again. There were the truly unfortunate few who, through fault or fate, fell and were paralyzed, like the actor Christopher Reeve. Finally, there were those who had fallen and died. That was the known risk of riding. Though Grace no longer event-jumped for competition, a misplaced hoof during any hunt or trail ride could send both her horse and her tumbling. A dear friend had died from a hunting accident just the year before.

Charles, however, had suffered more than his share of injuries, both minor and severe. He was only sixty-five, but he had the bones of an eighty-year-old. She couldn't bear to lose him. Grace was resolved never to see him fall again.

He stood buttoning his pajama top, staring out into the night, lost in thought. Finished, he turned and caught her staring at him.

"What?" he asked, seeming baffled, looking down. "Did I put my pants on backward?"

Grace smirked. "I know what you're thinking. And the answer is no."

"You're a mind reader now too?"

"No. I am a wife of thirty years. I think that qualifies." She paused. "I know you want to buy that horse."

Charles shrugged and walked closer to the bed. "Sure, I want to. Doesn't mean that I will."

Even this admission of desire was more than she could bear. "Charles, you promised me. No more jumping."

"Who said anything about jumping? I would ride Butterhead for dressage. You're the one who's been after me to find a horse."

"Oh, please . . ."

"I'd be fortunate if Angel let me buy her."

Grace huffed and set her hand cream on the bedside table. "Let you? He was hawking her like a traveling salesman."

Charles's face flashed with annoyance. He drew back. He could look very patronizing when he wanted to. "You're being ridiculous," he said with a sniff. "No one has to hawk a world-class horse like Butterhead."

"D or D. That's all I'm saying."

Charles tied the sash of his robe with a smart tug of pique. "Stop throwing that up at me," he snapped. "I find it insulting when you tell the world about what should be a private matter between us."

"Private? Your accident was in the news! You were airlifted to the hospital."

His drew himself up. "So, I had some minor surgery. What's unusual about that?"

"There are no minor spinal surgeries! They had to cut through nerves and muscles." Grace had been mulling this over in her mind for hours and had worked herself up. She'd told herself to remain calm, but she couldn't hide the impatience in her voice. "Come on. This is me you're talking to. We both know that if you buy that horse, one day you'll jump her. You won't be able to stop yourself. She's a Grand Prix jumper! Riding her over a jump would be the ultimate high for a jumper addict like you."

"What if I did?" he exploded. "Jesus, Mary, and Joseph! Why do you always have to control everything? It's *my* life. I'm not dead yet!"

Grace bolted upright, stung by hurt, fury pumping in her veins.

"You almost were!" she shouted back. "I was there. I had to watch you fall and not get up. I saw you lying there and I didn't know if—" She couldn't finish the sentence. "I waited the eight hours while you were in surgery and they fused your spine back together. I helped you struggle through the physical therapy. Practicing with you day after day. I held your hand when you weren't sure you'd ever get out of that wheelchair. Did you think all that only happened to you? It happened to me too!" she cried, her fist pounding her chest over her heart.

"You didn't know if you were ever going to walk again. There were times I didn't believe you would, but I had to be strong. For you." She stopped to wipe her eyes and collect herself. She'd been screaming so loud her throat felt raw. She couldn't remember the last time she'd been so hurt and angry. "You promised me!" she cried, rising up on her knees and pointing to him, then slumped back on her haunches. Her voice broke. "I told you I wouldn't go through that again. I can't." She paused to wipe the tears again. "I wouldn't survive."

Throughout, Charles remained quiet. He stood at the foot of the bed, face drawn, eyes haunted. Yet his very silence felt defiant.

His silence triggered her last sliver of belligerence. "You want to know the truth?" she asked, a last-ditch effort. She was baring her soul. "I don't just not want you to buy Butterhead." She skipped a beat. "I don't want you to buy *any* horse. I don't want you to ever get back on a horse again."

"Grace—" he said dismissively, as though what she'd said were a joke.

"I mean it, Charles. My family is my life. I will do anything to protect you and Moira. Even be the bad guy in this scenario. I'm not saying don't have horses. Have as many as you want. I know you need horses in your life. Take care of them. Love them. But you don't have to ride a horse to love them. I don't want you to ride anymore." She swallowed hard. "Love me more. Love me enough not to ride."

Charles's shoulders drooped in defeat. He came to Grace's side of the bed and placed a comforting hand on her shoulder. They were at an impasse. Spent.

"Please, don't cry. You know I can't bear to see you cry."

"Charles, I'm begging you."

"I can't promise you not to ride."

She pinched her lips, conceding that point. "Okay. But don't buy that horse. Butterhead is a wonderful horse, I admit. I'd love to ride her too. Who wouldn't? But she is a jumper. That's what she's trained to do. That's what you are trained to do. It's in both your blood." She shook her head. "You wouldn't be able to keep your promise not to jump. It would be inevitable."

He sighed heavily. "I won't buy the horse."

She heard his defeat and it saddened her. But there was nothing else she could say to change the way things were. She couldn't leave it at that, however. She needed to sound supportive. Grace searched her mind for words as she reached up to pat his hand on her shoulder.

"Come to bed," she said in a kindly tone. It was all she could think of.

Charles stepped back and his hand slipped from her shoulder. "Not yet. I want to walk out to the barn to check on the horses."

Grace rubbed her eyes. "Don't stay out too late. You're tired."

"I enjoy it," he said. "Besides, I want to stay up for the eleven o'clock update on the hurricane."

"Oh, God, I can't listen to another word about that storm today."

"Good night," Charles said, and turned to walk away.

The distance across the carpet felt like miles as she watched him make his way to the door. She turned with a heavy sigh to fluff up her pillows.

"Turn the light out, please," she called after him wearily.

Charles paused at the door, his back still to her. "I don't know why you're so worried about me jumping."

His voice was sharp and tinged with frustration. Grace went still and turned her head to look at him. She saw that his face was colored with suppressed emotion.

He met her eyes. "I can't even get back up on a damned horse!"

She stared, openmouthed, as Charles turned on his heel and shut the door behind him.

EIGHT

August 20, 11:50 p.m.
Freehold Farm, North Carolina
Hurricane weakens to Category Four over Cuba

It was late and the clouds had shifted, allowing the waxing moon and a sprinkling of stars to shine in the dark sky. It had been a roller-coaster day and night. The lows of the evacuation, the high of seeing old friends, and the whirl of getting horses and dogs settled. The dogs . . .

Elise laughed just remembering the equestrian elite's reaction to seeing a trailer full of rescue dogs yapping. And that smell! Still, everyone had rolled up their sleeves and helped. They were even cheerful about it. It was a new experience for them, she was sure. But also there was a good feeling that came from helping others in times of trouble.

Once the dogs were corralled in the yard and Grace had left for bed, she and Moira had filled buckets with soap and water and one by one bathed each dog clean of the sick and poop. It was a crazy collection of purebreds and mutts. There were three big dogs. One was a boxer mix named Birdie, the sweetest comic of a dog, who weighed in at about sixty pounds. His best buddy was Murph, a ninety-pound, goofy, easygoing hound mix whose powerful bark could rattle your insides. Then there was Jack, a McNab herding dog, an exuberant boy with big, soulful eyes. This dog was a natural leader.

The other five were smaller. Nacho, a small tan Chihuahua, strutted across the yard like he owned the place. He didn't take guff from any dog, big or small. Two terriers—an adorable Yorkshire mix named Benji, and Maybelle, a sleek white terrier mix with a black eye patch—chased each other, one trying to put paws on the other's back in a classic dominance move. Then there was Tut, a large Boykin spaniel who seemed to care more about people than other dogs. He stood by the gate with his yellowish, mournful eyes and whimpered to get out. Lastly, there was Izzy, the funniest little dachshund mix with the ears of a bat and the curly tail of a pig—an adorable total mess of a dog.

Together she and Moira had bathed, dried, and brushed all eight of the dogs, scrubbed their crates, and put in fresh bedding. Each crate was labeled with its tenant's name and history. In the hours of work, the awkwardness between them had dissipated, and in its place she felt the old kinship kindle.

Elise had no idea what time it was when they closed up the garage. Or if it was even still evening . . . it could well be the early hours of the morning. She couldn't remember ever being so filthy and exhausted. With unspoken cooperation, she followed Moira's lead across the yard with a sluggish gait, careful not to step in the dogs' land mines. She smiled in the darkness when she figured out where they were headed, as memories of nights when they were young flitted through her mind like bursts of starlight. They used to sneak out after a long night of talking, giggling and hushing the dogs, to quietly skinny-dip.

The starlight guided them to the shimmering water. The clink of the iron gate sounded in the night. Somewhere in the distance an owl hooted its eerie call, and the lamplights of the fireflies glimmered in the woods. Wordlessly they stood at the edge of the pool and began to strip. Their dirty clothes fell to the flagstone patio in piles at their feet. Moira glanced at her, a devilish smile on her face, her dark hair freed from its hold. Elise had always loved the glossiness of Moira's hair, how it fell like a thick waterfall down her shoulders. She quickly unwound her own skein of a braid, allowing her hair to drape her body. When done she smiled back at the woman silhouetted in the darkness, accepting the dare.

As one, the two women lifted their arms over their heads and dove into the black water. Oh, it was glorious how the silky warm water felt as it flowed across Elise's body, washing away the soil, the currents like gentle fingers loosening her hair. After a few leisurely laps, she flipped to her back.

They swam in tandem, synchronized swimmers, as the years washed away between them. Elise felt the loosening of her tension, as well as her inhibitions, like her hair flowing in the water behind her. She always felt the world was watching, judging, waiting for her to fail. With Moira, in this gentle moment under the stars, she felt that burden slide away and again was a young girl, without a care in the world. Above, the night sky winked at her.

"This is nice," she said on a sigh, breaking the long silence.

Beside her, Moira responded in her low, melodic voice, "Yeah. Like old times."

"Skinny-dipping." Elise snorted a laugh. "The last time I did this was with you. God knows how long ago."

Moira giggled. "Me too. It was your swimming pool in Florida.

I'll never forget how silky the water felt. But," she said with a shiver, "I'm getting cold. Let's get out. I'll grab some towels." She flipped over and began swimming with long-armed strokes to the steps.

Elise followed and grabbed the large towel Moira had handed her. It seemed remarkably white in the darkness. They dried their hair, unconcerned with their nakedness, then wrapped the towels around their bodies island-style, walked to the chaise longues. Then they lay back to look once again at the stars.

The breeze was like a soft and moist tongue lapping against her skin. Elise felt like her bones were melting into the cushions as the past and present coalesced. "I feel like we're back in college."

"What happened to us?" Moira asked, turning her head to face Elise. Her tone held the hint of sorrow. "I mean, to our friendship?"

Elise deflected the surge of emotion that rose up. She hadn't seen Moira since her wedding. She'd seen Grace in Palm Beach more often than her friend. She'd never felt their distance as a betrayal as much as the loss of a treasured, unique friendship that had diminished into a vague, sad acquaintance. "We're still friends." It was a lame answer, she knew. It was the best she could come up with.

"You know what I mean," Moira said, not accepting the ruse. "There was a time we were inseparable. We were always in contact, no matter where in the world we were. I called you, you called me back. I always knew what you were up to. And you, me. Then it all just sort of . . . disappeared."

"You got married."

"Well, yeah," Moira replied with a small frown. "So what?"

Elise brought the edge of the towel up to rub at her hair. She didn't want to delve into what Moira's wedding had meant to her. How it had solidified in her mind that Moira was going in one direction, and that it was time that Elise did, too. Once again she demurred.

"You got involved in your husband. Your new life. The married life. Hey, it's nothing new. It's happened to me time and time again. A friend gets married, and I slip into the singles crowd. It's a separate universe. We don't have the same interests, the same lifestyle." She dropped the towel and lifted one hand. "The marrieds hang out together, and . . ." She lifted the other, "the singles hang out together." Both hands flopped to her sides. "It's just the way it is."

Elise heard rather than saw Moira move on the cushion with a soft grunt. She didn't reply.

"Besides," Elise added, slightly upbeat. She didn't want Moira to feel rebuffed simply because she'd made her choice. "I started pushing hard in competition. I didn't have time for friendship."

"Thanks," Moira huffed.

"You know what I mean." Elise was unapologetic. "You competed once upon a time. You know the pressure. Hey, you made your world and I made mine. It doesn't mean we don't care about each other."

Moira was silent a moment, then said softly, "Yeah."

"Do you ever regret giving up competition?"

"No," Moira replied promptly. Then with more thought, "Not competition. I was done with all that. Though I do regret not riding much anymore. I don't know why I've let that part of my life slide. Even the horses . . ." She shook her head. "Listen to me. Even I can hear that's not good. Truth is, I let a lot of my interests slide."

"Interests? More like passions." Elise had heard the regret in Moira's voice, the uncertainty, and wondered about it. She ran her hand through her damp hair, feeling the weight of it. Then, digging a bit deeper, she asked in seeming nonchalance, "How's Thom?"

After a prolonged pause, Moira answered simply, "Good. I guess." She skipped a telling beat. "I really don't know. I haven't seen him in six weeks."

"Where is he?"

"Somewhere in Canada deep in some tunnel, checking out equipment. It's a big order so he'll be there for another week. Or longer. I really don't know, and I can't say I care."

Elise looked at her speculatively. "That's a mouthful."

Moira didn't answer.

"Trouble in paradise?"

Moira sighed. "I left Thom."

Elise startled and rolled in the chaise to lift herself on one elbow so she could look at Moira's face. "You what? When?"

"I left him," she repeated. "Just. He doesn't even know it yet." Moira lifted her left hand into the air and wiggled her pale-tipped fingers.

Elise squinted. Her eyes were growing acclimated to the dark. She was stunned to see that Moira wasn't wearing a wedding ring. How had she missed that?

Moira dropped her hand and folded it across the white towel that blanketed her body.

"What happened? Did he cheat on you?"

"No. Nothing like that. You know," she said with a short laugh. "He could . . . cheat. Traveling so much. I wouldn't know it. But I just know he wouldn't. He's not that kind of guy."

"I didn't know there was a kind."

"I could be naïve, but I don't think so. Besides, that's not why I left."

Elise didn't speak. She gave Moira time.

"You know, I haven't told anyone about this yet. Not even my mother. I'm still sorting it all out."

Elise felt chuffed that Moira would confide in her. Like the old days. She felt privileged, even honored. She leaned forward to catch every word and each nuance of tone and movement.

"When I boarded up the house to evacuate," Moira continued, "it looked so empty. Dark and closed-up. Lifeless. I felt like I was looking at my life. I decided then and there I wasn't going to live like that anymore. If I didn't leave, I was going to curl up and die in that house. And I wasn't thinking about the hurricane." She rubbed the empty space on her ring finger where the thick white-gold band and large diamond had so recently rested.

"I thought you two were so in love."

There followed a pained silence.

"We were," Moira said in a choked voice. "I don't know. I still love him," she confessed. "But what's love? Shouldn't it mean putting the person you love first? Ahead of anything else? There I was, alone in a big house with a hurricane barreling in, and I hadn't heard a word from Thom. Not one worried call asking how I was. Or what my evacuation plans were. Hell, forget the hurricane. Weeks go by without anything but texts. Not a single conversation. It's hard to feel love in that scenario." She took a deep breath and exhaled loudly. "I don't know him. And worse, I don't know myself."

Moira rested the back of her hand against her forehead as she stared at the sky. Elise wasn't tired any longer. She felt alert, keen to hear what Moira said next.

"You know me," Moira continued. "I've always been so sure of what I wanted in life. So gung-ho about everything."

"I know. No one could change your mind once it was made up."

Moira ventured a laugh, but it fell.

"I tried to make my marriage work. I truly did. But nothing's turned out the way I'd expected. The best-laid plans of mice and men, right?"

"Tell me about it."

Moira looked at her askew. "What do you mean? Looks to me like things are turning out pretty well for you."

Elise waved her hand. "Later. Go on. I want to hear."

There was a pause and she heard Moira sigh.

"There was no baby. That was the big disappointment. Then he started traveling a lot for business. Not for spite," she clarified. "He had to do it. I get it. But I'm stuck alone in a big house in a strange town with no career, no passion. Nothing."

"Why didn't you go back to riding?"

An irritated frown flashed across Moira's face as she shook her head. "Like I told you before, I don't want to compete." She shifted to her side as well, facing Elise. "I'm talking about *purpose*. Desire. See, that's the problem. I lost that. I'm thirty years old and I don't know what I want to do when I grow up."

She paused, her face growing resolute. Elise knew that expression well.

"But I'm going to find out." Moira's tone changed from what was dangerously close to a whine to the familiar, determined tone. Elise was glad to hear it.

"When you say you've left Thom . . . does that mean you want a divorce?"

"Yes. If things stay the same. Like I said, I haven't even told him yet. It's going to hit him like a ton of bricks."

"It should. Wake him up." Elise swallowed hard, trying to understand what all this meant. "Are you sure you still love him? Or is he . . . safe. Secure."

Suddenly tears sprang to Moira's eyes, making the dark-brown orbs luminous in the dim light. In the starlight, so close, Elise thought she'd never looked more beautiful.

"Oh God, how do I answer that? I thought I'd love him till the day I died." She shook her head in confusion.

"If you don't go back to Kiawah," Elise pressed, "where will you stay?"

"Here."

"Why run home? You could stay with me. Or, rather, us." She rolled her eyes. Always in the shadows was her mother. "In Florida."

Moira was silent, surprise at the invitation etched on her face. "Really? You have room?"

"Hello! You've been to the estate. You can stay in the main house, in your own wing. Or stay with me in the guest cottage."

"What would I do there?"

"Same thing you'd do here. Figure out what you want to do next."

Moira chewed her lip. "Thanks," she said a bit breathlessly. "I'll think about it. I'll need all the support I can get."

"I'll support you," Elise said with more verve than she'd intended. Suddenly, she wanted Moira to say yes. It felt like it could be a lifeline for her, as well. Her friend back. "There's so much to do in Florida. So many different people. Lots of opportunities." She reached out to touch Moira's arm. "I care about you."

Moira's face softened and she smiled. "I know. And I care about you. We're best friends."

Elise felt her insides swirl, making her feel a bit dizzy. Her brain was telling her to keep quiet. Not to bare her soul. But hadn't Moira just revealed her vulnerable side? Wasn't that what friends did? Her heart was urging her to speak now. She'd waited far too long already.

"We are best friends," she began hesitantly. Moira's head tilted, catching the tone. "I wasn't being completely honest with you when you asked why we'd stopped seeing each other," Elise said. "I mean, sure it's true about the marrieds and the singles. But, well . . ." She paused, then said, "My singles were all women."

"What?" Moira's face was perplexed.

Elise shook her head, surprised she had to spell it out. With a smirk, she said, "Moira, I'm gay."

Moira looked thunderstruck. Her mouth slipped open and she held herself very still, almost tensely.

"Don't look so shocked. I can't believe you didn't know."

"Elise, I don't know what to say," she said on a breath. "Sure, we were best friends—but how was I supposed to know? You never gave me any indication. We double dated! And you were almost always wearing riding pants and a polo shirt. It was your uniform." Then somewhat indignantly, "You should've told me. What did you think I was going to do? Not be your friend?"

Elise shrugged, not wanting to admit that that was exactly what she'd feared. "I meant to tell you. I never had the right opportunity. And, I guess I wasn't comfortable enough with it to admit until later and by then we'd drifted apart. I tried to work up the nerve before your wedding." She chewed her lip. "But I saw how happy you were. Friggin' glowing." She shrugged and looked away. "So I said nothing and instead played the good bridesmaid. Hey, it was the right thing to do." Her voice was low now. "You went off on your honeymoon, and I went off to competition. End of story."

"But it wasn't."

"No."

Elise looked at her hands. "I wish you'd told me. I don't know why you think the news would've made me feel any differently about you." She looked up. "Why tell me now?"

"I'm older. Not so shy. And, I want you to know."

Moira didn't speak.

Elise fell back on the cushion and squeezed her eyes closed. "If you want me to sleep in another room—another bed—let me know. Not that I'd, you know, do anything. But I'd understand." She turned her head to sneak a sheepish look at Moira. To her relief, Moira no longer appeared shocked. Her face was calm, and she even seemed moved by the confession. A soft, sad smile spread across her face.

"Don't be silly," Moira said. "This doesn't change anything. We're still best friends."

Elise ventured a shaky smile. "I'm glad."

"Though I have to wonder how close we really were. I mean, how did I not know this? I should've guessed."

"I was careful. Besides, how would you guess? Girls hug. I kissed your cheek, so what? It's not like I came onto you or anything. I love you. But, not in that way." She snorted. "You're as straight as an arrow."

Moira looked at Elise without guile. "So, you're gay?" she asked, as easily as if she were asking if Elise was happy.

Elise shrugged. "Yep." Then, "No matter how comfortable I am with being gay, it's still nerve-racking to come out to someone you care about."

"Does your mother know?"

"No!" The word burst out. "God, no. She's the reason I haven't come out to the world." Her lips twisted as she ruffled her hair. Then she admitted, "I'm already enough of a disappointment to her."

"How can you think that? Elise, you're killing it out on the circuit. She must be busting her buttons with pride."

"That's a reach," Elise said, bringing her knees up on the chaise. She chose her words carefully. "She expects so much from me. So much more."

"What mother doesn't? Is that a bad thing?"

"It is when you're having to fulfill your mother's dreams."

"*Her* dreams?" Moira's voice rose. "Not your own?"

"It all gets mixed together so I don't know what my dreams are anymore. You know she was working toward the Olympics when she had her accident."

"Yes, of course."

"She was good," Elise added. "She was a top contender for the German team."

"And you're good." Moira took her arm. "I thought you wanted the Olympics as much as she did."

Elise looked at Moira's hand, patted it with her own. "No. I don't want it as much as she did. Or as much as she wants it now. She's living vicariously through me."

"But," Moira slid her hand away to settle back on her cushion. "Elise, no matter how much your mother might want it for you, you have to have the goods to reach where you are now."

She rose up on her elbow and looked at Moira again, trying to explain. "I know I'm good. I work hard at it. Practice, practice, practice. But it takes a gold-medal drive to get there." She shrugged. "And I don't have that. I'm running out of steam," she confessed. "I'm not ready." She laughed derisively. "And I'm definitely not ready on Whirlwind."

"He's an amazing horse."

"No doubt. Magnificent. This is the year I'm supposed to intro-

duce him to the equestrian world. Like Edward Gal did with Totilas."
She lifted her hands. "Shock and awe. We wanted early wins, high
scores to get the attention of the Olympic team for 2020. That's the
horse my mother chose to take me there, and we've been preparing
for this moment for years. The horse is able. I'm a good rider." She
sighed and flopped back against the cushions. "But we're just not in
sync. To tell you the truth, I don't think Whirlwind likes me much."

"Elise—"

"I'm not being dramatic. Frankly . . ." She looked up at Moira and
found sympathy there. It encouraged honesty. "Whirlwind is bonded
to Karl. He'd do anything for him. I can see it. And so can my mother.
It makes her furious. In one breath she pushes me to work more with
Whirlwind. Then in the next she holds me back so I don't get hurt.
She's convinced there's something I'm not doing. Not giving. But,
Moira, you know that bond can't be forced. I'm trying. Really I am.
It's not all Whirlwind's fault. I'm not that fond of him either!"

Moira laughed sympathetically.

"Mother's forbidden Karl to ride him for dressage. She wants to
break that bond. As if she could. He can only act as groom for the
horse and trainer for me." She shrugged, and tears flooded her eyes.
"He's not a miracle worker. It's up to me, and I can't make it happen.
And the pressure is building. We're running out of time, Mother is
getting more demanding. She's spent so much money! And me . . . I
hate her for what she's making me feel. She's turned me away from
riding. It's getting so I hate to practice. I don't want to compete. I
just want all this to end!" She put her hands over her face.

Moira reached over to lightly take Elise's hands from her face.
Elise was ashamed of the tears there.

"What can I do?"

It was what Elise needed to hear now. Not suggestions. Not a lecture. Just her presence.

"Be here for me."

"I am."

Moira let her hands retreat and moved to sit on Elise's cushion. That small bit of closeness felt comforting to Elise.

"I don't know what else there is. It's all I've ever worked for."

"Well!" Moira announced. "Then you're like me. Hitting thirty years old and trying to find out what we want to do in life."

They both erupted in broken laughter.

"What a pair we are," said Elise.

"There are worse problems."

"For sure," Elise said. Then more soberly, "Like losing everything you own to this damn hurricane."

"Yeah," Moira agreed. Elise looked up at the sky. The stars still were visible, but wisps of clouds were moving in. "My house is on the coast too." She giggled. "Frankly, I wouldn't care if it got blown away!"

"Hey, it's not my house," Elise said with a short laugh. "I have no skin in the game. Here we're safe. We have our health."

"We have each other," Moira said, and reached out her pinky finger to Elise. "Friends forever," she said, quoting what they used to say as young girls.

Elise linked pinky fingers with Moira. "For evah!"

Then, for no reason in particular and a thousand others that were buried in their hearts, the two grown women laughed and giggled like schoolgirls again.

NINE

August 21, 6:00 a.m.
Freehold Farm, North Carolina
24 hours before expected hurricane landfall in the Keys
Hurricane warning issued

Charles arrived at the barn as dawn broke the darkness. A thin rosy line etched the mountains. The air wasn't as crisp as usual. Early bands from the storm were bringing water to the air, even so early.

He'd had a restless night and found the gentle nickers and whinnies of the horses soothing as he went about his chores. Though his body was calm, inside his head was a maelstrom of feelings. He didn't like to quarrel with Grace. They rarely did and both felt the repercussions deeply. But he knew this morning's deep disquiet was born from more than their terse words.

He felt lost. Having top equestrians at his home, Angel in particular, hearing him talking of international jumping events, hopes for the 2020 Olympics—events that Charles had once aspired to,

even participated in at his prime—made him feel both a keen longing that he thought he'd gotten past and, worse, a self-pity that
he despised. How far he'd fallen, literally and figuratively. He still
wanted to be a player. To ride the circuit, to compete. Goddamn it,
at the very least to ride again. The yearning churned inside like the
hurricane barreling toward them. He'd suffered worse than broken
bones. He'd broken his spirit.

At six Jose and Karl ambled in. They all shared a quick cup of
strong coffee as they divvied up chores. The horses were whinnying and kicking the walls of their stalls impatiently. Then they began
the morning routine. By six-thirty, the horses had their fresh water
and hay. By seven, they'd been given their grain, and by seven-thirty,
sated and quiet, they were ready to be turned out into the paddocks
and have their stalls cleaned.

Charles paused from his stall mucking and let his head rest on his
hands against the pole of the pitchfork, still plagued by his thoughts.
God help him, *he* was the evacuee. He was the man running from the
storm—a coward, too afraid to get back on the horse. Shame coursed
through him. He felt a complete and utter failure. An aging has-been.
A bystander worthy of nothing more than mucking stalls.

Once his chores were done and the horses had been brought
back in, he sought comfort from his horses. One by one he visited
their stalls and put his hands on his old friends, who accepted him
with equanimity. He brushed them, checked their water, talked to
them. He let the palms of his hands slide against their gleaming
coats, attuned to the rippling muscles, the turning of the heads, the
low nickers in a morning communion. He breathed them in, talis-
mans, so deeply he could almost taste the sweet hay.

On his way out he stopped to visit Butterhead, who welcomed

him with cool regard. He courted her, but her gaze was fixed on Angel as he strode through the hall, stopping to talk in rapid Spanish with Jose. She was devoted. Angel should never sell this horse, he thought to himself. It would break her heart. He meant to talk to Angel about it in a quiet moment.

The last horse left to visit was Whirlwind. Charles felt a bit of anxiety at approaching the big stallion, especially after the spectacle yesterday. *Damn,* he thought. *I'm not so much of a coward that I'm afraid of a horse in a stall!* Gritting his teeth, Charles left the barn and crossed the square to the second, smaller grouping of stables where the stallion was housed. He saw that Karl had already cleaned the stall. Good man. Whirlwind was out in the paddock especially designed for stallions, separate from the other paddocks and five boards in height rather than four to prevent the stallion from jumping out if enticed by a mare. Whirlwind's carefully groomed coat gleamed in the sunshine like a raven's wing, and his soft mane flowed in the breeze. Charles approached slowly, with no expectations. He simply wanted to pay his respects to his guest.

Whirlwind lifted his head from where he was grazing and watched him approach, his eyes fixed and his ears twitching. As he drew near, Charles looked for facial expressions to give him clues how to proceed with this spirited horse. Most people were not aware that horses had facial expressions, much less seventeen, three more than chimpanzees. He'd read studies, but it was his own experiences with horses that guided him the most.

Which was why when he saw Whirlwind raise his inner eyebrow, it revealed that he was nervous. So Charles stopped moving and waited until he saw the horse exhale a deep, quick breath through his nostrils, like a sigh. Charles felt inordinately pleased at this, as though he'd been granted a gift. He bowed slightly, smiling in return—a gesture he sensed was appreciated by the horse. Charles believed in showing all animals respect, especially in their own space. And what animal deserved it more than the noble horse?

When he moved forward once again, hesitantly, not rushing him, Whirlwind didn't back away. He continued to watch in a more relaxed manner as Charles spoke greetings in a calm voice. Reaching the paddock gate, Charles just stood there and let Whirlwind slowly approach. Curious, the horse tentatively lowered his head and sniffed him. With equal ease, Charles reached up to stroke Whirlwind's long neck. His fingers touched the quivering, soft coat, and Charles released a sigh when Whirlwind did not step out of reach.

Charles couldn't quite explain the emotions that began to swirl inside of him. It was an odd mix of tenderness and awe—and, yes, gratitude. He swallowed hard, then murmured thanks to the horse for his trust. He felt the horse shift his great weight, then lower his head to sniff Charles's shoulder. Charles felt the slight stubble of the horse's whiskers and smiled again, then relished Whirlwind's warm breath on his neck. As the horse breathed on him, all of the negative feelings that had weighed so heavily in his chest seemed to lift and blow through him, leaving him feeling light-headed. He looked up into the stallion's large, dark eyes, and his own breath stilled. He felt something shift inside. Open up. As unexpected as it was, with Whirlwind, this magnificent, proud, even diffident horse, Charles felt a profound connection.

"He likes you!" Karl said, sounding both surprised and pleased.

Whirlwind immediately jerked his head up to look at Karl.

Charles sighed. The moment was gone. He turned to face Karl, who approached in a limping gait. He was still wearing the heavy sock and sandal on his injured foot because he couldn't squeeze his swollen toes into his boot.

"I feel honored," Charles replied, trying to make light of his embarrassment at being caught in the private moment.

"*Ja,*" Karl replied with a great grin, "you should. That's rare with this big fella." He reached up and stroked the forelock between Whirlwind's ears with enviable familiarity. Karl carefully opened the gate to the paddock as Whirlwind stepped back. Charles stood by and watched as the horse lowered his head for Karl to slip on his halter and then attach the lead rope to take him into the barn.

Charles couldn't help but feel a bit jealous. There was no hesitancy between them. He readily saw the trust they shared.

"Especially today," Karl said, worry creasing his brow. "He's a little off. I don't know if he's sore from all the traveling or it's just the strange surroundings." He stopped to look up at Whirlwind and stroke his neck. "Maybe he needs a day off."

"No! He needs exercise."

Gerta's voice came from behind them. Both men jerked their heads to see her striding toward them. The horses watched her pass, and Whirlwind's ears went back and he whinnied. Charles held back a smile, thinking of how Moira told him that some people believed she stuck a crop in her boot. Unlikely, he thought, though he appreciated the effect she had on the horses. Gerta was casually dressed in jeans, boots, and a long-sleeved navy T-shirt, ironed. Her blond hair was pulled back into a tight bun. Without makeup, she was still striking.

"Where's Elise?" she asked, looking at Karl. It sounded more like an accusation.

"I don't know." Karl did not look at her.

Gerta looked at her watch and frowned in annoyance. "He is fed?"

"Of course."

Charles readily saw that there was no love lost between the two. Uncomfortable with the confrontation, he turned to leave, then spotted Elise and Moira approaching at a companionable pace along the road beyond the barn. They were both dressed in riding apparel, arms swinging and laughing at something. Seeing him, Moira shot up her arm in a wide wave. Behind them strode Grace in dark jeans and a bright white shirt. His heart eased at seeing her glossy hair bounce on her back as she walked; from this distance, she didn't appear any older than the girls.

He turned to Gerta. "Here they all come now." Then he looked to Jose with a nod of his head. "Let's finish getting the arena set up for dressage. Then we can put in a few jumps for the other horses after they are finished."

Elise strode toward the riding area dressed in breeches and boots. She carried her helmet under one arm and her gloves in her other hand. The sky was overcast, always better than a hot sun.

The riding arena was beautifully set overlooking the pastures below and surrounded by the enchanting Blue Ridge Mountains. Grace and Charles Phillips had created two arenas, one for dressage and the other, higher up on the hill, for show jumping. A large mirrored wall was erected at one end of the dressage arena, and presently Karl and Jose were putting down the final long white boards and letters that would establish the standard dressage arena for Elise to use for her lesson with Whirlwind.

Karl began finalizing the tacking up of Whirlwind when Elise reached her mother. Her body language spoke volumes. Gerta stood erect, hands on her hips. Elise crossed her arms at her chest like a block.

"Why were you late?" Gerta demanded.

Elise watched Karl lead Whirlwind from the barn toward them.

"Late? We didn't set a time. I came at eight, as usual."

"It's almost eight-thirty," Gerta shot back.

"So call out the guard." Elise began slipping her hands into her gloves. She added, "I was helping Moira with the dogs. There're a lot to feed."

"That's not your job. Your job is to practice on Whirlwind."

"I know what my job is, Mother," Elise replied with heat. "Now, if you'll kindly leave the ring, I can get started." Turning her back, she walked to where Karl stood by the mounting block trying to settle Whirlwind.

It was clear that Whirlwind was agitated. He was pawing as Karl tried to hold him in place and then circled him to reestablish his position by the mounting block. Elise tried to bring her heart rate back down with deep breaths. It was never wise to harbor negative feelings while riding a spirited animal like Whirlwind.

"Be careful," he said to Elise. "He's not himself. The tension of the storm, the trip. I don't know. We'll take it easy today."

Elise, already unsettled herself, nodded to Karl. "Okay," she said as she took another deep breath and approached the mounting block.

It was quite a feat to get Elise safely mounted. Each time she tried to place her hands on the reins and her foot in the stirrup, Whirlwind would lunge forward against Karl's strong hold. Finally, after several failed attempts, Elise was able to swing her leg around and ride the horse into the arena.

Charles returned from organizing the preparation for the other horses to be ridden after Elise's lesson. As he descended the grassy slope, he waved to Angel putting Butterhead up in the paddock. Closer to the arena, he spotted Grace at the railing of the ring with Hannah. They both carried a white mug. Grace's coffee would be black, he knew without looking. One of her boots rested on the bottom rung of the fence, one arm rested on the top. A few feet away, Moira stood beside Angel and watched the lesson as intently as a bird dog on a hunt. Charles was glad to see her interested in horses again. *Maybe seeing Elise ride will spark her competitive spirit again,* he thought with hope. Some distance away, Gerta stood wide-legged and held the top railing with her hands as she watched her daughter and Whirlwind in the ring. In the center Karl was shouting instructions to Elise. His tone was encouraging, but Charles detected a hint of impatience from time to time.

Elise began by just walking the horse around the arena for about ten minutes. She used this time as would any athlete to warm up the horse, but also to get his mind in work mode. Each stride, although it was just a walk, was deliberate and had purpose.

Karl called to her as she passed him, "Maintain a long rein, but have the horse march using his hind end more. Engage! Allow the rest of his body to become lighter and balanced. Yes, better!"

The pair then progressed to a posting trot, trying to get the horse to loosen up his body and reach more through his movements. Karl had them execute a series of serpentines back and forth across the ring, Elise using her legs, reins, and eyes to direct and engage the horse. As the pair progressed to the sitting trot, Karl called out, "Make the horse trot more forward. Go!" he shouted, lifting his arms. "You must create the required energy and power."

Charles was impressed with Elise's skills. She had a relaxed seat, nice and loose, and made the transitions appear effortless. He appreciated the years of training and competition it took to make it look like she was just sitting on the horse for a ride. As for the horse, though still young at nine years of age, he had developed the powerful hindquarters and that something indefinable that smacked of a winner. He couldn't take his eyes from him.

Watching them work, Charles felt that he too was learning lessons from listening to this brilliant young trainer and watching how Elise executed his orders with finesse. The competitive spirit sparked inside of him as he saw how one could perfect each transition, like a golfer perfecting his swing. The slightest change could make a world of difference.

Elise crossed the arena at a canter, turning at the corner and riding around through the middle to begin executing a spiral that would gradually become smaller and smaller until the horse would perform a pirouette.

Charles moved to stand beside Grace. She turned her head, and her dark eyes were full of questions. "You okay this morning?"

It was a loaded question. They both knew it. Charles let a smile ease across his face and leaned forward to kiss her cheek. "I'm good."

She looked back at him dubiously, then turned again to watch Elise.

Gerta came to stand beside them. After perfunctory good mornings, they all watched Elise ride Whirlwind.

"It's sloppy," Gerta said in judgment.

"I think she looks great," Charles said.

Gerta ignored his opinion. She exhaled sharply. "I think he's too much horse for her."

"Maybe," Charles said. "That's a lot of horse for most anyone."

"No," Gerta said sharply. "It's not the horse."

Charles cast an assessing glance at Gerta. Her lips were pinched with displeasure.

As if hearing her judgment, Whirlwind suddenly grew impatient with the exercise. He was raising his head, pinning his ears, and swishing his tail. All indications to Charles that he was in some pain. When the horse lost his step and kicked out behind, Charles sucked in his breath.

Flustered, Elise became rougher with her hands, locking her reins against his mouth rather than allowing, and jabbing her long spurs into his sides.

Karl was beginning to shout at Elise now. "Stop fighting with him! You need to allow. Stop and organize. Then start the exercise again."

Elise's cheeks were pink from the battle of wills. When she rode past, Charles could see beads of sweat. The horse's nostrils were flared, his mouth was open, and he appeared to be breathing fire. Charles was new to dressage, but even he could see that the tension was mounting. Perhaps it was that Elise was already on edge from her testy interchange with her mother. Or that both horse and rider were dealing with the long journey and new surroundings. And, of course, there was the pressure on Elise of trying to impress her hosts and childhood friend. He knew well that horses easily sensed their riders' stress and anxiety. Some horses were able to ignore it and work through it. But others—more sensitive horses like Whirlwind—became unsettled and agitated themselves.

Karl asked Elise to move again from the trot to the canter. Whirlwind had cooperated relatively well, but when Elise asked more of him, he'd had enough. The great animal suddenly reared up on his hind legs. Elise held tight to the reins as his front hooves pawed the air.

Everyone took a step back, breaths held. Elise held on, but Whirlwind seemed determined to get her off his back. He landed back on his front feet, dipped his shoulder, and kicked out both of his rear legs, sending her flying over his head.

Everyone gasped. Charles felt Gerta's hand grip his arm. Elise landed hard on her back, rolling in the dirt to a stop.

Karl hurried to Whirlwind, who was standing by Elise admiring his work, and reached up to grab the reins. Whirlwind seemed almost relieved to have Karl take hold. He pranced but didn't rear up. Gerta and Moira ran to Elise, who had risen to a sitting position and was spitting dirt from her mouth.

"Are you all right?" Moira called.

"*Ist alles okay?*" Gerta asked, bending toward her daughter, her voice high with worry.

Elise took Moira's arm and rose, then swiped the dirt from her pants. She also brushed away Gerta's outstretched hand. Her cheeks flaming in embarrassment, she reared on her mother. "I'm done with that horse!" she shouted.

Gerta stood back, eyes wide.

Elise cast a sharp, angry look at Whirlwind. It looked like the horse gave an angry look right back. Elise turned on her heel and stomped from the ring. "That's it!" she fired as a parting shot.

Everyone stood in silence for a moment, not sure of what to do next. Only Whirlwind paced with Karl, cooling down. Moira watched the horse with her hands on her hips, eyes squinted.

"I told you he was off today," Karl told Gerta with a flare of anger. "This storm has made everyone anxious. He feels that."

"I think it's more than that. He's got a problem," Moira said, walking closer to them. She indicated Whirlwind's hindquarters. "Look how he favors that hind leg. And how he shifts his weight rapidly from one foot to the other."

"Walk him," Gerta ordered.

As Karl walked Whirlwind away, Gerta studied the animal in silence, her hand at her chin. After a moment she called out to Karl, "She's right." She turned to Moira and said politely, "Thank you, Moira. You are very observant. Very good." Then to Karl, "You should have noticed that. Call the vet immediately. I want him checked out today. *Verstehen Sie?*"

Karl lifted his hand in a quick acknowledgment, then led Whirlwind to the gate, gently and without hurry. Whirlwind followed quietly, not balking or hesitating, eager to return to the barn.

Hannah couldn't find Angel anywhere. She had a phone conference call in half an hour and she needed to get back to the lake house where all her papers and files were. Running out of time, she asked Grace to tell him she'd be back for him and dashed to the Audi to head for the lake house.

She made her way down the winding tar and gravel drive through Freehold Farm, her mind filled with the incredible actions of the morning. She'd been stunned to see the power of Whirlwind. Hannah loved to ride, but she was certain she wasn't up to the task of riding such a spirited horse. Elise did a remarkable job handling him, but even she was no match for the horse's determination to get her off his back. It was like watching someone flick a fly from their shoulder. In her experience, a horse only behaved like that when something was wrong. Maybe the saddle was askew. Or perhaps he'd sustained an injury on the trip. She was glad Gerta had called a vet.

Hannah slowed to a stop at the end of the drive and flicked on her turn signal. She eased onto the dirt road and picked up speed. As she passed the lane to the cottage, she turned her head to look, as she always did, just out of curiosity.

She braked when she spotted Angel. He was walking up the stairs to the front door. A million thoughts ran through her mind, chief among them his reputation as an incorrigible flirt. She knew Gerta was not at the cottage—Hannah had just left her at Grace's house. The front door opened, and she caught a glimpse of Elise's blond hair. Hannah's hands tightened on the wheel. She held her breath—then exhaled loudly in stunned disbelief when she saw Angel walk into the cottage and the door close behind him.

Hannah faced the road and slowly began driving away. Her fingers tapped the steering wheel. What she'd seen could be perfectly innocent, she told herself. But her insecurities battled in her brain to be heard. Elise was younger. Pretty. Accomplished. Hannah swallowed hard. Rich. An altogether tempting morsel for a vigorous man like Angel de la Cruz. He loved women. Loved their company. He didn't sleep with all the women who fawned over him. No man could keep that up, she thought with a bitter laugh. But he managed to handle his fair share.

She was fairly certain he hadn't strayed with her, yet she had to admit that their relationship had been strained. Angel seemed restless, sniffing the air like a teaser stallion. And to be honest, lately she'd been focused again on her business.

As Hannah eased onto the highway, she'd already decided not

to confront Angel about his visit to Elise. Instead she'd wait for him to bring it up. And she'd watch.

A soft knock sounded on the cottage door. Elise was sitting on the brown leather sofa, elbows on knees and her face in her hands. Her britches were coated with dirt, her helmet tossed on the floor. She looked up at the sound and cursed. She didn't want to talk to anyone now—but it was probably Moira. She wiped the tears with a quick mop of her face, sniffed, and walked stiffly to the door.

The last person she expected to see was Angel de la Cruz.

"What are you doing here?" Her voice was unwelcoming, even hostile.

Angel smiled beatifically. It animated his face and lit up his eyes. And it had the desired effect at softening Elise's attitude.

"I came to see you, of course. Are you okay?"

"Never been better."

"We all take a fall. It hurts our pride more than our backside, no?"

Elise flushed and looked down at her mud-streaked boots. She hadn't removed them before entering, which she usually did. "I'm okay."

"Are you?"

Elise heard his doubt and looked up sharply, even suspiciously. "What do you mean?"

"Can we talk?"

The gossip about what a womanizer Angel was flashed through her mind. She was alone here. Then she mentally scoffed at herself.

Of course he wasn't hitting on her. She stepped aside and ushered him in.

Angel walked past her with an event jumper's confident stride. They all moved a bit like Mick Jagger, more a swagger than a gait. She watched his gaze sweep the room, the handsome wood floors and ceiling, the chic comfort.

"She likes hunting, no?"

Elise laughed despite herself. "Yeah. Grace is a big hunter."

"It's nice."

"My mom likes it here. She's close to Grace and"—her arm swept the room—"it's all one floor."

"Oh yes, her leg," Angel said. "I only just learned this. She is brave, your mother."

Elise's face clouded. She didn't want to talk about her mother at the moment.

"So, what do you want to talk about?"

Angel circled back to the sofa and sat. She thought he certainly made himself at home as he stretched his arm out over the back pillows and crossed his legs. They were long and lean, his black boots shined up to the knees. Elise sat in the big leather chair opposite. It was so cushy she sank into it, making her feel even smaller than she was. She hoisted herself up out of the donut hole and perched on the edge of the cushion.

"Tell me about Whirlwind," Angel began.

"What do you want to know?" Her tone bordered on insolence.

"He is a world-class horse, this, of course, we all know. Muscular. Full of intention. Stout. His potential . . ." He lifted his shoulders and spread open his hands. "Exponential. The horse has it all."

Elise's face expressed her bored annoyance. "So, what else is new?"

Angel closed his hands, then looked into her eyes. "All but the right rider."

Elise felt slapped. She sat straighter in her chair. He'd named her greatest fear, and she didn't know whether to be grateful or insulted.

"I mean this in a kind way," Angel hurried to add. "You are a fabulous rider. I've seen you compete. But on this horse, you are . . ." He searched for the words. ". . . out of sync, you know? When you ride him, it's like watching a couple that are fighting and don't want to be in the same room with each other."

"It's that obvious." She wasn't asking.

"Maybe not to some. But to me—yes."

Elise rose in a huff and paced across the room. "We're having difficulties," she said in a defensive tone. "If you're going to use the relationship analogy, we're working it out. It doesn't mean we have to divorce."

Angel spoke plainly. "Sometimes you can't work it out. It's best just to leave."

She halted abruptly, crossed her arms, and fired back, "You're good at that, from what I hear. Leaving." It was a mean swipe, she knew it. But she wanted to hurt him too.

Angel half-smiled in acknowledgment. "Women, yes. True. My horse . . . no," he said emphatically.

"What a lie. I happen to know you're trying to sell Butterhead to Charles. Everyone knows. You're hardly subtle."

Angel's smile fell to a frown, and he looked at his hands. "Yes," he admitted. "I am sorry for this. Brokenhearted. But . . ." He looked at her, his eyes wide with honesty. "I have no choice. I am, how do you say it . . . maxed up. No, that's not right. Out. I'm maxed out. I need not just any horse, but a remarkable horse, one as good as Butterhead, to prepare for the Olympics, and this is, of course, expensive. I dreamed of going to the Olympics with Rogue's Fancy. But it is not meant to be. She has given me her very best for a long time. But the sad truth is Butterhead is my only resource. I am not like you. So many horses at your disposal. So I must sell her to buy the new horse. It is not me leaving her. It is more me letting Mr. Charles have her. I know she will have a magnificent life with him, here at this farm."

"But—" She chewed her lip. "You'll break her heart too. You have to know that. Anyone can see how devoted she is to you."

Angel didn't reply, but his face appeared stricken.

Elise walked across the room and sat on the sofa beside him. "Angel," she began hesitatingly. "Please tell me. How do you build that bond? How can I make Whirlwind care for me the way Butterhead cares for you?"

This time, Angel's smile was sad. "You cannot. That bond just happens. It's like falling in love. You look into the eyes, and you just know. And when you ride the horse, you are in sync. The horse wants to please you. You want to help her to understand what you need. That's where practice comes in. Learning how to talk to each other, eh? But the will to learn . . ." He lifted his finger. "That cannot be taught. It comes from here," he added, touching his heart. "And this is what I did not see with you and Whirlwind." He paused. "I saw it, instead, with Karl."

A flush of anger swept through Elise at hearing Karl's name. No, not just anger, she thought as she processed her flaming emotion. Her ineptitude. Her inability to succeed with this horse that her mother had determined was the one that would take her—not Elise but Gerta—to Olympic victory. Once again, Angel had named her great fear: *Karl was better with Whirlwind.*

"What do I do?"

"You know. You already said it."

She looked at him, confused. "I said what?"

"You said you were done with that horse. With Whirlwind. Right?" He snorted a laugh. "You shouted it, actually. This is good. You know what you have to do, eh? Elise, you need to find another horse."

Elise laughed and shook her head. "Oh no. Don't try to sell me Butterhead."

Angel laughed with her. "No, no, not Butterhead. She is not up to your level of dressage. Mr. Charles, yes. She could be good for him. And he could be good for her. But you need to find your own horse." He changed his tone to convey gravitas. "Not let your mother choose your horse."

It was a slap, and it stung. But it was true. They shared a look of understanding.

Elise tugged at her hair as a niggling thought—one that had been playing in her mind since the previous night—resurfaced.

"I need to find myself more than a horse. I need to find a life."

They looked at each other, and Elise gave him a little smile.

Angel nodded. He put his palms together, then steepled his fingers at his mouth. At last, dropping his hands to his knees, he turned to pin Elise with his dark gaze.

"Have you ever thought about selling Whirlwind?"

TEN

August 21, 10:00 a.m.
Freehold Farm, North Carolina
*Noelle makes landfall at Key Largo
as a Category Four hurricane*

Moira was alone with Karl in Whirlwind's stall, save for an orange-and-white cat that sat in a rear corner of the stall licking its paws. She'd never seen that cat before. Everyone else had scattered like the four winds. Though the stall was spacious, Moira felt the confinement keenly.

Karl was a handsome man. Not in a pretty-boy kind of way— his cheekbones were too sharp, his forehead too broad. With his blond hair brushed back and his sinewy body, he had a leonine appearance. When he was angry, there was no disguising it. But when he smiled, the warmth that sprang to his blue eyes came as a surprise and was all the stronger for it. And, she'd discovered, he was reserved with his smiles.

He'd offered her one of those smiles when she entered the stall.

She'd smiled back, tucking a shank of her thick hair behind her ear. Moira knew that Elise both admired and resented Karl. His ability with horses and in dressage was, she said, brilliant. And it was just that ability that was the bone of contention between them.

Moira had no such argument with Karl. She found him kind, and that was the quality she prized most in men. That, and a natural ability with animals. This Thom was lacking, which worried her. How could she have married a man so disinterested in animals? It created a gulf between them. How could something so important to her mean little or nothing to him? Thom didn't even like animals. He tolerated Gigi at best. He didn't ride horses, and whenever she'd argued with him to try the sport, he countered that she should try loving cars, as he did. The argument always ended in a stalemate. Thus Moira found that she admired Karl. And, she admitted, she found him enormously attractive. *That* feeling, she realized as he caught her eyes and smiled, was mutual. There was no denying the spark between them.

Karl was changing out the water buckets when she walked in. Moira knew that Grace eschewed automatic waterers. She preferred buckets so she could verify how much water each horse consumed. He was doing the best he could, limping.

"Who's your friend?" she asked, indicating the large tabby cat in the corner.

He laughed and shook his head. "Beats me. I found him here this morning. Your father never saw him before either. Seems to have made himself at home. Whirlwind likes him, I think. He seems calmer with him around, so I let him stay. I call him Big Orange."

She looked at the large, long-haired orange-and-white cat. He stared back with that calm disdain every cat mastered. He had an unusual stripe of white that crossed his face like a lightning bolt that made him appear rakish.

"There's cat food in the tack room. Jose feeds the strays."

"Yep. Found it. Thanks."

She drew nearer, watching him limp with discomfort as he began grooming Whirlwind. He had a brush in either hand and worked them across Whirlwind's broad side in circular strokes.

"How's your foot?" she asked.

"The foot is okay. It's my pride that took the beating. Rookie mistake."

"It wasn't your mistake. Bunny is my parents' dog and he came out of nowhere. It was my fault." She dipped her head sheepishly. "I'm in charge of the dogs. I don't know how Bunny escaped. He's like a Houdini."

"I should've been more careful. But the doctor said it's not broken. It could be a nasty sprain or some other soft tissue injury, which won't show up on an X-ray, but whatever, it still hurts like . . . the dickens."

"You should stay off your foot," she said, then realized it sounded maternal. When he looked at her like she was kidding, she laughed and said, "Well, as much as you can. Seems like ice is in order. I'll get you some."

"Really, I'm good. It's *his* injury I'm more worried about." He straightened and limped closer to her. "So," Karl said. "What made you first aware Whirlwind might have an injury?"

Moira had to reflect on her answer. "In truth," she began hesitantly, "I'm not sure what came first. It all comes together into one picture in my mind."

He looked at her, seeming baffled.

"It's hard to explain." Moira paused, wondering how much she wanted to reveal. But really, what did she have to lose? She spoke from the heart. "I'm able to communicate with an animal. I always have, ever since I was little. It wasn't till I grew up that I realized it wasn't like that for everyone." She gave a self-conscious laugh. "It's like they are talking to me. Not in words," she hastened to add. "It's more an understanding of intention. Emotions. Or problems."

Karl stopped to look at her. She didn't see confusion or, worse, derision. Rather, curiosity. So she continued.

"I just knew that Whirlwind was hurting. He was radiating pain. That's when I watched him more carefully and noticed his hind leg was off balance. Then, when he kicked his leg out, it was a confirmation. The poor guy, he was really trying out there. Trying to do what Elise wanted. And you kept pushing him harder and harder till he broke. Unfortunately, it was Elise who took the fall."

Karl pursed his lips and tilted his head. "So you're saying I totally missed it."

She shrugged with a crooked smile. "Yep."

"So you are a Dr. Dolittle."

She frowned. There it was. Derision. "Never mind."

"Sorry," he said, and reached out to stop her. She felt the connection spark. "I'm sorry. I didn't mean to be rude. I'm fascinated, really. I've heard of people who can communicate, of course. But, I never believed." He smiled and dropped his hand. "I'm being honest. But I'm open to this. I can see you know something. Does he tell you? Where is his injury?"

Moira began again, hesitatingly. "Like I said, he doesn't talk to me. I have a picture in my mind of where the pain is. That's how it works. Then I explore."

Karl stepped aside to leave her room to approach Whirlwind. He gestured with his hand for her to go ahead.

"Will you hold on to his lead?" she asked. "Sometimes the horse doesn't appreciate me poking around his sore spots."

Karl complied and stood waiting.

Moira didn't move immediately. She stood looking at Whirlwind with her head slightly cocked.

"He won't hurt you."

She flashed Karl a quick smile. "I know. I don't like to barge into his space," she explained. "It would hardly be polite, would it? I'm waiting to be invited in."

Karl's brows rose, but she was grateful he didn't venture his opinion.

"You see how his ears have moved forward and his muscles relaxed some? Now I am welcome to enter. They are proud creatures, you know. I'm simply showing respect."

Karl's doubt slipped from his face, replaced by admiration.

Moira moved closer to the stallion and gently placed the palms of her hands on his neck. Whirlwind turned his head to look at her, then allowed her touch. Moira reached up to stroke his neck. In her mind, she thanked him for trusting her.

"He's really a beautiful horse."

"There's no horse like him." Karl looked at Whirlwind, and she could see love for the animal shining in his eyes.

"I don't like to rush. I want him to trust my touch. I begin with a gentle massage, before I move into more specific areas." She began stroking his neck, his back, his withers, just letting the horse feel her hand over his body.

"How did you learn this approach?"

"I took classes. My college degree was in equine science," she told him.

"Ah," he said, understanding more.

"And I used to ride dressage competitively. When I was in college. Elise and I were in shows together."

"She never told me that."

Whirlwind shifted his weight and stomped his foot. He seemed to be asking why they weren't paying attention to him. She smiled. "And my father was a professional. But you know that."

"Of course. Why did you stop?"

"I'm more like my mother," she told him, realizing in that moment how true that was. "I still love horses. I want to be connected to them. But in some other way."

"What way?"

She laughed in a self-deprecating manner. He'd just voiced the question she was battling with every day. "I'm trying to figure that out."

She moved closer to Whirlwind and placed her hands on the horse's flank. She spoke in a calm, soft voice near the horse. "I learned equine massage. I wanted something to back up all the mental messages I was receiving from the horses." She glanced back over her shoulder. Karl's bright-blue eyes were watching her intensely. Emboldened, she continued, "I found massage to be a remarkable diagnostic tool."

She reached higher on Whirlwind's neck, feeling Karl's presence beside her. She took a deep breath to clear her mind.

"Now that he's more relaxed, I begin searching for where he's in pain. I begin at the top of the neck," she said, letting her long, slender fingers glide alongside the spine, digging in deeper at points.

Whirlwind threw his head up in complaint. "There, see?" she said. "That's a sore spot." She flattened her hand and let her palm glide over his slightly sweaty coat. "With each new location, I watch how the muscles react, gently palpating. See, right there, how he shivers? This poor fellow is sore all over." She clucked her tongue sympathetically.

"I can see how he reacts," Karl acknowledged. "It is remarkable."

Moira continued manipulating the muscles along the spine, the tips of her fingers digging in slightly. She reached the point of the hips, then lowered to the flank. She stopped, feeling heat radiating into her palm. *Yes,* she heard in her head. *Here.*

"Karl, put your hand here, by mine."

Karl moved beside her and stretched his hand over hers. He was hovering over her, engulfing her, so close she could smell the sweat on his body, feel the pressure against her back as he leaned forward. The hairs on her arm straightened as pheromones flared. He felt it too. It was too powerful.

"Like this?" he asked in a low voice by her ear.

Moira moved her hand from under his to let his palm lie flat on the horse's back. "Do you feel heat there?"

Karl waited, concentrated, then shook his head. "No."

He didn't have the gift. She was sad for him, but it was rare, she knew. She could still teach him to manipulate and discover the trigger points. "That's okay. Move your palm along the lumbar muscles. Gently apply some pressure."

He did so. She watched his strong, slender fingers stretch out across the back. Whirlwind shuddered violently and kicked out his rear leg.

Karl dropped his hand. "There?" he asked, stunned. "That is it?"

"I'd say so!" she replied with a short laugh. "It's a clear diagnosis. Whirlwind is out of alignment. He was hurting out there, especially under the saddle. In my humble opinion, he'll need an equine chiropractor as well as a vet. My mother knows a good one."

Karl stepped back, and she appreciated the cooler air between them. "Good, good," he said, rubbing his jaw.

The emotions flaring between them had to be brought under control, Moira thought. She had to stop behaving like a schoolgirl. *I'm a married woman,* she admonished herself. She looked again at Karl. His eyes were like blue beacons searching hers.

But she wasn't a school girl. She was a woman. Searching and lost and lonely and desiring to explore new experiences and the depths of her feelings. She had been asleep so long she longed to re-awaken. And wasn't that the role of the kiss in fairy tales?

All her mental arguments were scorched by the fire racing through her veins. She watched him move closer and drew a quivering breath, knowing what was coming. She chose not to flee. Her breath sucked in when she felt his hand trace the delicate path of her jawline down to her chin in a movement not unlike her own on Whirlwind. When his thumb gently stroked her lips, she closed her eyes and parted them. She kept her eyes closed because she didn't want him to see her hesitation . . . her doubt . . . the *no* shouting in her mind.

When their lips met, Moira felt her breath leave her body as she molded her body to his. Hunger and desire swirled through her, and she slipped her arms around his neck. She knew it was wrong, but she wanted to feel passion again. To feel alive. It had been so long.

He pressed her harder against him as his tongue delved deeper. She felt his desire rising, and a sudden chill swept over her.

No, she heard in her mind, louder now. Viscerally, her instincts were on alert . . . and Moira was always attuned to her instincts.

She pulled back her head, drew away, and lowered her arms. "I'm sorry. I can't do this," she said in a soft voice.

Karl's brows furrowed in confusion. "Why not?" He moved closer again, tugging her toward him.

She disentangled herself from his arms and stood in front of him, arms loose at her sides. The silence stretched. "I'm married," she said at last.

She saw disbelief register on his face. Then disappointment.

"Married?" Karl pointedly looked at her ring finger.

Moira's face clouded as she darted a look at the white space on her ring finger where her wedding band and engagement ring had so recently been. She self-consciously crossed her arms, hiding her hands. After a pause, she looked at him at last. "Yes."

Karl's expression shifted to become impassive. It was a gesture of acceptance laced with pride. "Okay." He stepped back, widening the space between them.

"Karl, I—"

The sound of an engine interrupted them. Moira turned her head to see a white pickup truck pulling into the square with the emblem of the veterinarian emblazoned on the door. It was with some relief that she moved out of the confined space, and the conversation, to greet the vet.

ELEVEN

August 21, 2:00 p.m.
Interstate 26, South Carolina
*Noelle gaining power over warm water to become
an "extremely dangerous" Category Five hurricane*

D amn."

Cara swung her head to look at David's tense face. His brows were furrowed and his lips were tight as he quickly flipped on the turn signal and the hazard lights.

"What's the matter?"

David didn't respond. His gaze was flicking back and forth from the rearview mirror to the windshield in deep concentration as he made his way across two lanes to the exit. When he reached the right lane, he slowed down. Fortunately, traffic going south was sparse. Cara's stomach clenched when she saw the red warning light flashing on the dashboard. David gripped the steering wheel tightly as they pulled off the highway exit ramp. It only took a few minutes, but it felt like forever. Once there, she heard David release a heavy sigh.

"We have a flat tire," he said.

"I didn't hear it pop."

"Nah, it's a slow leak. We probably ran over a nail or something."

"Do we have to stop now? Can we change it?"

He shook his head. "I don't want to change a tire on the highway if I can avoid it. Thank God it's not a blowout. The flat tire acts as a cushion for a short while. There's a gas station up ahead. We'll take it slow and we should make it. But this tire's shot. We'll have to pray they have a replacement."

There were a few gas stations right off the exit, and David went to the one that had a service garage connected.

"That's a damn miracle," he muttered as he parked the car near the garage.

But all the gas stations near the exit were packed with lines of cars waiting for gas.

"They're all evacuating," she said. "A lot of the license plates are from Florida."

"That storm's coming," he said, "and they're running."

As they walked to the service station, Cara looked at the lines of cars. Many had two or more people in them, and some had dogs' heads poking out the windows. All of the cars were full of possessions. Mothers with children walked to and from the station. Folks were buying water, snacks. There would be, she knew, a long line at the women's restroom.

Inside the garage a television on the wall blared out the weather report. People gathered around it, listening for the latest update on the hurricane's progress. Earlier in the week the hurricane had wobbled one way and then another, sending people on both the Atlantic and Gulf coasts scrambling. Now the landfall location had been pin-pointed to the Atlantic side with relative assuredness. Hurricanes were wily. They remained unpredictable. The question in everyone's mind was, *Where on the coast was this one going to hit*? Fear and worry etched the faces of the men and women. Even the children appeared unusually somber, some leaning against a parent's leg. These travelers were not on vacation. They were running scared.

Inside the garage was filled with cars, most up on lifts, and all the mechanics were working feverishly. The smell of car oil and grease permeated the air. Even the line to simply check in the car was six people deep. David shook his head and glanced at his watch with a frown.

"You might as well get comfortable. This may take a while."

Cara chewed her lip, knowing that they were already on a tight schedule to make it to the house, board it up, and get off the island before the bridge was closed. Her anxiety bubbled up and she wanted to play the big-city executive, be pushy and get ahead of the line. She took a steadying breath, tamping down her frustration. There was a time to complain and a time to be silent; this, she decided, was a time for the latter. She tightened her lips against the things she wanted to say, nodded, folded her arms across her chest, and prepared to wait.

Twenty minutes later they were at the head of the line. A stout, middle-aged man with greasy brown hair and bushy brows offered a perfunctory smile of greeting. He wore a pale-gray uniform shirt that was stained and worn, but she could still make out that his name was Bobby. He looked up at David and said in a tired voice, "Can I help you?"

David explained what had happened. It was at times like these she appreciated his commanding voice and presence. No matter how much she might know about cars, and no matter how much she might hate it, in truth, in a garage the banter went better man-to-man. She glanced again at her watch. It was already 2:30. Looking at the fatigue on Bobby's face, she'd bet cash money that he was already working overtime. She glanced behind. Since they'd arrived, four others had joined the queue.

"You're in luck," Bobby said, looking at the computer screen. "We have a tire for the Range Rover. We can replace it. But," he said, again looking at David, "it'll take time. There are four jobs ahead of you."

"How much time?" Cara chimed in.

She knew she was beginning to sound a bit desperate. David turned his head to meet Cara's gaze. She could tell he was worried that she was about to lose her cool.

Bobby shot a look at the shop and all the cars being worked on. When he looked back at them his face wasn't encouraging. "You don't happen to live near here? So you can come back and not wait? Maybe tomorrow?"

They shook their heads. "Afraid not," Cara said.

"Okay then," he said with a weary sigh. "You can wait in the office." He gestured toward a small, uninviting room with metal chairs. "It's air-conditioned."

"I'll go grab things out of the car," David told them.

Bobby wiped the beads of sweat from his brow. The doors to the garage were open and the humidity was thick. As he checked them into the computer, he asked, more out of politeness than any real interest, "Where you guys headed?"

"Isle of Palms," Cara replied dully.

The man paused and looked at her. "You headed there *now*?"

She nodded. "I live there."

"You know what's coming, right?" he asked in disbelief.

She chuckled, expecting this response. "Yeah, I know. We're just headed back to board up the house. Then we'll leave."

"Missy," he began in a neighborly tone, "you don't want to go back there. Look," he said, indicating the gas pumps at the station. "See that long line of cars waiting for gas? And out there on the highway crawling along? Everybody's getting the hell out. Believe it or not, the traffic's only going to get worse. Once panic sets in, it'll be bumper-to-bumper. No gas. I swear to God, I wonder what would happen to all those folks if the hurricane came sweeping down and they were stuck in traffic! And, lady, they just announced it's likely going to be a Cat Five. That's Hugo kind of bad."

Cara saw the fear in his eyes that she was sure mirrored her own. She swallowed hard.

"Ain't no house worth that," he added for good measure. "You might just want to turn around and head back up north while you can."

Cara stared into his pale eyes and asked herself again if she didn't want to give up and head back to the mountains. Maybe the flat tire was a warning—a sign from above telling them not to go forward. Cara wasn't one to run, however. Her mother used to say her middle name should've been Stubborn.

"Thanks," she said. "We'll be fine."

Bobby looked at her like she was nuts, then just shook his head in a not-my-business manner and turned to the printer that was pumping out her receipt. When he handed the paper to her, however, his eyes were filled with concern.

"Tell you what. I'll see what I can do to get you outta here a little quicker. There isn't a hotel room for miles."

He turned and walked off before she could thank him.

The back office was a sorry, airless place with a sagging leather sofa, a row of metal chairs, old greasy magazines on a chipped faux-wood table, and a Mr. Coffee machine that was turned off, the pot rimmed with dried coffee. Most of the chairs were occupied by sunken-eyed travelers in the same predicament she was in, waiting for their cars to be repaired so they could get back on the road. True to his word, the serviceman did his best to push them through, but it still took three hours of waiting. Time was of the essence. Each hour's delay getting there was an hour closer to the hurricane's arrival.

Back on the road at last, Cara was more eager than ever to reach the beach house. They kept the news on, conversation stopping whenever a weather update came on.

The sun was already lowering by the time they reached the Connector to Isle of Palms. She'd crossed this span countless times in her life. She'd grown up in Charleston, and her family had their summer house on Isle of Palms. Back in the day, they'd crossed the old, narrow Grace Memorial Bridge from Charleston and traveled through the sleepy town of Mount Pleasant to the swing bridge over the Intracoastal Waterway and the wetlands to Sullivan's Island. There wasn't a direct route to Isle of Palms. They had to drive across Sullivan's, then cross the bridge over Breach Inlet to reach Isle of Palms. Sometimes they'd come by boat. But usually Mama packed up a cooler and bags of food and they'd motor to the small beach house facing the ocean.

Cara well remembered the debate about building the long expanse of Highway 517. They'd called it the Connector because it linked Isle of Palms directly to the mainland without visitors having to cross Sullivan's Island. Some of the islanders had fought against the Connector because they liked the fact that their island was harder to get to than Sullivan's Island, and argued that its inaccessibility would keep more people away. With Wild Dunes Resort at the northern tip of the island, that effort was already a lost cause. Still, after the terrible destruction on the island during Hurricane Hugo in 1989, it was clear that the islanders needed a safe means to flee. By 1993 the 3.84-mile highway with its fixed-span bridge connecting Mount Pleasant with Isle of Palms was complete.

Cara looked out the window as they made their way across. They were one of a mere handful of cars coming to the island. Everyone else was heading off-island, their cars packed to the gills with belongings, some pulling boats. The tourists were long gone. These were the die-hard residents who'd waited to see what the storm was going to do before deciding at the last moment to heed the evacuation warning.

Her gaze skimmed the wetlands below. The tide was rushing in, filling the mudflats. The tips of the cordgrass were beginning to turn golden, a first sign of approaching fall. The big car glided higher up the Connector to reach the apex. No matter the season, no matter the time of day, Cara's breath hitched at the sudden sight of the great Atlantic Ocean looming before her. The expanse of sea meeting the horizon in a line that seemed to stretch out to infinity never failed to fill her with awe.

It was the sky that dictated the color of the mercurial sea. On sunny days, the water shimmered a brilliant blue. When gray clouds filled the sky, the sea reflected its stormy colors. It seemed incongruous today to see a dull gray-blue ocean reflecting the sky. One wouldn't guess a hurricane was advancing toward them, save for the telltale gray cirrus clouds that streaked across the sky, forerunners of the ominous armada sailing in its inexorable path. Still, all one had to do to see signs of what was to come was to look at the sea and the way the water roiled in haphazard currents, small whitecaps forming.

Every time she reached this point, her heart opened to the welcome of the island—until now. For the first time, the island didn't feel welcoming. It felt threatening. Instinctively, she reached across the front seat to clasp David's arm.

David turned his head quickly, his eyes scanning her face. "We're going to be all right," he reassured her, moving his hand to squeeze hers. "We'll be gone before the storm hits."

Cara asked herself for the hundredth time why she'd felt the need to return to this precarious barrier island just as a hurricane threatened and everyone else was leaving. But she knew the answer. It was because of the beach house. Her beloved Primrose Cottage.

When at last they reached the beach house, her little cottage seemed so small and helpless sitting on a small dune facing a turbulent sea. What hope did it have against the impending fury of the storm looming from the ocean? This little house held so many of her childhood memories. Only the good ones.

Nestled between the large vintage Victorian of her dearest friends, Flo and Emmi, on the left and a larger contemporary mansion on its right, Primrose Cottage was a slight glimpse of the past. When it was built, this street had been oceanfront and all the small houses sat behind a line of large dunes. Old-timers knew that the job of dunes was to act as a barricade against waves and tidal surge. Today most of the vintage cottages were gone, cleared away to make room for the mansions that created a pastel wall blocking the view of the ocean. Cara's mother, Lovie Rutledge, had shaken her head in wonder why, after the devastation of Hurricane Hugo, they would mow the dunes down to build bigger houses even closer to the sea.

Primrose Cottage had been Lovie's sanctuary, a place where she could escape the pressures of Charleston society—and her husband—to spend quality time with her children and, later, her grandchildren. In her lifetime, Lovie had loved and protected the island's sea turtles and this beach house. On her death, Cara had gladly assumed that responsibility. And she'd tried her best. She was here now, wasn't she?

Cara felt a sudden shiver of apprehension. Though the beach house had withstood countless storms for more than eighty years, could it withstand what was predicted to be the fiercest one of all?

She stepped out of the car, and immediately the heavy humidity descended on them, thick and wet. Her pale-blue cotton shirt began to cling to her breasts and felt like a blanket around her back. David rounded the car to grab their two small bags from the trunk of his Range Rover. They hadn't packed much—this was a quick trip. Cara grabbed the cooler, and together they headed single-file toward the front porch, their feet crunching loudly in the gravel.

Cara dug into her purse and handed David the front door key. As he opened the door, she walked to the railing and gazed up at the twilight sky. She saw a few gulls struggling in the brisk wind. Many of the local birds had already flown from the path of the oncoming storm. Instinct was a powerful survival tool. There was an eerie silence on the island—no bird calls, no bursts of laughter from the beach, no cars passing on the road. Not even a dog barked.

But in the distance, the ocean roared.

"Cara?"

The sound of David's voice brought her back to the task at hand. She looked up with a quick smile. "Yes, coming."

She walked past him as he held the door open for her, stepping into the steamy, stale air of a locked-up house. She set down the cooler and stretched out her hand to flick on the lights, shedding an instant glow on her familiar surroundings.

Everything was as she'd left it. Truth be told, nothing significant had changed since her mother had lived here. It was still the same three-bedroom house. A small entryway opened into the spacious living room with its row of windows overlooking the ocean, heart pine floors, and shiplap walls, with a brick fireplace dominating one wall. To the left, a narrow hall lined with family photographs in black frames led to two small bedrooms. As a child she'd slept in the leeward room and her brother, Palmer, on the seaward side. To the right was a small galley kitchen and the larger master bedroom. Cara had done all she could to the galley kitchen save knocking down an exterior wall and adding on. But she'd never change the original design of the house that had been built by her grandparents. Instead, Cara had added a fresh bit of youth and color with pale ocean-blue paint and glossy white trim, and the new sunporch off the back of the house. That had been Brett's final contribution to the cottage. Though it wasn't a large house, she'd never felt crowded in it.

David returned to the house carrying the groceries they'd picked up before arriving. He kicked the door shut behind him as he made his way to the kitchen. "That's the last of it."

Shaken from her reverie, Cara followed him to the kitchen, feeling a little guilty for not helping more. "I was woolgathering. It's always this way when I come back after an absence. The memories rush in."

David plopped the two brown paper bags on the counter, then looked over at her. He was a tall man, broad-shouldered. His salt-and-pepper hair was gaining more salt since she'd met him four years earlier. But the thick eyebrows over his rich brown eyes were still black. He was one of those men who aged well, would perhaps even look better with the passing of time. His eyes crinkled.

"Well, we made it."

"We were the idiots heading *toward* the storm. Come to think of it, isn't that some bedrock of myth? The fire-breathing monster rises from the sea and all the people flee. But there's always the fool who rushes in to fight the monster."

"Yeah. That fool is called the hero," David said with a smirk.

"Fool, hero—he usually gets killed in the battle."

"He rises to the gods."

"*He* being the operative word. You're covered. What happens to the woman? She gets banished to Hades."

His chuckle rumbled low in his chest as he moved closer and gathered her into his arms. She felt his strength surround her and closed her eyes for a moment, breathing it in. Then she yawned loudly.

"Want to call it a night and start fresh in the morning?" he asked.

"We sat in that horrid waiting room for more than three hours," she said. "We lost so much time—we've got to get rolling. I don't want to be a heroine. I want to get out of here. Run!"

He kissed the top of her head, releasing her. "How about I pour us a glass of wine and we settle in."

Cara ran her hands through her short hair and rubbed her scalp. "Settle in? We just got here. I'll unload the groceries. You turn on the oven for the frozen pizza. After we eat, we can get started."

David pulled out a bottle of red and set it on the counter. As he fished in the drawers for the corkscrew, he said, "Honey, it's too late to start tonight. It's too dark."

"We can't just hang out. We came here to get this done and get out!"

"And we will. Tonight we can start by locating the shutters and tools. We'll make a plan. But we'll start putting up the shutters tomorrow. We're both beat, and"—he indicated the darkening sky— "we're losing daylight."

Cara rubbed her hands together, agitated. She couldn't wait to leave. Her phone rang, and grateful for the distraction, she grabbed it from her purse.

"Hello?"

"Cara? It's Grace."

"Hello!" She had met Grace Phillips waiting in line at the IGA grocery store, a small market not far from David's house in Tryon. Grace had an easy, outgoing manner and they struck up a conversation about the good meat at the shop, the Tryon movie theater, and within the space of five minutes Cara knew a great deal about the area and had struck up a friendship.

"I heard you went to the island. I'm worried about you. Is there anything I can do?"

Cara smiled. "Calling is enough. Your timing is perfect."

"How long are you there for?"

"A day. We'll be back in a jif."

"Promise you will. And call me when you get back."

"I will."

Cara walked into the living room, feeling buoyed by the call. She turned on the television. After a moment the picture formed and Cara switched immediately to the Weather Channel. She stood in front of the screen, arms folded, watching intently.

David approached with a glass of wine. "I doubt anything's changed in the last hour."

"Shh," she said, taking the glass. "It's the eight o'clock update."

She felt the walls close in around her as the news showed photographs of the damage Hurricane Noelle had wreaked in the Caribbean. The Virgin Islands were decimated and the storm had hit Cuba as a Category Four. When the meteorologist reported that the storm was likely to become a Category Five hurricane, confirming what Bobby had told her at the gas station, Cara felt her knees weaken.

"Oh, God," she said as a groan.

"We'll be out of here in forty-eight hours," David said, and reached out to turn off the TV.

"No, don't turn it off," Cara cried out.

"It's making you crazy."

"I need to hear it. Do you mind?"

He shook his head. "Not if you don't. But if you stand here watching it all the time, we won't get anything done."

Cara smiled, chagrined. "Right. I'll show you where everything is," she said, turning away from the television and returning to the kitchen. "Brett was always very organized about shutters and his tools, and I've kept it up. I've got all my important papers organized and ready to go in plastic files." She chuckled softly. "I call it my pack-and-go box. I've had that done since June. When hurricane season begins, I'm counting my flashlights."

David pulled the frozen pizza from the box and put it into the oven. "Sounds good. This should be easy."

"The hard part is deciding what else I'll take with me." Cara looked around her precious home. In her mind's eye she saw all the things that were dear to her. A few special pieces of jewelry. Photos. Hope's baby album. She shook her head. "I want to pack up the entire house and carry it to a safe place."

"I know," he replied, rounding the counter to refill her glass of wine. "We all feel the same. But that's the price we pay for living in paradise."

His attempt at humor went a long way to lessen her tension. They clinked glasses.

Cara felt the tannic cabernet slide down her throat, rich and full-bodied. "My mother always believed that somehow this beach house would survive whatever storms came its way. And it did. I mean, it's not like we haven't gone through this dozens of times before, right?" she said with enthusiasm she didn't feel. "We'll board the house up tight and it'll be fine. It always is."

Cara brought her glass back to her lips and drank deeply as from the other room she heard the meteorologist, a specialist in hurricanes, explain again about the hurricane's rain bands, the clouds moving counter-clockwise up to three hundred miles out from the hurricane. He went on to explain with graphics how the hurricane's right side was the most dangerous part of the storm because these bands had the added effect of the hurricane's swirling wind speed.

She leaned against David. He slipped his arm around her shoulders as they stood together, trapped once again by their hunger for news about the monster storm. They both knew that this wasn't just a hurricane coming their way. If rumors were true, this was the mother of all hurricanes. This was the storm that could sweep Cara's house away.

TWELVE

August 22, 5:30 a.m.
Freehold Farm, North Carolina
*Hurricane makes landfall at Key Largo
in northernmost Florida Keys*

H ello? Gerta? Are you awake?"

Blinking hard as she held the phone to her ear, Gerta barely recognized Grace's voice as she turned her head to look out the bedroom window. The red-patterned drapes were open and scant breeze came from the open window. Outside the sky was that hazy gray of dawn.

"I am now."

"Oh, did I wake you? I'm sorry. I thought you were up with the birds."

"I took a melatonin last night. I couldn't sleep," she added, rubbing the stump of her leg. It still throbbed from the long trip, less now, but enough to disturb her sleep.

"This is a call to action," Grace began. "I got an urgent call from Katherine Bellissimo. You remember her, don't you?"

"Of course." Gerta knew Katherine well. She was a partner of the Palm Beach International Equestrian Center and they often worked together.

"Then you know she's also one of the founders of the Tryon International Equestrian Center." Grace took a breath. "Hurricane Noelle is about to make landfall in the Keys. Then it's projected to go straight up the Atlantic Coast."

This news brought Gerta wide awake. She lifted herself on her elbows. *"Mein Gott."*

"The Gulf area is sighing with relief, but everyone on the Atlantic side who hasn't already left is running. An SOS is going out to everyone and anyone to help house evacuating horses. TIEC has already opened up their stables for as many horses as they can hold. They have up to five hundred stalls."

"That many?" Gerta said on a yawn, rousing further. She well understood what it would cost the center to open and house the horses, then clean the stalls again after they left. Her own horses were being boarded there. "That is more than generous. Katherine's a saint."

"She needs our help. The first of the horses are arriving this morning. She's pulled in all the grooms, but they still don't have enough help. So . . . will you?"

"Will I what?"

"Help feed and walk the horses. Deliver water. Muck stalls. Whatever it takes."

Gerta heard the force of Grace's words. She could be a bulldozer when she was on a mission for good. Gerta wanted to say no.

That was not the kind of work she did, not anymore, at least. She'd mucked a lifetime's worth of stalls. Her father had made certain his children would not be spoiled and that they knew every facet of the horse-breeding business. She and her two sisters rose at dawn and went out with the other stable hands, every morning before school. But that was then. Now she hired others to do it.

"But my leg—"

"Right. You won't have to muck stalls or carry bags of food, but you could walk the horses. I'm sure they'd appreciate your experience. Katherine's going to be out there too. We all are. It's all hands on deck. We all want to pitch in." She paused. "We need you."

Grace was right, of course. Besides, Gerta could hardly refuse her host.

She took a deep breath. "All right. I'll help."

The highway seemed to stretch clear to the distant peaks of the Blue Ridge Mountains. This early in the morning, with the mist settled around them, the mountains were the purple of ripe grapes. The clouds had moved in overnight, but the sun scraped through, allowing great shafts of light to spread out in dramatic beams across the dark foliage.

Gerta rode in the front passenger seat of Grace's big Mercedes. Her friends Caroline, Cornelia, and Rebecca crowded together in the back. Grace had given her the skinny on the women before they'd arrived at Freehold. They were her nearest and dearest and lived nearby. Caroline and Rebecca were equestrians, but Cornelia bred Wagyu beef cattle. They were bound together by their love of animals, great and small. Caroline was in the same hunt club with Grace, and they all worked on committees with her to find homes for rescued horses, maintain trails, and support the local humane society. All three were outgoing, smart, and warm. Bottom line: they'd all volunteered to help muck out stalls. They were the kind of women Gerta wished she could call friends as well.

A soft rock station played on the radio as they made their way to the Tryon International Equestrian Center. Sade was singing "Kiss of Life" and the women were unconsciously moving in time to the gentle beat.

The news broke the mood when it gave the hurricane update. Hurricane Noelle was approaching the Florida Keys. The meteorologists were giving a history of the destruction in Cuba and the Caribbean. Gerta took a breath, marveling at how, up in the mountains, one could feel so far from the enormous storm heading toward the shore—then, boom, reality broke through the façade and all their attention was riveted back on the coast as their heart rates accelerated.

"Could you turn it up?" Rebecca asked, leaning forward against the front seats and indicating the radio. "Did I hear that right? They said this hurricane might become a Category Six? That's a whole new category!"

The car went silent as they all zeroed in on the weather update. Hurricane Noelle would make landfall on the Florida Keys soon, then move up the Atlantic coast. The upper southeastern coast was now under a hurricane warning, the meteorologists warned, and preparations should be done—windows boarded and doors reinforced, trees trimmed and dead limbs removed, patio furniture and planters brought indoors to prevent them from becoming missiles in the fierce winds. The news also reported how the evacuation routes leading out of Florida were still dangerously packed. Farther up the coast as well—traffic was jammed all the way through Georgia and South Carolina. It seemed the whole southeastern coast was on the move.

"I worry about the people evacuating getting stuck on the highways," Caroline said. "What if they run out of gas? I shudder to think what would happen if a hurricane hit while they were all stuck there."

"Don't go there," said Grace. Her fingers tapped the steering wheel. "It's too horrid to consider."

"But it could happen."

"It's not the wind I'm most fearful of," said Rebecca. "It's the flooding."

"It's climate change," said Grace.

"It's not just the hurricanes," Gerta said. She spoke loudly so they could hear in the backseat. "With climate change, all the storms will become more intense. Winter freezes, scorching heat, drought . . . In Europe, my family tells me of the bitter winters."

Cornelia twisted her lips and asked, "Is it really as bad as they're saying? Haven't there been horrific storms for years? We just had a one-hundred-year flood. A hundred years," she repeated for emphasis.

"Except the one-hundred-year floods are happening every few years now," said Rebecca.

Caroline seemed on the verge of tears as she stared at her cell phone. "My calls won't go through to my mother. She's in Fort Myers."

"It's mayhem down there now. The lines must be down," said Cornelia.

"My parents are in assisted living." Caroline's slender frame seemed to fold into itself, her usually sweet expression worried. "I'm frantic," she confessed. "The facility didn't move them out. They claim they have a great hurricane facility. But how secure is it really? My mother says she's fine, but she always puts on a strong face. And my poor daddy, he doesn't know if it's sunny or raining anymore." Caroline wrung her hands. "I wanted to go down to get them once it looked like it was hitting the coast, but it was too late."

"Don't you worry, honey," Cornelia told her, patting her hands. "They're on the Gulf side. Besides, those folks know what they're doing. That's their job. They'll be fine. We all will." She paused. "I just hope it peters out some as it goes over land. Y'all know I have a house on Isle of Palms," she said with worry in her voice. She picked up a piece of paper and began to fan herself as she looked out the window. "I hope it survives." Her voice grew wistful. "We were planning on a family Christmas there this year. With the new grandbaby."

"You still might," Grace said consolingly. "My condo is in Palm Beach . . ." She shrugged, indicating *good luck with that*.

Cornelia's smile was wobbly. "I'm glad we have each other. We just have to take care of each other and anyone else we can."

"Makes me feel good we're helping with the horses," said Rebecca.

Grace added, "And pray."

Caroline laughed shakily. "I'm praying real hard!"

"Me too," said Cornelia.

Gerta listened in silence, staring out the windshield. She couldn't give voice to all that she had at stake with this hurricane. Her entire breeding facility—her life's work—was in the crosshairs.

She was accustomed to facing problems and solving them, getting things done. But in the face of nature, there was nothing she could do but wait. She had no control. It was a feeling she eschewed. She didn't like being helpless.

"I'll be honest," Gerta ventured in a lowered voice. She turned to look out at the countryside whizzing by. Trees. So many trees. "I am generally not one for praying. But perhaps . . ." She released a short, self-conscious laugh. "Perhaps I should start."

Caroline reached over from the backseat to touch Gerta's shoulder. "I'm with you, my friend."

Gerta sucked in a breath, feeling exposed—yet a half-smile played at her lips. Caroline had said "my friend." At times like this, that word meant so much.

A silence settled on the group as each considered what the aftermath of the Category Five hurricane could mean to them personally. And to their loved ones.

At last they reached the cloverleaf in the highway that provided them with a vista of the equestrian center. It spread out over some fifteen hundred acres in the mountains of North Carolina. Here, the 2018 World Equestrian Games had been hosted, a triumph for the United States equestrian world. It was complete with a six-thousand-seat outdoor stadium, multiple event rings, a separate sports center, and a covered arena—not to mention five hundred horse stalls. It was in these that the desperate owners fleeing the hurricane could house their evacuated horses.

When Grace's car approached the large wood-gated entrance

to the equestrian center, there was already a line of cars towing horse trailers checking in and heading to the stalls. As they drove in, Grace gave Gerta a quick tour of the facility. Gerta had been to equestrian facilities all over the world, and the Palm Beach International Equestrian Center in Wellington was superb, so she was not inclined to be impressed—but she had to admit that indeed she was as Grace wound past the numerous handsome buildings. The scope and vision of the equestrian center gave her pause.

Grace parked in the lot nearest the stables. Gerta pushed open the passenger door and, with a bit of a struggle, rose to a stand. She forced a smile as her prosthesis chafed against her still-tender skin. Early as it was, the air was already heavy with humidity. Like the other women, Gerta wore jeans and an old chambray shirt, prepared to get dirty. Boots were de rigueur—only a fool would wear tennis shoes or, worse, flip-flops when working with horses. She wiped a bead of sweat from over her lip.

"I'd expected it to be cooler in the mountains," she said with a hint of accusation.

"Oh, it's the oncoming hurricane," answered Cornelia, almost apologetically. "We're expecting rain tonight. I can feel it in the air like a bubble about to pop!"

"And climate change," chirped Grace again.

Caroline laughed and said, "Honey, it's just August in the South."

Grace and the other women talked among themselves as they walked ahead. Gerta held back at the entrance and removed her sunglasses as she perused the large building housing the horse stalls. It surprised her how barnlike the stables actually were. Too often show stalls were rickety and industrial. Gerta stepped inside and lifted her hawkish nose. One couldn't hide the smells of a badly run stable—urine alone could be pervasive. She sniffed, and caught a whiff of the unmistakable scents of pine shavings, leather, and horseflesh. All smells she welcomed. *Well done,* she thought approvingly.

"Welcome!" Katherine hurried from across the barn, her hand extended in greeting. She was a petite woman and wore her long blond hair pulled back in a ponytail. In her jeans, navy T-shirt, and boots, she looked as young as her daughter walking beside her. "Thanks so much for coming," she said, her hazel eyes reflecting her gratitude. "It's mayhem with all these horses coming. There's so much to do, I swear, we couldn't get it all done without your help."

"Y'all are the ones helping the most," Grace offered. "I mean . . ." Her arm swept out to indicate the number of horses already ensconced in stalls. "What would *they* have done?"

Katherine waved the compliment away. "Opening our doors was the right thing to do. Horses go the distance with us every day. Now they're the ones going the distance—literally. We have to help them."

Gerta heard the chorus of agreement and felt a sudden lightness in her chest. She went to greet Katherine, and the two women commiserated briefly over what might happen to their properties in Florida. But it wasn't the time to talk, and they kept it brief.

All the women gathered around the petite woman carrying a clipboard. Nancy Corte was the stable manager. Highly organized, she gave out instructions and divvied up the work. Nancy explained that some of the horses in this group of stalls were from a South Carolina riding center, while the others were rescue horses from a Georgia facility.

For once, Gerta was not the one in charge. To her surprise, she enjoyed feeling part of the group—part of something bigger than herself.

The barn hallway was unusually wide, with ample room for horses and people to pass. As she walked toward the stall of her assigned horse, her gaze swept the barn, catching details others might miss. There were water spigots and fans at each stall, as well as larger ceiling fans in the hall. A nice breeze ran through the barn, cooling it even on this steamy day. Tack rooms were on either end of the hall. Katherine did a nice job taking care of both the horses and those who tended them, she thought.

The horses seemed content, despite the turmoil they'd been through. They stood with their heads hanging out the stall windows and watched the humans with curiosity. Because of her leg, Gerta had been given the task of walking the horses. As she passed the stalls, one horse lifted its head and whinnied very loudly, demanding. Gerta stopped in her tracks and swung her head to look at him, as did most everyone else in the barn. She met his gaze, and he nickered in satisfaction.

"Well, hello," she called back.

The horse was a big dark bay with brown eyes that stared at her with unusual intensity. His ears were forward and his neck seemed to be craned toward her while his nostrils were wide, exploring. She liked the looks of him—and more, his attitude. When she smiled, he looked back at her with confidence that bordered on cocky.

"You have to wait your turn. But I'll be back," she said, and began walking away.

The horse whinnied again, more insistently, and kicked the stall door for good measure. Gerta stopped and turned back, questioning.

"Okay. You've got my attention," she said, putting her hands on her hips. "What's the matter, big fella?"

As though in response, the horse shook his mane and blew out air.

Caroline walked by pushing a wheelbarrow of hay. She chuckled and said, "I think he likes you."

Gerta huffed out air in derision. Of course the horse didn't especially *like* her. Most horses didn't. If anything, they respected her, as she respected them. But like? No. Gerta had hardened her heart against such emotions. She hadn't tried to get a horse to *like* her since Razzmajazz. There had been only one horse for her. Enough for her lifetime. She couldn't feel that way again for any horse. Never again . . .

Gerta frowned and turned to go. Once again, the big bay stomped his feet and neighed loudly, clearly demanding her attention. This time she turned and walked back to the horse and faced him squarely, giving the horse her full focus. The horse shifted his head so he could gaze at her from his right eye. Gerta smiled. She knew that because of the placement of horses' eyes, they could not see what was directly in front of them, but had to shift their heads to the side to get a good view of something straight ahead. So this horse was, in fact, staring her right in the eyes.

"What's going on with this horse?" Gerta called out to Katherine, who was filling the water buckets in the next stall.

Katherine stepped out of the stall and leaned against the gate. There was a sprig of hay caught in her hair and her cheeks were flushed. "I'm not sure," she said, then smiled wryly. "Other than that he wants your attention. Why don't you walk him first? I don't think he wants to wait," she added with a chuckle.

"What's his name?"

"If it's not tacked onto the stall, that means he's probably one of the rescues and doesn't have a name."

Gerta glanced at the front of the stall. No name. So he was a rescue. She felt a sudden pity for the horse. He had too much personality for such an uncertain future. She approached the bay's stall slowly, speaking soothingly. The horse's ears remained relaxed as he pulled his head into the stall and stood watching. And waiting. Gerta slid open the gate and got her first good look at him.

He was a bit thin—to be expected in a rescue, she thought. But he was indeed a good-looking horse with his rich bay coloring, elegant black stockings, and one white sock on his rear ankle. His black mane and tail were matted. Nothing a good brushing couldn't fix. Quite pretty, she amended, coming closer and narrowing her eyes in perusal. She placed a hand on his neck, calm and reassuring. He had to be more than sixteen hands with a rectangular build. She let her hand glide along the long sloping shoulder to the strong hindquarters, assessing. As she put on the halter and lead, she studied the finely chiseled head with its broad forehead.

"Katherine?" she called out to the next stall. She heard the *thwack* of water turning off, and a moment later Katherine rounded the stall.

"Yes?"

Gerta stood back from the horse and put her chin in her palm. "I'm not sure, and I'm not crazy, but I think I'm looking at a Trakehner."

Katherine's eyes reflected surprise, and she came closer to study the horse. If it was true, this would be a valued warmblood from Germany. Not something that one usually found among rescues.

"You never know with a rescue. Don't they usually have the Trakehner brand on them?"

"*Ja,*" Gerta said, feeling the thrill of the hunt. "Let's take a look." She moved to the hind flank while Katherine searched the bay's shoulders.

"Here," Gerta called out, her voice high with excitement. Her fingers had rolled over the small scar made by the brand on the right hindquarter. "See? This is the double moose antler." She bent to peer closer. "And yes, it has the dot in the center." She stepped back, stunned by this confirmation. "This is definitely a Trakehner. From Germany. The product of nearly three centuries of breeding. And here we find him in a rescue facility." She put her hand to her cheek. "It's quite unbelievable."

"You know German warmbloods as well as anyone," Katherine said. She gazed at the horse with wonder. "There's a mystery here. These horses just came in yesterday. Tell you what—I'll see if I can dig up his paperwork and get back to you."

"That would be wonderful," Gerta said. "Something is not right. A Trakehner should never have ended up a rescue. The Klugs have raised Trakehners in Bavaria for many years. The Germans are very protective of them." She looked at the horse, wondering what circuitous route he had taken to end up at this stable. "Don't you worry, Mr. No Name. I'll take care of you."

Gerta began talking to the horse in German as she led him out of the barn—knowing his origins, it just felt right. She didn't have to walk far to reach the grazing areas. They were spared a scorching sun as heavy cloud cover created a low gray sky. Strange how one forgot about the hurricane up here, she thought, until one looked at the sky. She shuddered at the realization that the storm was moving toward them in its inexorable path.

Still Gerta was able to put the storm out of the forefront of her mind and savor the lazy walk, the horse on his long lead occasionally dropping his head to graze. He seemed to enjoy the sauntering pace just as much, and at this slow walk her prosthesis didn't chafe. Pausing as the bay grazed, she let her gaze roam the grounds. Green summer leaves rustled in the occasional breeze. The few yellow ones presaging autumn fell and floated in the air. In the beds surrounding the buildings, pink pentas and purple salvia bloomed. Yellow sulphur butterflies fluttered from blossom to blossom.

Suddenly she felt the horse's muzzle close to her shoulder. It seemed to be sniffing her hair and blowing on her neck. The wiry whiskers and warm breath on her neck tickled, and she laughed lightly. She stopped and looked over her shoulder, so close that she was almost staring into the horse's eyes. They were a deep, liquid brown, and for a moment, she was mesmerized as old memories tugged.

Razzmajazz used to blow on her neck when they walked in the field. Horses showed affection for one another by gently blowing into each other's nostrils. They didn't usually offer their affection to humans, and never to someone they were not interested in.

"You certainly are a Romeo."

She turned and began to walk away. He followed, coming close again to nuzzle her neck with his velvety soft muzzle. Then he gave her a little push. She stopped and turned to stare at him. Gerta's face stilled as she looked into his eyes. This was a game Razzmajazz used to play. No other horse ever had.

What was happening? From deep in the recesses of her brain came a foolish, ridiculous thought. She didn't want to give it merit. It couldn't be. Not in the real world. Not in her neat and orderly world. But this horse . . . how could he know the game? Or to blow on her neck? The way he was looking at her, so intently, it was like he was looking into her soul. He seemed to be urging her. Even daring her. Toward courage. Toward faith.

"Razzmajazz?" Her voice quavered on the name.

The horse inhaled quickly, then puffed out a breath through his nostrils so they vibrated and made a loud purring sound. He shook his mane, excited.

Trembling, Gerta stepped closer to the horse. Hesitantly she reached up to run her fingers down the long white blaze on his nose, then back up. She lifted his wiry forelock and sucked in her breath. There was the small white star that had marked Razzmajazz.

Her neat, orderly world spun on its axis. She'd heard people talk about former lives, people who were convinced that their horse or their dog was really the reincarnation of their former pet. She'd scoffed at such nonsense. Who could believe that?

And yet, here she was. With this horse. This Trakehner, like Razzmajazz. Every instinct in her body told her that this was her beloved horse.

"Jazzy?" she asked in a soft voice. "Could it be you?"

In response, the horse lowered his head, bringing it toward her in a sign of complete and utter affection. He was giving her the cue this time.

Gerta lowered her forehead and brought it to rest against the horse's nose. They seemed to meld into one being. She felt a rush of love flowing through her bloodstream, pumping so hard it was like a deafening drumbeat. So fast and loud that, deep inside, she felt the ice that had formed around her heart all those years ago after her horse's death crack and splinter at last, filling her with warmth.

THIRTEEN

August 22, 8:20 a.m.
Isle of Palms, South Carolina
Mandatory evacuation warnings
for South Carolina coast

Cara and David awoke at dawn. The gray clouds dominated the sky, causing the sun to rise in drab colors over the steely ocean. It was not a morning for leisure. They gulped down coffee and power bars, eager to get the house boarded up as quickly as possible.

Cara led David to the shed beneath the front porch where the metal storm shutters were stored. There was no electricity here and in the dim light they dodged spider webs and stepped over garden pots and tools coated with a thick layer of sand. They moved a few rusting bicycles out and at last got to the shed in the back. David opened the creaking doors and smiled with relief. Cara's former husband, Brett, had the shutters neatly organized with a map in a plastic cover showing where each shutter should be placed. Each shutter was clearly numbered.

"Brett made this a whole lot easier," David said. He turned to smile at Cara but his smile fell at seeing her face.

"Honey, are you okay?"

Cara couldn't respond. Staring at the map, memories of Brett flooded her mind. She'd loved Brett and always would. He had always been her rock, the one sure thing in her life to cling to through storms and life's vicissitudes. For her, part of the pain of hurricanes was missing Brett. And still mourning him. Boarding up the house, preparing for a storm, brought the memories flooding back like a tidal surge.

Cara put on a brave smile. "I'm fine. All this hurricane stuff."

"I'm here. You're not alone. We'll get this house boarded and be on our way. Okay?"

"Yeah." She smiled and welcomed his quick kiss.

He picked up the first grouping of shutters. "Let's go!"

She gripped the sides of a tall steel shutter with leather gloves. It wasn't terribly heavy but its length was awkward. She made it out of the narrow shed and was carrying it along the grass to the stairs when a familiar voice called her name.

"Cara Rutledge! What in the name of God are you doing back here?"

Cara set the shutter down and turned to see Florence Prescott walking toward her from the house next door. At eighty-one, she was still spry, though her gait was slower. Her white hair was thinner now and not as snowy, but her blue eyes still shone bright. Flo was dressed in her ubiquitous nylon pants and a blue Turtle Team T-shirt.

Behind her, the screen door to the house next door slammed shut and she spied her best friend Emmi coming out, drying her hands on a towel. Her flaming red hair was pulled up on her head in a sloppy bun. She, too, wore the uniform of the turtle team. Emmi's weight went up and down like a yo-yo. She was in a heavier phase now but what caught Cara's attention was her wide, Carly Simon grin. Cara couldn't help but smile back as she slapped the dust from her hands and went to greet her friends.

"Why in the hell did you come back from the mountains?" Flo asked in her usual strident manner.

Emmi put a calming hand on Flo's shoulder. "Looks to me like she's putting up shutters. How are you, hon?" she asked and stepped forward to hug Cara.

"Okay. David and I are trying to put these up lickety split so we can head back to the hills. Why are *you* still here? Your house is all boarded."

"I know," Emmi replied and rolled her eyes.

"We're checking on the last turtle nests," Flo said with conviction. "We've got two that are due to hatch any minute. Both laid the same day. We put them right by each other at Third Avenue. We call them The Twins."

Emmi looked out to the ocean. "I'd hoped they would have hatched last night, but no luck."

"I told you we should've helped them a bit," Flo muttered.

"Oh, no you don't," Cara told Flo. "Michelle Pate is very firm on that point. We let nature take its course."

"Oh, for pity's sake," Flo shot back, her eyes blazing. "They're due now! And it's not like we'd be opening up the nests for our convenience. This is an emergency. If we don't get them out they may not survive. I don't know that I could bear that."

Cara looked to Emmi. She was the leader of the Isle of Palms/ Sullivan's Island Turtle Team. The final word rested with her, and she took her orders from Michelle Pate at the South Carolina Department of Natural Resources.

"I've told her," Emmi said to Cara.

"Lovie would've done something!" Flo said, almost beside herself. "She wouldn't let them sit in that nest to die. Remember the time we moved the eggs? She knew what had to be done. Yes, ma'am." She nodded her head, more a jerk, for emphasis.

"We got in a lot of trouble for that, too."

"Maybe. But the eggs hatched, didn't they? The turtles survived." Flo's pale eyes gleamed with triumph.

The memory flashed in Cara's mind. Her mother had brought into the house the last unhatched nest on the islands. She'd put them in deep sand in the red bucket, and this she placed in her bathroom cabinet, thinking to save them from being swept away by the storm. It was a serious transgression of the SCDNR rules. The likelihood of the eggs surviving the move was slim to none.

But survive they did. Even though her mother didn't. She passed soon after the hurricane. To this day Cara believed it was the spirit of her mother who protected the eggs and blessed them so the hatchlings did emerge. It was a miraculous event on a soft night after the hurricane. The whole Rutledge family had gathered around to cheer on her mother's final nest. It was a transformative night. Watching the hatchlings scramble to the sea, Cara had made her decision to remain on the Isle of Palms—at her mother's beach house—and to marry Brett Beauchamps.

Cara looked out to the ocean. The gray seas were turbulent, roiling in wild currents and swirling with whitecaps. Another hurricane was roaring in. A shudder ran through her.

"I'd love to debate this," she said to Flo, "but I have to get our shutters up. I support whatever Emmi decides." She looked at Emmi. "When are you leaving? It's mandatory now, you know."

"We know," Emmi said. "We're almost out of here. I expect we'll leave right after lunch."

"Do you have a place to go?"

"We're going to my cousin's in Columbia."

"I'll be at David's in Tryon with Heather and Bo. Text when you leave."

Emmi stepped forward to hug her. When she was close, Cara whispered, "Is everything okay with Flo? She seems a little agitated." Flo was well on her descent into Alzheimer's. Emmi was a saint being her caretaker and living with her. Cara did her part to help. Cara and Emmi were like Flo's daughters, the only family she had. But Emmi did the heavy lifting.

Emmi looked over her shoulder. Flo was picking up a shell from the ground. "I'll call you later," she said with meaning. "Be safe. Don't stay a minute longer than you have to."

"Hell no," Cara answered with a laugh.

Cara went to Flo and wrapped her arms around the woman's frail shoulders. Florence Prescott had always been bigger than life. Buoyant and loud speaking, she was a fearless protector of sea turtles, Cara's mother, Lovie, and both Cara and Emmi as children. She never married and had dedicated her life to her career as a social worker. It was hard seeing this woman in decline.

"I'll see you when we all come back home," she said, and kissed Flo's cheek. "Take good care of Emmi."

"I always do," Flo replied. Then her bright eyes shone with

clarity. "I know these hurricanes come hard for you. Memories stir. But you have David. Lean on him, now. I daresay he's up to it."

"I will. Godspeed."

August 22, 2:00 p.m.
Freehold Farm, North Carolina

Even after a long morning with the animals, Moira strangely didn't feel tired. Too many other emotions were swirling through her, indefinable but smacking of hope. She was on her way across the fields from the garage to a special place she often went when she needed to think.

Yesterday, the visit from the veterinarian had turned out to be one of life's moments that were a blessing, unexpected, thus all the more sweet. Dr. Kate Pittman was also a licensed equine chiropractor. She'd examined Whirlwind and agreed with Moira's diagnosis that the horse's alignment was out. Dr. Kate was a teacher at heart and appreciated Moira's study of equine massage. She took the time to explain each step of the chiropractic procedure. When she was finished, Moira and Karl both could see that Whirlwind was feeling better. It wasn't the validation of her suspicions that excited Moira, though in truth the respect she saw reflected in Dr. Kate's eyes was encouraging. It was more what the veterinarian had said, what Karl had echoed: *Have you ever considered being a veterinarian?*

She'd almost laughed in response. Consider it? It had once been her dream. She'd actually applied to veterinary school—and had been accepted. That dream, like so many others, had been tossed aside when she'd married.

Moira strolled at a thoughtful pace up the curve of the hill. The cut grass stuck to her boots, its thick scent filling her senses. Looking up, she saw the storm clouds hovering and she tasted rain. Her eyes were fixed on the hill's highest point. A sacred place.

When her parents had purchased the farm, they'd intended to build a house at that high point. It was a beautiful spot, open and grassy, with a spectacular view of the rolling pastures. But when the builders put out the stakes for construction, each morning they found that the stakes had been moved. There were a number of signs on the property that Indians had once lived here. An ancient beech tree bore Indian carvings marking treasure, and spearheads and rudimentary tools were uncovered in digging. Her mother had contacted the Bureau of Indian Affairs, and they came to inspect. The Phillipses had learned that the farm had once been the site of a fierce battle between Indians and settlers. The experts also told them that the three ancient trees clustered atop the hill marked a burial ground. At the foot of each tree was a semicircular alignment of rocks, pointing toward the clear view of the sky. It was sacred ground, likely the resting spot of royalty.

Moira didn't know if the word *royalty* was correct—maybe they meant chiefs, or even revered medicine women. She only knew for certain that they were women. She felt their spirits when she visited them. They spoke to her clearly. She didn't tell many people about her ability to communicate through the thin veil. For one, she didn't want strangers showing up at the site. Secondly, she was well aware of the skepticism about all things psychic. Only her parents knew about her communication with the three women—and

Elise—and they believed completely in her ability. Her mother told her she'd been prescient ever since she was a little girl, how it was a gift, one to be treasured. Moira had always felt that their faith in her was the true gift.

She made her way to the top of the hill. The sky was foreboding, and in the distance, thunder rumbled. A brisk breeze blew up, scattering leaves and caressing her face. Moira approached the three trees with respect. In the middle stood the tallest oak, broad at the base with large roots curling in the ground, secure and strong. This magnificent tree's branches spread out far and wide in a great embrace of the sky. Moira reached it and bowed at the waist.

"Daughter," she said, then stepped forward to touch the thick, striated bark. She closed her eyes and waited for some sense that this tree had a message. Only the birds sang from above. She withdrew a small piece of quartz from her pocket and placed it at the tree's roots as an offering, then moved to the left to a modestly smaller tree. This noble tree's roots also curled thick and strong over rocks. Again, Moira bowed and placed her offering of quartz.

"Mother." As before, when she put her hand on the deeply ridged bark, she felt no strong sense of communication.

She crossed to the opposite side of the grassy arena, admiring the view of lush green trees and fields below, some spotted with horses. She approached the smallest of the trees with special reverence. This tree was bent and scarred by what was most likely a lightning bolt. Some of its branches were already dead. Moira bowed, hoping that this tree would have some much-needed advice today. She set the quartz at the base of the tree. Its roots were not as large or thick, but this tree was by far the oldest.

"Grandmother," she said, and stepped forward to place her

hand on the dry, thick bark. This time Moira felt a sudden gush of maternal love. The emotion enveloped her, causing tears to flood her eyes, bringing her to her knees. She placed her cheek against the bark, feeling as though it were her grandmother's breast. In this moment, she felt connected to the divine, in the presence of all beings and linked at a cellular level to all of nature and the world around her.

"Grandmother," she cried chokingly, awash in emotion. She felt all the myriad questions swirling inside of her. Should she leave Thom? Should she fight for her marriage? Should she—did she dare—go to veterinary school or was it too late? "What should I do?"

She closed her eyes and waited for the vision. In her mind's eye came the clear image of a tree's roots growing deep in the ground. The roots were strong and healthy. Nourished by Mother Earth. She heard the words in her mind: *You know what you have to do.*

"I don't," she cried, sounding like a child to her own ears.

You know what you have to do, came the reply once more, as gentle and sure as the wind in the leaves above. And again, the image of the tree roots floated through her mind. Roots. Her roots, she thought. Then, with more clarity, *My roots.* And suddenly all became clear.

Moira always looked at what other people needed from her, what she could do for others to help them, to nurture them. The tree was telling her that it was time she listened to her own needs. To grow her own roots deep into a fertile soil. *Be rooted*, she heard.

Moira kissed the tree bark, feeling its roughness on her tender lips. A black ant crawled into her field of vision, stopping in caution. Gripping the tree, she rose to her feet. She felt light-headed, as though waking from a dream. She breathed deep and took a final sweep of the vista, letting its peace and power fill her. Then she bowed once more to the old tree.

"Thank you, Grandmother. I know what I have to do."

August 22, 4:00 p.m.
Isle of Palms, South Carolina

The pounding as David set the hurricane shutters into place continued throughout the day. Cara had moved the planters and porch furniture indoors and trimmed bushes and limbs that were close to the house. At three o'clock a policeman stopped by to remind them that there was a mandatory evacuation going on. Cara had assured him that they were just going to finish up and head out.

"You put your life at risk staying," he'd told them. "Once that bridge closes, no one gets off. And we can't come to save you."

It was an onerous message, one that added adrenaline to their efforts. There were a few hitches they hadn't planned on, one big one being running out of the right screws for the shutters. David had to make a dash to the hardware store in Mount Pleasant and they, of course, did not have the right size. So he had to drive across town to another where thankfully he found what he'd needed.

But David was nearly done now. Cara was in the bedroom, packing a few final things into her suitcase. She'd placed a jewelry pouch that contained her mother's pearls in first. She'd seen her mother wear these pearls more times than she could count. There were a few other nice brooches and earrings, but Lovie had never been one for jewelry, and she'd given the bulk of her inherited pieces to Julia, Cara's sister-in-law. Palmer was the eldest son, after all. But in truth, Cara wasn't much for jewelry either. She'd claimed, instead, her mother's collection of local paintings. Those, it turned out, were a real treasure trove. Unfortunately, she could only fit one into David's car. She selected her favorite, a Jonathan Green. She was zipping her suitcase shut when a knock came on the door.

Cara thought for certain it was the policeman back to warn her again, but when she opened the door she was surprised to find Emmi. Her face was wild with worry. Cara felt her stomach clench. This wasn't good news.

"What are you still doing here?" Cara asked. "Why aren't you gone?"

"Flo's missing."

Cara felt her throat tighten. "What?"

"I've been looking for hours. She went out for the nest. Ugh, she's so stubborn," she fired out with anger born from worry. "I didn't realize she'd left the house until I was ready to leave. I went straight to Third Avenue, expecting to find her there opening the nests. But she wasn't there. So I ran home and looked around in every room in the house, just to be sure. Then I went out looking for her. I didn't find her so I came here." Emmi's voice was ragged with fear.

"Did you call the police?"

Emmi shook her head. "The police? No! I didn't think . . ."

"Oh, Emmi, why didn't you call me, at least? We've lost precious time." She heard the accusation in her voice and, seeing the guilt on Emmi's face, regretted it.

"I didn't want to bother you. You were trying to get out. And I thought I'd find her. But when I didn't, I came right over."

"Of course," she said with a quick smile. Cara's mind began to sort out possibilities. It was moments like these that Cara shone. She could make quick decisions and act forcefully.

"We have to call the police immediately. They may be busy with storm preparations, but they'll help us. We're running out of time."

"Okay," Emmi said, calmer. She had Cara to tell her what to do.

"Where do you think she might be?" Cara asked.

"Like I told you. The nests at Third. But she wasn't there."

"Which means she got lost."

"That's what I'm afraid of."

Cara put her hand to her forehead. "Do you remember years back when this same thing happened to her mother, Miranda?"

"Flo's mother?" She shook her head.

"Sure you do. She went out looking for the hatchlings. She had Alzheimer's and got lost. It took hours to find her. We found her wandering the beach, trying to find her way home."

"That's what is happening with Flo. Lately, she's been getting lost more often. I don't let her out on the beach by herself anymore. It's been hard. She sneaks out."

"I'm sorry this has fallen on you, Emmi. When this storm is over, I'll do more."

"I know you're there. But for now, I'll call the police."

"And I'll call David. We need all hands on deck."

. . .

August 22, 5:30 p.m.
Freehold Farm, North Carolina

In Grace's kitchen, the Rolling Stones were crying out that *sometimes you get what you need* over the speakers. Her friends were standing around the kitchen island, wineglasses in hand, moving to the beat of the Stones. Her friend, Laura Rombauer, had shipped a case of her vineyard's chardonnay and zinfandel to Grace as a birthday gift with the note "to drink on the occasion of a celebration." Grace couldn't think of anything more worthy of celebration than the coming together of friends to help the horses. When they'd finished their work, Grace had corralled her friends over to share the wealth. They were still wearing their soiled work jeans and riding pants and danced in stocking feet, having left muddy boots at the door. Everyone knew Grace liked a clean floor. From time to time they burst out laughing as they shared a story from their day at the barns.

Hannah brought out her makeup kit and set it on the kitchen table with flair. "Girls!" she called out. "Gather 'round." She began spreading out tubes of lipsticks. "I've got some great new colors. Help yourself! Who wants a makeover?"

Rebecca hurried to the table and claimed a chair. "Me! I've always wanted a makeover."

The rest of the women gathered around, drawn to the free samples on the table, eager to scrounge through the lipsticks and try on different colors. They passed around the hand mirror, asking each other, "How does it look? What do you think?"

Only Gerta hung back, almost shyly. But she was smiling, enjoying the company.

I love these women, Grace thought as she watched them. Gerta, Hannah, Katherine, Caroline, Cornelia, and Rebecca—her posse. Her pals. She'd called and they'd come running, no questions asked, as she knew they would. There were only a handful of people one could count on to show up in times of trouble, and those people were here in her kitchen today.

Grace made a final check of the big pot of spaghetti sauce simmering on the stove. Garlic bread wrapped in aluminum foil lay on the counter beside boxes of pasta. A big green salad waited in the fridge. It wouldn't be a fancy dinner, but tonight, after a hard day's work and the worry of the hurricane hitting Florida, they all needed some comfort food.

She grabbed a bottle of red and a bottle of white and joined her friends at the table. When she'd filled the last glass of wine, she lifted hers and tapped the crystal with a spoon to draw everyone's attention. She saw their faces smiling up at her, curious.

"To the horses!" she said.

This was met with a chorus and clinking of glasses.

The music changed and Cyndi Lauper began belting out "Girls Just Want to Have Fun." It was too perfect. Instantly the women were back on their feet, laughing, dancing around the kitchen floor, hip-bumping and joining in together to belt out the chorus.

Moira and Elise had heard the laughter and loud music and came downstairs to check it out. They had changed from jeans to yoga pants and baggy T-shirts for a relaxed evening. They stood at the entrance to the kitchen, mesmerized by the sight of their mothers and their friends drinking and dancing and whooping it up like teenagers. They turned to each other at the same time, eyes agog. Then they started to laugh.

"I hope we're as cool when we're their age," Elise said.

"Oh, we will be," Moira said with a smug smile. "We will be. Come on!"

Raising their arms, they entered the kitchen dancing.

"Who started a party and didn't invite us?" Moira called out.

Everyone turned toward them and shouted out greetings and called the girls in, waving their arms. Grace rushed to grab two more glasses. She poured the wine and handed each of the girls a glass.

"Darlings!" Grace was beaming to see them. "I poured you the zinfandel," she said. "It's so rich I can almost chew it."

"*Delicioso,*" Moira crooned, sipping. She began moving her hips to the infectious beat. She met her mother's gaze, feeling as she always did the rush of love, and they bumped hips.

"You and me, baby," Grace said, wrapping her arm around Moira with a strong squeeze.

Grace spotted Elise dancing by Gerta's side, her long braid swinging. She danced to them and they clinked glasses. Gerta was more reserved than the other women, but Grace knew that for this mother and daughter, it was a good moment.

"Gerta!" Katherine called out. "Tell everyone what happened to you at the barn today." She turned to the other women. "Really, everyone, quiet. You have to hear this. It's unbelievable."

"That's the problem," Gerta responded drily. "It *is* unbelievable."

"Grace, could you turn down the music?" asked Caroline as politely as she could while shouting over Cyndi Lauper.

"I'll get it," said Moira, and she hurried out to the family room. A moment later, the music dropped to soft background noise as Irene Cara started singing the theme to *Flashdance*.

They gathered around, all eyes on Gerta. Reluctantly, she began telling the story of the Trakehner horse. The women fell silent as the tale unfolded, leaning forward to not miss a word.

Grace had never heard Gerta talk in such hushed tones, as though cautious to venture her beliefs. The Gerta she knew was authoritative, even bold with her opinions, as though daring anyone to question her. Clearly this incident had shaken her to the core. Then Grace remembered far back to when they were young, when Gerta rode Razzmajazz. There had been a devotion between them so profound that Grace doubted she'd ever feel that bonded with a horse. When Razzmajazz had died that terrible, painful, public death at the show, the audience had all recoiled in horror as the horse's legs kicked spasmodically in the air. Medics and others had come rushing to help the horse and try to move him, even as he was seizing, to pull the woman out from under him. Gerta had been crushed beneath Razzmajazz, but she had only cried out in worry for her horse. Grace would never forget her anguished screams.

"I know it sounds crazy," Gerta said in conclusion. "I, of all people, can hardly believe this." Her nose rose a tad, and she added unapologetically, "But I do. I *know* it's Razzmajazz."

"I find it especially interesting that this horse is a Trakehner," added Katherine. "Finding the brand means he had to have a German sire. I'm looking into it."

"You really believe all that?" asked Cornelia. "That this horse is your Razzmajazz reincarnated? Couldn't he just be a horse that happens to do some of the things your horse did?"

Rebecca leaned forward. "Why not be open-minded when we don't know whether it's true or false?"

"But we do know, logically at least," said Cornelia. "No one has ever died and come back to life to tell us about it."

"Except Jesus," Caroline added with a meaningful tone.

"Well, yes," Cornelia replied quickly. "But that's faith. There is no empirical proof of any normal human who claims they have been reincarnated into this day and age. Much less an animal."

Gerta heard the skepticism and saw the somewhat amused spark in Cornelia's eyes. She couldn't blame her. Cornelia was pragmatic, as Gerta was. Before today, Gerta would have been the first to voice her doubt.

Gerta picked up her wineglass in both hands and looked at it. "It's hard to explain—much less prove—why I believe it to be true," she replied, then looked up. "I read once that *A great horse will change your life. The truly special one defines it.* We've all heard that in a rider's life there is that one special horse. That doesn't mean we won't have other horses that teach us or touch us. But most riders can point to the one horse that did more than just change their life. As the quote says, that one special horse defined it."

"That's true," Hannah said and Caroline nodded as well.

"Razzmajazz was that horse for me. I *knew* this horse. I may not understand reincarnation. But yes. I absolutely believe that this horse is my Jazzy." She shrugged and smiled. *What else can I say?*

Cornelia smiled at her, moved.

Grace was eager to join in the discussion. "I absolutely believe in reincarnation. I think I've had many lives, and all of them involved horses. You never know," she added with a smirk, "I might've been a horse in another life."

"That I can believe," Rebecca said with a laugh while Hannah brushed blush across her cheeks.

"Or maybe a mule," chided Hannah.

The women laughed, no one more than Grace. "You know that Freehold Farm has had its share of paranormal influences. I'm not saying I can explain them. But I've witnessed them."

"You young girls are being quiet. What do *you* believe?" Cornelia asked.

Elise smirked and shrugged.

Moira responded with alacrity. "Oh, I believe in reincarnation. One hundred percent."

Gerta held back her smile at the look of surprise on Cornelia's face. Moira had the reputation of being levelheaded and her uncanny ability with animals was well known.

Katherine nudged Cornelia and said, "What she's really asking is whether any of us think this is all woo-woo."

A gentle laughter filled the room and the mood began to flow again with the wine as Grace refilled their glasses.

"Why would we think reincarnation is"—Moira lifted her hands to make air quotes—"woo-woo." She paused, letting that sink in. "I believe animals have abilities to sense things—or see things—that we cannot. We humans have become so-called evolved. Fact-based. We rely on our left brain for accuracy. For what we see. But it's our right brain that informs us of instinct, and that sense of knowing something is true, *without* seeing it." She looked meaningfully at Cornelia. "Faith."

They smiled warmly.

Katherine asked, "Horses rely on the right brain for their fight-or-flight instinct. I wonder . . . how many of you evacuated from the storm not just because of the weather warnings, but because you sensed an urgency to flee?"

The women looked at one another.

Hannah raised her hand. "Javi has impeccable instincts. You've seen him with horses. He *knew* we had to go."

Caroline said, "I always listen to that uh-oh voice in my head. I learned that when I don't, I regret it."

"I'm very sensitive about such things," Grace said. She looked at Gerta and Hannah. "I called each of you to get out, right?"

Gerta tipped her head with a half-smile and raised her glass.

"That sixth sense is within all of us at birth," continued Moira. "Some humans hone this gift and have more access to auras or visions or experiences like Gerta had. These people are called shamans or visionaries." Moira offered an uneven smile. "Or kooks. We all are judged for our external knowledge and not for internal wisdom. I stand in awe of our potential, if we choose to explore it." She turned to Gerta. "Good for you."

Gerta offered a tremulous smile in return. Her pale face flushed. "Honestly?" She let her gaze sweep the faces of the women in the room. "These feelings are new for me. Totally out of character. But I feel"—she laughed self-consciously and looked at her wineglass—"rather suddenly, like a window has opened and fresh air is blowing in. My left brain is telling me to stop being such an idiot. But my right brain is whispering, *Go! You know this is right.*" Gerta glanced up, seeking out Elise's face. Her daughter stood still, listening intently. Gerta laughed lightly, as one making light of her confession.

Grace chimed in and said in a matter-of-fact voice, looking at the women, daring them to deny her. "Gerta's right. Another thing I know for sure is that we were all meant to meet. This day has been special for me, too. For all of us. Maybe this hurricane brought us together for a reason. Don't you feel the energy?"

"I do," called out Caroline. "It's almost tingly."

Rebecca and Hannah were nodding their heads.

Katherine's eyes shone. "I know we were."

Cornelia grinned wide and clinked glasses with everyone. "Absolutely."

Gerta brightened, feeling not merely validated, but included in the group of friends. Welcomed.

Grace turned to the two young women. "And that includes you, too."

Rebecca was drawn by a sudden burst of howling and yapping to the collection of dogs hovering outdoors at the window. Some stood on hind legs, staring almost frantically inside.

"What on earth do these dogs want?" she asked.

Moira chuckled as she set her glass on the counter and rushed over to the window where Bunny and Gigi sat calmly staring out at the near hysterical dogs on the other side of the glass. She swooped up her little Cavalier King Charles spaniel and returned to the group. The pretty tricolor dog was wearing pink ruffled pantaloons. "Gigi's in heat."

"Good heavens, girl. Why haven't you spayed her?" asked Caroline, rising from the table.

Hannah laughed boisterously. "I love it. Look at those boys lined up out there. They're all in love!"

The mood shot upward as everyone laughed, back on safe ground.

"I co-own her with a breeder," Moira explained. "I have to see if she wants to breed her one time before I spay her."

"With the way those dudes are looking at her, good luck with holding out," said Katherine.

"Oh. My. God," exclaimed Caroline on a long sigh. She was standing by the window staring out. "Who is *that* dog?" she asked, pointing.

"Which one?" Elise asked, moving closer to peer out.

"That big one with the brown and white coat, standing by the planter. I swear, he's staring at me with those big eyes. It's like he's looking into my soul."

Elise squinted. "That's Jack. He's the leader of the bunch."

"He's my dog, is what he is," Caroline declared. "I know it." She looked up, her eyes twinkling. "It's my instincts at work, right?"

"That's a perfect segue into what I wanted to talk to all of you about," Moira said, walking back to the window. Predictably, the moment the dogs waiting there spied Gigi again, they commenced scratching at the window and howling. "Look at all the dogs out there. Good, friendly, healthy dogs. That hurricane is battering Florida, and Danny and Ron will be rescuing a lot more dogs from flooded homes. I have to find homes for these dogs, and I need your help."

Rebecca, looking quite pretty with her makeover, tilted her head and wagged a finger at Moira as she walked to the window. "Are you trying to rope us into adopting a dog?"

From beside her, Moira heard Elise mutter teasingly, "Busted."

Moira's mouth eased into a wide grin. "At least think about it. You know Danny and Ron let the dogs live with them in their house, so they're all socialized and ready to go. Come on," she pleaded. "Y'all spent the day helping horses. How about helping these dogs? They need you too. And they're great, I promise you."

Katherine moved to the window to peer out. She pointed at one of the terriers. "That little dog looks just like that Benji dog in the movie. I've always wanted a dog like that. You know, my Lucy died a few months ago. I've been thinking of getting a dog."

Cornelia joined the others at the window. "We've got a big farm. And my husband loves a good hound. I'll just bet that coonhound can hunt."

Rebecca pointed. "What about the cute little dog sitting by its lonesome by the pool. Isn't she sweet with those big ears? I just know she's a girl."

Hannah sidled beside Cornelia to look out the window. "Oh, she is sweet. But I've got my eye on that Chihuahua. Talk about attitude."

Elise turned to her mother with one brow raised and asked challengingly, "Are you going to adopt a dog?"

Gerta shook her head. "You know I'm not a dog person. Besides, I just adopted a horse."

Elise appeared confounded. "You adopted a horse?"

"Honey, we were just talking all about it," Caroline said kindly.

Elise's face clouded with belligerence as she brushed her braid from her shoulder. "You didn't mention you were *adopting* it. You never want any animal without a pedigree. And now you're adopting this horse?"

"Yes. He's in the barn right now."

Elise covered her surprise by lifting her chin. "Well, cool," she declared. "I've always wanted a dog, and you always said no. I'm adopting Birdie." She said the words as a challenge and stared at her mother, bowed up for her response.

Gerta only smiled serenely. "Okay."

Elise appeared nonplussed by her mother's calm response. With a curt nod, she rose and left the room.

Moira covered the awkwardness with forced cheer. "How about we all go out and see if a dog speaks to you?"

Grace set down her wineglass and shot from her chair. "I call dibs on the white terrier with the black patch!"

Everyone laughed and followed her out, including Bunny, who trailed at their heels, barking.

Moira paused, noting that Gerta hadn't moved from her chair. "Are you all right?"

"Oh, *ja*," she replied, slipping into German in her fatigue.

"You don't want to join us?"

"I'm going to walk down to the barn. It's my night and I want to check on Jazzy. Tell your mother not to hold dinner for me. I would like some time to myself."

Moira rested a hand on Gerta's shoulder. "Later, when you have time, will you introduce me to Razzmajazz? I'd love to meet him."

Gerta's eyes kindled with affection. She wondered how Grace had raised such a thoughtful daughter. And why Elise was always so angry.

FOURTEEN

Cara's heels dug into the cool, damp sand as she pushed against the gale-force winds howling on the beach. Above, the clouds had thickened and felt so low she was sure she could reach right up and touch them. They made the early evening sky appear as dark as night.

The tide had turned into a wild thing, spitting out water and roaring as it prowled closer, devouring beach. Its vastness was covered with choppy, white-capped waves like scales on some mythological water beast. Sea foam lined the shoreline in surreal, spongy stretches. There was no horizon over the ocean, no difference between water and sky and earth. Everything was a gray, swirling mass.

Cara brought the collar of her raincoat higher to her neck, clutching it there, as the first bands of rain began to fall. Reports of squalls spotted in the area threatened tornadoes, one of the hidden dangers of hurricanes.

When at last she reached the Isle of Palms pier, she pulled out her flashlight. This was the end of her assigned search area. The wind pushed at her back as the yellow beam of light searched under the pilings. There was only a scant amount of beach left as the sea encroached. Soon, the dunes would be gone. They'd have to leave as soon as she got back. Time had run out for them all.

"Flo!" she screamed out at the top of her lungs. She felt desperate. She'd run out of places to look. She'd run out of time. "Flo!" Her throat was raw from screaming and she doubted she could be heard against the pounding of the surf. Fear snaked along her spine and tears, not rain, flooded her eyes.

Flo wasn't here. No one was fool enough to be out on this beach. Exhausted, she gripped the pilings and lay her cheek against the wet wood. It'd been nearly two hours since the police had divided up the area around the beach for the search. They were calling off the search at six-thirty. In ten minutes. The police would be closing the bridge and they all had to leave. There was nothing more they could do in the wake of a hurricane.

She was crazy to be out here, to have waited this long. She knew it. She of all people! She'd vowed never to stare a hurricane in the eye again. But what choice did she have? Flo was out there somewhere, alone and afraid and lost, and she couldn't— wouldn't—leave until she'd been found. "Mama, please help us find Flo," she prayed.

She felt her phone vibrate, and turning her back against the wind, she held it to her ear.

"Cara?"

"David!"

"We found her."

. . .

Minutes later David's Range Rover rolled up to the curb at the pier to pick her up. Front Beach, usually jam packed, was deserted. She climbed into the car and fell against him, relishing his strong arms around her.

David raced down Ocean Boulevard, ignoring speed limits. The houses on both sides of the street were boarded up and deserted. Cara didn't see a single car. On the way, David informed her that Flo had been found wandering on the far northern point of the island on the Wild Dunes golf course. She was carrying the Island Turtle Team's red bucket used for moving eggs and hatchings. She was weak and exhausted, but okay. Cara's relief knew no bounds and she began to cry, great heaving sobs, releasing all her pent-up worry. David reached out across the seats to hold her hand.

Arriving at the beach house, they saw Emmi tossing luggage into the trunk of her SUV. Flo sat quietly, spent, in the front seat. Their good-byes were quick, emotional yet spare. Time was of the essence. A police cruiser stood by to escort them across the bridge. The wind gusted and rain fell in bursts.

Cara ran to the police cruiser window and waited for them to lower it. "We need a minute. You go ahead with them," Cara shouted.

The policeman was new to the island. Fear shone in his eyes and she wondered if this was his first hurricane. When he spoke, his voice shook. "Don't delay, ma'am. We're shutting the bridge down. This wind is getting wicked."

"Got it!" she called back with a thumbs-up.

Debris was airborne in the gale-force winds as Cara and David raced into the house. Cara threw things into a suitcase. Her worst fear was that the wind would pick up and they wouldn't be able to cross the Connector. When she went outdoors to load the car, she saw that Emmi and the police car had left. She squeezed the final suitcase into the already jam packed car. The big Range Rover was filled with everything she could get in. Slamming the back door, she lowered her head against the wind and ran into the house.

The relative quiet indoors was a sharp contrast to the mayhem outdoors that battered her. She took a second to catch her breath. It was then she heard the pounding. What? Was David working on the shutters? She hurried through the back hall, oblivious to the puddles she was tracking on the floor, to the bedroom that faced the sea. She found David, his hair wet from the rain and his clothes damp, lifting the final shutters onto the window.

"Leave it, David," she cried. "We have to go."

"I only have one more window. It's the seaward window."

"David . . ."

"It's almost done. Hand me that screwdriver." He reached out his hand.

Cara took a breath, then ran to pick up the battery-operated screwdriver and place it in his hands.

"Thanks, babe." David was intent on finishing the last window. Beads of sweat mingled with water dripping from his face but he didn't slow down. When the shutter was screwed in place he reached up to swipe away the water from his eyes as he strode across the room to grab the next shutter.

"Is the car packed up?" he asked.

"Yes."

"Good. Five minutes and we're out of here."

The wind howled at the window, rattling the old frame. It sounded menacing. Cara looked at her watch. It was nearing seven o'clock. "Hurry, David . . ." she said in a keening voice.

He was true to his word. Five minutes later the last window was boarded. He didn't wait to pack up the tools but carried the battery-operated screwdriver as he grabbed her hand firmly.

"Let's go."

They scooped up the final items by the front door and, holding hands, they went out into the storm. Noelle was coming, breathing hard, howling like a banshee and spitting rain. Cara could barely stand up against the wind.

"Get in the car!" David shouted, pointing. Then he turned and began closing up the final shutters at the door.

Cara fought against the horizontal wind as she crossed the gravel path to the car. Once inside she checked her watch. It was 7:05. She blanched and said a quick prayer that the bridge was open. The last few minutes waiting for David in the car were the longest in her life.

Finally, the car door opened and he slid inside, soaking wet. He pushed the hair out of his face and without saying a word, fired the engine. No sooner had they reached Palm Boulevard than the rain began to pour in torrents. Water raced down the side of the road and in spots there was already flooding.

"Stay out of the flooded areas," she warned. She knew in this torrential current the car could become a coffin.

"I know."

The windshield wipers were going full blast but the rain and fog were so thick they could barely see the road. David leaned over the steering wheel, occasionally reaching out to wipe the film off the windshield with his large hand. As they crawled along the road at a snail's pace, Cara pinched her lips as memories of another night, years before with her mother, flooded her mind. That night Cara had been driving as they'd tried to evacuate the island. It had been last minute, like now.

Suddenly, David brought the car to a stop. He swiped the moisture from the window and peered out. Cara did the same. Ahead, she saw yellow-and-white-striped police barricades in front of the Connector. Their reflector lights shone bright in the glare of the headlights.

Cara let out a soft cry. "It's closed."

She turned to look at David. His face was like granite, still and stony. For a moment he didn't move. She could almost hear his brain clicking. Rain pounded the roof of the car like drumbeats. Then he turned to look at her, a fierceness in his eyes she'd never seen before.

"I'm sorry. We should have left."

Cara could only stare back. This was déjà-vu. That fateful night with her mother, the bridge had been closed as well.

He swallowed hard, his focus sharpening. "We'll go back to the house," he said in a low voice. "Cara, I'll protect you. I won't let anything happen to you. Do you believe me?"

The last time she'd been stuck on the island, she'd had to take care of her sick mother. This time, David was offering to protect her. She'd done a pretty good job taking care of herself these past fifty-four years. She'd learned, when the chips were down, to count on herself.

"We'll protect each other," she said. "Now turn this sucker around and let's get back to the beach house. We have to prepare."

. . .

August 22, 6:30 p.m.
Freehold Farm, North Carolina

Gerta walked from the house down the winding driveway toward the barn. The wind was picking up as the outer bands of the hurricane pushed the rain forward. Where the driveway curved near the front of the house there was a spotlight in the grass that illuminated a very large modern work of art. The sculpture was made of large pieces of metal to form a grazing horse. Very Picasso, she thought, and for a moment wondered if it was.

The driveway wound past an ancient beech tree that bore Indian carvings, barely visible in the dim light. Grace had told her the drawings indicated a treasure was located here. Seeing the stream of water skipping over rocks alongside the tree, she thought the wise men might have meant the fresh spring water. Certainly that would be a treasure in the future as fresh drinking water became rarer. Or they could have meant this beautiful piece of land with its rolling hills. Or, as Moira suggested, it might simply have been a signal to other Indians that tools were buried there. Whatever the answer, Gerta found the possibilities only added to the magic of the property. As Grace had mentioned tonight, this farm was a place of supernatural power.

The barn was quiet save for the soft music playing on the Internet music station. Mozart's Adagio in E was soothing against the noise of the wind outdoors. The horses were deep in their clean stalls, fed, watered, and ready for the night. She found the sweet smells of the barn comforting. As were the soft, vibrating nickerings of the horses. For her, they had the same effect as listening to a cat's purr. She could feel the tension seeping from her body. A barn was always home for her.

She went first to Razzmajazz's stall at the far end. Seeing her approach, Jazzy came to the window to hang his head out, ears alert. He strained his neck to get closer to her, blowing through his muzzle in a soft nicker of welcome.

Gerta's heart melted. She set down her purse and walked to his side. She gave his neck a good scratch, something she used to do to Razzmajazz. "Look what I've brought for you." She reached into her pocket and pulled out a carrot. Jazzy immediately helped himself from her flattened palm. She chuckled as he chewed loudly. When he was done, she brought her cheek close to the soft hair of his neck, breathing in the scent of him. Jazzy moved his neck to almost wrap around her body like a hug and nuzzled her shoulder—the same way horses showed affection to other horses. Gerta closed her eyes, smiling. She had not been imagining this horse's affection.

She stepped back to open the stall and walked inside. Slipping a brush over her hand, she took her time currying him, enjoying the contact. She brushed until his coat gleamed a burnished dark red. She moved on to the tail, working out the knots, and then to the mane, and finally the forelock, seeing again the telltale marking of the small, white star. She ended with a gentle scratching around his ears. This was where Razzmajazz had loved to be scratched the most. Sure enough, he released a low-pitched guttural sound, like a sigh.

Jazzy lowered his nose and sniffed her prosthesis. Gerta held her breath, wondering if he was simply checking the leg out—or if he was remembering the accident. He sniffed it for a long while.

"It wasn't your fault," she said, patting his neck. "You tried to roll away from me, but you couldn't. It wasn't your fault."

Jazzy lifted his head and looked out the stall. What did he remember? she wondered. This was going to take time. She smiled and thought, *Damn the schedules and demands*. She could hire more help. This was her life. She'd make the time.

She didn't know how long she spent in the stall, brushing and talking to Jazzy. It was a stream of consciousness, sharing with the horse all the feelings pent-up about that horrible accident, her fears and the devastation of watching them inject him with drugs. How his legs kicked in the air, then went still. Tears flowed in torrents down her cheeks as she remembered. These were not tears of sadness, but of catharsis. At last, the dam was breaking. Through it all, Jazzy stood stoically and listened. She didn't want to be rushed or interrupted. This was a private time of reconnection between her and Jazzy. A time to sort things out between them, to remember the past, and to familiarize themselves with the person and horse they were today.

It was Mother Nature who told Gerta it was time to get going. The wind was building up, shaking the leaves in the branches and sending great gusts through the barn. In the distance she heard the low rumble of thunder. She gave Jazzy a final pat, then left the stall and went to close the rolling entrance door of the barn. The air held water; rain was imminent. Then she went about the night check, moving from stall to stall to top off the water buckets and feed the last hay meal of the day. She took note of each horse, his or her attitude and condition, drawing on a lifetime of experience.

When she walked into Butterhead's stall, she knew immediately that something was very wrong.

Butterhead was restless, shifting her weight as though in discomfort. Drawing closer, Gerta saw she was covered in a fine sweat and her breathing was rapid. Looking around the stall, she found no feces. She went immediately to the tack room and found the stethoscope. Walking at a fast clip, she returned to Butterhead and listened to her gut. She sighed with relief. Noises were churning. But a check of her gums revealed they were pale. Gerta felt sure it was colic.

She'd lost a horse to colic years back because she hadn't caught it. She'd walked away, thinking she'd check on the horse after doing an errand. The horse had taken a sudden turn for the worse and died. Gerta had never forgiven herself for her negligence. Since then she'd been hyperalert for any possible symptoms of colic in her horses. Taking her phone from her pocket, she pulled up Grace's number and hit the dial icon. Grace would have the number of the local vet. Nothing happened. She looked closer: the phone wasn't dead, but there was no service.

"*Scheisse,*" she swore. Pausing, she noticed that the music had stopped. The Internet was out. It had to be the storm, she thought. Grace had told her how every storm knocked out the connection. Gerta pinched her lips as her heart raced. Time was of the essence. She had to get word to Angel. Someone had to call a vet.

"Don't you worry," she told Butterhead. "I'll be right back."

Her leg might be gimpy, but she'd have to make it back to the house as fast as she could. Even if it was uphill all the way. She closed the stall gate behind her and walked quickly to the barn door. Grunting with the effort, she slowly rolled the big barn door open just as the sky opened up. The rain was torrential, a whiteout of water that looked like someone standing on the roof was emptying buckets. The pounding on the roof was deafening. She put her fingers to her cheeks. *What to do . . . what to do.*

Gerta set her chin and went back to Butterhead's stall, deter-mined not to lose her. Butterhead was swishing her tail and her ears shifted back in warning as she approached. She was in pain and didn't want Gerta near.

"I know you don't feel like walking," Gerta said evenly as she opened the gate. "And it's a shitty night for it, but it's what we're going to do." She picked up the halter from the peg on the wall and slowly moved toward the horse. Butterhead's ears laid back, but Gerta continued with calm, measured movements, speaking sooth-ingly to her all the while. She slipped the lead rope over the mare's neck in one smooth move, then the halter over her nose.

Making clucking noises, she walked Butterhead at a slow pace back and forth along the hall, but it was too short. She needed more room to walk her. Outside, the powerful rain had passed as quickly as it had come. There was only a drizzle now.

"Come along, *Schatzi*. We don't mind a little rain, do we?"

She led Butterhead out of the barn, feeling the cool mist on her face. She guided the horse farther out, feeling her boots sink deep into the mud, trampling the grass. She looked up at the clouds. They were rolling fast, bringing the hurricane. Her leg would punish her later, but she had to walk the horse for at least fifteen to twenty minutes. *It is what it is,* she thought. She could only hope that when she returned the Internet would be back on.

Angel was looking for Gerta. She had been gone for a long time and no one seemed to care. He didn't feel right that she—a woman—was taking barn duty tonight, especially during this storm. It pricked his conscience. Not to mention his manliness. The others sat at the dining table and talked over plates rimmed red with spaghetti sauce and littered with bits of pasta and bread. Charles kept the wine flowing, and everyone seemed to be ignoring the rush of wind and the frantic swaying of the great trees outside the windows. If anything, the storm heightened the emotion of the evening, making everyone laugh harder, louder, as if in defiance.

In the family room the omnipresent weather station showed current pictures of the hurricane. Angel watched as the meteorologists traced the cone of Hurricane Noelle's path. The hurricane had hit the Florida Keys as a Category Four and was now moving north along the Florida coast. He returned to the dining room and stuck in his head. The candles had burned low. The guests were relaxed in their chairs, sated, and their eyes glistened in the candlelight. Angel knocked on the doorframe, drawing their attention.

"Oh, sit down," called out Hannah with a hint of frustration. "Your pacing is making us nervous."

Angel looked directly at Hannah. "Come, look. You should come see this. Palm Beach . . . it's, like, getting pounded."

Wood chairs pushed back as one as everyone rose and hurried to the living room. They clustered around the television as Charles reached for the remote to turn up the sound.

The news showed pictures of Palm Beach getting the brunt of the storm. Hurricane Noelle was whipping the palm trees, scattering beach chairs and sending them flying. The weatherman stood in a covered patio, rain and wind battering him. He was fighting just to stand as he made his report.

"I hate it when they do that," Elise said, making a face. "He should just go inside and tell us what's happening. Do they think it makes it more exciting? It's just stupid."

Grace came to put an arm around her shoulders. "Your farm will be fine," she said in a reassuring voice. "Your mother builds a strong house."

"No one ever expects a hurricane to hit home," Elise said softly.

"But look," Charles said reassuringly, "it's dropped to a Category Three. Florida has weathered a lot worse."

"Dad, a Cat Three is still one hundred eleven miles per hour," said Moira.

Angel looked to Hannah and offered a smile of reassurance. Her Palm Beach condo faced the ocean.

"What do you think? Will it get here tomorrow night?" asked Hannah. Her voice rang with worry but she was trying hard to remain upbeat.

"Most likely. Tropical-force winds at most," Charles answered. "Nothing like this," he said, gesturing to the television report. "It probably won't be as strong as what we've got right now. Not to worry. It'll be nothing."

The wind gusted, whistling at the windows and rattling the branches of the shrubs outside. Outdoors something fell over, clattering loudly. With a sudden burst, a deafening rain pounded on the roof. Everyone turned to watch rain fall in sheets outside the windows.

"That doesn't sound like nothing." Elise brought her wineglass to her lips.

Charles tried to make light of it. "It's the rain bands passing through. It comes and goes. See?" He pointed upward. "The rain's already slowing." He smiled like the Cheshire Cat. "For now."

"Gerta shouldn't be alone in all this at the barn," Angel said, a frown creasing his face.

"She's safe down there. It's dry and warm. And built like a tank," said Charles.

"But she can't get back in all this rain. With her leg, you know?" Angel argued. "She walked. Her car is still up here."

"She walked?" Grace's face puckered in worry.

Elise's face clouded. "What if she gets stuck down there?"

"She can go into my loft," said Karl. "It's very comfortable. I'll text her and tell her that." He pulled out his phone, paused, and then looked up. "There's no service."

Grace groaned and put her hand to her cheek. "Not again. I swear, the Internet goes out if a mouse farts up here."

"Let's be fair," Charles said, "it's pretty bad out there. We should all stay put until this blows over."

"I'm going to pick her up," Angel said decisively. He looked to Hannah. "Where are the keys?"

She looked at him questioningly but didn't argue. "In my purse."

"I'll be right back," Angel said as he trotted out.

Angel slipped into one of Charles's rain jackets that hung by the door. He found Hannah's keys and headed out. No sooner did he leave the house than the rain came pouring down again. Ducking his head, he ran for the Audi. He was drenched by the time he got into the driver's seat. The rain pounded the small car like a drum. Even with the windshield wipers going full tilt, he had to crawl along the driveway at a snail's pace. He leaned far forward over the steering wheel, squinting and reaching up to wipe the condensation on the windshield with his palm. He couldn't see more than a few feet ahead of him. He cursed the crazy weather.

Somewhere between the house and the car, the rain slowed again. He blew out a sigh of relief. He could see the road, even though there was thick fog. Still creeping along, Angel turned at the fork onto the driveway that led to the barn. The fog swirled and the rain was beginning to pick up again. As he rounded the bend to the parking area, out of nowhere a woman leading a horse appeared in the headlights. He stomped on the brakes, coming to an abrupt halt that jolted him forward.

"*¡Madre de Dios!*" he shouted, and slammed his palm on the steering wheel. His heart thumping, he leaned forward and peered through the clicking windshield wipers in fear he might have hit her. He was stunned to see that the woman was Gerta Klug, looking like a drowned rat. And the horse was Butterhead.

Swearing in Spanish, he turned off the engine and leaped from the car. He had to squint to see her. Gerta was soaked to the skin.

"What, are you crazy?" she shouted at him. "You almost hit us!"

Angel's gaze was hungrily studying Butterhead. She looked sickly, with her head lowered and her wet mane flattened against her body. Reaching out, he took the lead from Gerta.

"What are you doing?" His tone was accusatory.

"What does it look like I'm doing? I'm walking your horse."

His eyes widened. "Is it colic?"

"Yes," Gerta said, "I believe it is. I tried to call the vet but there is no service."

Angel understood all now. In a rush he recalled how Butterhead had been acting off this morning, but he'd attributed it to all the stress of travel. He'd let her relax and didn't put her through her morning exercises. She hadn't looked bad when he'd brought her back to her stall from the pasture—but he hadn't taken the time with her that he usually did. Guilt washed over him as he realized he'd not paid attention and missed the signs.

His gaze returned to Gerta. *She* hadn't missed them. She'd caught the symptoms. And she'd been out walking Butterhead, in this horrible storm. With her bad leg. She might have saved Butterhead's life.

When he was this upset, his mind worked only in Spanish. He began talking rapidly to Butterhead in soothing tones as he led her back to the barn. Gerta followed more slowly. Her limp was far more noticeable. His gaze swept over Butterhead, noticing her tired gait, as well, and the drooping of her head. His heart beat fast with worry. If anything happened to her, he thought, he couldn't bear it. His fear was a testament to his love for the horse.

"*Jesucristo*, how long have you been walking in this rain?"

Gerta's voice was haughty. "Not more than half an hour. To good results. She had a bowel movement," she announced triumphantly.

He stopped and turned. "*¿Ella hizo caca?*" This was an important sign that the worst was over.

"Twice!"

"That is such good news," he exclaimed. "Fantastic." He turned and led Butterhead into the barn. Once inside he saw the fresh hay and water. Gerta had done her job well. He walked the tired mare into her stall, then hurried to the tack room to fetch a stack of towels. He began toweling off his horse, rubbing hard to get her circulation going. When he was done, he put his ear to her gut and was rewarded by the strong sound of vigorous gastric activity.

When he felt sure Butterhead was well and resting comfortably, he came out of the stall and closed the door. He turned to see Gerta standing in the hall, pale and unmoving, as though frozen. Angel went still and looked at her. Really looked at her.

Her white blouse clung to her breasts, revealing soft, creamy mounds and the slender straps of her bra. Her blond hair had slipped from its hold and drooped, soaking, to her shoulders. And her face. Water dripped down her cheeks along with mascara. As his gaze traveled down her body, her soaked jeans revealed where the socket of her prosthesis came to the groin, just below her hip. She was shivering and stared back at him with wide, voluminous eyes.

He'd never seen anyone more beautiful in his life.

His voice softened. "Now it's your turn." Angel went to grab two of the towels and carried them to her. He dropped one to the floor and reached out to wrap her in the other.

Gerta stepped back, eyes hard. "Don't touch me."

"Shh," he said, and gently placed the towel on her head. "You need help too." He carefully rubbed her hair dry, the towel covering her head. When he moved it from her face, her blue eyes stared back, bulging with restrained fury, her nostrils flaring. He smiled and dabbed delicately at her face, wiping away the mascara. She continued to glower as he continued to smile, amused by her spirit.

"Do you do this with Hannah?" she asked, testing him.

Angel paused. "Honestly, I haven't touched Hannah like this in months."

Gerta's brows drew together, but she didn't speak. Her eyes watched him with the stillness of a cat. If she had a tail, he felt sure it would be twitching. *Careful of claws*, he thought to himself as he brought the towel down to wrap it around her shoulders. Then he began to rub her arms vigorously.

"We've got to get the blood flowing," he said in the tone a father might use to his child. "There," he said when finished, wrapping the towel tighter around her shoulders. "Feel better?"

Unexpectedly, Gerta's stony façade suddenly crumbled. She stared back at him with tears flooding her eyes as her lower lip started trembling. He saw in the blue pools a vulnerability he'd never seen in her before.

When her face at last crumpled and she broke into a sob, Angel swiftly gathered her into his arms. He made soothing sounds as he had to Butterhead earlier.

"Shh . . . shh. It's okay," he murmured as he smoothed her wet hair from her face with his palm.

She laid her head on his shoulder, still shivering. "I-I was doing the barn check," she began haltingly. "When I went into Butterhead's stall, I saw right away something was wrong." She released a long, shuddering sigh. "I tried to call Grace. So she could tell you and call a vet. But there was no service."

"I know."

"Then I was going to walk back up the hill, but the rain hit. Terrible rain." She shook her head against his chest. "All I could think of to do was walk her."

"You did the right thing. You saved her life."

She sniffed and laughed weakly. "I was never so happy to see a horse take a dump in my life."

He enjoyed the sound of her laughter.

She pulled back, wiping the tears from her face with quick movements. "I'm sorry I cried. I don't know what came over me."

She sniffed. "Well, perhaps I do. It's been an emotional day." She raked her hair from her face with her fingers. "I must look a fright."

Angel held on to her shoulders, looked into her eyes, and said, "I think you are the most beautiful woman I've ever seen."

She wiggled free from his hold and took a step back. "Now you're just being ridiculous," she said sharply.

Suddenly the music began playing. Their eyes met, and they both grinned with relief. The Internet was back!

Angel dug into his pocket for his phone. "I'll call the vet. I got her number this morning. It's in my favorites."

"I'll call Grace."

When their phone messages had been delivered, Angel slipped his phone into his pocket and held out his hands.

"What now?" she asked, bringing her hand to her hair.

"Let's dance."

Gerta's eyes widened. "Dance? Me?" She shook her head while backstepping. "Oh, no. I can't dance."

"Everybody can dance."

"Not me. You don't understand. I'm a bit lame. I wear a prosthesis."

He moved quickly, taking a step closer to wrap his arm around her waist before she could escape. "No excuses," he said, pulling her closer to his chest.

The music changed, and a piano played Debussy's "Clair de Lune."

Gerta had no fight left in her. She loosened and let him take her right hand as his arm tightened around her waist. He guided her gently in a swaying motion, left to right, repeated in slow, rocking steps. At first she was stiff in his arms, resisting. He didn't push her.

He let her take her time, to listen to the music and grow accustomed to the feel of him against her. In his experience, handling a woman was a lot like riding a horse. A good rider didn't force his horse to do something; he gave the animal a chance to *want* to do it. And perhaps most importantly, a good rider was able to follow what the horse asked him to do as well.

Angel watched for her signals, attuned to her movements. Gradually he felt her relax in his arms, and the more she did, the more she tuned in to his lead, and the transitions came easier. Neither of them spoke. They swayed as around them Debussy's haunting melody played, and the horses nickered their soothing, sensual sounds. It was a natural symphony, and Angel closed his eyes and smelled rain in her hair and shampoo that hinted at roses. When the music ended, he stopped and moved his head to look down at her. She tilted hers upward. Her eyes were soft now. Trusting.

He stared at her lips, desire welling inside. He waited for her signal. Gerta brought her hand up to the stubble on his chin, then let it glide up to the soft, shorter hairs along the back of his neck. She studied him, as though memorizing each detail of his face, before she moved her hand higher into the softness of his hair. Then she brought his head toward hers.

He measured his approach in breaths. Her lips slid open, and in a final breath his mouth was on hers. She closed her eyes and pressed herself against him. The connection was so strong he felt something inside of him shift. The taste of her, the smell of her— he couldn't get enough. One kiss would never suffice. When a soft moan escaped her lips, he pressed her tightly against him, lifting her slightly as he deepened his kiss.

Then he thought of her and held himself in check. She was

feeling vulnerable, he knew this. It would be wrong of him to press. When he moved back, she took a long, shuddering breath and opened her eyes. They were wide and her pupils were glazed with desire. And then she released a slow, knowing smile. He smiled too, a wonder-filled smile.

Neither noticed the sound of a car pulling up to the barn, the slamming of doors. They stopped dancing and took steps apart only when they heard Grace's voice calling out, "Hello!"

FIFTEEN

August 22, 9:15 p.m.
Freehold Farm, North Carolina
*Hurricane Noelle weakens to Category Three
as it approaches the coast of the Carolinas*

Showered, refreshed, drained, Gerta stood before the bathroom mirror in the cottage. She grimaced from the phantom pains in her leg. They were pulsing shock sensations, like a taser that came on with too much stress and not enough sleep. She groaned softly and rubbed her prosthesis as though it were a part of her. Most people didn't realize that for her, it took 150 percent of the energy of someone with both legs to walk. Exercising Butterhead had drained a lot from her. She needed to find time to rest . . . a weakness that was an anathema to her.

The house was quiet. Elise was still out somewhere, most likely with Moira. Gerta wasn't worried. Elise had once told Gerta that ten o'clock was just the beginning of the evening for her age group. Gerta's sigh ended with a light laugh. Had she ever been that young? she wondered. Her whole life had been a series of challenges met and conquered. There had been little room for carousing.

But, she thought, watching the slightly wicked smile forming on her lips, perhaps it was time in her life for a little fun.

She studied the face in the mirror, swiping away the condensed steam on the glass with her towel. Her eyes stared back at her, blue and luminous. A wonder shone in them that she had not seen in so very long. She tilted her head and brought her fingertips to her cheek, pulling the skin back at the eyes. There were wrinkles forming there, and on her forehead. Worry lines, people called them. Signs of advancing age, she called them. Still, she didn't look too bad for fifty-five. Her skin was smooth. Maybe all those moisturizers and creams were worth the ridiculous prices. More likely, she could thank genetics. And sunscreen.

Gerta didn't usually muse on the condition of her face or how young she looked. Such things mattered little to her—until now. Tonight, she appraised her attributes because of Angel de la Cruz. She was embarrassed to admit that she wished she were younger. She wanted to look younger. For him. How old was he, anyway? she wondered. Forty? Forty-five? *Too young,* she thought with a dash of her hopes and looked down from the mirror.

"The only thing worse than a fool is an old fool," she told herself.

She put a shaky hand to her forehead. It was late, the hour when she doubted herself most. She still couldn't completely process what had happened in the barn. They'd danced! Another laugh of disbelief. She hadn't danced since she'd lost her leg. Granted, it was only a back-and-forth stepping, but afterward she felt she could twirl! What was it about him that one couldn't say no? He had an energy about him, a confidence she found annoying. Invasive. Charming . . . And he had the most beguiling smile—so genuine, almost childlike the way it lit up his face. She closed her eyes, picturing it, and smiled.

A warmth swept through her, titillating, arousing. She felt again his arms around her. Saw again the way his pupils quivered like dark pools when he became excited. The way he looked at her lips. She opened her eyes and saw desire reflected in the mirror. Her fingers trailed from her forehead to her lips, feeling the tenderness.

Remembering.

A few miles away, Angel slipped quietly back into the lake house. The rain had stopped but the night remained as thick as mud. The house was pitch-black. Hannah had not left a light on for him.

When he opened the door Max gave off a low *gruff* of warning. Angel could hear the clicking of toenails as he crossed the tile.

"Come on, boy," he said, bending at the waist to embrace his dog. "Good boy, eh? You missed me. I'm back. I always come back to you."

Max rubbed against his leg like a cat, his rear shaking in joy.

Angel straightened and flicked on a light. Charles's waxed cotton jacket was damp and heavy. He slipped it off and tossed it on the chair as he walked to the refrigerator. The bottles clinked on the door as he jerked it open and light shone from the interior. The fridge looked cold and barren. An open bag of carrots was meant for the horses. Bottles of kombucha, vitamins, and serums for Hannah. Bottles of beer for him. His mind flashed to the fridge at the cottage. He'd peeked into it when Elise had offered him a drink. He was blown away to see how stocked it was—cheeses, fresh fruit and vegetables, those little deli containers filled with various salads, and wine. Good wine. He knew it wasn't Elise who shopped.

Gerta. The memory of her gave him pause. He stood in front of the fridge, opened a bottle, and drank thirstily. *Gerta,* he thought again, confused by the emotions running through him. He closed the fridge and leaned against the counter, drinking his beer, lost in his thoughts. The woman had been a complete and utter surprise. He could live to be a hundred and he'd never forget the sight of her, drenched and limping, her eyes blazing with determination as she walked Butterhead—*his* horse—in the pouring rain. She was a warrior! Fierce and powerful. He loved that about her.

He sighed, shaken again by the memory. But it was the vulnerability he'd discovered in her eyes that had brought him to his knees. He knew that seeing such emotion was rare. She'd let him see the woman behind the regal mask she wore for the rest of the world.

Gerta . . . She was the whole package. Beautiful. Smart. As regal as a queen. Wealthy, yes, he thought, wincing. He hated himself for even having that thought. But that was not why he was so drawn to her. He was, in fact, hopelessly attracted to her. When he'd held her in his arms, he wanted her. *Her.* Gerta, the woman.

He preferred older women. Always had. He was dating Hannah, after all—weren't she and Gerta about the same age? Yes, he realized with a smug satisfaction, as though that proved his point. He enjoyed younger women too. But older women had a clarity and substance he appreciated. And they gave him space. They had their own thing going, knew who they were and weren't so needy. Young women could act foolish and immature. It was all about them and how they looked and they were forever wondering what they wanted next. He didn't have time for that. Older women knew what they wanted, often had it, and were eager to ask him what *he* wanted.

Yet Gerta was at a whole different level—the highest level. She was like a Grand Prix horse, an international champion. Full of elegance and talent, spirited, self-driven—oh yes, and temperamental. She couldn't be forced. No, no. She needed to be coaxed. She needed the right partner—a skilled rider—to help her become receptive and responsive. To bring out the dance within her. He drank again, enjoying the refreshing taste of bitter hops.

Sadly, Hannah was no longer a challenge. She was wonderful—kind and funny and drop-dead gorgeous. But the spark was gone. They were friends more than lovers. Gerta, on the other hand . . . He reached up to rub at the stubble on his jaw. There was a woman who would be a challenge for a long time.

He scratched his head vigorously and blew out a plume of air. *"Basta ya,"* he said, setting his bottle on the counter. He sighed, feeling a great heaviness in his chest, a sadness that the time had come. He had to face it. It was over between him and Hannah. It had been for some time. He'd hoped that after this hurricane they could work things out. But tonight only confirmed that it was time to break up.

He reached out to pat Max on the head. The dog was so big that when he sat, his head was at Angel's waist. Angel let his eyes travel to the stairs. He couldn't put off the inevitable any longer. He had to talk to Hannah—tonight. *Man up,* he told himself. She deserved honesty.

With a resigned sigh, he took off his boots and went up the stairs to the master bedroom. The door was closed and no light shone from under the door. He paused, debating whether to awaken her. *Let her sleep,* he decided. *We can talk tomorrow.* He gently opened the door, cringing at the squeak. Sticking his head in, he spied Hannah lying in bed. He took one step forward when suddenly a small dog leaped from the bed, yapping hysterically.

Hannah's eyes sprang open and she stretched out for the bedside lamp.

Light flooded the room and she saw Angel jumping back from the snarling Chihuahua. Max hovered at the door, seemingly afraid to enter.

"*¡Mierda!*" Angel exclaimed.

"It's about time you showed up."

"What is this?" he shouted, hands out to the incessantly yapping dog darting at his feet. The little body jumped up with each bark. "*¡Este perro esta loco!*"

Hannah clapped her hands and whistled. "Nacho! Come!"

The fawn-colored Chihuahua cast Angel a withering look with his large brown eyes, then turned and effortlessly leaped up to the top of the bed and pranced across the mattress to settle in Hannah's lap.

"He's my dog," she told Angel. "I adopted him."

Angel ran his hands through his hair. "I thought you hated dogs."

"No. I only hate your dog."

Mumbling in Spanish, Angel came farther into the room, keeping a wary eye on Nacho. He pulled off his dirty T-shirt and began unbuckling his pants.

"He reminded me of you," she said with a smirk.

Angel didn't think that was funny. His scowl deepened. "You could've warned me."

Hannah looked at him coolly, stroking the dog's head with her coral-tipped fingers. "You were preoccupied. With Gerta Klug. You left me at the house without a car. I know you were worried because you called." She made a face to let him know she was miffed that he did not. "Moira drove me back. Thanks."

He shot a cautious glance at her but didn't reply. She leaned back against the headboard, Nacho in her lap, and watched Angel step out of his pants and kick them across the floor. She admired his beautiful body, as lean and taut as a jockey's with the rock-hard core muscles required of a jumper.

"Thank God I was," he said, lifting his palms to emphasize the point. "Do you know what I found when I got to the barn, eh? In that raging rain?" He stood before her, naked but for his slim black briefs. "She was out in the storm walking Butterhead. She had colic!"

Hanna paused her petting. "Gerta or the horse?"

Angel waved his hand dismissively. "You don't care. I know you don't care. You only care about your makeup."

She would have been angry except that she knew he didn't mean it. He was supportive of her makeup line, always bragging about her business to his friends and influential acquaintances.

"That's not true," she said without rancor. "You know I care." She patted the mattress by her side. "Tell me."

He sighed and came to sit on the mattress. "The doctor said it was the combination of stress and the long trip. She checked Butterhead very well and said she's okay now." He shrugged. "She pooped."

"Praise the Lord," Hannah said, lifting her hands.

Angel looked down at the dog with disdain. "Can you get rid of that rodent?"

"Don't call him that," she said, holding Nacho closer. "I think he's adorable." She kissed his head.

"How can you love that dog and not Max? He's a perfect dog. Devoted, loving—as a dog should be." He smirked. "As a woman should be."

"Don't," Hannah warned, giving him a shove.

"I'm kidding," he said with a laugh. "That's just my Latin machismo coming out." He made a whining groan. "Oh, but at least take him off the bed when I'm in it?"

Hannah looked at Angel's face. He really did look exhausted. His skin was chalky; he had rough stubble on his cheeks and above his mouth. His dark hair was disheveled from scratching his head, as he did when he was upset. She gathered Nacho and lifted him to her cheek. He licked her face.

"Sorry, my little *perro*, but there's only room for one dog in this bed." She kissed the top of his head and, bending over, set the Chihuahua on the floor and gave him a gentle nudge toward his dog crate. Nacho looked over his shoulder at her, sulking.

"So, Gerta is okay?" she asked. "You were so worried about her."

"Yeah," he said dully, looking at his hands. "She's good."

Hannah paused, then cast him a sidelong glance. "Does Gerta know about you and Elise?"

Angel's head jerked up, his eyes alert under furrowed brows. "What? What are you talking about?"

She heard a defensive tone that validated her suspicions, and felt her muscles stiffen. "I saw you go into the cottage this morning. Alone. Elise opened the door. I know Gerta was not there because I'd just left her at the main house." She glared at him.

He seemed oddly relieved by the accusation. "Yes, I saw Elise. I went to check on her. She had a bad fall."

"Please . . ."

"What do you think? That I slept with her?"

"Yes."

"She's a child," he replied dismissively.

"She's twenty-nine years old."

Angel made a frustrated sound in his throat.

"You've slept with lots of women—young, old, married, single."

"Not since I've been with you," he fired back, pointing at her. "Not once."

"You flirt with everyone."

"I like women," he admitted. "But I'm not interested in Elise, not in that way. Besides, she's gay."

"Wait. What?" Hannah gaped at him.

"Everybody knows that."

"I didn't!"

He shrugged. "So, I'm not sleeping with Elise. I'm not sleeping with *anyone.*"

The last word he said with import. Hannah understood his message—she couldn't remember the last time they'd had sex. If it was true that he hadn't cheated on her, and she believed him, then this proved his love. This reasoning worked to mollify her.

"I made a decision tonight," he said.

Hannah heard the seriousness in his tone and waited.

"Tonight, when I saw Butterhead so sick, I went crazy thinking I could lose her. And the relief when the doctor said she will be okay . . ." He sighed. "I knew. I will never sell her."

Hannah was surprised. And not. Angel was a man of passion

and quick decisions. Genius in some ways, childlike in others. But smart—always smart.

"I'm glad to hear it," she said, and meant it. "I'm very fond of Butterhead. I sometimes thought of her as a kindred spirit." She paused. "I don't know if she could've survived you dumping her."

Angel frowned at the insinuation. He sat back on the mattress, leaning on his arms. "I was never dumping her."

"What will you do now?" she asked. "You still need a horse."

"I have to come up with a new plan," he said with a fatalistic sigh.

"You will. You always do."

He chortled. "I do. . . ."

Hannah pushed back her hair and studied him. She sensed something was off. His mind was on something else. "Javi, is there something you're not telling me . . . ?"

He snorted and sat up again. "You know me too well. *Sí*," he admitted, "there's something I'm not telling you. Something I meant to talk to you about."

Hannah went still, watching him expectantly. She wasn't aware she held her breath.

He turned his head toward her. "*Querida*, you know I would never hurt you."

She didn't speak, but all her senses were on high alert.

Angel climbed from the bed and began pacing the room. He was scratching his head, and she braced herself for what she knew could only be bad news. He stopped in front of the bed and put his hands on his hips. He hung his head in thought. But when he lifted it, his eyes were clear.

"Tonight, I kissed someone."

Hannah pounded the mattress with her fist. Nacho jumped up in alarm. "I knew it. Who?"

"Gerta."

Hannah's mouth slipped open. "That sour lemon? I can't believe it." She released a short, bitter laugh. "Well, I can believe you would kiss her. *That* I can believe. But that she would allow you to kiss her?" She shook her head in disbelief. "She's frigid."

"Don't say that," he said. "It isn't nice."

"Wait!" she said, narrowing her eyes. Her anger made her mean. "Now I know how you're going to get your new horse. You're going to get a Klug horse. That's your plan. A stallion for a stallion. Well done."

"No," he said, his eyes flashing with insult, "that is *not* true. It is not worthy of you to say that to me. Or about her. The simple truth is that there's something about her." Angel bowed his head. "It just happened. We did not plan this. How could we? But I . . . could love her. Say what you want about me. But leave her out."

Hannah swallowed hard. Angel had many sides. He could be the angel one moment, the devil the next. She was pretty good at being able to tell when he was being sincere. In that moment, Hannah believed that he really did care about Gerta. Her anger dissipated, replaced by sadness that he no longer felt that way about her.

"Then it's over between us."

He looked at her with sad eyes. "It's been over for a long time."

She looked at her hands, ring-less, and nodded. "I know." She took a breath. "Thank you for telling me right away. I appreciate not looking the fool in front of my friends."

"I would never do that to you. I hope you know that." He smiled at her, that damned, sweet, innocent smile. "I will always love you."

There it was. The final good-bye. "And I will always love you," she said, sealing the breakup. It was all over but the packing. She reached over to grab a pillow from his side of the bed and stuffed it into his stomach. "Now, go sleep on the couch."

He chortled and bent to kiss her cheek. She held up her hand, refusing it. "Good night, *querida*." He straightened and quickly walked around the room, grabbing his clothes. Even his shoes.

Hannah smacked her lips and patted the bed, calling, "Nacho, come."

The Chihuahua leaped to the bed and took his place in her lap. Hannah petted the silky fur and realized she didn't feel anger or resentment, nor even any great sadness at seeing Angel's back at the door. He was right. They'd both known this relationship was coming to a close. Their gazes had shifted elsewhere—his to Gerta, hers to her company. That was where her heart lay now. Hannah looked down at Nacho. He stared back at her adoringly. And her dog.

She looked up as Angel was leaving the room.

"Javi?"

He turned and looked over his shoulder. *"Sí?"*

"Close the door."

Moira and Elise settled Tut and Birdie in their crates. They were keeping the boys in the family room downstairs with Maybelle—away from Gigi. Elise's boxer mix was neutered and not the least fazed by the pheromones in the air. Tut, however, was intact and pining for Gigi. He was frantic, scratching at his crate, and refused to eat.

Back in Moira's bedroom, Gigi jumped onto the bed and wagged her tail, ready for play.

"Gigi, you're such a flirt," Elise told her as she held back the Cavalier from licking her face. "How much longer will she be in heat?"

"Another week or so. She's starting to show interest in Tut now. I'm on high alert."

Once Moira put Gigi into her crate, the women showered, changed into pajamas, and climbed into Moira's queen bed. Elise lay on her back, shoulder to shoulder with Moira as her gaze swept the bedroom.

"I don't think this room has changed since college," Elise said.

She'd often visited Freehold Farm in the summer when the girls toured the United States in competition. There were the same white French Provincial furniture, pale-blue-and-white striped silk curtains, and a pastoral painting of horses grazing in a field. There was also a wall of framed photos of Moira in competition, reaching over the neck of Quicksand as they took a jump, her face shining with intensity and drive. With her dark hair and slender, long body, she looked smart in her black jacket, boots, and helmet.

Moira yawned and said sleepily, "Who had time? I haven't stayed here long enough to make changes. I was in shows with you. It wasn't that long after college that I got married."

She paused to rub her eyes. Elise knew she was thinking about Thom.

Moira dropped her hand on the bed. "I don't think Mama wants to change it. She probably likes to think I'm still just away at college."

They both laughed at that. Grace's devotion to Moira was a running joke between them.

Outside the wind was picking up again. It was a strange night—wind and rain one moment, quiet the next.

"It's wild out there," Elise said, looking out the window at the weather. "I thought it would be quiet up here in the mountains. Not so . . . well, stormy. We're so far from the coast."

"Well, we are safe, compared to the coast," Moira said. "That's why we're here."

"Don't hurricanes lose strength as they move over land?"

"They do, but they still carry vast amounts of moisture, which causes thunderstorms and thus . . ." She indicated the window. "The main problem for us up here is the flash floods. But we'll be fine here. Trust me."

Elise was silent for a moment. "Do you mind if I ask you a personal question?"

"No."

"Do you find Karl attractive?"

Moira appeared astonished by the question. "Me?"

Elise rolled her eyes. "Yes, you. You're so obvious."

"What?" Moira asked, her voice rising. "Don't be ridiculous. I think he's very nice. And he's a very good teacher." Turning to meet Elise's teasing eyes, she couldn't help but laugh. "Okay, yes. I do find him attractive. So what?"

"I think he finds you attractive too. I've seen the way he watches you. When you're in the same room, there's an atmosphere."

"He does not."

"Don't pretend you don't know. I've seen you smile back at him."

"Why shouldn't I smile? I smile at everyone."

"Come on, Moira, it's me you're talking to. What are you thinking? Do you like him?"

Moira was silent for a moment, chewing her lip. She rose to a sitting position. "I kissed him," she blurted out.

Elise scrambled to sit up. "You kissed him? As in kiss, or you hooked up?"

"Kissed," Moira affirmed.

Elise scrunched up her face in distaste. "Karl . . ." She shook her head. "So, does this mean you're splitting with Thom?"

Moira shifted back against the pillows. "No. I kissed Karl—and it was a good kiss," she admitted, "but it made me realize that I love Thom. I'm not playing innocent. I let Karl kiss me—I wanted him to. But smack in the middle of the kiss, I realized I didn't want it to go any further. I still love Thom. He's my husband. But I've been the walking dead. That kiss brought me back to life. I might love Thom, but he has to accept that I'm making choices now. And first of all, I'm choosing me."

In a sudden shift of mood, Moira bolted off the bed and said with a burst of enthusiasm, "Let's not waste our time talking about Karl or kisses. There's something so much more important I want to share with you. Wait a minute."

Elise had no idea what Moira was on about, but it was fun to see her so excited about something again. She fluffed up the pillows then stretched out as she watched Moira dig papers out of her desk drawer and hurry back to the bed. She jumped on the mattress like a schoolgirl. They sat face-to-face, Moira resting back on her heels and clutching a sheaf of papers against her breast. Elise had never seen her eyes so bright. There was a radiance about her that pushed away the sounds of the storm outside the windows. Her joy was infectious, making Elise smile too.

"What?" Elise asked with a laugh.

"I've given this a great deal of thought," Moira began. "It's not a rash decision. But I've made up my mind." She smiled pensively. "I know what I'm going to do." She handed the papers to Elise.

Shifting her weight on the mattress, Elise held them closer to the light on the bedside table. She looked up, questioning. "This is an application to veterinary school."

Moira nodded. "Yes. I'm applying again. I talked to the admissions department. Because I'd applied before and was accepted, they don't feel I will have any difficulties getting accepted again."

Elise was shocked. "You were accepted?" When Moira nodded, she added indignantly, "And you didn't go?"

"Water under the bridge. I'm going now. That, my dear friend, is the salient point." She brought her hands together. "Oh, Elise, I feel like my old self! So full of purpose. I'm bursting with enthusiasm. I can't wait to go back to school. To study. Oh. My. God." She turned and fell back on her pillows with a plop. "I can't tell you how good it feels to know what I want. It's empowering. I want to dance in the streets, shout it out from the rooftops." She laughed and kicked her legs. "I'm back, baby!"

Elise laughed, happy to see her friend so full of life again, so full of purpose. But even as she smiled, deep inside she felt a pain that shamed her. Jealousy. *She* wanted to feel that sense of purpose, that excitement for tomorrow. For the last couple of days, she'd felt closer to Moira because they were both going through the same malaise. She hadn't felt so alone, so out of step, knowing that they were both lost. Now, once again, Moira was pulling ahead. She'd grabbed her brass ring and was going full-out to win. And again, Elise felt left behind.

"Elise?" Moira's smile slipped as she rose up on her elbow to look closer at Elise's face. "Are you crying?"

"No," Elise said with a huff, wiping her eyes. "I'm just happy for you."

Moira rose to grab Elise's shoulders and give them a gentle shake. "But you're upset. What's the matter?"

"Nothing's the matter. At least, nothing I can name. It's just . . ." Elise shrugged, embarrassed by her show of emotion. She felt like a spoiled child.

"Just what?"

"I just wish I knew what I wanted to do with my life."

Moira was quiet, considering. Then she said, "Go to the hill to visit the Queens."

"The trees?" Elise grew wistful. "I haven't thought about them in years."

"They're still there for you."

"I wouldn't know what to ask them."

"Ask them for their advice. I'll go with you."

Elise shook her head. "No, thanks," she said with condescension. She saw Moira cringe, and realized she'd been rude. "I'm sorry. It's just, I'm not like you," she said in a gentler tone. "I'm not into that kind of thing."

"That kind of thing?" Moira tightened her lips.

Elise could feel the chill settle around them. "You know what I mean," she said with a sigh.

"Suit yourself. But, Elise, if you don't mind my saying so—"

"Uh-oh, here it comes."

Moira ignored her attempt at humor. "I'm serious. If you don't want to listen to the trees, I get it. But listen to me—your friend. You've been trying to make your mother proud for as long as I've known you. Maybe it's time to find out what will make *you* proud. You told me you weren't sure you wanted to do dressage anymore. That's huge! Immense. You know what you *don't* want to do. So why are you still doing it?"

Elise felt her throat closing. She shrugged.

"Wait." Moira held out her hand in an arresting gesture. "Don't tell me. I already know the answer. Because your mother wants you to do it."

Elise didn't want to hear this anymore. "Okay. I get it. Let it drop, Moira," she said, a tone of warning in her voice.

But she wouldn't. This was the Moira Elise knew too well, trying to make her friend feel better. If only she knew that all Elise wanted right now was for her to stop talking so she could lie in her own misery! She gritted her teeth as Moira went on.

"You and I, we both try to please others," Moira said. "We always have. When I went to the trees today, they told me it was time to please myself."

"Yeah, well, self-pleasure is never a bad idea."

Moira didn't laugh. She seemed deflated. "Go ahead, make jokes. But don't tell me you're jealous because *I'm* making decisions and moving forward while you don't even try to change."

"It's not like I can just chuck my equestrian career."

"Why not?"

Elise threw up her hands in frustration. She was mad now, and when she got mad, she had no filter. "Why not? God, Moira, you should know why not. Or has it been so long since you've had anything real to give up that you've forgotten?"

Moira looked shocked. "How can you say that? You know I've been struggling."

"Sure. But think about it. What have you done since I last saw you?" She raised her eyebrows, daring her to answer.

Moira stared back at her, blinking rapidly.

"You got married and—oh yeah, you bought a house. A house you don't even like. And me? Poor loser me? I've been winning show after show around the world. And I'm shortlisted for the Olympics. I guess that's not important in your playbook. You can hold on to your failing marriage. But me? I should just toss up my hands on my ten years of day-in and day-out goddamn hard work and just chuck it."

"Okay!" Moira said, swinging her legs off the bed onto the floor. "I'm sorry. Forget I said anything. I was just trying to be supportive. I didn't mean to make it sound like you weren't successful. I know you are. I'm jealous of you."

"Don't," Elise said, putting her hands up to ward off Moira's words. They were both on high horses now and needed to climb down. "Shit. I'm sorry too. You hit a nerve. Please, just let it drop." Elise rose from the bed and grabbed her clothes. She began ramming her legs into her jeans, almost losing her balance.

"Don't go," Moira said. All the joy was gone from her voice. Now she sounded defeated.

"I need some air."

"You can't go out in this storm."

Elise grabbed her bag. "Watch me."

SIXTEEN

August 22, 10:30 p.m.
Freehold Farm, North Carolina
*South Carolina residents warned to move away from water
as a life-threatening surge of ten to fifteen feet is forecast*

Angel helped himself to a third beer. He sat on the burgundy-and-white checked sofa, his pillow in his lap, his legs stretched out. He started peeling the label as thoughts of Gerta crowded his mind. Her vulnerable blue eyes haunted him.

Max jumped up on the sofa beside him and stretched out on the cushions, his giant body crowding Angel to the corner.

"*Dios*, Max," he exclaimed, waving his hand. "What's that smell?" He stood up and took a few steps back. Back on his feet, he felt the need to stretch his legs. "Come on, boy. I need some fresh air. Want to go for a walk?"

Max lifted his head barely enough to look at Angel and thumped his tail.

Angel noticed how sedentary Max was becoming. There was

more gray salting the dog's wiry black hair—especially at the chin and along his belly. His heart lurched as he recalled the harsh reality that dogs aged seven years for every human year. And these big dogs didn't live as long.

"Max," Angel said gently, scratching him behind his cropped ears. "You're getting old and fat and lazy. Come on. Don't you want a walk?" He slapped his thighs to motivate him.

Max plopped his head back on the sofa as his answer.

Angel put his hands on his hips and sighed with resignation. He turned his head and looked out the window. The rain had stopped. All the houses around the lake were dark and seemingly empty. The lamplight cast eerie shadows on the living room walls. Angel tapped his fingers on the bottle and pursed his lips. He was antsy. He had to get out of this house.

There was only one place he wanted to be. He swallowed the dregs of his beer, then walked to the door, grabbed the car keys from the table, and went out into the night.

The lights of the cottage were still on. The blinds were down and he didn't see any shadows cross the windows. He put the car in first and slowly went up the driveway. The gravel driveway was slick with rain, mud, and fallen leaves. At the top of the hill he stopped and idled when he saw that the vintage Mercedes was gone. But the lights were on, so someone might be home. But who? Elise or Gerta?

He turned off the engine and sat a moment to get his head straight. If Elise opened the door, he could tell her he'd come to talk about selling Whirlwind. She'd been open to the possibility, and he had a few people he knew who would be interested in such an important horse and willing to pay the minimum two million dollars the horse was worth. Angel would get his percentage of the sale. A little off the top, enough to help him acquire a horse he could develop. Could he go through with the sale of Whirlwind now? he wondered.

He closed his eyes and shook his head. Why did life always have to be so damn complicated? He was at a turning point in his career. He should be, as Hannah had told him repeatedly, more sensible. A businessman. Or, as his father had told him, "You deal the cards and play your hand." If he thought in these terms, Whirlwind was his ace of spades.

Angel huffed out a wry laugh. Who was he kidding? He might be clever, even occasionally devious. But he was not hard-hearted. In this deal, Gerta was the trump card. If she played it, he was out.

Angel gazed again at the small cottage shining with yellow light in the darkness. After all that wind and rain, the air was calm. He chuckled to himself. No doubt the calm before the storm. He felt that his future lay in that house. Who would be inside?

He exited the car as a gust of wind shook the branches overhead. Droplets of water sprinkled down, cool and refreshing. He stuck his hands in his pockets and walked to the shelter of the small front porch. Standing between a planter filled with red geraniums and a pair of tall, black rubber boots, he raked his hair with his hands, the best he could do without a comb. Then he cleared his throat, straightened, and knocked three times, firmly, on the hunter-green door.

He waited a minute, but there was no answer. He could hear music in the house. Edith Piaf was singing "La Vie en Rose." Someone must be home, he thought. Determined, he rang the bell. Tapping his foot, he looked out at the shadows of trees in the woods and waited another two minutes. Then three. Could they both be gone? He knocked again, louder this time. Still no one. He felt awash with disappointment. He very much wanted to see Gerta tonight. With a sigh, he turned to leave when the door suddenly swung open.

Gerta stood in the doorframe, backlit by the house lights. In the darkness she seemed to glow in the simple white cotton nightgown. For the first time he caught a glimpse of her prosthesis beneath the hem—a metal foot. Her blond hair was pulled back from her freshly scrubbed face with a black headband. With her hair falling loose around her shoulders and the prim gown, she looked like a fair-haired schoolgirl.

Gerta's eyes were wide as she stared at him, her fingers at her lips, too stunned to speak.

Angel's face was grave as he stepped into the house. Gerta took two steps back. He closed the door behind him. They stood still, silent, each gauging what those few feet between them signified. Once he crossed the divide, he couldn't turn back.

He held her gaze, waiting.

Wordlessly, barely perceptibly, she nodded.

In two long strides Angel swept her into his arms. He looked down into her face. Their kiss earlier had been one of discovery—cut off abruptly by the arrival of Grace and Charles, and soon after that the vet. This time, he wanted to explore her more. He held her face in his hands so he might kiss her more deeply. Her pupils flickered, inviting him. As he lowered his lips to meet hers, he thought that this time, there was no hurry.

· · ·

Elise just wanted to go to bed. She felt weary and depressed. She climbed into her mother's Mercedes and fired up the engine. As always, it purred into action. She hated fighting with Moira. It left her with a weight in her chest that made it hard to breathe. One she knew was tied to guilt. Moira had been so happy, and Elise? She'd been a downer.

She was happy for Moira, even proud of her for fighting so hard for this self-discovery. Did she have to suffer longer and drag out her misery? Of course not. It was as if the hurricane had put them all in a pressure cooker up here and sped up the process. Why was Elise such a brat just because she felt sorry for herself? Her fingers squeezed the leather-covered steering wheel.

She shouldn't have gotten so mad. But sometimes Moira didn't know when to shut up. Why did she always have to have the last word? The last thing Elise needed from her best friend—who was feeling pretty good about herself—was a lecture about what a loser she was.

She shifted gears and headed down the driveway toward the road. The night was thick with fog and as black as tar, but at least the rain had stopped. The headlights carved out a yellow beacon, enough to see twenty feet ahead at most. Branches littered the driveway, ripped from trees during the windstorm; Elise wove around a few of the bigger ones. It was a good thing she was driving slowly, because when she made the final curve by the pasture, eight or nine white-tailed deer startled her as they crossed the road. After she caught her breath, she enjoyed the final sight of the white tails of the does flagging high in the air as they gracefully leaped away.

It was a short trip to the cottage. Elise yawned as she pulled up the gravel driveway, hearing the crunching beneath her tires. Then she rubbed her eyes, squinted, and did a double take at spotting the Audi parked in the driveway. What was Hannah doing here so late? she wondered. Then another person sprang to mind.

She turned off the engine and sat in darkness chewing her nails. Yellow light shone from the house, carving out the black night. Would Angel tell her mother that she was thinking of selling Whirlwind? A chill ran through her. No, she couldn't believe he'd do that. After all, it was *he* who'd come to her with the idea. He'd asked her to be quiet about it, to keep it between them until he learned more.

Only one way to find out, she thought, resigned, and climbed from the car. The damp gravel was littered with fallen leaves. She walked around potholes filled with water and stepped up onto the porch. She'd started kicking off her boots when she heard the soft murmur of a man's voice. She put her ear to the door.

Definitely Angel's voice.

Elise pushed open the door and stepped into the front room, blinking in the light. At first glance, the room appeared empty. But then she froze. There was Angel de la Cruz all right, sitting on the sofa with her mother. But he wasn't talking to her. He was kissing her. Elise grimaced. More like making out.

Her first sensation was embarrassment at catching them like this. Thank God they were just kissing. Her second was a sweep of nausea. This was her mother. She couldn't remember ever seeing her mother kissing anyone. Not even her father. *What the hell?* she thought, dazed. Her mother and Angel? She couldn't put them together. She stood for a moment, staring with her lips parted. When had this happened? Her third reaction was an old fallback for her:

anger. Well, maybe not anger so much as a sense of betrayal. Her mother was sneaking around, and Angel . . . Was he cheating on Hannah? She'd thought Angel was her ally. Now she saw that he was just using her.

Her mother must have sensed her presence because she suddenly looked up. Their eyes met, and Gerta's widened with surprise. She awkwardly pulled away from Angel, who had very good instincts himself. He looked over his shoulder. He froze for a fraction of a second before he straightened up and backhanded his mouth. They scrambled to collect themselves.

"Elise," her mother said, bringing her hands up to adjust the headband that was sliding from her hair. "How long were you standing there?"

It pleased Elise in an odd way to see her mother so flustered. It was the first time she'd ever had any sense of power over her mother. "Long enough."

Angel frowned with worry and darted a glance at Gerta. He seemed more concerned about her than about himself. But she didn't care about Angel. It was her mother who drew her focus. And she wanted to exercise the power she was feeling.

"Ask lover boy about the deal he and I are working on about Whirlwind."

Elise had the satisfaction of seeing Angel's face constrict and Gerta swiftly turn her head to face him before she closed the door.

Elise stumbled back to the car, feeling the aftershocks. She wasn't aware that she carried big chunks of mud clinging to her boots into her mother's pristine Mercedes. Her hands shook as she put the key into the ignition and roared the engine. When she got back on the road, she pulled to the side and laid her head on her hands against the steering wheel. She felt her chest constrict and her heart was racing.

She sat back in the leather seat and closed her eyes, taking deep breaths. Then she barked out a laugh imagining the conversation that Angel and her mother were having right now. If she looked back, she'd probably see fireworks going off from the cottage.

Elise brought to mind the conversation *she'd* had with Angel about Whirlwind. He'd asked her if she did, indeed, own the horse. When she confirmed that she did, he'd asked if she would ever consider selling him. He said he knew someone who might be interested. They had discussed how much she could get. He'd take a bit off the top, of course, as a finder's fee, but the sum she'd pocket was considerable. Elise had told him she needed to think about it. They'd agreed to keep the conversation private—with them all being together in this fishbowl, as Angel put it, it wouldn't be good to get people upset. At first, she'd told him she didn't think she was interested. But since that time, she'd begun to consider the possibilities.

Whirlwind was her only asset. Everything else was in her mother's name. Her mother gave her an allowance, like some child. She was so damn controlling. It was demoralizing to be nearing thirty years old and realize she didn't even own her own car.

She opened her eyes and stared out at the black night. In her heart, she knew money wasn't at the core of why she was so upset about her mother and Angel. Why she was having some kind of anxiety attack. She brought her fingers to the bridge of her nose. Yes, that was it, she told herself, taking deep calming breaths. Anxiety.

What was going on with her mother?

She was making changes, claiming what she wanted—adopting the horse Razzmajazz, taking on a lover, Angel. There would be more changes in the future, Elise felt sure. Wasn't this good? Wasn't this what she wanted for her? Yet all these changes left Elise feeling anxious that her mother's discovering her separateness, her *I* in their relationship, would distort their carefully crafted *we*.

Elise looked out at the road ahead. Where was she going to go now?

An hour later, Elise found herself standing in the barn at Karl Reiter's door. It was the last place in the world she'd expected to end up. When the door opened, the expression on Karl's face told her he was thinking the same thing. He was wearing hunter-green and blue boxers with horses on them, a ratty T-shirt, and a look of confusion. She held back a laugh at the sight of his hairy legs. She'd never seen his legs.

"What are you doing here?"

Elise deadpanned, "I don't know what I'm doing here. But I need a drink."

He stepped aside, and she walked into the loft apartment. Her head moved from left to right, taking the apartment in. She hadn't expected it to be so grand. Then again, Grace didn't do anything halfway. Elise whistled softly when she saw the two-story windows. Looking around at the chic, rustic décor, she thought it had been done up by Restoration Hardware.

"This is a nice place," she said appreciatively.

"Much better than I'm used to," he chided—a dig at her mother. "I'd Airbnb it."

"I don't think they want the trouble or need the money." He gestured with one hand—the one holding a glass a third full of amber liquid over ice. "How about that drink?"

"What's that?" she asked, pointing.

"Bourbon. The guy at the liquor store gave me a quick tutorial. It's supposed to be the man's drink up here in the mountains. Ever try it?"

She shrugged. "It's like scotch, right?"

He laughed. "Except that scotch is made in Scotland and bourbon is made in the United States. And scotch is made from malted barley. And bourbon is made from corn. Want to try some?"

"Sure. I'm game."

They walked over to the small bar, where Karl began to make her drink.

"Water, over ice, or neat?"

"Over ice."

A moment later he handed her the glass.

"Where do the stairs lead?" She indicated a narrow flight of steps against the back wall leading to the second floor.

"That's the loft. It's pretty big. There's a king bed, a TV and sofa, and a nice desk. Best of all, it has windows that overlook the barn. I can stand there and look down and see the horses." He smiled, clearly infatuated with that. "Amazing. I spend most of my time up there. Want to see it?"

Elise didn't want to go into his bedroom. She shook her head with a smirk. "No, thanks. It's nice down here." She looked at her drink. She wasn't much of a scotch whiskey fan, so she wasn't hopeful. She took a taste and wrinkled her nose. Handing back the glass, she asked, "Do you have a beer?"

He chuckled as he poured the contents of her glass into his. "I'm German. Does a bear shit in the woods?" He went to the fridge, pulled out a Kölsch pale ale, and handed it to her.

"So, are you going to tell me why you're here, or are you going to make me guess?" He at last smiled at her, and it was like a dare.

Elise shook her head. "It's a long story." She covered her dodge with a sip of her ale.

"So you want me to guess," he declared with sarcasm. He crossed his arms and studied her. "You had a fight with your mother."

She frowned and pursed her lips. "Well, no . . . but, yeah, kinda."

"So what else is new?"

"Well . . . I had a fight with Moira."

"Really? This does surprise me. You two are best friends. And I think it would be hard to have a fight with Moira."

"Oh. But not with me?" She shook her head. "Don't answer that." Elise took another swig of her beer and walked over to the brown leather sofa, plopping into the cushions. It was then that she noticed the mud streaking her boots. "Oh no, I didn't take off my boots. I'm so sorry," she said, her voice muffled by being bent over to remove her boots.

"Nothing I can't sweep up. We're in a barn. I'm sure this place has seen mud before."

"Yeah, but there aren't oriental rugs in the other part of the barn." She set the boots together at the base of the couch, pulled her braid from her back, and watched him settle into the red upholstered chair across from her. He was a good-looking man, tall and lean. It occurred to her that this was the first time in all the years she'd studied under him that she'd ever seen him in a casual setting.

"So you had a fight with your mother *and* with Moira."

"Let's not leave out Angel."

"Him too?" Karl muffled his laugh by bringing his glass to his lips. Then he asked, "Did you come here to fight with me? Perhaps you want a grand slam?"

She laughed. "Nah. I fight with you every day. Why would I come for that?"

They both laughed and took a drink. He smiled at her over the rim of his glass.

"What happened? Can I ask?"

Elise sobered quickly and looked at the bottle in her hand. "Karl," she began in a dramatically philosophical tone, "I think I'm at the proverbial fork in the road."

"Yeah? Where do the roads lead? And do you know which one you want to take?"

She chewed her lip, then nodded. "Yeah, actually . . . I think I do. One road leads to the Olympics." She held out her hand to indicate that he'd be traveling that road with her. He nodded in agreement. "The other"—she flipped her hand palm-up and spoke succinctly—"the other is the road not taken. And I suspect taking it will make all the difference."

Karl swirled the ice in his glass. His eyes sharpened with interest. He knew that they'd crossed the line from joking to a serious conversation.

"You'll have to explain."

Elise set down her bottle and brought her legs up to the sofa to sit cross-legged. She began unconsciously to stroke the long braid that lay over one shoulder. Karl noticed, however, and smiled at the familiar gesture she made whenever she felt anxious.

"Well," she began, "after my fight with Moira, I left the main house to go back to the cottage. I just wanted to go to bed." She hesitated. Should she tell him about her mother and Angel, she wondered—or was that too private? Her mother was Karl's employer, after all. Loyalty won out. "I got into an argument with my mother." She shrugged as though to say, *as usual.* "So I went out for a long drive."

"You went out for a drive in this weather?" he asked with disbelief.

"It stopped raining," she said in her defense, then laughed self-consciously. "I got lost," she admitted. "Do you know how often the GPS goes out of service up here? And it's so fucking dark. I thought I'd never find my way back. But somehow I did. Once I reached the gate, however, I realized I had nowhere to go."

Karl's face grew soft. "So you ended up knocking on my door."

She shrugged. "A lost sheep," she said with a wry grin. "Can I stay here tonight?"

"You are my student. You can crash anytime you want. My door is always open."

She tilted her head and said, "You know I'm gay, right?"

"*Ja*, of course. So what?"

She smiled, liking him a lot more. "You know, it seems to me that part of the problem between us has been that we haven't been having these kinds of conversations. Heart to heart. You're my trainer. We spend more time with each other than with almost any other people. What took us so long?"

"We were in competition, I think."

"Over Whirlwind's heart."

He nodded. "*Ja*. And your mother's."

"Ja," she replied, drawing out the vowel and nodding with emphasis, mimicking his accent.

"I think this is why you fight with her so much. You are a little bit afraid of her. She tells you what to do, and you do it. But you have this look on your face when she gives you an order." He made a face, tightening his lips while his eyes bulged.

"Stop." She laughed. "I do not."

"You do! She gives you your marching orders and you are the good soldier. March, march, march. I think one day I'm going to see you do the goose step."

Elise slapped her hand to her forehead. "It's that bad?"

"Do I have to tell you?"

The joke was on her, she realized, and she shook her head.

"I think, Elise, it's time for you to march to your own drum."

Her face fell and she reached out to pick up her bottle. She felt her heart begin to race again. At the heart of the problem was the fact that she needed to work harder at the task of clarifying her own separateness and independence from her mother. If she did so, she might be less angry and less fearful about voicing her own wants and needs. To be less afraid to stand separate and alone on her own two feet.

She lifted her bottle in a mock toast. "And *that* pretty much was exactly what Moira and I fought about." She lowered her arm. "I didn't realize it was so obvious."

"Only to those of us who care." His eyes shone with a new tenderness. "To the world, you are Elise Klug, the fabulous young dressage rider on a meteoric rise."

"Like my mother."

"Yes. And no."

"You know she had her accident at about my age?" When Karl nodded, she went on, "She got pregnant with me soon after she was married. After I was born, she began competing again. My father gave her Razzmajazz to train. I don't think he knew how good a horse he was. But it soon became obvious to everyone that those two had that intangible something special together that made them pure magic. She too had a meteoric rise, winning show after show. She catapulted toward the Olympics. It was only a few months before the Olympics during a trial when Razzmajazz took that jump and had his heart attack. He died right there on the spot."

"And crushed her leg," Karl finished for her. "This is a story every equestrian in Germany knows. The German team dedicated their gold medal to her."

Elise paused and said, "What they didn't know, what no one fully understood, was how much riding in the Olympics meant to her. Not just the win, but the performance. The ultimate test. It was one thing for her to lose her leg. It was another thing altogether to lose that experience. So she turned to me. Her little mini-me," she said with a wobbly smile. "I've been groomed for this from the moment I first got on a horse."

"That's not so unusual. Many mothers are stage moms."

She cast him a loaded glance. "There's a stage mom, and then there's Mommie Dearest." He looked at her questioningly, and she realized that as a European he hadn't caught the reference. "No matter how hard I try or how many ribbons I win, I'm never going to be good enough for her. I could win a gold medal at the Olympics and it still wouldn't be enough for her. Because in the end, it still wasn't Gerta Klug who won the medal. That was *her* dream. And only she can fulfill it. I can't do that for her. I'd have to do it for me."

"And you can. You're good. Very good. You'll make the team."

"I believe you're right. I could." She looked him in the eye. "But not on Whirlwind."

Karl went still, then gave one curt nod of his head. "No. Not on Whirlwind." He shifted forward on his seat, resting his elbows on his knees. "I wish Whirlwind responded to you more, Elise. I truly do. You must believe I am not trying to interfere."

"I know that—now," she admitted. "I wish I could connect with Whirlwind, but I've come to accept it's not going to happen."

Karl gave her reply some thought. "Your mother has many excellent horses. I think Wagner's Dream could be a good match for you. She has enormous potential. We could work with her."

Elise shook her head. "My mother would never agree to that. She bought Whirlwind to take to the Olympics."

Karl's eyes flickered with frustration at Gerta Klug's iron will. But he persevered. "Then we'll have to work harder. Whirlwind is such a terrific horse. He has great heart and the will to win. He's young yet. Give him time. Maybe the next Olympics."

Elise could hear in his voice how much he loved Whirlwind. He'd do anything for the success of that horse.

"I don't think you understand. I'm not going to ride Whirlwind *at all*. Not to practice. Not to the FEI. Not to the Olympics. Not anywhere. I don't want to compete anymore. I'm giving it up." She smiled. "I'm taking the road not taken."

Karl looked stunned. "This can't be true. Elise, listen. Don't make a rash decision because you're angry at your mother."

"I am angry at my mother. But Whirlwind declared his decision when he tossed me in the dirt. I heard him loud and clear. And now I'm declaring mine."

"It's not that easy to give up a lifetime of training. What will you do?"

"I'm not sure. I just need to get off this train. Take some time to do a lot of things I put on hold. I'm hoping it will help me figure out what I really want to do. Karl, I want to find my own dreams. And who knows? The road may lead back home and I'll come back to riding."

"If I can help you. Anything . . ."

"You can help me by helping Whirlwind. I know he's a great horse. And I know he's best with you."

"Thank you, Elise. From you, that means a great deal."

A look was shared. A white flag raised and graciously accepted.

"Have you told your mother?" His eyes gleamed with curiosity. This was, they both knew, the million-dollar question.

"Not yet. But I think she's catching wind of it," Elise said with a satisfied smile, thinking of the conversation Gerta and Angel must be having. She laughed out loud and took a long swig of her beer. "I think I'm going to bob and weave until I'm ready for the knockout punch. I'll tell her I'm gay, too."

Karl hooted, and they both laughed long and hard. Elise's braid fell forward across her chest. She looked at it and suddenly hopped to her feet. She felt energized.

"Do you have a pair of scissors?"

Karl rose more slowly and stretched his back. "I'm sure there's a pair here somewhere. Grace has thought of everything. Check the bathroom-slash–laundry room." He gestured toward the room in the back.

"Well, come on," she hollered over her shoulder. "I need your help."

"My help?" His voice rose. "For what?"

Elise stuck her head out the door and snapped the scissors open and shut with one hand. With the other, she held up her braid. "I've wanted to do this for a long time."

"Mein Gott." Karl set down his drink and rubbed his jaw before following her into the back room.

SEVENTEEN

August 23, 3:00 a.m.
Isle of Palms, South Carolina
*Noelle hits Isle of Palms
as a Category One hurricane*

It was a fitful night of howling wind, screaming louder and louder as the hours progressed. Cara lay curled up beside David on her queen-size bed in what was once her mother's bedroom and was now hers. Her head rested on his shoulder, his arm around her.

They'd arrived back at the beach house only to find they had to reopen the door's shutters in the punishing rain. David had opened only a few slats of the shutters, big enough for them to slide through before shutting the door against the raging storm.

Once inside, they discovered the electricity was out. Cara had her flashlight in her pocket and they spent the next few hours setting up lanterns, filling the tubs with water, and laying out matches, candles, and other emergency supplies. After that, all they could do was wait.

As the storm approached, the little beach house swayed and with every surge of wind that roared past she heard huge trees snapping and glass breaking and the thump of something being carried in the air and unceremoniously dropped. The windows were boarded so they couldn't look outdoors at the storm. But in her mind's eye she saw the palm trees bending half over in the wind and rain.

Throughout the night the wind screamed at the windows. They lay together in bed, exhausted from the physical work of putting up shutters and walking miles in the fretful search for Flo in the storm, and the mental strain of fear and worry. Somehow they'd managed to fall asleep, growing accustomed to the incessant gusts and retreats of the wind, in and out, like the heartbeat of a beast.

It was the silence that woke her. Cara opened her eyes to utter blackness. Not a single beam of light permeated the dark of the sealed house. She took a shaky breath and moved David's arm from her chest. The humidity was like a wet blanket. In the eerie silence, the phrase *silent as the tomb* sprang to mind and rattled her. She rose up on her elbow.

"David," she said.

He was lying on his back, snoring softly.

Cara gently shook him. "David."

He awoke with a start, instantly alert. "What's wrong?"

She put her hand on his chest. "Listen. It's quiet."

It took a moment for him to catch her meaning. She could barely make out his visage in the blackness, but she saw a movement and imagined him wiping his face, waking further.

"Is it past?"

"I don't think so."

"It must be the eye of the hurricane."

"Oh my God," she said, breathless.

"Come on. Grab your flashlight."

Cara froze. For a moment she was thrown back to the last time she'd been trapped in this house during a hurricane. The time with her mother. That night when they'd awakened, they'd stepped out of the bed into murky ocean water. The fear of wind had quickly grown more insidious as the terror of the tidal surge's water rose.

A second later she saw a beam of yellow light and David's form visible.

"Is it dry?" she croaked out.

"As a bone."

She started breathing again. They had both slept in their clothes. She grabbed her flashlight from the bedside stand and said a prayer of thanks when her feet hit the dry floor. She set the beam on her watch.

"It's a little after three." She slipped on her shoes and followed him to the front door.

The house was quiet and seemed intact. No wind howled outside. At the front door, the small opening space from the removed shutters was still there. David had never gone back out in the storm to the car for the battery-operated screwdriver to put them back up. For all the hammers and Phillips-heads they'd found in the house, there wasn't a single screwdriver. Cara was frustrated but David had kept his cool and only said, "I know what I'm getting you for Christmas." The front door had held strong during the storm, though a puddle of water had formed at the base.

They pushed open the front door and slipped out through the narrow opening.

The night inside the eye of the hurricane was eerily beautiful. Hauntingly strange. They walked hand in hand no farther than the front of the house, not knowing how much time they had in the eye before it passed and the wind picked up again. Cara's eyes scanned the beach house, looking for damage. With relief, her little house seemed relatively unscathed. Branches of trees lay scattered on the road and in the yards, a neighbor's laurel oak tree had split and half lay sprawled across their garage, and garbage cans and debris scattered the earth. She didn't see any roofs blown off, no boats in front yards, none of the horror stories she'd heard from folks who'd survived Hurricane Hugo.

"The hurricane must have lost power over land," David said. "This isn't too bad."

"Thank God," Cara said, but even as she spoke, she wondered which town bore the brunt of the hurricane's landfall.

They stood and looked around them at a dreamlike world. It was as if time had stood still. The air was deliciously warm and humid—tropical. Looking up at the sky, the clouds formed a ragged circle around them, as though they were standing in the middle of a stadium.

Cara squeezed David's hand. "David, I can see the stars!"

It was true. Inside the eye, surrounded by raging winds, was a tranquil sky, crisp and shining with stars. They both felt swept up in the power of the moment.

David faced Cara and brought her hands to his lips and kissed them, holding them tight. "Cara, we are in the eye of the hurricane. This is a moment we'll likely never see again."

"I know," she said, looking into his eyes.

"We've both been through storms in our lives. We've endured

the loss of our spouses and all the pain associated with that. And then, we found each other." They both smiled. "Life became good again. Placid, peaceful, like here and now. The bad part was we had to go through half of the storm to reach this eye. And"—he smiled again—"we will have to go through the other half once the eye passes."

She laughed lightly, but remained quiet. Something was happening. She looked into his eyes and saw a storm brewing there, a squall of emotions. She took a small breath, pensive.

"I know I can weather any storm with you by my side. As long as we are together, we will always be in the eye of the hurricane. You and me. In our hearts. In our love. In our commitment."

David lowered to one knee, sinking deep into the soggy earth, not giving it any notice. Cara's breath hitched and she felt her heart race, not with fear, but joy.

"Cara, will you marry me? Be my wife."

Cara felt her life flash before her. The only other proposal she'd had was Brett's and she'd said no. Though in time she'd finally acquiesced and they'd married, she'd blown the moment. This time, she wanted to get it right. There would be no questions or hesitations. There was only one answer she would give.

"Yes!"

David rose to sweep her in his arms. As the gunmetal clouds rotated around them in thunderous majesty, they sealed their commitment with a fervent kiss.

Then the winds shifted and thunder rumbled. Their moment was over.

Laughing, he took her hand and they ran back to the beach house, slipping through the aperture and sealing the door against the oncoming storm. As the winds began to pick up and howl once again, Cara no longer felt fear. She was in her beach house. With David. Confident of her future for the first time in many years.

Cara swore she would never be afraid of a hurricane again.

August 23, 6:30 a.m.
Freehold Farm, North Carolina

Charles arrived at the barn a little earlier than usual. The hurricane had left the coast and been downgraded to Tropical Storm Noelle. It was now traveling a slow path inexorably north toward North Carolina. It was due to hit them sometime around midnight.

Charles felt a strong pride of ownership in Freehold Farm. It was more than just a place to him. It was his home, where he'd raised his daughter, and where he hoped his grandchildren would visit. If a human could set down roots, this was where he'd dug in. He felt the singular presence of positive energy in these hills. Indians had walked this property. They'd lived, fought, and buried their queens here. When his time came, he wished to have his ashes laid to rest up on the plateau overlooking the valley. Grace would rest beside him. Together in life, together in the afterlife. And when beloved horses and dogs passed, he'd bury their remains up there as well.

Nothing escaped his gaze as he walked down to the barn. It was the first clear morning in days—not sunny, but not nasty either. The cooler air and breeze, not to mention the cloud cover, would make it a good day to exercise the horses. He picked up branches and sticks that had been blown down the night before. Checked to see that rainwater was flowing down the culvert. The weatherman had said some of the rain and wind from the bands might've been worse than what they should expect tonight. He thought that was likely wishful thinking, but hope sprang eternal.

As he rounded the back of the barn and approached the entrance, he stopped in his tracks, seeing odd movement inside the barn. He stepped out of the direct sightline into the central hall—not hiding, he told himself, that wouldn't be seemly, but curious. He waited and watched as the door to Karl's loft opened slowly, stealthily. "Huh," he uttered, both amazed and amused when out stepped Elise.

Charles did a double take. Or was it Elise? He craned his neck and squinted to see in the dim light of the barn. The woman looked like her, same height and build. But this woman had very short, spiky blond hair. Not the skein of a braid Elise usually wore. A doppelgänger. The thought popped into his mind and he tossed it aside, amused. She leaned against the loft door to slip on her boots, then picked up her bag and scurried out the opposite end of the barn as silent as a mouse. He heard the sound of a car engine igniting. He walked quickly to the opposite entrance of the barn and peered out in time to see Gerta's vintage Mercedes winding down the road.

Well, well, well, he thought. Not a doppelgänger at all. But what on earth had Elise done to her beautiful hair? He chuckled at the vagaries of youth and headed back to the barn. He couldn't wait to tell Grace about this.

The horses recognized him and immediately began a chorus of insistent whinnies and muffled snorts. "Good morning, my lovelies," he called out as he began the morning chores. The warmth of the horses' greeting, their excitement at seeing him, was his morning shot of adrenaline. These glorious animals never failed to lift his spirits, even when a storm was bearing down on them.

He'd just started organizing the feed when Jose arrived in his silver sports car. They greeted each other warmly and set about the usual division of chores. There was always so much to get done in the mornings—delivering fresh water, feed, and hay, riding and exercising the horses, putting them out to pasture, mucking out the stalls. Then cooling down the animals, grooming them, and, at the end of the day, putting them all back into their stalls for the night. He loved it. Caring for horses was both his vocation and his avocation.

When Karl came out of the loft yawning and scratching his belly, obviously still sleepy, Charles called out a good morning, his eyes twinkling. Karl never spoke much. He waved and grabbed a bale of hay with enviable ease. Most people were unaware of the strength most riders possessed. He carried it over to where Charles waited to spread the hay into a wheelbarrow.

Charles cut the cords binding the hay together, then opened the bale. Karl returned with a second bale of hay.

"Did you sleep well?" he asked Karl with nonchalance.

Karl dropped the bale, then shrugged. "*Ja*, okay. It's a nice bed. Firm mattress."

Charles swallowed his smile. "Yes. I always like a firm mattress." He shook out some hay. "It sure was a stormy night. Did you sleep through it?"

Karl mopped his weary face. "I had a few . . ." His smile was quickly hidden by his hand. ". . . distractions."

I'll bet, thought Charles as he lifted the handles of the wheelbarrow. He released his grin across his face as he pushed the wheel-barrow down the hall to deliver the hay to the waiting horses.

Grace came to the barn later in the morning. She hadn't slept well the night before and couldn't get enough caffeine into her system. She wanted to be alert this morning to watch the Grand Prix–level riding that would happen right here in the horse rings of Freehold Farm. Angel de la Cruz would be riding Rogue's Fancy, but no one was sure of how well she was after her bout of colic.

The big question was what would happen with Whirlwind. Was the stallion well enough to ride? And would Elise ride him again? It seemed everything was up in the air on this hurricane morning. She could feel the change in the atmosphere.

When Grace stepped into the barn in her black jeans, boots, and a crisp white shirt, she spotted Charles in Superman's stall, brushing him down. He stuck his head out on hearing her and waved. Their eyes met, and in that quick gaze she felt the soul-stirring support that could only come from a long marriage and the countless moments shared.

Last night had been one of those moments. Moira had come knocking on their bedroom door. She'd perched on the edge of their bed as she often had as a teenager when she had a matter of the heart to discuss. Grace could see that she'd been crying, and she immediately was on high alert. She'd closed her book and set it aside, removed her reading glasses, and folded her hands. Charles had done the same.

Moira had told them that she'd left Thom. The news would

have been more startling except that she'd gone on to tell them how she still loved him and that—maybe—they could work things out. If he supported her decision. Charles had cast his wife a surreptitious glance, brows raised. Grace had lifted her shoulders in a shrug. Then, taking a breath, Moira told them that she was applying to veterinary school. For all the possible things that Moira might have told them with such a serious face, the announcement of school came as an enormous relief. They were, in fact, delighted.

Grace entered the office of the barn with thoughts of her daughter filling her head. Moira's life was in a state of flux. Too many pieces whirling in the air. Grace wanted to help her organize them, nail them down. But Charles had made her promise to let Moira deal with the changes on her own. It was a promise she'd find hard to keep.

She went directly to the automatic coffee machine and, after cleaning up discarded trash and filling the machine's tank with spring water, punched the button and made herself a cup of coffee. She took a quick sip and frowned. It was a mediocre brew at best, compared to the freshly ground and brewed coffee she served from her fancy Italian espresso machine up at the house. But it was caffeine.

She heard a noise, turned, and saw Gerta walking into the office. Grace had to stop and take her appearance in. She looked crisp and stunning. Her hair was pulled back in a sleepy ponytail and her face was natural save for a bit of lip gloss. She wore a black polo shirt and specially designed, slim, cream-colored pants that fit neatly over the stump of her leg, allowing the world to see her prosthesis. She couldn't remember a time she'd seen Gerta's false leg uncovered.

"Gerta! Good morning. Want some coffee?"

"What's so good about it? Everything is a damned disaster. Let the hurricane come. Let it take everything. I don't care."

"For heaven's sake. Whatever is the matter? I've never heard you talk like this." She turned to the coffee machine to pop in a fresh cup.

"I've never felt like this. You might as well know. I kissed Angel de la Cruz."

Grace stilled. This took a moment for her to process. She turned to face Gerta. She was standing shoulders back, chin up, waiting for Grace's response.

Grace didn't disappoint. "You kissed him?" she exclaimed loudly, disbelievingly. "When?"

"Yesterday, in the barn." She crossed her arms and said a bit defensively, "It just happened. It had been such an emotional day. Jazzy . . ." she said in way of explanation. "I was at the end of my rope, frantic about Butterhead and her colic, there was that godawful rain . . ." she added with a wave of her hand.

"And?"

A smile twitched her lips. "And it was wonderful."

Grace couldn't help the smile of delight that lit up her face. Then her face clouded. "But Hannah . . ."

"Yes. Hannah." Gerta released a sigh. "They broke up. No," she quickly inserted, seeing Grace's face, "it wasn't because of the kiss. They were on the verge of breaking up anyway. Otherwise I don't believe the kiss would have happened."

"Okay," Grace said, deciding to believe this—though she made a mental note to go check on Hannah. "But I don't understand. Where's the fiasco, then?"

Gerta went to the coffee machine and pushed the button. The

machine clunked and began to brew. She rested her fingertips with their unpainted nails on the counter then lifted her eyes to face Grace. "Angel came to the cottage last night. We kissed again."

"Oh."

"It's not what you think. We were kissing when Elise walked in on us. She saw us."

"Oh," Grace repeated, only this time she let the word slide in understanding.

"She didn't yell or fuss."

"Why would she? She's not your mother. It's not like you're married."

Gerta returned a small smile of appreciation for Grace's defense. "Elise wasn't angry. She looked more . . . hurt. I could have handled her anger." She laughed curtly. "That emotion is my old companion. But this was different. She seemed hurt. Lost. I'm worried about her." She went to retrieve her coffee and leaned against the counter, taking a sip.

"Ach," she said with her nose wrinkled. "This tastes like black water."

Grace could count on one hand the number of times she'd seen Gerta Klug appear shaken and vulnerable. Once was after her accident, of course. Grace had flown to Switzerland and stayed with her for weeks after she lost her leg. The second was when her poor excuse for a husband divorced her. Gerta had told her then, in her inimitable style, that divorce was like a war. People had to choose sides. She'd discovered who her true friends were, and they were precious.

And this time was the third. Grace drew closer, understanding that her friend was facing another turning point.

"How can I help?"

Gerta cradled her coffee cup and blew on it. But she didn't sip. She lowered the mug and lifted her face to Grace. Her eyes were troubled, and again Grace saw the unusual self-doubt in her expression.

"How can I be a better mother?" she asked. "I'm such a failure. I look at you with Moira, the closeness you share. The honesty. I want that with Elise."

Grace was taken aback. What a question! She'd never thought about it before. Mothering came easily to her, like breathing. "I have to think about that," she said with a quick smile. "First, thank you. Let me think . . . I guess I have to say I treat my daughter like I treat my friends. I hold her close, try to think of what she might need and how I can get it for her. Not big things—not always. But little things like a bouquet of flowers when she's feeling blue. A quick hug. An ear when she needs a good chin-wag. Yes, I think that's the most important thing: communication. We tell each other things."

Gerta listened intently. "Well," she said as in summary, "I can see why we are in trouble. We never talk."

Grace pinched her lips. Dare she say what was on her mind? She didn't like to judge or give unasked-for advice. But, she thought with a mental shrug, hadn't Gerta just asked for her advice?

"Gerta, please know I'm not criticizing you."

Gerta's eyes flashed with alarm.

"Maybe you could . . . ease up on Elise." She paused. "You hover."

"I don't." Gerta looked away.

Grace's laugh rang with skepticism. "Honey, you control her

life! She's bound to you so tightly I don't see how she can breathe. Ease up on her—let her make her own choices. Do you even know what she's so angry about? Because she is, all the time. She tries to mask it, but underneath there's a simmering fury that one of these days is going to erupt."

Gerta turned to look at her. Grace knew she was listening.

"How do I begin?"

"Just tell her you'd like to talk to her. Or rather, *with* her. See where that takes you. And, Gerta—let her fail. Let her fall flat on her face. Then be there for her when she gets back up. She'll thank you for that."

Gerta took in a shaky breath. "And I thank you. For being honest. I like that. I can't stand people mincing about. Just tell me the truth."

"That's the German in you, I think."

"No," Gerta said with a smirk, "don't stereotype. It doesn't suit you."

"Speaking of stereotypes, is Angel a Latin lover?"

"Oh, *mein Gott im Himmel*. I can't believe you said that. Shame on you."

"Yeah, yeah," Grace said, laughing. "So tell me."

Gerta's smile fell. "It is not going to work out."

"Why not?" Grace challenged her.

"It's complicated," Gerta said sulkily. "It appears that Elise has been talking with Angel about selling Whirlwind."

"But she can't," Grace said, utterly shocked. "You own him."

Gerta shook her head. "No. Elise does. Do you remember I gave him to her for her birthday? The papers are signed."

Grace had forgotten. This changed everything. But it still didn't make sense. "Why would Angel get involved? What's at stake for him?" And then, feeling indignant for her friend, "Why would he do that to you? Seems rather underhanded."

Gerta sighed with resignation. "He tried to explain to me."

"Please explain it to *me*."

"He went on about how Elise confessed she didn't bond with Whirlwind. He agreed. He said it was obvious to him they weren't a good match. That she would never be the right rider for Whirlwind. And other things . . ." She waved her hand dismissively. "Just excuses. I cannot be with a man who lies to me."

Grace realized that Angel had the strength to voice to Gerta what everyone else was thinking. "Was it a lie? This is something you and Elise have to talk about. It's that communication thing."

Gerta's eyes sparked. "Do you think it is acceptable for Elise to sell Whirlwind?" She brought her frustration under control and spoke in an even tone. "Even if it is her horse, that horse represents a substantial investment by the Klug stable."

Grace knew that tone and wasn't having any. "First of all, this isn't a boardroom—so you can drop the attitude. Second, you're talking about your *daughter*. Not some investment. Money isn't the issue here—or it shouldn't be. You might be asking yourself *why* Elise, knowing that, still would want to sell Whirlwind."

Gerta stared at Grace with dismay. She put a trembling hand to her head. "I feel like my world is spinning around me. Everything is happening so quickly. What I thought was grounded is suddenly up in the air."

"It's this hurricane," Grace replied. "You're displaced, worried. Even your past is pushing into your present with Razzmajazz. It's no wonder our emotions are heightened. Darling, it's not just happening to you. Moira is in something of a personal hurricane as well. Elise too. Hannah and Angel. Talk about a whirlwind!"

They both laughed at the double entendre.

"Honey, we'll just have to hold on tight to each other, weather the storm, and see where the chips fall when it's all over."

Gerta tilted her head and looked across at her. "What about you? No whirlwind for you? You always seem to have it all together. Do you ever have problems? Come to think of it, I can't remember you ever coming to me with a problem of the heart."

"Oh, I've got my ups and downs, don't worry about that."

"Oh no—you don't get to blow me off. Your turn. Tell me. What's a downer for you?" She pointed her finger like a school matron. "Communication. This is how it works, right? Give and take, sharing?"

Grace chuckled and nodded. "I suppose you're right." She took in a breath, considering. "If I'm to be completely honest, I've been worried about Charles."

"Is he all right?"

"His physical health is fine. It's his mental health. He's been fixated on buying Butterhead."

"But Angel is not going to sell her."

"But he is," Grace countered. "He's practically begged Charles to buy her. Though why he'd want to sell his beloved horse is beyond me. She's given him the best years of her life—she deserves better. But more to the point, I don't want Charles to buy her. Forget that stuff he was saying about her doing dressage. Come on . . . I wasn't born yesterday. Butterhead's a jumper—a Grand Prix jumper! You know as well as I do once he's on the back of that good a horse, he won't be able to help himself. One day he'll take that jump."

"So what if he does?" Gerta said. "He knows the risks. That's what he does."

"He could fall," Grace blurted out. Suddenly her pent-up emotion came pouring out. "I couldn't bear seeing him hurt again," she cried. "Everyone thinks I'm so strong. I'm not that strong. Not about him. He's my whole life. I don't want him to ride again, not ever. Much less jump." She sniffed and wiped her eyes. "That's why I gave him the choice. D or D. Divorce or dressage."

"Yes, yes," Gerta said impatiently. "I know what it means."

"I figured I could endure his riding if he didn't jump. But he hasn't been able to find a horse, or even get back on one. He's getting depressed. He doesn't talk about it, but I can see it's wearing on him."

Gerta had listened without speaking. Now she set her coffee cup down and fixed her attention on Grace. "You think *I'm* controlling?" she scoffed. "Listen to yourself. I'm a piker compared to you."

Grace took a sharp little breath.

"Charles is a grown man. You are emasculating him."

"I am not."

"You stand there and tell me to let Elise make her own decisions. *Schatzi*, take your own advice. Let Charles make his own decisions. If you don't, he'll come to hate you. Like Elise hates me. And, Grace, it will break your heart. I can tell you."

Grace felt like she'd just been hit with a sucker punch. She was stunned. Speechless. The truth hurt. She leaned against the counter beside Gerta, then rested her head on Gerta's shoulder. She relished the sensation of Gerta's head moving to lean against hers.

. . .

Charles stood at Whirlwind's stall, waiting for Karl. He would be exercising the stallion this morning to give him a good workout before the storm. Charles came every morning to pay his respects to Whirlwind, and again in the afternoon when the horses were brought back from the pasture. And again in the evening. Whirlwind knew him now and even accepted him warmly with soft, vibrating nickers. Charles heard it as "Good morning! Nice to see you." He was utterly besotted with the stallion.

He stroked the horse's neck and chatted with Whirlwind about nothing in particular, just whatever came to mind. He longed to brush him, to walk him, to become more involved with this horse that had claimed his heart. Whirlwind was not his horse, however, and to do that would be wrong. So he contented himself with communicating with the stallion in the only way he could.

"Good morning, Mr. Charles!"

Charles turned to see Angel emerging from the main barn with Butterhead on the lead. She walked at an easy pace and held her head comfortably. She looked nothing like the dejected, weak horse he'd seen in the barn the night before.

"How's she feeling this morning?"

"Great!" Angel exclaimed with enthusiasm. "It's like she's never been sick."

"As the song says, what a difference a day makes."

"I'm going to give her some light exercise today. To get the gas out. It's been too long in the stall."

"I have to say, she's looking good."

Angel tried to pass at a safe distance but nonetheless Whirlwind caught wind and stomped his foot and grew agitated at the proximity of Butterhead. He stretched out his neck toward her with his head held high. His upper lip curled back, baring his upper teeth, and he began inhaling deeply.

Butterhead also grew restless, her tail high, eager to approach Whirlwind.

"That there is a classic flehmen response," said Charles with appreciation. "I haven't seen that in a long while, not being around many stallions. Nature is magnificent, isn't it? He's caught the scent of her pheromones, all right."

"These two, eh?" Angel said with a light laugh as he walked Butterhead farther away. "Get a room, eh?" he said to his horse.

"I can't say as I blame you, old boy," Charles said to Whirlwind. "Butterhead is one sweet filly."

Angel stopped and looked at the mare with affection. "She feels so spirited today. I think she knows that I made a decision."

"Oh?"

Angel turned to face Charles. "Mr. Charles, I've decided I am not going to sell her."

Charles nodded to indicate his understanding. He liked Angel de la Cruz, much to his surprise. He'd been prepared to dislike him right from the start, but Angel had proved to be respectful, hard-working, cooperative, a great storyteller. Not at all the self-centered rock star Charles had expected. And, as in any herd, the younger horse appreciated that Charles was the stallion here.

"Good decision," he called back. "Glad to hear it. A horse like that only comes into your life once. If you're lucky."

"You seem interested in *that* horse." Angel gestured to the stallion.

Charles looked back to Whirlwind. The horse was calmer now, but he kept his eyes on the mare. "Who wouldn't be? What a magnificent animal. But poor me. I finally fall in love with a horse and I can't have him."

"You don't know that."

"Gerta would never sell him."

"Never say never," Angel replied. "Remember Totilas. Whoever thought he'd be sold, eh?"

Charles had always been a great fan of what was arguably the best dressage horse of all time, one who'd brought a new level of interest to the sport. Charles had thrilled to the genius of Totilas's performance. Watching videos of Edward Gal and Totilas sweeping the gold medals at the FEI World Games had helped to convince Charles to give up jumping and give dressage a go. Unfortunately, the fairy tale of Edward Gal and Moorlands Totilas hadn't ended well. The sale of Totilas had stunned the world. Afterward, Totilas had been plagued by injuries and pulled out of competition.

"I don't think Totilas was ever the same after he left Gal," said Charles. "They were a team. A bond of trust was made and broken."

"I think riders everywhere, in every discipline, felt their hearts break a little bit with that one," said Angel.

"You know, you might've been criticized for the same thing if you'd sold the famous Rogue's Fancy."

Angel met his gaze, then turned to stroke Butterhead's neck. "*Nunca,*" he replied. "I will never." Then, with a nod, he started walking Butterhead to the jumping ring. "Oh," he said, pausing to make one more statement.

Charles looked up.

"You should know. Gerta does not own Whirlwind. Elise does."

EIGHTEEN

August 23, 8:15 a.m.
Freehold Farm, North Carolina
Hurricane Noelle is downgraded to a tropical storm

The two riding arenas at Freehold Farm lay parallel to each other on two level plateaus up the hill from the barn. The upper arena was used for jumping practice. The white-fenced arena had all-weather footing and a series of jumps and obstacles. A tractor with a drag sat ringside. Lower on the hill, the dressage arena was a long rectangle equipped with low white boards and cones with markers set at particular distances.

Charles walked up the hill at a leisurely pace. His boots were wet with dew and the world was lush green from all the rain. He looked up at the sky. The weather station reported that the tropical storm was continuing to rapidly weaken as it moved over land. This was hopeful news. But they were not out of the storm's threat yet. He used to feel that being in the mountains, they were safe from storms. After all, Tryon was in a unique microclimate in Polk

County, North Carolina, called the thermal belt. Frost and freezing temperatures were less likely to occur, giving them milder temperatures and a longer growing season. And it was good for riding horses, too.

Here in Tryon they were far from safe from hurricanes, however. Hurricanes' outer bands often brought days of tropical wind and rain and flooding. For North Carolinians—and many people living inland in the South—the wind wasn't the factor they were most fearful of. It was the rain. No, he decided. Never good to let one's guard down when it came to storms.

There was no rain yet today, though the sky was gray and an armada of clouds was amassing again in the far distance. A small breeze harkened the storm, and feeling the cool moisture on his cheeks, it was welcome. It would be a nice morning to ride.

And today, everyone was turning out for what they hoped would be some spectacular showmanship.

Charles heard Grace call him and he turned to wave. She was coming out of the barn. He was eager to tell her about Elise's kinky haircut, but then he spotted Gerta behind her. Later, he decided. He wouldn't be the one to bring the subject up to Gerta. It wouldn't be right.

"Good morning!" he called out.

Grace returned a wave, and he waited while the two women trudged up the hill. He caught sight of a glimpse of metal beneath Gerta's breeches. He was mightily impressed by her ability with the prosthesis. She'd told him this one had changed her life. There were microprocessor computers in the leg that sensed movement. She could walk uphill, in the rain, even swim. There was no stopping her.

Grace's eyes were sparkling with anticipation. "I'm so excited. Let's go watch Angel."

"He's not jumping today," Charles reminded her. "He'll just do gentle flat work. Because of the colic."

"I know. But I still want to watch the master ride."

Gerta let them go ahead. She watched them walk arm in arm, her heart beating faster not from the climb, but because of the proximity of Angel. Grace and Charles were, she knew without doubt, her very best friends. She felt she could share almost anything with Grace. Still, she wanted to be alone while watching Angel de la Cruz ride this morning. Her feelings for that man were jumbled up between her heart and her head. She had much to think about.

She also kept her eye open for Elise. She didn't come home again last night. She probably slept at Moira's again, but Gerta had waited up quite late in hope she would. Grace was right. They did need to talk. Perhaps today they could have a new beginning.

She looked at her watch. Speaking of late, Elise was late for her dressage lesson.

She spotted Moira higher on the hill near the jumping arena, in black riding breeches and boots. She veered off to talk to her. She was such a delightful girl, always so wise. She hoped she'd also glean some information about Elise. As she approached, she read the words of Moira's gray Caroline's Cakes T-shirt: EAT CAKE. BE HAPPY. Gerta chuckled and wished life could be so easy.

Moira's hair was down, glossy in the sun. The occasional breeze teased the ends, lifting them in the air. She, too, wanted to observe one of the world's finest athletes in the sport. But her face appeared troubled.

"Watching the master?" Gerta asked when she reached Moira ringside.

"He makes it look so elegant. Natural. Even just walking," Moira said with a sigh. "See how collected they are?"

"That's what the best do," Gerta replied. She looked into the arena. Angel looked desperately handsome on Butterhead in all black: his breeches, polo shirt, and helmet. As he rounded the arena his chiseled features looked straight ahead. His hands had his horse in complete control. She couldn't deny the stirring the sight caused her.

She took a breath and turned to Moira. "You look exceedingly pretty today," she told her. "Positively glowing."

Moira's brown eyes lit up. "Why, thank you, Mrs. Klug. I feel good inside. I made a big decision. I'm going to vet school."

"How wonderful! You'll make a wonderful vet. Your parents must be so proud."

Moira smiled. "They are. As you, I know, are proud of Elise."

Gerta's smile wobbled. "Yes." She paused. "Do you know where she is? She's supposed to be riding Whirlwind this morning."

Moira's brightness dimmed. "Uh, no. I haven't seen her. Not since yesterday."

"She didn't stay with you last night?"

"No. She left around ten."

Gerta's face stilled as her mind wildly searched possibilities. Where could she have spent the night? This bit of news she needed to keep between herself and Elise.

She was relieved to have the conversation interrupted when Grace came over to join them.

"Look at him," Grace said. "He reminds me of McLain Ward, the way he holds his reins. Don't you think?"

"Yes," Gerta said, turning her attention back to Angel. "I was thinking the same thing."

"Not too shabby to be compared to the number-one rider in America," said Moira.

Angel was giving Butterhead a light workout, flatting rather than jumping. He spotted Gerta and smiled. She did not respond. But Gerta's experienced eyes missed nothing. Angel was a very composed rider. He sat perfectly on the horse, strong, straight, and knowing just when to guide the horse to a turn.

She also appreciated just how amazing a horse Rogue's Fancy was. There was a joy in Butterhead today. She looked light on her feet and her ears were always up. It was a shame that they didn't jump. She would have liked to see them work together. She felt sympathy for Angel's position of losing his mount. And she admired Angel's horsemanship. Not only his decision to let Butterhead retire when she was at her prime, rather than let her slowly diminish her reputation in the public's eyes, but also for not selfishly pushing his horse so soon after colic. Anyone could see the mare wanted to take the jumps, but Angel deftly guided her away.

As she watched him, Gerta was ashamed for the thoughts she had. The rocking motion of his hips was highly suggestive. There were so many seemingly sexual expressions that equestrians used all the time to innocently describe the horse world and yet could be taken out of context. Several of them ran through her head now. *You must push harder. He was a good ride. Sit deeper and move with the rhythm.* She covered her smile with her hand and blushed, imagining Angel as a lover. As a woman, she appreciated his sex appeal.

As a businesswoman, she recognized his talent. Angel was young, experienced, and able. And currently without affiliation to any stable. She tapped her lips with her finger. All he needed was the right horse.

A short while later, Angel finished exercising Butterhead and dismounted. Jose stepped forward to cool down Butterhead and bring her back to her stall. Angel handed him the reins, then turned to look for Gerta. Spotting her, he lifted his hand in the air, indicating that she should wait.

Gerta turned her back to him. "Shall we go to the dressage arena?" she asked Grace, taking a step forward. "Where is Elise?"

Suddenly, Grace grabbed her arm and gave out a short yelp of surprise. "Jesus, Mary, and Joseph!"

Gerta swung her head in the direction of the barn and felt the blood drain from her body.

She hardly recognized her own daughter. Elise's beautiful long hair was gone, cut in a pixie cut, close to the scalp. Gerta didn't speak. She couldn't speak. She merely stared, stoically, as Elise sauntered toward them up the hill in tight black jeans and a bright yellow daisy–patterned shirt. A garish paisley scarf looped through her belt loops and hung down to her knees, flapping in the breeze. She looked like a vision from the 1960s. A thousand questions burned in Gerta's throat.

When Elise drew near, her smile could only be described as insolent. Gerta knew she was testing her, seeing how her mother would react to this show of defiance. *Oh, Elise*, she thought. There were so many ways she could have tested her. Why did she have to cut her beautiful hair? Gerta mourned the loss of it as though it were her own.

Gerta understood that Elise was upset about many things. If she'd only come to her, as Moira went to Grace. Seeking advice, distraught, even crying. Perhaps Gerta would have reacted differently. But Elise's thinly concealed anger was a trigger for Gerta. Old patterns died hard.

She took a step forward, coming face-to-face with her daughter. She heard Grace murmur something from behind her, but Gerta didn't listen. Even as the words came out of her mouth, Gerta wanted to take them back.

"You're not dressed to ride. And you're late!" She lifted her nose, eyes blazing, daring her to answer.

Elise's face showed disbelief, followed by a flash of hurt before her smile shifted to derision. Her lips twisted in disdain, and she turned her gaze away. When she looked at her mother again, her eyes were like blue chips of ice.

"You haven't figured out that I'm not riding?"

"Why not?"

Elise gave a little shrug. "I don't want to."

Gerta closed her eyes and felt the burn. There it was. The gauntlet thrown. She took a breath, fighting for control, then opened her eyes. "So I see."

Elise's hand went up to grasp her braid, then fluttered in the air. Gerta noticed the gesture, a habit of insecurity. Her heart lurched as she remembered the child.

"What have you done to your hair?" Gerta asked, her voice softer now.

"What do you care?"

There was the hurt, she thought. It had the effect of water over the flame. "I care," she said softly.

Elise's shrug this time was more timid. "I just wanted something different."

"You succeeded." Gerta ventured a small smile.

"You hate it," Elise spat out, defensive.

"No, I don't hate it," Gerta said, taking in the way the shorter hair made Elise's eyes appear bigger and Elise more womanly. Not so girlish. "It's very chic. I just need time to get used to it. Did you cut it?"

"Yes. Karl helped."

Gerta's brows rose. "So that's where you spent the night."

"Yeah. On the couch." She paused, then blurted out, "Mom, I'm gay."

Charles swung his head, his expression confused.

"Yes, I know, dear," Gerta said.

Elise stared at her mother, dumbstruck. "You knew?"

"Of course. I'm your mother. I was just waiting for you to tell me in your own good time."

Tears sprang to Elise's eyes as she offered a watery smile. She reached up to let her fingers graze the short hairs of her neck. "It will grow. In time."

As their relationship would grow, she thought with hope. Gerta smiled and nodded. What was hair? She wanted her daughter to be happy. There were far bigger discussions they needed to have together than the length of her hair.

Elise's anger had seeped from her like helium from a balloon. She looked over her shoulder to see Karl riding Whirlwind up the path from the barn to the dressage arena. She chewed her lip, then said, "Karl's going to ride Whirlwind today. He's very good with him. Please, watch before you say anything. It's better that you see for yourself the difference between him and me on Whirlwind."

Karl was riding Whirlwind? That felt like another defiance.

Gerta had specifically ordered him not to ride the horse. She watched Karl riding Whirlwind toward them through narrowed eyes. Was it defiance? she thought. Or . . . was she overreacting? Calm down, she told herself. It was Elise's choice not to exercise Whirlwind. Karl was his trainer. He was just doing his job.

She looked into Elise's eyes and saw again the flicker of fear, like one watching to see if a firecracker would go off. Was that how she wanted her daughter to feel around her? Fearful? Hesitant?

Gerta managed the best smile she could. "Okay," she said, and then, in a gracious sweep of her arm, said loudly, "Shall we watch?"

"Great," Elise said and offered her a bright smile before taking off for the dressage arena in long strides. Gerta saw Moira trot up to Elise's side. The girls' heads drew together in an impassioned discussion.

Charles walked up to her with Grace on his arm. He gallantly offered his other arm to Gerta. She thanked him, and they began the trek down the hill to the dressage arena. She was very aware of Angel's presence a few feet away.

Grace leaned forward to catch Gerta's eye. She lifted her hand to a thumbs-up gesture.

"You done good, girlfriend."

Charles's eyes were fixed on the glistening black stallion as he swung the gate open to the dressage arena. Karl nodded at him with a smile and tapped his helmet as he passed through.

He brought the stallion into the arena with a calm, steady gait. Today there were no theatrics or drama. Whirlwind appeared calm and content to enter the long rectangular arena.

Charles closed the gate and leaned against it, resting his elbows on the top rung and his right boot on the bottom. Everyone else found a spot to stand and watch. There was a subtle excitement in the air, a simmering expectation to see what could happen. The last time, Whirlwind had been in pain and intolerant. He'd tossed Elise into the dirt. Was this horse temperamental? Too spirited? Even unwilling? The question running in everyone's mind was though this horse was undeniably gorgeous, was he trainable?

As for the rider, no one knew what to expect. Karl was still nursing an injured foot and limping. Charles wondered how he got his swollen foot into the boot. Looking at his face now, however, one would never know he was most likely in pain. What would they see today? Charles wondered. Two wounded warriors? Or two potential champions?

Karl began walking Whirlwind around the perimeter of the arena. Every athlete, no matter the sport, knew the importance of a good stretch and warm-up to get the muscles supple. Karl had confided to Charles that in his opinion, most dressage tests were won in the warm-up.

Eventually Karl moved Whirlwind into the trot, a jogging pace faster than walking but slower than a run. It was a flashy gait, a chance for a horse to strut his stuff. Charles loved the sound of the steady hoofbeats on the ground and the huffing sound of the horse when he passed. To the observer one would think that Karl was just sitting on the horse, along for the ride. But Charles was attentive to the practiced placement of Karl's hands, his impeccable seat position, the rolling, rhythmic movement of his hips in pace with the horse. It was all a dialogue between horse and rider. Karl's subtlest movements communicated to Whirlwind his intentions.

For his part, Whirlwind was on fire. He was a frighteningly strong horse, with powerful hindquarters and muscles that rippled beneath his polished ebony coat. Yet he harnessed his energy into correct movements, in complete sync with Karl. It seemed to Charles that Whirlwind was intent on showing the world that he chose Karl as his rider. There was a strong communication between them. A trust and even devotion that was palpable. Whirlwind was declaring he would follow this man's lead wherever he wanted to go.

The loyalty and panache only served to make Charles want Whirlwind all the more. *What a showman*, Charles thought, his heart quickening. What spirit. He wanted to be connected to this horse in some way. Whirlwind had that certain something—the *it* factor—that a horse couldn't be taught. He had to be born with it.

Their transitions were remarkable, from a collected walk to an expressive trot and finally to a brave canter. As Karl took Whirlwind through the exercises, a feeling of awe spread through the group. They all knew they were witnessing something special. Possibly the beginning of a magical combination.

After the exercise, the group came together to share their thoughts. Charles could see in their eyes that they all had felt the incredible power of the team as much as he did. In an odd way, Charles felt a paternal pride for Karl and Whirlwind. He'd become very fond of them both. Their success felt like his success.

Elise turned to Gerta. There were tears in her eyes, not of sadness, but, rather, pride.

"You see, Mother," she said triumphantly. "Whirlwind *is* a magnificent horse. I was simply not the right rider."

Gerta couldn't think of the right thing to say, so she simply offered a quick smile.

"He's truly a wonderful horse," Charles agreed in a wistful tone. "One in a million."

"Interesting choice of words, Mr. Phillips," Elise said. "Though in truth, he's worth a bit more than that."

"What are you talking about, Elise?" snapped Gerta. "He'll be worth *much* more than that when he's proven."

"Perhaps," she said. Then she paused. "But I've decided I'm selling him now. For two million."

Charles rubbed his jaw. "Selling him? But what will happen to Karl? Didn't you just see what a team they make? That doesn't just happen."

Elise looked stricken. "Of course I'll recommend Karl as the trainer to whoever buys him," said Elise.

"Trainer?" Charles said, feeling the injustice of her statement. It seemed too cavalier since it involved Karl's future. "He just proved he's so much more than a trainer. He deserves the chance to show Whirlwind. They will only help each other. Divide them, and who knows what you'll get. Remember Totilas."

"I hear what you're saying. But I can't control what will happen. You know as well as I do that the person who spends that kind of money on a horse will likely be buying it to ride for him- or herself."

Angel cleared his throat and leaned closer to his side. "Mr. Charles, you should buy him."

Gerta's blue eyes were like flames as she found the target for her building anger. She turned on Angel. "What are you saying? It is not for you to suggest such a thing. Who do you think you are? This is the end of this discussion. Whirlwind is not for sale."

"Actually, Mother . . ." Elise turned and looked at her. In that moment she was no longer a little girl. Her short hair indicated a new power, like armor, and she stood strong. "Yes, he is. I've decided to sell him. Not for spite," she assured Gerta. "Certainly not to hurt Karl. I have only the greatest respect for him. Not for any reason other than I do not want to ride him. I do not want to ride at all. Not for a while. And Whirlwind is my only asset. My ticket to ride, so to speak." She smiled at her mother, sincere. "And for that, Mother, I thank you."

Gerta stared at her daughter, torn. On the one hand she wanted to fight with Elise, with Angel, with them all to keep Whirlwind. Wasn't she the one who'd found him? Went to Germany to purchase him?

On the other hand, what would be the point of fighting? The horse was not hers. She had given Whirlwind as a gift to Elise. Perhaps the gift she could give her daughter now was the power of choice.

Her shoulders lowered, and she felt defeated as she looked out across the arena. Karl was walking the topic of their heated discussion to cool him down. The rhythm was easy and steady, like a heartbeat.

She put her hand to her heart. "Is this really happening?"

"Oh, it's happening," Grace said loudly.

Everyone turned to look at Grace.

Grace strode forward and put her hands on Gerta's shoulders. "I'm buying Whirlwind."

Gerta's eyes widened. "*You?*"

Elise chirped out a laugh and slapped her mouth with her hand. "Don't be so shocked. You so much as told me to. Remember?"

Gerta's mind fled back to their discussion that morning. What had she said, she wondered wildly, that would make Grace think that?

Grace released her and walked to Charles. The breeze was blowing his graying hair and his large blue eyes were wide. He looked as though he was trying to figure out if his wife was going mad. She smiled and framed his face in her palms.

"I love you, Charles. I'm buying him for you."

The arena was empty. Hoof marks scarred the dirt and from the sky a few fat raindrops fell in heavy splats, leaving circles in the dust. Gerta stood alone in the field between the dressage and jumping arenas—a metaphor for her life, she thought. She'd made her mark in jumping events and her daughter in dressage. And now it appeared that she wouldn't make it to the Olympics in either arena.

She was fifty-five and once again her life was changing course, through no decision of her own. It was humbling to realize that despite all the control over her life that she liked to think she had—the hours of practice on a horse or the hard work on her business—fate could come along and intervene and change the course of one's life in the breath of a moment. One tragic fall, a bitter divorce, a child's decision, a hurricane.

The one constant in her life had been horses. She'd spent a lifetime with them and they'd helped develop her confidence and perseverance. She doubted she could have overcome the loss of her leg were it not for refusing to back down from challenges. She would not let the loss of a leg define her. She would show the world that she was much more than a limb. She had to admit she wasn't the most flexible of people. She'd heard the jokes in the stable about where she put her crop. But she'd never wanted their affection. She wanted their respect.

Living in that ivory tower, however, could be lonely. Her inflexibility and refusal to back down when she thought she was right had alienated most people in her sphere. Including—most especially—Elise. And now, too, Angel.

She just witnessed today that a strong ego or *being right* was ineffectual when dealing with a horse. If Whirlwind made a mistake, Karl's correction was immediate and without a sense of right or wrong. It was a dialogue developed on a foundation of trust.

That was pretty phenomenal, when one thought about it. In nature, horses were a prey animal. Humans were predatory. That didn't set up a relationship geared for success. And yet humans had six thousand years of history with horses. The horse had made a powerful impact on the evolution of the human world. If history taught her anything . . . if the horse taught her anything . . . it was that holding too tight to the reins, using spurs, and forcing one's will on the horse would never create a bond or a partnership.

The rain began to fall harder. Gerta walked down the hill to the barn, careful not to slip and fall. By the time she arrived, her clothes were wet and her hair was plastered to her head. When would she learn to wear a slicker in weather such as this? Some of the horses were still in the paddocks. On entering, she inhaled the heady, welcoming scents of a barn and was welcomed with a few nickers. As she walked down the barn hall, Butterhead poked her head out from the stall. Gerta smiled and went to pet her but stopped when she spotted Angel in the stall.

He was bent over her rear hoof, picking out mud with a hook. On hearing her, he turned his head to look over his shoulder. His face immediately broke into a smile of such delight that it touched her heart. He released the hoof and approached her. They stood on either side of the stall gate. His hazel eyes searched her face and his smile widened.

"Look at you. Soaked through again. What am I going to do with you?"

"I'm going to get a towel," she said, and turned to leave.

"Wait," he called after her. He came out from the stall, closed the gate, and walked at a fast pace toward the tack room, removing his work gloves en route.

Gerta pushed a shock of damp hair from her face, cursing herself for being a fool to be caught in this position again. Instead of waiting, she walked to Jazzy's stall and smacked her lips. The big dark bay immediately came and hung his head over the stall window. He nickered and blew air through his nostrils. Her heart softened again at seeing him.

Angel returned with a towel. He reached out to dry her hair but this time she took the towel from his hands.

"Thank you. I can do it."

Angel raised his brows but relinquished the towel and put his hands behind his back.

"You are angry with me."

Gerta rubbed her head vigorously. "Of course I'm angry with you. You lied to me."

"When did I lie to you?"

She lowered the towel to glare at him through locks of hair. "A lie of omission."

"What is this lie of omission," he asked, not comprehending the English word.

"Omission!" she snapped. "Not telling me about the sale of the horse was as much a lie as telling me you knew nothing."

"This is crazy," he fired back, insulted. "I did not lie of omission to you. Yes, I talked to Elise about selling the horse. *Madre de Dios*, everyone saw that she was not right for the horse except for you. You had blinders on," he said, putting a hand at either eye. "I told her I would make some inquiries. But," he said louder to stop her interruption, "I told her she had to tell you before I did anything!"

"You dropped the bug in Charles's ear about buying him."

"What is this dropping the bug? I told him I thought he should buy the horse. Yes. Because he loves the horse."

"And you don't get a referral fee? A little off the top?"

He didn't speak.

Gerta felt her fury bubble. "I thought so."

Angel opened his palms. "I had planned to get a fee, yes. I need the money. I'm not rich like you. I've made some bad mistakes. I'm not so good with money, eh? But I am not selling Butterhead, and I need a horse. This is my career, Gerta," he said with the hint of a plea for her understanding. Then he sighed and shook his head. "But that is not the reason I thought Charles should buy the horse. Did you not see him with Whirlwind? He pined for him. And," he added with enthusiasm, "he just hired Karl to work for Freehold Farm. Not just as a trainer. But as a rider. He's going to let Karl show Whirlwind."

This took the wind out of her argument. It was the right thing to do. She should be happy. But she felt even more deflated.

"That is what I should have done," she said softly. "If I had not had the blinders on." She looked up at him and gave a short, desperate laugh.

"Gerta, I told Elise and Charles I am not taking the referral fee. Charles did not buy the horse, eh? Grace did. You should collect the fee."

Gerta laughed, feeling a heaviness leave her chest. Angel did not make a deal behind her back. That cut had gone the deepest.

"Well," she said by way of a declaration, stepping away and draping the towel over the gate. She reached up with both hands to comb her hair back with her hands. "I guess Whirlwind is going to the Olympics after all."

Angel tilted his head. "Maybe not in 2020. They'll just be starting to do shows."

"Don't underestimate them. You might be surprised. When I was Karl's age, I catapulted to the Olympic team in months. And look at Charlotte Dujardin with Valegro. It's possible. And I truly hope they make the team. And if not this time, the next." She sighed. "I just wish it could have been Elise."

"That wasn't her dream."

"No. It was mine."

Angel drew near and took her hands. "You don't need Elise. She's not even a jumper. Like us." He commanded her gaze and she held her breath. "You have me. I'll take you to the Olympics. Let me be the one who gets you there."

Gerta moved her right hand and placed it over his heart. "My gallant man. You have great heart." Her smile was shaky. "Yes. I accept. I will go with you to the Olympics."

"Not only go with me," he said. "I will go with you."

"Well, yes, of course."

"No, I do not think you understand. You will be in the Olympics."

"What are you saying?" she said, pulling her hand away. The dreamy atmosphere was suddenly lost. "You're insane."

"Hear me out. Maybe not jump. But you can do para-dressage. I know you. You have Razzmajazz back, you have the drive and the talent. You can do anything."

Gerta blinked rapidly as this new possibility exploded in her mind like fireworks. She had Jazzy back. She could begin dressage training.

"I'm not afraid of hard work," she said.

"No!"

"Do you think I could really do this? At my age?"

"Julie Brougham of New Zealand is sixty-four. And Mary Hanna in Australia."

Gerta released a short laugh. "What are they eating down under?"

"There's an old superstition at the track. If there is only one gray horse in a race, that's the horse to bet."

Gerta scoffed. "You and your superstitions."

Angel took her in his arms and kissed her hard and fervently. When he drew back, they both were breathless.

Angel transmitted a surge of confidence in her. In them.

"You can do this," he told Gerta. "I believe in you. This is your dream. Go for it."

NINETEEN

August 23, 8:20 p.m.
Freehold Farm, North Carolina
*Gusty winds and flood watches called for
North Carolina as Tropical Storm Noelle approaches*

The candles burned low, several wine bottles sat empty on Grace's dining room table, and they'd made serious headway into the rich chocolate cake from Caroline's Cakes. Most all the guests were gathered at the table except for Hannah, who begged off because of work. Boots were at the door, the attire was casual, and dogs were sitting under the table. Elise was shamelessly feeding Birdie bits of her dinner, while nearby Gigi and Bunny sat beside Moira and Charles, eyes round and begging. The faint whimpers of Tut and Maybelle in their crates sounded from the family room.

"Well, I'm off," Angel said, setting his napkin on the table. He rose from his chair. "I'm doing the barn check."

"I'll go with you," Charles said, pushing back his chair. "I want to check on Whirlwind."

Gerta's sigh was audible.

"I can do that for you, sir," Karl said with alacrity.

"No, no," Charles said, his hand waving Karl back into his seat. "I want to go."

"He's in love," Grace said with a chuckle.

"True," Charles acknowledged with a meaningful glance at Grace. He nodded his readiness to leave to Angel.

"Don't be too long," Gerta cautioned. "The storm is heading this way."

"No," Angel replied, and offered her a knowing smile. "Not too long."

Angel again borrowed Charles's rain jacket and they headed out into the night. Conditions remained fair. He could feel the drop in barometric pressure and looked at the sky. Only the faint outline of cumulus clouds was visible in the darkness. The two men stopped to look at the sky.

"What do you think?" Angel asked Charles.

Charles looked in the sky and rocked on his heels. "Midnight. Maybe later."

They drove in a relaxed silence in Charles's pickup truck the short distance to the barn. The evening had been saturated with conversation already. Both men enjoyed the stillness of the dark interior of the car. The headlights cut through the darkness and Charles, familiar with each curve of the road, made good time.

The gravel crunched beneath their boots as they walked toward the barn. At the entrance Angel stopped, seeing a black feather lying on the gravel. He bent to pick it up.

"That's a turkey feather," Charles said on stepping closer to inspect. "We have a nice breeding pair wandering around here."

Angel held the feather between his thumb and forefinger. "My mother used to tell me that if you found a black feather, it was a sign that you were about to embark on an exciting adventure." He looked up at Charles and said in a cheeky manner, "Maybe a scary one, too."

"I'd say that sounds about right. Love is never easy."

"You heard?"

Charles chuckled. "You forget who my wife is. Grace knows everything that's going on. She's faster than Twitter." He waited for Angel to finish laughing before asking, "So, you and Gerta . . ."

Angel's lips eased to a thoughtful smile. The question didn't surprise him. He'd been getting surreptitious looks all through dinner. "*Sí.* I can hardly believe it."

Charles looked at the ground. "I don't mean to sound like a father, but she is an old friend," he began. He looked Angel in the eye. "Do you love her? I don't want to see her hurt."

Angel didn't flinch. "I do. It is fast, I know. We both know. But it is real. I would never hurt her."

"And Hannah?"

Angel heard the challenge in Charles's voice, and it was fair. She, too, was their friend. "I will always love her. She will always be my friend. We are good."

"She didn't come to dinner."

Angel shook his head, acknowledging this. Her presence was missed by all. "I wish she did. She feels, I think, a bit, how do you say it . . . awkward? She doesn't want to talk about it to everyone."

"I don't like her feeling excluded. Stuck alone at the lake house."

"She knows that. She has been talking to Grace. And she's

working. She's very excited about a new product line. I am happy for her. She needs this. It's what she wants."

Charles took a breath and then exhaled. "Okay, then." He pointed to the feather. "It seems the angels have given you and Gerta their blessing."

Angel smiled, hearing Charles's blessing in the comment. He was a good man. A good friend to have in your corner when the chips were down.

The two men went their separate ways. Charles made a beeline for the other, smaller barn of stalls where Whirlwind was kept. Angel stepped into the main barn, rich with the smells of warm animals, hay, shavings, and manure. The horses nickered at hearing him enter, expecting treats. He first greeted Butterhead, his gaze sweeping over her, assessing. He pulled a carrot from his pocket and enjoyed her muzzle against his palm.

He completed the list of night chores, checking each of the horses. When he was finished, he walked out to the stalls across from the barn. The light was on in the stall and he saw Charles's gray head bobbing as he brushed the horse's coat. The sight gave him pause. Charles's energy and obvious joy was like watching a boy at Christmas receiving his most eagerly awaited gift. Angel smiled and approached them. Whirlwind saw him first and his head came up, his ears forward.

"Mr. Charles," he called out. "How's your new horse?"

Charles stopped brushing and sauntered closer to the gate. His grin stretched from ear to ear. "I can't believe he's mine. One piece of paper signed and I'm a made man."

"I see you've also got a new cat." Angel pointed to the exceptionally large orange tabby licking himself on the fresh hay.

"Him." Charles laughed and nodded. "Yep. He seems to like it here and Whirlwind seems to like him. Karl named him Big Orange."

"That's a good name for him," Angel said. "In my country, cats in the barn are a good thing. Except black cats," he hurried to add. "Cats keep the rodents out and also keep the horses calm."

Charles reached up to stroke Whirlwind's neck. The big horse turned his head to gently nuzzle Charles's shoulder.

"He really likes you."

Charles replied modestly, "So it seems."

"Have you gotten on him yet?"

"No." Charles shook his head and took a step back.

"You should. You don't buy a car before you take it for a ride."

"I will . . . When I'm ready."

Gerta had told Angel that Charles had stopped riding. Angel thought it was merely until he was healed from his accident. Gerta had confided in him that he might have PTSD about the fall. Grace had told her Charles had not even gotten back up on a horse. For horse people, this was the line in the sand. After a fall, one either got back up on the horse, or never rode again.

"Maybe, Mr. Charles, it is time," he said solemnly. "If you don't get back on, you have too much time to think about it. You know, the fall, the pain. Your mind builds up this fear. It can make you crazy. And the longer you wait, the more afraid you become. It is . . ." He paused, struggling for the word. "*Es irracional*, eh?"

"Not irrational," Charles replied soberly. "The fear is very real. I've been seeing a psychologist. We are trying to desensitize me. Working with the horses every day, being near them, feeding them. This helps me see them—and their size—as approachable."

"How's that working for you?"

He raised his shoulders briefly. "Pretty good, up to a point. I've gotten so I can get up on the mounting block. But then . . ." He shook his head. "Perhaps it's the fear of getting hurt again. Of not being able to walk again." He paused. "I stop." He looked at Whirlwind who stood relaxed, his rear left hoof cocked as the orange tabby wound around his legs. "When I met Whirlwind, something changed. I think you might understand when I tell you that the horse chose me. Not the other way around."

When Angel nodded, Charles continued in a contemplative tone. "Do you understand what we mean in English when we say we gentle a horse?"

"When you work with a wild horse to tame it."

"That's part of it. Back in the day, they said a wild horse had to be broke, meaning to get him trained to do work. Usually quickly. Sometimes brutally. I suspect *broke* is the right term. We broke their spirit. Today, there's no need to break them by rough handling. With time and training we've learned a wild horse will become responsive. But that term still hangs around to mean a horse that can be ridden or driven. One that's under control." He rubbed his jaw in thought and looked again at Whirlwind.

"I don't much care for that term. Don't like the connotation. I prefer to say a horse is finished. Gives the horse more respect, don't you agree? Words are a powerful tool." He shook his head. "Anyway, when a horse is trained, we try to keep the horse from getting its flight-or-fight instinct worked up. To help keep the emotions under control. To trust. To feel safe."

He looked at Angel. "What I'm trying to explain is, you might say Whirlwind tamed me, or rather, my fears." He reached up to pat the long, black neck. "This big, splashy galumph of an animal has the gentlest spirit. He might be that one special horse. The once-in-a-lifetime horse that Gerta talks about. My soul mate."

Angel witnessed the bond between them and understood Charles's meaning. That bond would be the tool that allowed Charles to get back on a horse. He left one thing out, though: leadership. Horses were herd animals and instinctively needed a leader. Whirlwind felt safe with Charles, as well. A bond went both ways. And Charles was, quietly and effectively, a leader.

"If he is your soul mate," Angel said, "do you think, then, that you could get on Whirlwind?"

This gave Charles pause. His gaze swept over the horse. Angel saw the deep lines coursing through his tanned face. They spoke of a rich and full life. One that had seen its fair share of trials. Every professional rider could talk of their falls the way a veteran soldier went on about old war injuries or women prevailed upon listeners the aches and pains of labor. But Mr. Charles Phillips had experienced more injuries than his share.

"I just might," Charles replied thoughtfully.

"Then let's do it."

"What? Now?"

"Yes, now. No time like the present, eh? Why wait another minute?"

"The storm is one good reason."

"Excuses. You told me midnight." Angel checked his watch. "It's only after ten. We have much time. What do you say? I'll help you. Come on, Mr. Charles. Don't put it off. Carpe diem."

"Yes," Charles replied haltingly. Then, as though working himself up, he fisted his hands. "Let's do this."

Together they saddled Whirlwind, who appeared eager to step out of the stall. Charles flicked a switch and lights lit up the lower dressage arena. The wind was picking up, but it was not too bad. It was, Angel thought, rather exhilarating. Charles walked at a determined pace. As they reached the gate, however, Angel saw his hand closing and unclosing nervously around the lead. Angel began to worry if this was such a good idea, after all. He knew Charles's anxiety was building. Angel thought to keep Charles talking would stop the panic from building up in his mind.

"You're thinking of the accident, no?"

"Yes."

"Okay. Do you remember the day of your accident?" he called out.

"Of course." He stopped walking. "I was in a show. Like so many others. It wasn't even the highest jump." He paused. "I didn't see it coming. Selectro just bailed. Stopped short and over I went."

"Was anything going on that day in your life? Were you thinking of something else? Maybe a fight with Grace?"

Charles walked a while, his helmeted head bent in thought. He then stopped again to look over his shoulder. "Actually," he said, in a tone that implied he was having a revelation, "we were going to fly to Europe the next day. For another show. I remember arguing with her about the time push. We still had so much to do before we could leave."

"There you are. Something was on your mind. You may have missed some cue from the horse. You may not have been focused on the jump. It happens."

Charles didn't reply. He turned and began walking again. They went through the gate and on to the interior of the dressage arena.

Charles walked Whirlwind to a level area then stopped and stood silently a moment, staring at his boots.

"Mr. Charles? Are you okay?"

Charles looked up and his face was contemplative. "Actually, I was just remembering. I've never been angry at Selectro for the fall, because I believe he saved my life that day. If he hadn't balked at the jump and I hadn't fallen, the doctors wouldn't have discovered I had a blood clot. Like I said, we were scheduled to fly to Europe the next day. I might've broken my back, but if I'd gotten on that plane, I would've died. I've always felt in my gut that Selectro somehow knew I had a blood clot."

Angel was deeply moved.

Charles took a deep breath. "One horse saved my life physically. And now, another is going to save me mentally." He looked up at Whirlwind and stroked his neck. "Let's do this."

Angel carried the bright yellow mounting block close to Charles and set it before the horse, making sure it was settled solidly on the ground. He stepped aside, allowing Charles room to mount.

Charles stood on the block with one hand on the saddle and the other holding the reins. He paused, collecting his wits. When he felt ready he lifted his foot tentatively in the stirrup. Whirlwind shifted his weight. Charles immediately pulled his leg back in.

"It's all right. He'll wait for you," Angel said encouragingly. "He loves you, right? You have nothing to fear. Think soul mate."

"Right."

He watched Charles take another breath and harness his focus. Angel mentally urged Charles on: *Go . . . go . . . go . . . You can do it.*

But Charles didn't move. He stood with his hands on the saddle, battling with his fears.

"Do you want me to give you a leg up, Mr. Charles?"

Charles shook his head. "No. I'm good."

Angel prayed Charles wouldn't accidentally kick Whirlwind with his foot as he swung it over the horse, startling him.

Charles put his foot into the stirrup again and waited. Angel held his breath. This time Whirlwind didn't budge. He was patient, waiting for Charles. In one smooth move Charles hoisted himself up and swung his leg over the back of the horse, sliding smoothly into the saddle.

Angel released his breath. He wanted to whoop out loud, but of course he didn't. The last thing anyone wanted to do at this miraculous moment was spook the horse. Charles wasn't smiling. His face was a picture of concentration. He began checking the horse's girth.

"I brought the lunge line," Angel told him. "We can go that route. This first time," he added. His having some control over the horse might help Charles feel more relaxed in the saddle while he met his fears.

Charles looked up. His eyes were crinkled and his cheeks rose in a smug smile.

"No, thanks," he said buoyantly. "I've got this."

"Remember, if a mistake happens, forget about the mistake and keep going."

"Not a bad lesson to remember for life, eh?"

Angel smiled and gave Charles the thumbs-up. As Charles led Whirlwind to the outer perimeter, Angel hurried to retrieve the mount. He moved it to the side rail then crossed his arms and watched as Charles smoothly walked Whirlwind around the arena. Charles had a good seat and Whirlwind exhibited none of his high-stepping anxiety. This was akin to a first date. They were checking each other out, learning the cues, beginning a dialogue.

After a while Whirlwind shifted easily into a trot. The trot was a flashy movement and Whirlwind's legs stepped high. He looked like he was on springs. With the wind gently blowing and the coolness of the night air, the horse seemed to be enjoying the evening outing. Angel watched the pair as they began to dance together. Granted, it couldn't be compared with the fluent, effortless ballet that Whirlwind shared with Karl. That had come from countless hours of practice. Whirlwind understood each subtle movement Karl had offered. But with Charles, it was relaxed and easy. Angel's grin widened. And both horse and rider seemed to be having so damn much fun.

Charles rode no more than twenty minutes, but it was enough. When he dismounted, he took off his helmet and Angel could see the man was practically busting out of his skin with happiness. His eyes were bright and his face flushed. He wrapped his arms around Whirlwind's neck and hugged him.

"Thank you," he said to the horse, unabashedly choked up. Releasing the horse, he stepped toward Angel and wrapped his arms around him as well. "Thank you," he said again. "Thank you, my friend."

When he stepped back, Angel could see the tears flooding his eyes. They made his own eyes water.

"It was time!" he exclaimed. "That is all. You know," he teased, "you look so good, maybe *you* will be the one to take him to the Olympics."

Charles smiled at the joke then grew serious. "No, Whirlwind is going to make me the best dressage rider that I can be." He paused. "But Karl will make Whirlwind the best dressage horse he can be."

He looked at Charles and beamed. "*Sí. Es perfecto.*"

Charles lit up. "I've got to tell Grace," he exclaimed, and swung his head back toward the house, as if he could see her there.

"Go to her, my man. Go now! I'll take care of Whirlwind."

Charles hesitated, though it was clear he wanted to take off whooping and hollering down the hill. "How will you get back to the house? No, I'll wait."

"Go! I'm not going up the hill." He smirked. "I'm heading to the cottage. It's not so far. I can walk."

Charles understood and slapped Angel on the back. "Very good then. I'll take you up on your offer." He was already walking away when he said more for politeness, "You're sure?"

"Yes, I am sure. Go!"

Angel laughed to himself, not at Charles but with pure love for the man, as he watched him hurry down the hill then sprint to his truck. He heard the engine fire up, then a moment later saw the red pickup speeding up the hill. *Grace is going to ride a stallion herself tonight*, he thought with another laugh.

"Come on, you magnificent horse," Angel said, patting Whirlwind. "You've done your good deed for today."

Elise sat across from Karl at a pub in Landrum. A local band was playing "Sweet Home Carolina" and the locals were joining in with the chorus. She couldn't believe Karl had never heard of the song.

"I'm going to make a southern boy out of you yet," she teased.

"What do you mean?" he asked, leaning across the small round table to be heard over the band. "I've lived in Florida for almost ten years."

Elise laughed. "Florida ain't the South," she said. "Now that you're moving to North Carolina, you have to appreciate the delicacies of southern living."

"*Ja?*" he asked, and downed his beer. He lifted his hand and gestured for the waitress. "Like what?" he asked Elise.

"Oh, like barbecue. You should know, southerners take their barbecue seriously. Different regions have their own take on what makes theirs the best. Here in the Carolinas, they like to use the whole hog, slow-cooked and smoky. North Carolina might fight with South Carolina over whether tomato or mustard sauce is the best, though. You'll have to come to your own mind on that. And biscuits." She rolled her eyes in ecstasy. "You haven't lived till you tasted a southern biscuit. You'll come to love collard greens and pies, oyster roasts, fried chicken—all fried foods." She smacked her lips. "Especially fried green tomatoes."

Karl made a face.

"Trust me. You're going to love them. And sweet tea. So sweet it can make your teeth ache. In fact, you know you're in the South if you get sweet tea without having to ask for it."

The waitress brought two more beers and cleared away the two empties.

"I'll stick to beer." Karl raised his bottle to his lips. After drinking he cocked his head and asked disbelievingly, "You really got two million dollars for Whirlwind?"

"Minus taxes, expenses . . ."

"And what you have to pay Angel."

She shook her head. "No. He wouldn't take a penny. Something about his honor."

"Really?" Karl took a long drink and looked around the room, thinking. "That's cool," he decided.

"He's a good guy. I guess I can see him with my mother." Then she shook her head and in unison she and Karl said, "Noooooo."

Elise looked at the band. They were playing in a cleared area in the back of the room, encircled by wooden chairs and small circular tables. The three men wore scruffy beards and played guitars and drums. The woman had long black hair, wore a floral skirt, and played the fiddle. They were young and cool in their cowboy boots. Elise listened and wondered what it would be like to play an instrument. Maybe she'd try to learn guitar.

"I still can't believe you got two million," Karl said again, drawing her attention back.

"Why?"

"That horse is unproven. I mean, two fucking million dollars."

"Stop repeating the amount. I know how much it was."

Karl picked up his beer and looked at her over it. "Sorry. I just never dreamed he'd fetch that much. Not yet."

"A thing is worth what someone is willing to pay. Mr. Phillips wanted that horse. He probably would've paid more. But I like him, and that wouldn't have been right. I asked for what we put into him. That was enough. Plus, he hired you. That's got to be worth something to you."

Karl put down his beer and nodded hard. "I tell you . . . I'm still in shock."

Elise tore at her label and said, "I know you will be good to

Whirlwind. And so will Mr. Phillips. No matter what you might think, I do care about Whirlwind."

Karl looked at the tabletop. "I know." He lifted his head and said with a mischievous grin, "What are you going to do with all that money?"

Elise released a giggle. "I've no idea. Travel. Go to school. Rescue horses." She shrugged.

Karl lifted his bottle toward her to toast. "Here's to the road not taken."

Elise tossed her head back and laughed freely. They clinked bottles. "To the road not taken!"

Hannah sat at the computer. Her fingers flew over the keyboard. A few more sentences and she'd finish this report. She typed the last word and placed a period. Then she sighed and reached for her wine. It was a lovely white wine, chilled. She took a sip and smiled. She'd forgotten how much she loved chardonnay. Angel drank only red wine and so she'd joined him. Now, with him gone, she went back to white. There were lots of little things like that, all of which made her feel freer. Delightfully selfish. And, she had to admit, despite the occasional bout of pain, happier.

She closed her computer and rested her fingers on the top. Her new makeup line was drawing some important attention. She'd set up some meetings in New York. As soon as this storm passed, she could pack up her car and go. God, she couldn't wait. It'd only been a few days up here in the mountains but it felt like a frigging lifetime. She swirled her wine, watching the liquid form peaks and valleys on the glass.

A lot happened in these few days. The hurricane had hit the Florida coast, and there was some serious flooding and wind damage further north in the Palm Beach area. Her condo would be covered by insurance. But she feared Gerta's farm might have been hit hard.

She couldn't stop the sudden feeling of pleasure at the thought. It was terrible of her to feel that, she scolded herself. She should be ashamed of herself. She took another drink to swallow her smile.

A scratching on her leg brought her attention to the little fawn-colored Chihuahua begging to be picked up. She reached down to pull him to her lap. He kissed her face while she laughed and half-heartedly told him to stop. Then he settled in her lap while she petted him behind one of his very large ears.

"You're my hot little boy now, aren't you?" she crooned.

There is something in the air tonight, Angel sung in his mind as he slowly walked across the grassy hillside, Whirlwind's great breadth behind him. The sound of the wind rustling the leaves in the trees filled the night. It was soft and moist and the branches were swaying. There were no ominous signs of the storm's arrival. Just a heightened tension. A sense of expectancy that was almost sensual.

He was walking Whirlwind past the paddocks when the horse became unusually animated, stopping and sniffing the air. Then he heard the high, insistent whinny of a mare from the paddock.

It all became suddenly clear. Angel cocked an ear. That was

Butterhead. Earlier, he had turned Butterhead out in the paddock to give her some fresh air and grazing time after being cooped up for so long. He planned to bring her in after he settled Whirlwind.

It was no wonder Whirlwind was pulling back, jerking his head up, ears twitching. Angel had to maneuver him in circles to get him to calm down. As he did so, he admired the remarkable strength and sinewy definition of the stallion's muscles. They glistened with a fine sweat. In the dim light of the distant arena he saw the horse's wild, bright eyes and prancing hooves. This was a magnificent horse, in his prime and ready to perform. There was no doubt in Angel's mind that someday Whirlwind would stun the equestrian world. With Karl riding him, this horse would become an international champion, maybe one for the books. If so, when he retired, he would also gross millions of dollars as a stud. Charles and Grace would multiply their investment many times over.

What a horse, he thought again, as Whirlwind settled. It was Gerta who first saw the potential in the two-year-old. Gerta who had brought Karl to America to train the young horse. She'd been the orchestrator of Whirlwind's forthcoming success. And yet, she would not reap a penny from it. Nor he, he thought ruefully.

Butterhead whinnied high and loud from the shadows, followed by an insistent kicking of the gate. Whirlwind responded immediately, pulling away from Angel and threatening him with his hooves. He was determined to reach the mare. Angel pondered how there was no questioning that this stallion and this mare certainly liked each other. It had been love at first sight. *Like him and Gerta*, he thought.

He looked up at Whirlwind as an idea set root in his mind. The natural affinity of these two horses for each other increased the fertility and decreased the odds of aggression or injury. They had, as it were, chemistry. It seemed to him that nature was calling.

No, he told himself, pushing where this idea was heading out of his mind. He paced farther away from the paddock, feeling the stallion's resistance. Could Butterhead even conceive at fifteen years of age? He did the math in his head. If Butterhead did conceive, she would produce a foal in the spring. An excellent time. Fortuitous.

He heard the cry of his mare and stopped in indecision. He reached up to vigorously scratch his scalp. *Ayyyyy*, he groaned. What was he thinking? Did he dare do this? he wondered. If something should happen to Whirlwind, Charles would never forgive him.

But, he thought, stopping his scratching and standing still, what a gift it would be to give Gerta a foal from Whirlwind.

Angel looked up at the stallion. His nose was high in the air, doing the flehmen response. Oh, yes, he was ready. Eager. Across the field, he could hear the restless stomping and screaming of his mare. The sweet songs of love, he thought to himself.

It was wrong. Of course it was, he thought as he began leading Whirlwind back to the paddock. Once at the gate, he removed the tack from the anxious horse. The wind gusted, seeming to inflame the stallion all the more. He heard Butterhead before he saw her. Her golden form was pressed against the fence, waiting.

Angel stopped at the gate and looked up at Whirlwind. "Okay, my man," he told him. Then he pointed his finger. "But if you do anything to hurt my little girl, I'll come after you. *Comprende?*"

Whirlwind whinnied and stomped his foot impatiently.

Angel stood before the gate. He made a quick sign of the cross. Then he opened the gate and released Whirlwind into the paddock.

The stallion bolted and disappeared into the night. He listened to the sound of hooves running in the distant darkness.

Angel locked the gate securely and took a long, deep breath. He walked at a slow pace to the saddle and gathered the tack into a pile. When he was finished, he sat on the saddle, stretched out his legs, and pulled a pack of cigarettes from his pocket.

He smiled, thinking of what was likely happening in the paddock behind him. Then his smile widened as he thought of his impending visit to Gerta. He lit the cigarette, took a long drag, and exhaled. All in good time, he thought. All in good time.

Now, all he had to do was wait.

Moira stood in the screened porch of her mother's house, arms crossed tight around her chest, and listened to the storm. It was very late, sometime after midnight. The much-anticipated storm had arrived and it turned out to be more water than wind. The rain fell steadily, heavily, drenching the earth. She heard the thundering of raindrops on the roof and felt the moisture dampen her skin and hair. It felt cool and refreshing.

Standing here, outdoors but sheltered, she felt alive, part of something bigger than herself. The rain smelled sweet and she breathed deep. She couldn't see the trees but she could hear the deafening rattling of the wind surrounding them. Rather than frightening, she found the sound of the steady rain comforting. Everyone, all creatures great and small, were indoors and safe. For all the fears and anxiety of the past week, in the end, this storm would pass.

A noise from inside drew her attention. She turned her head to see Tut running across the living room. What was that dog doing outside his crate? Moira wondered. Then, sucking in her breath, she spotted Gigi. Annoyed, she uncrossed her arm and took a step forward to fetch her when she was distracted by headlights in the driveway. Peering out into the night she saw a car she didn't recognize pulling up in front of the house. *Who could that be?* she wondered and stepped close to the screen to squint in the faint front porch light.

The car stopped at the front door. She saw a man in a raincoat step out. He darted to the trunk and pulled out a suitcase, closed the lid, and tapped it in a signal. The brake lights went off as the car drove away, and in that flash of light Moira saw who it was.

"Thom!" she called out.

Her heart raced as fast as her feet as she tore through the living room to the front door. She swung open the door just as he was about to knock. His hand was frozen in mid-air. In the soft yellow porch light they stared at each other. His short, dark hair was slicked to his head, his broad chin was covered in stubble, and his brown eyes, though wide with wonder, revealed his fatigue. For a second they both stood frozen in surprise, then in a sweeping move he dropped the suitcase and stepped forward to wrap Moira in his arms in a possessive, fervent kiss.

Moira was swept away by emotions as raw and wild as the storm outdoors. She felt the rain on his coat soak her skin, cold and wet. His arms were so tight around her she couldn't breathe. And his lips, oh, his lips. They trembled as they devoured her whole.

"Thom, what are you doing here? Now?" she cried out when the kiss was finished and he moved his head back. He kept his hands on her shoulders and was staring at her with eyes filled with relief.

"I was mad with worry. I hopped on a plane to get here."

"You came," she said, capturing his words in her mind, a dawning of wonder. "But wait," she said when he stepped forward to kiss her again. "There's something I have to tell you. Something we have to talk about."

"Later. Right now I just want to hold you. My God, Moira," he said, pulling her closer. His brown eyes were as dark as the night. "I thought I might lose you."

She held his face in her hands, memorizing each detail. "No," she replied. "You won't lose me."

PART THREE

DEPARTURE

TWENTY

August 24, 9:00 a.m.
Freehold Farm, North Carolina
Tropical Storm Noelle headed out to sea

The sun was shining and the damp earth was a brilliant green. Puddles of varying sizes lined the driveway. Once again the birds sang in the trees, which seemed to stand straighter after the good watering. Grace looked up into the brilliant blue streaked with wispy white cirrus clouds and said a prayer of thanks. It couldn't be a more beautiful morning, she thought. The air was fresh and sweet-smelling, and it seemed there'd been no damage to the farm.

They'd heard on the news reports of flooding throughout the region, some of it sadly serious. There were calls for the state to be better prepared against heavy rains in the future. The mudslides, overflowing rivers and creeks, and the terrible dumping of animal waste into the water couldn't happen again. These were all very real problems that the state would have to address. But for this morning, Grace was thankful it wasn't worse.

Grace whistled for Bunny and Maybelle. The two dogs didn't respond. She cursed herself for trusting them and cupped her mouth and called their names. A vintage, buttercream-colored Mercedes came cruising up the driveway, and alongside it were the two dogs, barking like crazy. The car parked in the circular driveway before the house. The dogs ran around the Mercedes still barking and having the best time.

"Bad dogs," she called, clapping her hands as she ambled over to the car. The passenger door opened and out stepped Gerta, looking younger and more relaxed with her blond hair down around her blue linen shirt. Angel hurried around the hood from the driver's seat and kissed both Grace's cheeks.

"We all survived, eh?" he said in a grand manner. Then, frowning, he looked down at the two dogs jumping up on his legs. "¡Basta! Take it easy." He wore jeans and his usual polo shirt, this one white. "Little dogs," he muttered with disdain.

Angel went to open the back door and tried to lure a reluctant Max out of the car. Maybelle and Bunny wagged their tails, tongues hanging out in anticipation. As soon as Max had all paws on the ground, the three dogs took off running, Max dragging his leash.

"Oh God, there they go," said Gerta with despair.

"They'll come back." Angel put two fingers in his mouth and let go a piercing whistle. Max turned and came running back to his master.

"You have to teach me that whistle," said Grace. She bent and scurried after Maybelle, scooping her up. "Got you. Gerta, can you grab Bunny?"

Gerta, the accomplished horsewoman, looked helpless when it came to dogs. Angel handed her Max's leash. "Here, hold this. I'll get him." He was quick and athletic. In a few steps he had the terrier under his arm.

"Come in," said Grace. "Breakfast is buffet style, and the coffee is hot and ready."

They headed to the back door, past the fenced yard. Grace stopped to deliver the dogs into the confined area. Seeing them, Tut raced over to check them out.

"I heard you were up to no good last night," said Grace.

Angel's eyes flashed. "What did you say?"

Grace smirked. "The Boykin spaniel, Tut. He found Gigi last night and did the dirty deed."

Angel's laugh burst from him. "Oh, the dog! Really? Good dog," he exclaimed, smiling down at Tut.

"Don't say that to Moira. She is mighty pissed."

"There was something in the air last night," Angel sang as a tease.

Gerta slipped her arm into his. "Let's go," she said with a tug.

Once inside the house Charles and Thom rose from the chairs. They'd been sitting, deep in conversation. Moira shouted out a joyous greeting. In a playful mood, she grabbed a tray filled with mimosas and came to offer one each to Gerta and Angel.

"Come in," she exclaimed. "We are celebrating the end of the storm. Grab a seat. Everything is buffet. What kind of eggs do you want?"

The room smelled of bacon and coffee and hot biscuits. Moira was glowing as she waved Thom over to be introduced to Gerta and Angel. Grace watched, still not quite over the shock of seeing Thom appear in the kitchen this morning. One look at the two lovebirds and she knew all was well. Thank God, she thought, overjoyed.

The front door blew open and Elise rushed in, bright eyed and full of energy. She was chic in torn jeans and a ball cap at an angle over her short hair. Dark kohl lined her eyes, making them appear bigger and dramatic.

"Hi and good-bye, everyone. I'm heading out."

"Already?" cried Gerta in dismay.

"Gotta go," she said as she hurried to her mother's side. She gave Gerta a hug, closing her eyes. "I love you, Mutti," Elise said by her ear, using the affectionate German term. "I'll call you when I get there."

"Where?" Gerta asked, worry on her face.

"I don't know. Don't worry." Elise said in a lower tone, "Is it okay for Karl to drive me to Greenville in your car? I have to pick up my wheels." She turned to wave at Karl at the door. He lifted his hand in greeting. He stayed by the front door, clearly eager to go.

Moira shuffled closer and leaned in close to Elise. "What's this? You bought a car?"

"Yeah," Elise said, eyes sparkling. "I bought one online yesterday. So," she said, turning back to her mother. "Is it okay? He'll bring it right back."

Gerta looked like she was in a daze. "Sure, *ja*. Why not?"

Elise kissed her mother then turned to Moira. "Where's Birdie? In the back?"

Elise hugged and kissed everyone good-bye as Moira went out to the yard to help Elise collect her dog. The group gathered at the front porch to send Elise off. They called out their good-byes. Karl tapped the horn twice in farewell as Elise waved, and then they were gone.

As the others returned inside the house, Grace searched for Gerta and found her standing alone, watching the car disappear down the driveway. Her fingers were at her lips.

She came to her side. "She'll be fine, you know that, right?"

"I hope so. She's my baby."

"Let's go inside." They turned to go back into the house when another car motored up the driveway. Grace stopped to see an approaching black Range Rover, splattered with mud. It circled the driveway, parking in the spot the Mercedes had vacated. "Who on earth is that?"

The tinted window rolled down and she was stunned to see the face of Cara Rutledge.

"Well, hello!" she called out with surprise, arms up in the air as she walked to the car.

Cara stayed in the car. "I just had to stop and say hello and thank you for being my lifeline. We're heading back to David's house. We were driving right by."

Grace bent at the waist to peer into the window. Cara's hair was pulled back in a ponytail, and her face was pale and drawn. But who wouldn't be tired after what she just went through? The tall man driving the car leaned across the seat and offered Grace his hand.

"Hey, I'm David."

"My fiancé," Cara said.

"What?"

"We got engaged in the middle of the hurricane. How romantic, right?"

"Congratulations!" Grace exclaimed. "Come in. We've got champagne."

Cara shook her head. "Thanks, but I can't. I haven't seen my baby yet. I can't wait another minute. I just stopped by."

"Okay, but first I want you to meet Gerta Klug."

Gerta came to the window. "How nice to put a face with the story," Gerta said. "Grace told me all about your trip to Isle of Palms. I'm so glad you're all right. We were all so worried. Did you have much damage from the storm?"

"Some, but nothing we can't fix. It's part of living on a barrier island. And you?"

"We had some wind damage. And there was some bad flooding. But all the animals are safe. That's most important."

"Cara?" David said her name in that tone that implied it was time to go.

Grace stepped up to the window again. "Give that precious daughter of yours a kiss from me. And when you're settled, come for dinner. I've been cooking up a storm. No pun intended."

"I will." Cara smiled. "Thanks again."

As she drove away, Gerta turned to look at Grace and said, "You have such an eclectic group of friends."

Grace smiled. "Some people collect china or paintings. I collect interesting people." She changed the subject. "By the way, how serious is the damage to your farm?"

Gerta's face clouded. "Considerable."

"Oh, Gerta. I'm sorry."

"I didn't want to bring it up in front of Elise. She'd want to return home and help, but it's her turn to take care of herself. Besides, I have Angel. He's very resourceful."

"Please," Grace said with a laugh. "I doubt he knows which end of a hammer is up."

Gerta smirked. She let her gaze travel across the property. When it returned to Grace, she appeared thoughtful. "You know, I've become quite partial to this area. And the people. I might look at property while I'm here."

Grace linked her arm through Gerta's and gave it a squeeze. "I'd love that. In fact, I know the perfect place. . . ."

Once inside, they joined the others in the dining room. They were standing around the buffet and adding food to their plates. The conversation flowed easily, everyone sharing news they'd heard about the aftereffects of the hurricane. Grace was putting a bit of biscuit in her mouth when she looked over to the front door to see Hannah stepping in. She paused in the entry, looking insecure about coming farther in. Grace set her plate on the table and hurried to the foyer to greet her.

"There you are! I would've been very hurt if you'd slipped away without a good-bye."

"I'd never do that to you."

The two friends hugged, longer than just a hello.

"You okay?" asked Grace.

"Yeah," Hannah said, and she sounded like she meant it.

She looked beautiful, as usual, with her long hair flowing like rivers cascading down her shoulders and back. She wore a soft pink blouse that complemented her skin tone, and Grace could see she had taken extra care with her makeup and appearance. Her heart softened when she caught Hannah's gaze float across the room, then settle on Angel and Gerta, together in the dining room.

"I just stopped to say good-bye and give you your key."

"Nonsense. Have some coffee and breakfast. We're all saying our good-byes."

"No. Really. It's too awkward."

"No one feels that way. In fact, we'll all feel worse if you don't come in. Please, you're my dearest friend. We love you."

The decision was made when Angel strode up to Hannah, arms out to embrace her.

Hannah stepped back, hands up. "Forgive me if we skip the hug."

"I am so glad to see you. You look beautiful. As always, eh?"

Hannah returned a cold stare.

Angel could not be dissuaded. "Come in, let me get you coffee. Or maybe a mimosa?" he asked as he put his arm around her and guided her into the dining room.

Gerta rose to her feet when she spotted Hannah approaching. She put a smile on her face, but it was easy to see her eyes shone a bit too bright.

The room quieted as everyone pretended not to be watching the interaction between the two women.

Gerta began. "Hannah, I'm glad to see you." Her drink was in her hand, sparing her from having to extend it.

Hannah pinched her lips and forced a hard smile.

Gerta persevered. "Are you leaving today?"

"Yes. I just came to say good-bye . . . to Grace and Charles."

The dig was intentional and Grace cringed hearing it.

Gerta's face remained impassive. "Will you be returning to Florida?"

"Not right away."

Grace jumped in. "I hope your condo wasn't damaged."

"I don't know yet. First I'm going to New York for business. I have several meetings scheduled. There's interest in my new line."

"That's great news," said Angel.

Hannah ignored him.

"Congratulations," said Grace.

"We'll see," Hannah said with a quick, fatalistic smile, but her eyes danced with hope.

"Is that your new line of makeup you're wearing now?" Gerta asked.

Hannah's voice cooled again. "Yes."

"It's very pretty. Makes your skin appear so creamy. This is a good thing as we age."

"Some women know how to wear it."

"I liked the lipstick you gave me very much." Gerta pointed to her coral-colored lips. "It has lip balm in it, right? Brilliant. Perhaps you can send me some information? I might be interested if you are still looking for investors."

Hannah frowned slightly. "You don't need to do that. I'm good with you and Angel. He's all yours. I have a strict no-return policy."

"I never mix business with personal," Gerta said in a faintly haughty tone that, in this instance, came across as reassuring. "I think you're a good investment." She paused. "As for the other . . . I'm sorry, Hannah. I never meant for this to happen."

Hannah looked pained but said nothing.

Angel slipped an arm around Gerta's waist. "It is my fault. I am the one who is sorry."

Hannah snorted, "You got that right."

Grace came forward with a flute of mimosa for Hannah. "For you. Come in and grab a plate. You don't want breakfast to get cold."

Charles came behind Grace and slipped his arms around her waist and kissed her neck. Grace smiled as she leaned back into him.

Thom had his arm around Moira, and, seeing her parents, he gave her a nudge to notice. She smiled and kissed his cheek.

Hannah looked around at the three couples and said, "I have a feeling that everyone here is getting laid but me."

This broke the ice and everyone laughed as Charles herded them toward the dining table, where copious amounts of food waited.

Moira turned up the music and the sound of Motown filled the air. Feet shuffled and hips swayed as people put food on their plates.

"So when are y'all leaving?" Grace asked. "What are your plans?"

Hannah raised her voice over the music and said, "In the words of *The Big Chill*, we aren't leaving. We're never leaving."

Grace and Charles looked at each other with wide eyes, then burst out laughing.

"Did I tell you we get ice storms?" Grace said. "We're going to evacuate to your house!"

ACKNOWLEDGMENTS

The equestrian world is unique, complex, generous, and exciting. I am eternally grateful to so many involved in event hunting, show jumping, dressage, horseback riding, and horse care. I am now a devoted fan of equestrian sports and hope my novel offers a peek into the heart and soul of the amazing, noble horses and the people who are devoted to them.

Much like the hurricane adventure my characters go through in *The Summer Guests*, I endured a whirlwind of experiences as I wrote this novel and have come through with a collection of new, very dear friends I'll treasure for life. First, heartfelt love and endless thanks to Cindy and John Boyle and Mary Steele for embracing the original concept of the book, brainstorming with me, checking on my progress, taking me to events, reading pages, and guiding me to the right people over the past several years as I progressed on my steep learning curve. Finally, I'll always be indebted to the Boyles for hosting me (and my myriad of pets) not only for the original hurricane evacuation when the book was born, but for all the visits to North Carolina when I did research. I felt embraced by your family. Truly, I could not have written this book without you.

I am also beyond grateful to Katherine Kaneb Bellissimo for the brilliant foreword of the book, which sets the tone and brings to readers' mind the spirit of the novel. Thank you, too, for generously hosting me at the 2018 World Equestrian Games at the Tryon International Equestrian Center, and also at the Palm Beach International Equestrian Center. Thank you for reading my pages, encouraging me, and catching errors I would have missed. Most of all, thank you for your friendship.

Love and thanks to Leslie Munsell and Beauty For Real Makeup for generously sharing with me your ideas and the makeovers that made me feel beautiful inside and out. Thank you to Katie Jackson for your inspiration and guidance in creating the character of Gerta and understanding the issues facing one who wears a prosthesis. Meeting you and discovering your strength and courage truly defined this character. Much love and thanks to Kate Pittman for your wisdom, support, and an education on understanding the depths of connection with animals.

The efforts of those who rescue horses in the United States are heartfelt and impressive. My sincere thanks to all of you who fight to protect these beautiful animals, especially Heather Freeman, who let me help on her farm. And Sara Lyter who opens her heart and farm to rescue mini horses. Awe and thanks to Julio Mendoza, the brilliant dressage rider and teacher for allowing me to sit in on dressage classes and listen to the master.

Heartfelt hugs and thanks to the North Carolina women who became characters in the novel and who welcomed and supported me, and more, offered me friendship: Caroline McKissick Young,

Cornelia Alexander, Rebecca Hedges, Kim and Ting Oliver. And to
Lillian Stransky and her family.

I am honored to be an ambassador of Brooke USA, a worthy charity that strives to reduce the immediate suffering of the
world's most vulnerable working horses, donkeys, and mules and
to make sustainable improvements for the animals and the people
they serve. Thank you, Emily Marquez-Dulin, Kendall Bierer, and
Amanda Miller for supporting me and my books.

I am also delighted to be a new citizen of Tryon and thank the
welcoming community, the Tryon International Equestrian Center,
the Foothills Equestrian Nature Center (FENCE) for your continued support. Also to the Lanier Library. Much love and thanks to
Linda Tinkler, my realtor, and her husband Chris, friends and advisors on all things Tryon. Sincere thanks also to John Cash at Nature's Storehouse and to Julia Calhoun of Tryon Toymakers.

Danny and Ron's Rescue is a wonderfully unique dog rescue
in Florida and South Carolina. I appreciate their tireless efforts and
great hearts. Many of the dogs—and the cat—in the book were, in
fact, rescues. I thank the owners of all the animals mentioned for
generously donating to charity to see the names of their beloved
pets in print. I hope you enjoyed seeing your darlings in my novel.
They're all truly characters!

The writing of every book is a dedicated collaboration of the
editorial team and the author. In this I've been blessed. This book,
in particular, is about connection and it's hard to fully acknowledge the one I share with my editor, Lauren McKenna. We've been
through many book journeys together. Being a Floridian, Lauren
understood the chaos and heartache of hurricanes! And of course,
I appreciate the sparkling, creative, hours-long phone calls as we

discussed the story. Love you! I'm grateful to my publisher, Jennifer Bergstrom, my champion at Gallery Books, for believing in this story from the beginning and for supporting me and all my books with such heart. I am so fortunate to have a fabulous team at Gallery/Simon & Schuster, and I owe all of you my heartfelt thanks, especially Michelle Podberezniak, Jennifer Long, Jennifer Robinson, Abby Zidle and Maggie Loughran, Alexandre Su, Anabel Jimenez, Mackenzie Hickey, and Tara Schlesinger, and to Lisa Litwack and the art department for another fabulous cover. Finally, a special note of gratitude to Joal Hetherington for the excellent and perspicacious copyediting.

I'm so fortunate to have Faye Bender of The Book Group by my side, especially in the past intense year of work. Thank you for your quiet, firm presence, constant support, and the encouraging words when I most need them.

My home team makes my career a joy. I am humbled by your dedication and support. Thank you, Angela May, for holding me up with joy, wisdom, business savvy (and food), in so many ways every day. I appreciate more than I can say the dedication, hard work, ingenuity, and friendship of Kathie Bennett, also one of the Tryon evacuees. And my love and thanks to the whole team at Magic Time Literary Publicity: Roy Bennett and Susan Zurenda. A big thank-you to Meg Walker at Tandem Literary for your creativity and continued support.

I am the luckiest of women to have friends that care about me, my work, and our collective creative spirit. A special thank you to Patti Callahan Henry and Mary Kay Andrews for our work retreats where we truly work! Your suggestions are invaluable. And Patti, thanks for the blurb and the title of the book! Thank you to my tribe—you know I love you: Signe Pike, Cassandra King, Marjory Wentworth, Patti Morrison, Dorothea Benton Frank, Ellie Davis, Lindy Carter, Nicole Seitz, Nathalie Dupree, Linda Plunkett, Leah Greenberg, Pat Denkler. And my pals on the Turtle Team: Barbara Bergwerf, photographer extraordinaire, and Mary Pringle, Tee Johannes, Barb Gobien, Bev Ballow, Cindy Moore, Christal Cothran, Jo Durham, and my cuz, Christiana Harsch, and all at the incomparable Long Island Cafe, my favorite hangout.

One of the joys of book tours is being able to meet the booksellers. I am grateful to all for your welcome, for hosting events and hand selling my novels. A special note of thanks to my local bookstores. Over the years, we've become friends and I'm so grateful for your generous support: Buxton Books, Blue Bicycle Books, Indigo Books, Edisto Books, and Barnes & Noble, Mt. Pleasant. Thanks also to Buzzy Porter, Jackie K. Cooper for all you do. Love you.

Sincere love and thanks to my beloved ARTists. You are always there for me and I feel so fortunate to have your support, comments, and unfailing encouragement. You brighten my days!

Very special love and thanks to Marguerite Martino for her wisdom and the many hours of conversation over coffee and wine at Windover as we dug deep to create complex characters as well as the novel's themes. Heartfelt thanks to Jim and Kris Cryns for reading my pages and for your edits that brought honesty and humor to the story. And a nod to Gretta Kruesi, who on the day I was evacuating to North Carolina for a hurricane, brainstormed with me a book about evacuation and the influential women who were "forces of nature." What a thrill that it actually became a book.

I close with those who come first in my heart. Markus, you know you are the wind beneath my wings. Thank you for taking care of me, especially when I push hard under deadline, for listening to my ideas, even in the middle of the night, and for loving me. Finally, in this novel my characters discover what they treasure most in life. This I already know—my family. Love always to Claire, John, Jack, Teddy, Delancey; Gretta, Patrick, Henry; Zachary, Caitlin, Wesley, Penelope.

the
Summer
Guests

Mary Alice
Monroe

DISCUSSION QUESTIONS

1. Each chapter opens with a location, a time stamp, and a weather update. What effect does this information have on the tone of the book, and the mood going into the chapters? Why do you think the author chose to communicate this information this way?

2. Early on, we learn that Hannah has been through a divorce. She says that "marriage to an older man was confining." (p. 24) The Hannah we know now is vivacious and independent; how do you think her marriage and its end impacted her dating habits, and her drive to pursue her dreams? What do you think she meant by "confining?"

3. When Cara is planning to leave the mountains and return to her home in Isle of Palms, she recalls her mother's advice: "a wise woman never turn[s] her back on the ocean." (p. 43)

What does this advice mean to you? Do you think Cara has turned her back on the ocean?

4. Gerta and Grace share the kind of lifelong friendship many women aspire to, but few have. Their meeting at boarding school got off to a rocky start, but they eventually developed a mutual respect: "they compared grades, medals, points at competitions. Nonetheless, they were also each other's top cheerleaders." (p. 78) How do you think this shaky beginning shaped their friendship in the long run? What do you think has made their friendship work after so many years?

5. Charles's weakened health is a major point of conflict between him and Grace. During a heated confrontation about it, Grace tells Charles, "I held your hand when you weren't sure you'd ever get out of that wheelchair. Did you think all that only happened to you? It happened to me too!" (p. 120) At the same time, Charles bristles at Grace's attempts to let her fear control his life. How did you feel reading this exchange between them? Who do you think makes the stronger case for buying or not buying a jumping horse, and why? How much say should a person's loved ones have when it comes to decisions about his or her well-being?

6. Supernatural forces play an important role in the book. Moira has a strong spiritual connection with both her family's land and with the animals she encounters; when she visits the

sacred hilltop on her parents' property, she thinks back to the Native American women who once lived there and "she felt their spirits . . . They spoke to her clearly." (p. 201) Even Gerta comes to believe in reincarnation when she meets a horse with whom she has an instant connection. What was your initial reaction upon reading about Moira's gift? Did you believe that Gerta's new horse could be Razzmajazz reincarnated? Do you think it's possible to experience this kind of spiritual connection in real life? Discuss why or why not.

7. Both Charles and Gerta suffer from life-changing injuries before the book begins. Charles's serious fall confines him to his bed for months, and Gerta's amputation ends her Olympic dreams. How do these characters respond to their injuries differently? How is Grace's attitude toward these two accidents different?

8. Several of the characters grapple for control—Elise struggles to command Whirlwind, and Gerta struggles to rein in her headstrong daughter—all while an out-of-control weather system upends their plans. How do the characters approach the things they think they can control, like horses and each other, and how do they approach things they know they have no control over, like the weather? Which tactics seem more effective?

9. Throughout the book, Moira struggles to decide what direction to take in her marriage. Her story begins with her resolute

decision to leave her husband Thom; mid-book, she tearfully confides in Elise that she feels lonely and unloved—"Weeks go by without anything but texts. Not a single conversation. It's hard to feel love in that scenario." (p. 129) Finally, Thom shows up at Freehold Farm to reunite with Moira, who is now determined to make things work. Were you surprised when Moira chose to stay with Thom? What aspects of their relationship did you think worked well, and which aspects needed an overhaul?

10. Sexual tensions run high in the book. Characters make up, break up, couple up, and come out. When the characters first come together at Grace's home, Angel's mare is in heat, and so is Moira's dog; stallions are restless with desire, and dogs are constantly howling out in the yard. How does this heightened state among the animals mirror the characters' relationship woes and triumphs? Did it surprise you that the author chose to include these details about the animals?

11. Several of the women in this story reinvent themselves after a major life change. Hannah launches her makeup company after her career as a model ends, Gerta finds success in her breeding program after her divorce, and the end of the book finds Moira and Elise making significant career changes too. How is the theme of resilience and starting over on display here and throughout the larger arcs of the book? How does

the threat of destruction from a hurricane—the preparation for that damage, and the anticipation of rebuilding once it has passed—parallel the kind of rebuilding the characters have done in other areas of their lives?

12. Grace refers to this hurricane retreat as a "fishbowl" and Gerta tells her "I feel like my world is spinning around me. Everything is happening so quickly. What I thought was grounded is suddenly up in the air." (p. 293) Grace responds that the "past is pushing into [the] present" and each of the characters is undergoing something of a "personal hurricane." What does Grace mean by this? What is it about extenuating circumstances that brings underlying feelings to the surface, both in the book and in life? How do past and present clash in *The Summer Guests*?

13. Cara and David's journey to the Isle of Palms takes place outside of the "fishbowl" at Grace's house, underlining how isolated the two really are. Why do you think the author chose to keep Cara's story line largely separated from the other characters'? How did you feel reading Cara's chapters, not knowing what was happening at Grace and Charles's house?

14. The relationships between the characters and their animals is central to the story. Humans and animals bond, compete for attention, and find new homes—Angel fawns over his dog Max, while Max butts heads with Hannah; Elise strug-

gles to command Whirlwind, while Whirlwind's bond with Karl grows stronger; Gerta finds a cosmic connection with a rescue horse; Hannah brings Nacho the Chihuahua into her home and her heart. How do the animals' big personalities play out on the page? How do their bonds and conflicts with the human characters impact the story's plot?

15. After many conversations where Grace encourages Gerta to let Elise be independent, Gerta finally tells Grace to take her own advice and to let Charles make his own decisions about riding. Did this moment surprise you? How did this conversation change the relationship between the characters? Did you agree with Gerta's advice? Why or why not?

16. *The Summer Guests* has a large cast of characters, and alternates between multiple points of view. Who did you view as the main character? What was it about that person's arc that made you view it as the central plot line of the story?

ENHANCE
YOUR BOOK CLUB

1. Bring your pet to your next book club meeting. *The Summer Guests* explores the strong bond between humans and their animals, particularly dogs and horses. Meet at a dog park to discuss the book, or follow up your book club meeting with a volunteer trip to a local animal shelter.

2. Dive in to your own beach house memories. Bring a few family vacation photos or videos to your next book club meeting. Discuss your favorite beachy vacations, and your memories of beach houses (or any vacation houses!) you have loved over the years.

3. Host a dinner party or luncheon. Grace is host extraordinaire during Hurricane Noelle. From flower arrangements to wine pairings to comfort food, Grace leaves no stone unturned

when it comes to making her guests feel at ease. Sit around a lovingly set table and discuss the book over a home-cooked meal and your favorite wine.

4. Get back in the saddle. Find a local horseback riding stable near you, and spend an afternoon on the trails. Enjoy the fresh air, the gentle sway of your horse's gait, and the feeling of reins in your hand. Think about the importance of the bond between horses and humans in the book, and be open to observing the unique personality traits of the horse you are riding.

5. Read more from Mary Alice Monroe. *The Summer Guests* can be read on its own, but explore the rest of the Beach House series to learn more about Cara Rutledge and her emotional connection to her home on Isle of Palms. To find more books by Mary Alice Monroe, visit MaryAliceMonroe.com.

Keep reading for a sneak peek of
the next book in Mary Alice Monroe's
New York Times Bestselling
Beach House Series

Summer of
Lost and
Found

Available now from Gallery Books!

chapter one

Beware the Ides of March.
William Shakespeare, *Julius Caesar*

March 2020

HOW COULD THIS happen to her? Again?

Linnea Rutledge drove her vintage gold VW bug across the vast expanse of marshlands on the arching roadway known as the Connector. It was the main route from the mainland to the small island she called home. Below, the tide was low, revealing marsh grass that was just beginning to green at the bottom—one of the lowcountry's first signs of spring. When Linnea reached the apex of the roadway, she caught her first glimpse of the Atlantic Ocean. Today she didn't feel her usual euphoria. Rather, she felt numb.

She crossed onto Isle of Palms and drove the short distance seaward to Ocean Boulevard. Less than a mile more until she reached the quaint house she called home. Primrose Cottage was one of the few remaining 1930s houses on the island. It sat now dwarfed by the luxury mansions that dominated the boulevard.

Pulling into the gravel driveway, hearing the crunch of stone under tires, Linnea climbed from her car and walked swiftly to the front door, struggling with tumultuous thoughts of the injustices of fate. She didn't take in the first signs of wildflowers dotting the dunes or stop to enjoy the heady scent of honeysuckle along the fence. Linnea climbed the stairs with savage purpose, seeking safety. She pushed open the door, then closed it behind her and leaned against it, as one holding back a storm.

Closing her eyes, she panted, mouth open. She'd held herself to-gether by sheer force of will while she gathered her personal photo-graphs and belongings and carried them out in a cardboard box from her cubicle office at the South Carolina Aquarium. Her face muscles ached from hoisting a smile and bidding teary farewells to her fellows. It was a mass exodus of nonessential personnel. The aquarium was closing its doors to the public because of the pandemic.

She collected her breath and opened her eyes. Looking around the dimly lit house, Linnea felt the quiet familiarity embrace her. This was her aunt Cara's beach house, left to Cara by her mother, Linnea's beloved grandmother, Lovie. Linnea had grown up visiting here, be-coming part of the group of women who loved the beach, sea turtles, and each other with an abiding devotion. This little beach house had been their sanctuary from whatever buffeted them outside the clap-board walls.

It was her house now, albeit by rental from Aunt Cara. She let her eyes glide across the creamy-white and ocean-blue walls of the small rooms, along the fireplace mantel where sat silver-framed photo-graphs of the Rutledge family that went back generations in Charles-ton, across the shabby-chic white slipcovered furniture.

Linnea feared she wouldn't be able to stay here any longer. She dug through her purse and pulled her phone to her ear. Within mo-ments, the familiar voice of Cara answered.

"Hello, Sweet-tea. You're home early today."

Linnea loved the nickname her aunt had called her since she was little. "I, uh . . . was let off early. Can you come over? I have to talk to you."

A pause. Then in a more cautious tone, "Of course. I have to get Hope gathered. She has a doctor's appointment. I'll be there in ten."

Linnea tucked her phone away and strode directly to her bed-room. Sunlight poured in across the pine floors and oriental rugs. Her gaze swept the view of the ocean beyond; seeing it, she felt an immediate connection. Bolstered, she unzipped her pencil skirt and laid it on the mahogany four-poster bed that dominated the small bedroom. A simple skirt and crisp blouse constituted her uniform at the South Carolina Aquarium where she worked as the conservation education director. It was a style adopted from Cara.

Linnea had been Cara's assistant at the aquarium. After Cara resigned, the position as education director was offered to her. It was her dream job. Linnea loved teaching and inspiring others, as she had been taught and inspired by the women in her life. Though Linnea emulated Cara's sleek dress at work, at home she changed into her favored vintage look.

She went to the bathroom and, with efficient movements, washed the makeup from her face, then unpinned her blond hair, letting it fall to her shoulders. Scratching her head vigorously, she tried to shake off the tension that had held her taut since the news. Feeling a bit better, she put on cuffed jeans and a worn pink sweater, finally stepping into blush Capezio ballet slippers, a favorite since she'd taken ballet lessons as a girl.

Feeling more comfortable, she went out onto the porch from her bedroom and took in the view of sea and sky. The power of the vista had a calming effect. Then, hearing the crunch of tires on the driveway, Linnea hurried down the deck stairs and rounded the house to the driveway to see Cara's car parked there.

"Thank you for coming!" Linnea called out.

Cara's long legs, encased in black jeans, slid out from the car. She offered a quick wave. "I can only stay a moment. I was on my way out for Hope's physical."

Linnea waited while Cara removed her precocious six-year-old from her car seat. Hope's dark hair was tied in two braids and she wore a blue-gingham smocked dress.

"You look like Dorothy in *The Wizard of Oz*," Linnea said, placing a kiss on Hope's cheek.

"Who's that?" asked Hope.

Linnea looked at Cara with mock indignity. "She doesn't know *The Wizard of Oz*?"

Cara lifted her shoulders. "She's only six. Those evil trees and monkeys . . . I think Baum had older children in mind."

"Oh, please. Let me read it to her. It's a classic." Linnea lowered to meet Hope's eyes. "You're not afraid of witches or scary trees, are you?"

Hope's eyes were round, but she shook her head. "No," she said with a hint of doubt.

Cara laughed. "If she wakes up in the middle of the night, it's on you."

"Oh, she won't," Linnea said, then turned to Hope. "It has a happy ending. Let's read it." Then looking back at Cara, she added, "Even if the Wicked Witch of the West tells me not to."

"Who's that?" asked Hope.

"Later," Linnea answered with a wink. Straightening, she asked Cara, "Want to go to the deck? I have wine? Coffee? Water?"

"Nothing. Thanks. I have to leave in a few minutes." As they began walking to the oceanside deck, Cara's dark eyes focused on Linnea. "So, tell me, what's up?"

Linnea gestured to the patio chairs under the pergola. They sat while Hope hurried through the porch doors into the house to the toy bin that was filled with Hope's playthings. Linnea pulled her hair back into her hands, then let it go with an exhale.

"The aquarium is closed until further notice. I'm furloughed."

Cara's face reflected her shock. "My God. But of course they had to. The coronavirus is shutting down everything. They can't allow people to gather. Still, it's a shock." Always practical, she asked, "How are you fixed financially?"

Linnea shook her head. "You know what my salary is. I'm in trouble."

"Savings?"

"None to speak of. Even with you helping with rent, I'm not sure how long I can keep afloat."

Cara waved her hand. "Forget the rent for now."

Linnea was awash with relief. "Seriously? Are you sure?"

"Don't be silly. These are hard times." She put her hands on Linnea's shoulders. "Back when I was in financial"—she lifted her shoulders and her lips in an ironic smile—"and emotional trouble, my mother welcomed me into this little house, knowing I'd find my way. And I did. And now, it is my turn to offer the same to you. This is what we Rutledge women do. We take care of each other. And other women as well. It's a tough world out there for women, as you've just experienced." She let her hands drop. "So, darling girl, no thanks necessary. This is your legacy. And the purpose of this dear house. With so many blessings, we pay it forward."

Linnea felt the responsibility of her aunt's mandate profoundly. This was a passing of the torch. There were no words, so she remained silent.

Cara said, "Frankly, I'm more worried about the aquarium. How long will they be able to survive with their doors closed? They still have all those animals to feed and house."

"They've kept on a skeleton crew. I know it was a hard decision for Kevin to furlough us."

"He had no choice. Bosses have to make the tough decisions and do what's best for the institution." She sighed then shook her head and said wryly, "Beware the Ides of March."

Linnea looked at her aunt sitting across from her. Always cool and practical, she had a long history in management. She'd left Chicago almost two decades ago to settle in the lowcountry, but even on the island, she maintained her city chic. In jeans and a crisp chambray shirt, she looked elegant. Her hair was cropped short again and framed her face in a style that flattered her cheekbones and dark eyes.

Cara had the dark Rutledge looks of her father, Stratton. Linnea, like her father—Cara's older brother, Palmer—had the softer, petite, blond genes from Grandmother Lovie. As always, Linnea was taken by the way her aunt casually waved her hand in the air as she spoke or raised her fingers to tuck a wayward lock of hair behind her ear. Linnea studied the subtle and refined gestures, wanting to emulate this woman she admired. Cara was not merely elegant or in possession of a razor-sharp intellect, she was generous. Family came first with her. Cara might look like her father, but in this, she was most like her mother, Lovie.

Cara glanced at her watch. "I really must go," she said, rising. "Don't worry, Sweet-tea. Keep the faith. We always pull through somehow, don't we?" She looked over toward the house. "Hope! Time to go, honey."

From inside they heard a wail: "I don't wanna go to the doctor."

Cara met Linnea's eye, smirked, and went to fetch her daughter. Linnea heard a brief complaint before Cara walked out of the house with her daughter's hand firmly in hers.

"Come for dinner Sunday?" Cara asked Linnea as they walked together down the gravel driveway to Cara's car. "I'm hoping David will be home."

"I thought he was back."

Cara's lips tightened as she shook her head. "Not yet. The coronavirus is hitting London hard and he's been trying to get out for days. Flights are packed and there's talk of shutting down the airports."

Linnea heard the worry in her voice. "If anyone can get home, David will." She smiled. "He's like a homing pigeon."

Cara met her eyes with a grateful smile. "He's pretty resourceful." Then she said in a more upbeat tone, "Shrimp and grits sound good?"

"I'll be—" Linnea broke off. Catching a movement from the second-floor window of the carriage house next door, she stopped short, gripping Cara's arm.

"What?"

"There's someone in the carriage house," Linnea said sotto voce.

Cara looked up to the window and broke into a wide grin as she waved. "That's John."

Linnea felt her throat grow dry. "John Peterson?"

Cara laughed and looked at her with amusement. "Of course, John Peterson."

Myriad emotions flooded Linnea. This shock threatened to break the dam of her emotions, already brimming over with worry over being laid off.

"What's *he* doing here?" she demanded, her cry sounding petulant to her own ears.

"He had a conference in the area and stopped to visit his mother. Emmi, of course, was over the moon. She dotes on that boy. While he was here, he got word one of his colleagues in San Francisco tested positive for coronavirus. So, rather than take a chance of infecting others, he put himself into quarantine in his old apartment. He's worried not only about his mother, but about Flo. In her eighties, she's vulnerable. I admire him for that decision."

Linnea's brain was stuck on the fact that John was back. Living next door. She hadn't seen him since their breakup a year earlier. She'd thought he was the love of her life. And then he wasn't.

"Why didn't Emmi tell me he was back?" she asked.

Cara's brows rose. "Why would she? You've made no secret of the fact that you don't want anything to do with John. He is her son. That put her in a tough position."

Linnea crossed her arms. "She could have at least given me fair warning." Her gaze shot up to Cara along with her temper. "Wait. *You* knew. Why didn't you tell me?"

She felt the tension flare and saw the spark of indignation in Cara's eyes, the slight lifting of the chin.

Cara waited to speak, considering her words. "I suppose I could have told you. And might have if I wasn't so preoccupied." She paused. "Excuse me if I'm worried about my husband. The fact is, I just didn't give John's being here much thought."

Linnea swallowed, awash with shame for her show of pique. "I'm sorry. I shouldn't have jumped at you like that. I'm all off-balance, thinking only of myself." She reached out to place a hand on Cara's arm encircling her daughter. "Is there anything I can do for you? Watch Hope for a while? Make you a casserole?"

Cara's shoulders lowered and she quickly shook her head. "Please, no casseroles!" She smiled. "You know what I really need?"

Linnea shook her head.

"A nanny."

Linnea's heart sank. "Oh?"

"I have to get the house ready for David's arrival and Hope is cranky. She hasn't been able to play with anyone since they've closed the school. Not even her cousin Rory. Heather is under lockdown with him and Leslie." She sighed dramatically. "Hope is clinging to me. Honestly, I could use a break to get something done. I'll pay you, of course. And"—she raised a brow—"don't you need a job?"

"I do. And of course I'll be your nanny."

Cara looked skyward. "Thank heaven. I'll take her to the doctor's for her checkup, then could you watch her for a few hours? I want to spread plastic in the hallway, spray things down, get everything ready."

"Just drop her off."

"Thanks. Better go." Cara looked meaningfully at the carriage house window. "Be nice," she said cajolingly, then leaned forward to kiss her.

"How long is John going to be here? Gordon is coming from England in April. I don't think I can bear the battle of the beaux."

Cara raised a brow. "I didn't think John was still in the beau category."

"He's not," Linnea said firmly. "At least not in my mind. But I haven't seen Gordon since he returned to England, what . . ." Linnea did a quick count on her fingers. "Over six months ago. That's a long time to be apart. I don't want my ex hanging around when he finally gets here."

"You and Gordon are still together, right?"

Linnea nodded.

"Then it's only a problem if you still care about John."

Linnea felt a prick of uneasiness. "Right."

Cara looked at her watch. "Really must go. Thanks so much for being Hope's nanny. It's only temporary."

"I'm her aunt. 'Nuff said."

Cara smiled and climbed into the car.

Linnea waved, then stepped back from the Range Rover as it backed out of the driveway. Then, because she couldn't stop herself, she glanced up at the large arched window of the carriage house. In the light of midday, she saw John clearly. His dark auburn hair caught the light but his face was shadowed. In her mind's eye, she could see him smiling his crooked smile.

John lifted his hand in a wave.

Linnea reluctantly raised her hand and gave a halfhearted wiggle of her fingers. Then she turned heel, rolling her eyes, and walked resolutely to the rear deck. Once out of his sight she grabbed her phone and texted her friend Annabelle. She was on the staff of the sea turtle hospital and was also a victim of this morning's layoffs at the aquarium.

Can you come over? Must commiserate. I have wine.

She went indoors to pull out two wineglasses. As she set them on the counter, her phone pinged with a return text.

On my way.

LINNEA SETTLED BACK into the wicker chair, tucked her feet up, and crossed her arms. The large wood deck extended seaward from the house over the wild dunes of the Rutledge property. Most of the yards on Ocean Boulevard had been manicured with grass and plantings to resemble mainland lawns. Her grandmother had adamantly refused to alter the natural landscape so their property was a riotous collection of wild grasses, plants, and flowers. Across the road, a large lot was held in conservation, allowing the sand dunes to roll on unimpeded to the beach. It was a rare view on the developed island.

Looking at the sea, Linnea realized how grateful she was for the friends in her life. She remembered what her Grandmother Lovie had told her: *In life you'll have many acquaintances. But consider yourself lucky to have one or two true friends.*

Linnea had always been popular in school. She'd had a dozen girls she'd called friends. But none of them had gone in the same direction she had after graduation. Some were married with children; some had moved elsewhere. Linnea had been part of the latter group. When she'd returned home from California last year, she found she had less in common with her old friends. It had been hard to realize how friendships shifted over the years. She'd made new friends—Pandora James and Annabelle Chalmers. No two women could be more different. They were like oil and water and didn't get along. Still, a tenuous, new friendship had developed.

Pandora was high style, gorgeous, fun, and flamboyant. She was in graduate school for engineering in England and, Covid permitting, planned to fly back to her grandmother's beach house on Sullivan's Island for the summer.

Annabelle was a local girl. She and Linnea had attended the same private high school in Charleston but had never been friends. Linnea was part of the South of Broad elite society of old Charleston. She and her friends had hung in the same circles since the nursery and seemed destined to continue throughout their lifetimes. In contrast, Anna was a scholarship student who lived with her mother in a poorer part of the city. She'd never blended in with the popular group at Porter-Gaud. Though she and Linnea had had a rocky start last summer, over the past year working together at the aquarium they'd experienced a tidal shift in their relationship. Annabelle's habitual resentment of Linnea's privilege had ebbed, and in turn, Linnea's ability to open up, as a true friend must do, began to flow.

Linnea heard the crunch of Annabelle's car pulling up in the driveway. She got up to go greet her but hesitated at the edge of the deck. She sighed with annoyance. She didn't want to get tangled up with John again. Once burned/twice shy and all that. Instead of walking out on the driveway where John could see her from his window, Linnea crossed her arms as she waited for her friend to arrive. *This could make for an annoying few weeks,* she thought. When was John to hightail it back to his beloved California?

"Just go," she muttered. Then lifted her frown to a smile as Annabelle's face appeared from around the corner.

"I come bearing wine!" Annabelle called out as she climbed the deck stairs, a bottle of red in one hand, a bottle of white in the other. Her long red hair hung straight past her shoulders and large gold loop earrings. She was dressed, as usual, in jeans and a black T-shirt that read Save the Seabirds.

"Bless your heart!" Linnea called back, grinning. They walked together into the house in search of wineglasses and a corkscrew.

"Red or white?" Annabelle asked, corkscrew in hand.

"Today we're going to need both."

Annabelle chuckled in her low-throated fashion. "I hear you."

Linnea watched with awe as Annabelle twisted off the capsule around the neck of the bottle. She made it look so easy.

"How do you do that?" Linnea asked. "I'm pitiful trying to scrape that wrapper off."

"Comes with practice," Annabelle replied smugly. "Perks of being a bartender. Interesting fact: the original capsule was wax. Each bottle had to be dipped in wax to seal the end to prevent mold growth. The next innovation was lead. No surprise, that didn't work out, for obvious reasons, but it took them till the 1980s to switch to these polylam ones."

"So, if you collect old wines . . ." she said, thinking of her father.

"Yep. They still have those lead capsules."

"That explains a lot," Linnea said with a laugh. She gratefully took the offered glass of white wine. "I'm sorry, but I'm going to be tacky and add ice cubes. I can't drink warm chardonnay."

Annabelle shuddered. "I'll put this bottle in the fridge—and pour myself a Malbec." She worked on opening the new bottle as Linnea plopped ice cubes in her wineglass. "So, let me guess—you got laid off too?"

Linnea said with a groan, "*Again*. I can't believe I'm back here."

"At least we weren't fired."

"We're not getting paid. . . ."

Annabelle frowned while pouring out her wine. "Jeez, I hope it's not for too long."

"No one knows. That's the scariest part. It could be a while."

Linnea brought her glass to her lips. "If the aquarium gets in trouble, people will have to be let go permanently."

Annabelle's finely arched brows narrowed deeper and she took a long sip of wine.

"Let's sit outside," Linnea suggested, hoping the fresh air would lift the sudden drop in mood.

Annabelle grabbed the bottle of wine and followed her. "How are you holding up?"

"Same as you, I expect."

Annabelle settled in the chair recently vacated by Cara. She crossed her long legs. "Not quite the same." Leaning back in her chair she tossed out, "I'm guessing your family will help you out."

Linnea paused to sip rather than rise to the bait, recognizing Annabelle's knee-jerk reaction to the wealth difference between their families. "They'll try, I'm sure," she replied in an even tone, then sidestepped. "Seriously, are you okay, money-wise?"

Annabelle's shoulders lowered as she stared into her glass. She exhaled loudly and shook her head. "No. I'm worried."

"I am too. I have zero savings."

"Savings?" Annabelle snorted. "What's that? I was barely making rent with my extra bartending job. Thank God for catering gigs. That's how I ate most weekends. It's so damn expensive living in the city—hell, even *near* the city—that there's no hope of putting money away. I don't know how I'm going to make next month's rent."

"I'm guessing you won't be bartending much, will you?"

"Nada. Zip. Restaurants are closed. No one is having events."

Linnea looked at her friend's face. Annabelle's normally serious expression had a deeper edge bordering on desperation.

"Can you move home?" she asked.

"Good God, no. My mother's remarried to this creep," she said with a hint of disgust. "Who knows how long this one will last?" She rolled her eyes. "I can't go there."

Linnea licked her lips as a thought played in her mind. Part of her balked at the idea. But the other part, the one that made her think of Aunt Cara as inspiration, won out. In a rush, the words came pouring out.

"I have an extra room here, and Cara is giving me a break on the rent until this virus thing blows over. Seems only right to pay it forward." She paused. "You can move in here with me if you want. You wouldn't have to pay rent. But we'd split utilities and food. That way we'd help each other out. What do you think?"

Annabelle's eyes went wide. "Are you serious?"

"Never more serious."

Annabelle put her glass down on the table, resting her hand there as though to steady herself. Relief flooded her face and she replied, "Yes."

Linnea smiled and felt that gush of joy born of one woman helping another. She lifted her glass. "Well, then . . . here's to being roommates."

Annabelle's face lit up. She lifted her glass, and they clinked in the air.

"Roommates!"

Linnea sipped her chardonnay, then settled back in her chair. As she swirled the glass in her hand the ice cubes clinked, and she wondered if this was the best of ideas . . . or the worst.